WWW.BEWAREOFMONSTERS.COM

PRAISE FOR JEREMY ROBINSON

"[*Hunger* is] a wicked step-child of King and Del Toro. Lock your windows and bolt your doors. [Robinson, writing as] Jeremiah Knight, imagines the post-apocalypse like no one else."

—The Novel Blog

"Robinson writes compelling thrillers, made all the more entertaining by the way he incorporates aspects of pop culture into the action."

—Booklist

"*Project 731* is a must. Jeremy Robinson just keeps getting better with every new adventure and monster he creates."

—Suspense Magazine

"Robinson is known for his great thrillers, and [with *XOM-B*] he has written a novel that will be in contention for various science fiction awards at the end of the year. Robinson continues to amaze with his active imagination."

—Booklist

"Robinson puts his distinctive mark on Michael Crichton territory with [*Island 731*], a terrifying present-day riff on *The Island of Dr. Moreau*. Action and scientific explanation are appropriately proportioned, making this one of the best *Jurassic Park* successors."

—Publisher's Weekly - Starred Review

"[*SecondWorld* is] a brisk thriller with neatly timed action sequences, snappy dialogue and the ultimate sympathetic figure in a badly burned little girl with a fighting spirit... The Nazis are determined to have the last gruesome laugh in this efficient doomsday thriller."

—Kirkus Reviews

"*Threshold* elevates Robinson to the highest tier of over-the-top action authors and it delivers beyond the expectations even of his fans. The next Chess Team adventure cannot come fast enough."

—Booklist - Starred Review

"Jeremy Robinson is the next James Rollins."

—Chris Kuzneski, NY Times bestselling author of *The Einstein Pursuit*

"[*Pulse* is] rocket-boosted action, brilliant speculation, and the recreation of a horror out of the mythologic past, all seamlessly blending into a rollercoaster ride of suspense and adventure."

—James Rollins, NY Times bestselling author of *The 6th Extinction*

PRAISE FOR SEAN ELLIS

"What follows in *Savage* is much more than a political thriller. Robinson and Ellis have combined technology, archeology, and even a little microbiology with the question they ask better than any other authors today: what if?"
—Suspense Magazine

"Sean Ellis is an author to watch closely."
—David L. Golemon, NY Times bestselling author of *The Mountain*

"Sean Ellis has mixed a perfect cocktail of adventure and intrigue, and [*Into the Black*] is definitely shaken and not stirred."
—Graham Brown, NY Times bestselling author of *Ghost Ship*

"Some books are just plain unbridled fun; others are edge of the seat gripping entertainment. Some make you think; a few open your eyes. Sean Ellis is a magician, doing it all with a deftness that pulls you in and draws you along from page one breathlessly to the end of the book, offering mysteries galore, bad guys with the blackest hearts and a good old fashioned hero to kick their evil arses. I had a blast."
—Steven Savile, international bestselling author of *Silver*

"Sean Ellis writes action scenes that rival those of Clive Cussler and James Rollins."
—James Reasoner, NY Times bestselling author of *Texas Rangers*

"Sean Ellis delivers another high-octane romp [with *Magic Mirror*], exploring mythical lost civilizations and alternative histories, with the unrelenting pace of your favorite summer blockbuster."
—Stel Pavlou, bestselling author of *Gene*

"I'll admit it. I am totally exhausted after finishing *Oracle*, the latest Jade Ihara page-turner by David Wood and Sean Ellis. What an adventure! I kept asking myself how the co-authors came up with all this fantastic stuff. This is a great read that provides lots of action, and thoughtful insight as well, into strange realms that are sometimes best left unexplored."
—Paul Kemprecos, NY Times bestselling author of *Medusa*

"[*Dodge Dalton* is] high flying adventure at its best. Cleverly conceived, original, and multi-layered, the action literally jumps off the page and takes the reader through unexpected twists and turns."
—Rob MacGregor, NY Times bestselling author of *Indiana Jones and the Last Crusade*

ALSO BY JEREMY ROBINSON

ALSO BY SEAN ELLIS

Jack Sigler/Chess Team
Callsign: King
Callsign: King – Underworld
Callsign: King – Blackout
Prime
Savage
Cannibal

Mira Raiden Novels
Ascendant
Descendent

The Nick Kismet Adventures
The Shroud of Heaven
Into the Black
The Devil You Know
Fortune Favors

The Adventures of Dodge Dalton
In the Shadow of Falcon's Wings
At the Outpost of Fate
On the High Road to Oblivion

Cerberus Group Novels
Herculean

Novels
Magic Mirror
The Sorcerer's Ghost
Wargod
(with Steven Savile)
Flood Rising
(with Jeremy Robinson)

Novels with David Wood
Hell Ship
Oracle
Destiny
Changeling (2015)

Secret Agent X
The Sea Wraiths
The Scar
Masterpiece of Vengeance

HERCULEAN

A Cerberus Group Novel

JEREMY ROBINSON
AND SEAN ELLIS

Visit Jeremy Robinson on the World Wide Web at:
www.bewareofmonsters.com

Visit Sean Ellis on the World Wide Web at:
seanellisthrillers.webs.com

Jeremy dedicates Herculean *to Ray Harryhausen, who made myths come to life.*

Sean dedicates Herculean *to Nancy Osterlund. Teachers matter.*

HERCULEAN

PROLOGUE
TWELVE

PROLOGUE

A distant land, long ago...

At last, **he** thought. *The end of my journey is in sight.*

While that was not entirely true, the location on the map was indeed close at hand. But reaching that destination would not mean the end of his quest. Finding the Source—Echidna, the Well of Monsters—would merely be the halfway point. He would also have to make it back home, to the other side of the world.

To come this far, he had endured stormy seas and worse, entire oceans, where there was no wind at all. He had crossed deserts where no rain ever fell and climbed mountains so cold that breath froze into snowflakes. He had ventured into the eternal darkness of the Earth's bowels, where only monsters dwelt. To return whence he came, he would have to tread those paths again, face the same perils one more time.

The return trip would not be as difficult though. The path was already traveled, the unknown stripped of its mystery. He knew the way now, knew which roads led to danger and which winds would blow him to safe harbor. He had the map to guide him.

And he was not the same man that had set forth on this desperate quest.

He was stronger now. Almost as indestructible as the lion whose impervious skin he now wore as a cloak. His trials had refined him, melted away the base impurities of his being, left him stronger, purer...god-like.

He had been worshipped once or twice along the way. At first, the adoration had pleased him, but the novelty of the experience did not last. Yet, there was nothing the simple folk could give him that he could not just as easily take for himself. Their adulation was empty, rooted in fear more than anything else. Worse, their sacrificial offerings were always accompanied by endless supplications for divine assistance. Destroy our enemies. Bless our harvest. Restore my virility. Marry my daughter.

No wonder it had taken him so long to make it this far. The return journey would go more swiftly. Of that, he was certain.

But first, this one last labor. A journey into Erebus, the primal darkness. The Underworld, realm of the dead.

More superstitions for the simple-minded.

But not even he could deny that this was a cursed place. A few days previously, he had strode through a sea of golden grass, pasture for the great horned beasts that roamed in herds, stretching from one edge of the horizon to the other. But here the ground was scorched and lifeless. He could feel the heat rising up from the earth, burning the skin of his feet even through the leather soles of his sandals. Fumaroles belched out a poisonous fog. The rivers boiled. If there was a place where the wicked dead wandered in misery for all eternity, then this surely was its doorstep.

But the Underworld was *not* inhabited by the forsaken spirits of the dead.

It was a source of life.

He paused, and consulted the map again. The scale was too broad to show him the way now, but he knew he was close. He turned in a slow circle, his sharp eyes searching the landscape until, at last, he saw the path marker.

He moved in the indicated direction, maintaining a straight line to the extent the treacherous terrain permitted. There was no trail. It had been a long time since anyone had walked this ground. The living rarely had business in such a blighted place. There were, however, a few signs of more ancient travelers. Footprints, stamped in soft mud long ago, baked by the sun and the terrible heat of the Earth itself, until the mud was as hard as stone.

Had Typhon walked here once? He did not know the answer to that question. Perhaps the man who styled himself both a sorcerer and a god had procured the source of his power in some other way, not daring to brave the terrors of the Underworld. That would be so like him. He was a coward, who used others to accomplish his ends. There were braver men in the world, men willing to face such danger for the right amount of gold.

Some of the prints did not belong to a man, or even, judging by their size, an ordinary beast of the Earth. Those prints, if he read the signs correctly, led *away* from the entrance to the Underworld.

He found a second marker, then another, and then, as if drawn like iron to a lodestone, he entered a hollow depression in the scorched earth, where more ancient symbols indicated that he had arrived, warning him to proceed no further. It was a warning that he had no intention of heeding.

He consulted the map once more to find the words. They were strange, like nothing he had ever uttered before, and yet when he spoke them, the earth...changed. He was a learned man, far more knowledgeable than anyone who walked the world—even Typhon, the 'divine intellect,' was a mere child in such matters—yet he did not understand how it was possible for mere words to change the fabric of the physical realm.

When this task was complete, he would make a study of the matter, but for the moment, he could spare no mental energy investigating.

He spoke the words.

The rough stone wall shimmered like a waterfall.

He set his club on the ground by his feet and took a bundle of tightly wrapped dry grass from the leather sack that held his provisions. He coaxed an ember to life, and then touched it to the end of the torch. The resulting flame was paltry in comparison to the mid-afternoon sun's glare, but it would be more than enough to light his way.

He dared not linger now. He had four more torches in his sack, but they would burn quickly, and he had no desire to face the darkness beyond the gate without a light source. If he could not accomplish his task before a second torch burned out, he would have to turn back.

After retrieving his club and hefting it onto one shoulder, he started forward, stepping into the shimmering wall of rock as easily as one might walk through a heavy fog. The darkness closed upon him. Not even the torch could light his way as he passed through.

A moment later, he saw the flickering light again, and he knew he was now in what some believed was the realm of Hades.

He paused there, holding the torch aloft to orient himself.

The cavern had formed from molten stone, which had cooled and left a hollow lobe-shaped cavity at the center. The perfectly round tunnel led deeper into the interior. If he had any doubts about the volcanic origin of the cave system, the stifling heat and vile sulfurous atmosphere wiped them away.

One more reason not to tarry.

He had taken only a few steps into the tunnel when he heard a low rumble. A growl perhaps. Or the Earth clearing its throat in preparation to vomit a mass of superheated steam and liquefied rock.

He eased the club off his shoulder and raised it high, ready to meet whatever the Underworld decided to throw at him.

He glimpsed movement ahead. With a thunderous war cry, he charged and swung the club one-handed, driving down into the enormous, shadowy mass. There was a loud *thunk* as wood conn-ected with...something solid. The impact rang through the iron-hard wood of his bludgeon, and buzzed through his forearm. Had he merely struck a large rock? Had the movement been an illusion, caused by the flickering light of his torch?

He jabbed the torch forward at the shape, even as he hauled back the club for another swing.

His first thought was that he had been right to attack, for the shape was most definitely not a rock. His second thought was that he had been foolish to attack, for the beast in front of him was immense beyond comprehension. As big as the elephants that roamed the African plains. No...bigger even than that, and covered in black fur that devoured the light of his guttering torch.

The beast did not move.

His blow had struck true, caving in the thing's skull, striking with such force that one of its eyes had popped out of its orbit, dangling alongside a canine snout. It would have been a killing blow, even for a creature of such prodigious size, but for two things.

First, the skull he had cracked open like an almond was only one of three the beast possessed. Three heads—each vaguely resembling one of King Eurystheus's *molossus* hounds, albeit on a monumental scale—sprouted from a broad-shouldered torso. His club had smitten only the one on the monster's left. The other two were completely intact. Yet, before he could swing again, he realized the second thing.

The hellhound was already dead.

Or so it appeared.

Because of its enormous size, he had not realized that it was sprawled out on the tunnel floor. Had it been standing, he probably would have been able to walk beneath its belly. He studied the thing, wondering if he should smite the other heads anyway, just to be sure. There seemed to be the faintest flutter of movement at one of its remaining nostrils, but this too might have been a trick of the light. He lowered the club, then jabbed the torch at the beast's open but unmoving eyes.

No reaction.

The appearance of the hellhound was not completely unexpected. He had fought creatures such as this before, twisted things, Typhon's creations. Chimeras. This beast was different only because it was not the product of Typhon's warped imagination, but rather a natural occurrence—if such an animal could be considered natural—spawned from the Well of Monsters, the very thing he sought.

A closer look revealed the truth. The blow from his club was only the latest in a series of grievous injuries the creature had sustained. There were numerous scars on its two remaining heads, burns and gashes that had healed, leaving ugly masses of scar tissue. Some looked recent, only a few days old and barely begun to heal. They told a tale of life in the lightless depths of the Earth, a story of constant struggle with no respite.

He wondered what manner of creature would have dared challenge a behemoth such as this, and then he wondered if that other monster had survived the encounter. Was it still here, somewhere close? Were there others like it?

Almost certainly.

He edged around the stricken beast, still not certain that it was dead. If his earlier battles with chimera had taught him anything, it was that such creatures were extraordinarily hard to kill. As he passed along its immense flanks, he reached out and laid a cautious hand on its belly.

Still warm.

Though given the stifling environment, that counted for little. If it was dead—and surely it must be—then it had expired recently, a day or two at most, but possibly only a few hours.

The low growling noise repeated, and he felt a faint vibration against his palm. He drew back as if scalded and raised his club again, but the creature remained completely still. After recovering from being startled, he ventured closer once more. It was dead. Of that he felt sure. And yet the noise *had* come from the beast.

Curiosity replaced both his sense of caution and urgency. He leaned his club against the tunnel wall, knelt down and tried lifting one of the massive front paws. It was stiff and heavy, but he managed to raise it as high as his own waist.

The growl came again, and this time he realized that the sound was not *from* the beast, but from beneath it. He pushed against the forelimb, straining with all his might. The carcass rolled onto its side, revealing a second, much smaller hellhound, with all three of its jaws clamped tight on the exposed breast of the first.

A mother and its pup.

He stared at the thing for several seconds, wondering if it would attack. The noise repeated, much louder now that it was no longer muffled by the bulk of the dead mother, but the little creature had no intention of letting go. Nor did it appear capable of doing much harm. Despite its size—it was as large as a year-old ox—it was wasting away. Any milk the mother might have produced was long since gone.

He felt a pang of sympathy for the strange-looking pup, and then frowned it away. Sentimentality was a weakness, and in a place such as this, a fatal one. Better to crush the creature's skulls, spare it the misery of a slow death by starvation.

Yet, as he started to reach for his club, intent on delivering a killing blow, something stayed his hand.

Not compassion.

He felt none for the hellhound, but something else.

There was an opportunity here.

This creature was a scion of the Well of Monsters.

It was a living vessel in which the essence of the Well might be transported back to his home on the far side of the world. A self-sustaining supply of blood and tissue that he might study and experiment with at his leisure, to develop a weapon against

Typhon and his creations. Perhaps he would make even greater discoveries.

It was the very thing for which he had come.

He reached out slowly with his free hand. The pup growled again but did not unclench its jaws to snap at him. He stroked the side of its rightmost head, scratching gently beneath the ear.

A low, steady, terrified rumble issued from its throat, and he could feel the creature's rapid breathing, its heart fiercely pounding. But after a few long minutes, long enough for the torch to burn nearly down to a stub, the growling ceased.

"Well, that's progress," he murmured softly. "But what am I going to feed you?"

It occurred to him that the journey home might not be so easy after all.

THREAD

ONE

Liberia

At the top of the low hill overlooking the narrow trail cutting through the rain forest, Nils Van Der Hausen wondered why anyone would choose to build a village in such a place. He understood why settlements and cities sprang up along coastlines or on the banks of a river, but he could not fathom what madness possessed people to hack out an existence in the middle of the jungle, miles from the nearest road.

'Village' was too generous a term for this collection of huts that occupied the small clearing. It was a five mile walk to the nearest road and two miles from St. Paul River. There were dozens more just like it scattered throughout the river valley. Hundreds, even. The government in Monrovia was vaguely aware of their existence but made no effort to regulate them or provide even the most basic of services to their inhabitants. The people who called the place home subsisted on bush meat, which included anything that walked in the rain forest. The exact whereabouts of the villages and the names of the families who lived in them were unknown to the outside world.

It had taken him the better part of a day to reach this place, even with his GPS unit pointing him in the right direction. Finding these villages was like a mad scavenger hunt, a lesson he had learned during his first visit to the West African republic during the 2014 Ebola outbreak.

A genetic engineer by trade, Van Der Hausen had been part of the World Health Organization's response team deployed to Liberia to combat the spread of hemorrhagic fever. Once on the ground, he had discovered that the team had little use for his scientific expertise. Instead, they needed people on the front lines, trekking out to the rural villages, isolating the infected, educating the superstitious villagers about quarantine measures and how to safely dispose of corpses. He had spent weeks tramping around the jungle, in constant fear of the deadly virus, wild animals, bandits and ignorant villagers who were suspicious of everyone.

It had been a life-changing experience.

He had come to Africa with a burning zeal to help the afflicted, to make the world a better place. He had left with the realization that sometimes the only way to fix a thing was to burn it down and start over.

That and one other thing. He had also brought a little souvenir of his stay in West Africa: an ampoule of human blood teeming with the Ebola virus.

He could still recall the heady mixture of exhilaration and panic he had felt when smuggling the sample out. It had been much easier than he had anticipated; everyone trusted the scientists. Of course, things had not exactly gone according to his plan after that. His fumbling attempt to sell the sample might have gotten him arrested, if not for the intervention of the man who now stood beside him, staring down at the nameless village.

"That's the place?" Vigor Rohn asked.

Rohn was Bulgarian—Van Der Hausen recognized the distinctive Sofia accent. His voice was gravelly and irritable, like someone who had woken up with a hangover, except Rohn always sounded that way. He was big—six-foot-two, with the broad-shouldered physique of a footballer—and ugly. His face was pock-marked, like someone who had taken a double-barreled shotgun blast of rock salt. One of his ears looked like a cauliflower floret. Van Der Hausen felt quite certain that the man was no scientist, but Rohn always asked the right questions. He was either more intelligent than he appeared or he was being coached by a remote mentor. Probably both.

Van Der Hausen nodded and waggled his GPS unit. "I tagged the devices, just to be sure that no one tampered with them."

"And we will be safe here?"

"Technically, we could get a lot closer. This isn't some run-of-the-mill infectious bio-weapon." He smiled, recalling how Rohn had used very similar language two months earlier during their first meeting.

Rohn had found him, just five minutes before his first attempt at selling the Ebola virus to a man in the Stockholm underworld. Rohn had appeared out of nowhere, warning Van Der Hausen that the meeting was a set-up. They had left together, narrowly escaping the tightening police dragnet.

"My employer has noticed you," Rohn had told him. "You are an amateur, playing a dangerous game with no idea of the risks you face. But my employer admires your initiative."

Van Der Hausen, still in shock, had managed to ask whether Rohn's employer might be interested in purchasing the virus.

Rohn had laughed. "Ebola is nothing. A run-of-the-mill threat, good for creating a panic, but almost useless for strategic purposes. You should know this better than anyone."

"Then what—"

"You have something of even greater worth that my employer is willing to pay for."

"My scientific expertise?"

Another derisive laugh. "There are many scientists in the world. But only a few of them are..." Rohn paused as if searching for the right word, "...unscrupulous enough to sell a deadly virus to the highest bidder. That is what makes you special. My employer is interested in research and development. Genetic engineering is the new frontier. Those who are the first to blaze trails into unexplored territory reap the greatest reward. You want that, don't you?"

Van Der Hausen most definitely did.

"Then you must continue to impress my employer."

With a generous advance of seed money, Van Der Hausen had taken a leave of absence from the University of Stockholm and set up his own genetics lab, outfitted with state-of-the-art equipment purchased off the Internet. At first, he had felt like a frustrated artist, staring at a blank canvas, waiting for inspiration to dawn. Then he had remembered his earlier ordeal, and an idea had come to him.

Rohn had been right. Weaponizing infectious diseases by tweaking various gene sequences to increase lethality and communicability was *so* twentieth century. This was the new world, where the old limits of DNA and RNA no longer applied. Genetic engineering was a playground, where men like him spliced nucleic acids together like Lego blocks. The only limit was his imagination, and he had a very vivid imagination.

"Unless you're standing at ground zero," Van Der Hausen explained, gesturing toward the village, "within about fifty feet of the device when the spores are released, you could simply walk away and not be affected. If, that is, you knew what was happening."

Rohn grunted. "And you are ready to demonstrate now?"

Van Der Hausen waggled the GPS again. "Say the word, and I'll press the button."

"One moment." Rohn took out a satellite-enabled smartphone and tapped the screen to place a call. There was an audible ringing—the phone was in speaker mode—and then a voice spoke.

"Yes?"

"It is Rohn."

"Ah, time to see if our Swedish friend is worth the money we've spent." The voice was high-pitched and wheezy.

An old man, Van Der Hausen decided.

"Show me!" the man commanded.

Rohn held the device up so that its built-in camera was oriented down toward the cluster of huts. "You may proceed," he told Van Der Hausen.

The geneticist nodded and then turned his attention to the village as well. At a distance of almost three hundred yards, the villagers were barely discernible.

Like ants, he told himself. *That's all they are.*

He felt no remorse at what he was about to do. These were not people, not fellow human beings... They were a plague of insects, breeding and consuming with no regard for the consequences. Ebola was nature's way of trying to restore the balance, a fact that his fellow volunteers at the WHO had never understood. They had swept in like crusading knights, intent on slaying the dragon without ever stopping to consider that the dragon might have a role to play in the natural order of things.

His only regret was that this was merely a demonstration. One village. A drop in the ocean. Rohn's employer—his employer, too, he supposed—wanted a product, not wholesale devastation.

A countdown seemed appropriate. He started at five, and when he got to zero, he tapped the transmit button on the GPS.

He thought he heard a distant popping noise, like a balloon bursting or a cork shooting from a bottle of champagne, but it was probably just his imagination. The aerosol devices that disseminated the spores were more like garden sprinklers. There might have been a faint hiss close to the source but nothing audible at such a distance.

The wheezy voice issued from the phone. "Is something supposed to happen?"

"You must be patient," Van Der Hausen answered. "It may take a few minutes for the first generation of spores to mature. Growth will be exponential once the spores encounter a source of...ah...nutrients."

Several seconds passed, but still there was no visible change.

The voice spoke again. "I had expected something a little more dramatic, Dr. Van Der Hausen. This is rather disappointing."

"We may be too far away to see the results," Van Der Hausen replied, unable to hide his anxiety. They *should* have been able to see something. The outcome of the test in the laboratory had been quite dramatic.

"Rohn, take our friend closer so that we may get a better look." The voice of the old man on the other end of the phone was noticeably impatient and tinged with sarcasm.

Closer? Despite his earlier assurance, Van Der Hausen felt a twinge of panic at this prospect. Now that the spores were circulating, moving closer was definitely a bad idea. He looked at Rohn, hoping to see the same apprehension that he now felt, but the man's face was an emotionless mask. Rohn nodded in the direction of the village and spoke a single word. "Go."

Van Der Hausen swallowed nervously, forcing down the impulse to protest. "Very well." He knew what to look for. He would stop at the first sign of propagation.

As they descended the hillside, they were once more engulfed in the jungle thicket. Van Der Hausen scanned the vegetation, looking for any signs of new growth. After just a couple of minutes of pushing through the foliage, they reached the edge of the clearing. Though still a good hundred yards from the nearest hut, Van Der Hausen could hear the sounds of daily village life—children playing and babies squalling in their mothers' arms.

Something was wrong.

"There may have been a malfunction in the aerosol devices," he said, his tone more hopeful than disappointed. That explanation was preferable to the alternative. Yet, he had placed four of the devices—one at each corner of the building that had been set aside for use as a clinic—and the likelihood that all of them had failed was marginal at best. Which meant that the problem was with the organism itself. "Or possibly some environmental counter-agent that I didn't account for."

"I've seen enough," the old man replied. "Rohn, I have need of you elsewhere. Get to Athens as soon as possible. Kenner believes we may be on the verge of a breakthrough."

"What about him?" Rohn's eyes flashed toward Van Der Hausen.

"A bad investment. Cash him out."

Van Der Hausen was quick to protest. "Now wait just a minute. This is a minor setback. The whole point of a large scale test is to work out the—"

The words caught in his throat as he spied the glint of sunlight on the knife in Rohn's other hand. He brought his own hands forward in an instinctive gesture of self-preservation, even as the blade slashed toward him. He felt something tugging at his shirt, but then Rohn took a step back and sheathed the knife.

Van Der Hausen sagged in relief. Rohn's display of menace was only a reminder of the stakes in this dangerous game he had decided to play, nothing more, and unnecessary at that. Van Der Hausen hardly needed an incentive. He wanted to know what had gone wrong even more than Rohn and the old man.

A strange sensation hit his gut, a hollow feeling, similar to the experience of a rapid ascent in an elevator. Then he heard a wet sound as something hit the ground at his feet. He realized Rohn's slash had not been a mere threat after all. Darkness swelled at the edge of his vision, and pain bloomed in his abdomen. As he crumpled to the ground alongside his entrails, it occurred to Van Der Hausen that his worst fears had caught up with him. He *was* going to die in this horrible place.

TWO

Heraklion, Crete

The black-clad figure scrambled up and over the top of the six-foot high, metal fence, dropping down into an isolated corner of the wooded courtyard behind the Heraklion Archaeological Museum. He crouched there for a moment, concealed in the shadows, where the glow of streetlights did not quite reach. Then he extended a hand in a beckoning gesture.

On the other side of the fence, eighteen-year old Fiona Sigler took a deep breath, glanced around to make sure there were no witnesses and then launched herself into motion. Two seconds later, she was hunkered down in the shadows beside the first intruder, her uncle, George Pierce.

He was not *really* her uncle, just the best friend of her father, Jack Sigler...who was not *really* her father either, but such distinctions meant little to someone whose life to date was as screwed up as hers.

"See," Pierce whispered from behind his black ski-mask. "That wasn't so hard."

"Climbing the fence? Piece of cake," she replied, with just a hint of sarcasm. "It's the trespassing that's going to take some getting used to."

"Don't worry," he promised. "It gets easier."

"And so begins my life of crime."

Strangely enough, she was enjoying herself. Her heart hammered in her chest. She was terrified that a policeman or security guard would appear from out of nowhere, flashlight in one hand, gun in the other. But the fear was oddly exhilarating, like the thrill of a roller coaster ride. Given the sort of life she had led, a little late-night breaking-and-entering was actually pretty tame. If getting busted in the Greek Isles was the worst thing that happened to her tonight, she could deal. She had been through a lot worse.

They stole across the courtyard to the back of the building. The museum was housed in an unremarkable modern-looking structure at odds with the rest of the picturesque port city. They had spent the last two days in Heraklion, familiarizing themselves with the museum. 'Scoping the place out,' was the phrase Pierce had used. Being in the town was like traveling back in time. There were statues and fountains, old fortresses, churches and mosques, crumbling ancient walls sitting side-by-side with modern high-rise buildings.

Fiona thought the museum—which had been designed to withstand the frequent earthquakes that rocked the region—was ugly by comparison to the rest of the city. It had all the charm of a high school campus. But what did she know? Architecture really wasn't her forte. She was fascinated by languages, and while she was by no means fluent in Greek, she could read the Greek alphabet almost as easily as traditional Latin letters. The best part about the walking tour had been trying to decipher the signs, though surprisingly, many of them were in English.

She wondered which language would be on the signs in the local jail.

Pierce led her to an unmarked metal door, then he knelt before it, illuminating the doorknob with a flashlight clenched between his teeth. The intensely bright LED bulb in the MagTac tactical flashlight was muted to a warm red glow by the addition of a snap-on filter lens. Enough light to work by, but much harder to detect from a distance. Pierce produced a slim black wallet and took out a strip of metal that Fiona recognized as a lock-pick. He held the pick up to the keyhole, but then stopped and raised his eyes to her, mumbling something around the flashlight. "Awn oo eye?"

It was not a foreign language, but she had no trouble interpreting. *Want to try?*

Hell, yeah, she thought, but she merely shrugged, worried about appearing overly eager to engage in this criminal act, even with his approval. "Sure."

Pierce passed over the tool set and then moved aside, removing the light from between his teeth and holding it low, to illuminate the lock.

"Tell me about the Herculean Society while you do it," Pierce said, flashing a grin.

"What? Why?"

"Since tonight is an initiation of sorts, your first field mission, I want to be sure you know what led us here."

"You want a history report *while* I pick a lock?"

"Mind and body on separate tasks." He nodded. "It's an important skill."

Fiona inserted the pick. "The Herculean Society was formed in 800 BC, maybe earlier, by Hercules, hence the name. But he wasn't a demi-god. He was a man who used science to extend his life, tapping ancient secrets—and DNA, long before modern scientists even discovered it—to make himself immortal."

She raked the pick's tip along the keyway, feeling the pins move against the springs. She then removed a small tension lever from the kit and placed it in the cylinder, applying gentle but steady pressure, just enough to hold the pins in place as she teased them up, one by one.

"Over time, Hercules witnessed how mankind abused certain powers, and he realized that most of us couldn't be trusted with certain knowledge, artifacts or creatures. So he created the Society to hide, alter and protect history from humanity, and sometimes humanity from history. And he protected his own existence by exaggerating the truth about his life until it reached mythological proportions."

Each move of the lock-pick was second nature. One of her father's friends had taught her how to do this years ago. She had practiced until it was drilled into her muscle memory, along with hand-to-hand combat, shooting and some simple computer hacking techniques—all useful skills for cat burglars and government agents. Her father and his friends were the latter, all members of an elite paramilitary special operations team.

"In more recent years, Hercules went by the name Alexander Diotrephes, who I first met four years ago, under...interesting circumstances. Not long after that, he passed leadership of the Society on to my father, and *he* passed it on to you, what, six months ago? With that turnover rate, I'll be in charge by the time I'm nineteen." The cylinder rotated. The bolt slid away with a click. She grinned. "So are we here to protect history from people, or people from history?"

Pierce returned her smile. "It's usually a little of both."

She reached for the door knob, but Pierce shot out a restraining hand. "Alarm," he whispered.

She grimaced. *Of course there's an alarm. Stupid.*

Pierce reached into a pocket and took out a black plastic box that looked like a cross between an ohmmeter and an electronic stud-finder. It wasn't the kind of thing the average professor of archeology carried, but he wasn't the average professor of archeology. Not anymore. Those calm days were long behind him now. He missed the quiet sometimes, but he had no regrets. He was living every archeologist's dream, which sometimes included breaking into a museum. He held the device close to the door and moved it along the edge of the frame. As he swept the device across the top of the door, a red LED began to blink, and then it remained steadily bright. Pierce gave a satisfied nod and pressed a button on the device. When he lowered his hand, the device remained in place, magnetically affixed to the door.

"Open it," he said. "Slowly."

She turned the knob and eased the door open an inch, then another. There was no clangor of bells or sirens alerting the world to their unauthorized presence. The door was equipped with a contact-circuit—the idea was that when the door was opened, the circuit would be broken, triggering the security alarm—but the electro-magnetic induction field generated by the black box ensured that the circuit remained unbroken, even though the contacts were no longer touching. Of course, the alarm was not the only security measure they would have to worry about. The museum also employed a night watchman.

Pierce pressed his face close to the gap. "All clear."

He gripped the door and slipped inside. Just before he disappeared completely, he waved her forward. Once she was inside, Pierce reached up to the top of the door and carefully slid the black device around to the inside of the door frame. With the door firmly shut and locked, he deactivated the box and removed it, slipping it back into his pocket.

The service door opened into what appeared to be a supply room. Pierce shone his red flashlight around until he found a door leading deeper into the museum. He motioned for her to follow.

They entered a corridor lined with several more doors, but Pierce passed all of these by and went to the double doors at the end of the hallway. After a quick check to ensure that the doors were not rigged with an alarm, he cautiously opened them to reveal a dimly lit room.

Fiona recognized what lay beyond from their visit earlier in the day, a gallery of sculptures, some of the pieces life-sized and dating from the late Hellenistic and early Roman periods. The sculpted likenesses of gods and mythical heroes represented the tail-end of Crete's history, at least as far as archaeologists like Pierce were concerned. The museum contained antiquities dating back more than seven thousand years, to the Neolithic period, long before the rise of Classical Greek civilization.

Most of the collection in the twenty-one exhibition rooms of the Heraklion Museum was dedicated to the ancient Minoan culture, which had not only dominated the island of Crete but much of the Mediterranean up until about 1200 BC. Then their society vanished so completely that, by the time of Alexander the Great, the Minoans were remembered only in myths, a forgotten kingdom. One contributing factor had been the catastrophic eruption of a volcano on the nearby island of Thera—the largest volcanic event in recorded history, an order of magnitude greater than the eruption of Krakatoa in 1883. Many scholars believed that the Minoan culture had been the inspiration for the legendary Atlantis, described in the dialogues of Plato as a highly advanced but arrogant civilization, wiped out by angry gods in a single day.

Although later civilizations had occupied the site of the ancient Minoan capital, it remained buried until 1878, when the ruins of the ancient palace of Knossos were found, just three miles from the site of modern day Heraklion. More than a century later, archaeological excavations continued to shed new light on the Minoan culture, and it was one such discovery that had attracted the attention of the Herculean Society.

Fiona knew much of this from her own studies, but strolling the galleries with Pierce the previous days, he had been unable to resist the urge to lecture, and he had filled in the gaps. He was silent now, communicating only with hand signals. He pointed to an opening in the center of the far wall. Fiona nodded and crept through the gallery to the arch that led into the adjoining room. She edged out, looking and listening for any signs of the roaming watchman. When she detected nothing, she turned back and signaled a thumbs-up to Pierce, who was checking out the doorway in the opposite corner. He returned the signal and then motioned for her to join him.

The room beyond the doorway contained relics recovered from the ruins of Phaistos, a Minoan palace thirty miles away on the south shore of the island. The artifacts were arranged in simple glass display cases, with very little supplemental interpretive information. Most of the pieces were simple—bits of pottery, tools and jewelry. Irreplaceable items to be sure, but with very little intrinsic value, which no doubt accounted for the sparse security measures. But there was one artifact in the room that was truly unique. The reason for their after-hours 'visit.'

The Phaistos Disc was mounted in a circular metal bracket that reminded Fiona of a two-sided swivel mirror, secured behind panes of glass in a free-standing display case, in the center of the room. The artifact was a pancake-flat circle of glazed and kiln-fired clay, almost six inches in diameter, decorated on both sides with a series of symbols that spiraled from the center.

Almost from the moment of its discovery in 1908, in the basement of the Phaistos palace complex, the Disc became one of the greatest mysteries in archaeology and language studies. The symbols, forty-five distinctive pictograms, arranged into different 'word' combinations, were the source of the mystery. The pictograms, which were very similar to Egyptian hieroglyphs and depicted the shapes of people, animals, plants, tools and weapons, formed a message of some kind. Some believed it was an ancient zodiac horoscope or a child's board game. Some even believed it was of Atlantean origin.

For more than a century, all attempts to decipher the message had been unsuccessful. There was no way to know for sure if the images on the Disc even represented a real language. The meaning of the symbols was so perplexing that a few embittered researchers believed that the Disc was a twentieth century hoax. But in late 2014, a team of scholars led by Gareth Owens, a linguist working at the Technological Educational Institute of Crete, announced that they had cracked the code, using the Minoan Linear A script along with Mycenaean Linear B to identify several keywords. The working hypothesis was that the Disc contained a prayer to a Minoan mother goddess.

Yet while the mystery of the message had been solved, what could not be explained was the uniqueness of the symbols themselves. Each of the pictograms had been stamped into the soft clay using carved seals, one of the earliest known instances of typographic printing. Some ancient craftsman had carved the forty-five seals, used them to create the Disc, and then evidently destroyed them so they could never be used again. The symbols on the Phaistos Disc were unique, appearing there and nowhere else.

Or so it was believed.

Fiona knew differently.

They closed in on the display, and Pierce shone his red light on the keyhole of a cabinet lock, which was partially concealed in the base of the display. Fiona selected the appropriate tools from the pick kit and went to work on the lock. It took less than two minutes for her to defeat the simple mechanism, and this time she double-checked for an alarm before opening the case.

Pierce moved the beam of his light to the shadowy interior of the display, illuminating the Phaistos Disc. It looked so ordinary, a slightly irregular pat of clay, like a grade school art project stamped with what looked like decorative images. It was hard to believe that something so ordinary could be so mysterious, and potentially dangerous.

Fiona reached a hand in and grasped the Disc between thumb and forefinger. She eased it from the bracket and brought it out. Pierce took the artifact from her, and then proffered something with his other hand: an exact replica, created using 3-D molecular printing technology, precise down to the microscopic level. A scientific analysis of this duplicate disc might reveal it to be a fake—or it might not. The technology at the Herculean Society's disposal was truly that good—but because such a test had never been conducted on the real McCoy, no one would suspect that a substitution had been made. The assumption would be that the infamous Phaistos Disc had been a hoax all along.

With equal caution, Fiona reached back into the case and placed the duplicate where the original had been. She made one final adjustment, rotating the bogus disc a degree or two, then closed the display while Pierce slipped the authentic Disc into a cloth pouch, which he then stowed in a small satchel slung over one shoulder.

Behind her black ski-mask, Fiona allowed herself a satisfied smile. They had done it. Now all they needed to do was get out without—

Her smile died along with the hopeful sentiment as she caught a glint of white light, reflected in the glass pane. She looked up just as the source of the light, a flashlight in the hands of a uniformed man, appeared in the doorway. Then it shone right into her eyes.

THREE

Pierce gave the end of his MagTac a quick twist to remove the red filter cap and aimed the naked light directly into the face of the startled watchman. The man flinched, throwing his hands up and looking away, too late to prevent temporary blindness. The high intensity LED bulb would leave him seeing bright green spots for the next few minutes.

Pierce grabbed Fiona's shoulder. "Run."

He sensed her hesitation, so he gave her a shake to snap her out of her paralysis. "Remember the plan."

The exhortation broke the spell. She whirled around and bolted for the exit. Pierce was just a few steps behind her, but as they reached the door, he slowed and glanced back at the guard. Despite being unable to see, the man stumbled through the maze of display cases, intent on pursuing them. Pierce checked to make sure that Fiona was still moving toward the door, and then he turned back toward the night watchman, sweeping the room with the beam of the MagTac to make sure he had the man's attention.

The 'plan' Pierce had spoken of, which had been worked out in detail during their earlier reconnaissance, was simple. In the event that they were discovered, they would split up and leave the museum by different routes to confound pursuit. Because she had no experience with such things, Fiona accepted the plan without protest. This break-in was, after all, her baptism by fire. It was her first taste of what being an agent of the Herculean Society really meant.

As missions went, this one was pretty tame, but even so, allowing Fiona to accompany him and get her feet wet had been a tough decision for Pierce. She was an adult now, in both the legal and literal sense of the word. Old enough to vote and enlist in the military, old enough, as she all too often reminded him, to make long-term life decisions for herself. Nevertheless, she was still young and immature, and more importantly, she was Pierce's responsibility, which meant that if anything happened to her—if she was caught and arrested, or God forbid, injured—it would be on his head. The fear of what might go wrong hadn't been enough for him to leave her behind, though, especially since she was eager to take on greater responsibility. But that did not mean Pierce would throw all caution to the wind.

Some discreet inquiries had revealed that the museum utilized only one watchman for the night shift. He walked the galleries and manned a security station at the locked front entrance. Because there was no way to completely eliminate the possibility that the guard might stumble upon them, they had rehearsed several egress routes. The escape plan hinged on giving the guard two targets to pursue, each going in a different direction. Pierce, however, had not told Fiona the whole plan—specifically, his part of the plan. After splitting up, it was his intention to draw the guard after him, to give Fiona the best possible chance for a clean getaway. Unfortunately, he was the one with the Phaistos Disc, which meant that if he was caught, there would be hell to pay.

He definitely had the watchman's full attention. The man cursed loudly as he collided with a display case, rattling pieces of three-thousand-year-old pottery off their shelves, but he managed to keep his flashlight trained in Pierce's general direction. Pierce moved along the wall of the gallery, toward the opening in the corner that led to another room, but he didn't turn and run until he was certain the guard would follow.

The next room contained artifacts from other major Minoan palace sites, but Pierce kept his focus on the spaces where there were no relics on display. There was an arched opening to his left, and the archway ahead led to the gallery where treasures from the Stone Age were exhibited. Beyond that room lay the entry foyer and one possible exit from the museum.

He glanced back and glimpsed the dancing beam of the watchman's flashlight only ten steps away.

Okay, maybe this part of the plan is working a little too well, Pierce thought, returning his gaze forward. *No more fooling around.*

He flicked off his light and sprinted toward the lobby. The museum was not pitch black, but the abrupt absence of illumination from the MagTac made it seem that way. Pierce knew that there were no obstacles ahead but he had to fight an almost primitive urge to slow down and grope in the darkness like a blind man.

Once he reached the relative openness of the lobby, he hooked left, away from the main entrance, which was too close to Fiona's exit. He darted through another gallery full of Minoan antiquities, making a beeline for the stairwell on the other side of the room.

He risked a glance back as he veered toward the stairs and saw that his lead on the security guard had shrunk to just a few steps.

This isn't working, he thought. *Change of plans.*

As he ducked into the stairwell, Pierce grasped the central handrail and vaulted over it like an Olympic gymnast. He felt an abrupt strain in his forearm as his forward momentum stretched the limb, but then like the business end of a bullwhip, he was flung around 180 degrees, right into the path of the watchman.

At the instant of collision, Pierce curled into a fetal ball, protecting his head and vital organs. His shoulder caught the unsuspecting guard squarely in the chest, and the man was driven back as if hit by a wrecking ball. The impact sent Pierce flying as well, but because he was prepared for it, he recovered quickly, regaining his feet and whirling around to mount the stairs.

Beneath the knit weave of his ski-mask, Pierce was grinning like an idiot.

Growing up, he had not exactly struck an ideal balance between intellectual and physical pursuits. While the dream of being a two-fisted adventurer like his hero, Indiana Jones, had set him on the path to a career in archaeology, he had avoided athletic pursuits and focused on academic excellence, which had made him a top-notch professor but a piss-poor action hero.

Fortunately, since taking the directorship of the Herculean Society, he had been working to correct that deficiency, with a regimen of exercise and mixed-martial arts training. It was slow going, but evidently it was possible for an old dog to learn a few new tricks.

He bounded up the stairs, shaking out the mild pain in his shoulder. As he rounded the landing, he saw no sign of pursuit. The watchman was either still recovering or knocked out cold. Pierce's elation faltered a little as he considered the possibility that he might have seriously injured the man.

Nothing you can do about it now, he told himself. *Focus on the mission.*

The mission.

Burglary and brawling weren't the only new tricks he'd had to learn since taking on his new role as the leader of the Herculean Society.

As an archaeologist and a historian, he had been committed to advancing the cause of knowledge. Only by learning about the past could mankind chart the course to a better future. Or so he had always believed. But experience had taught him a lesson that no textbook ever could. Some secrets needed to stay buried.

Six years earlier, this point had been driven home when the truth he had wanted so badly to discover had nearly cost him his humanity.

Ultimately, only the intervention of the Herculean Society had saved him. Alexander Diotrephes had pulled him from the brink. Only later would Pierce learn another astonishing secret: Diotrephes *was* the immortal Hercules, and he'd created the vast organization, which had literally rewritten history over the course of thousands of years. Pierce had made a career of uncovering history, but it had now become his job, his mission, to conceal it. The old saying about being doomed to repeat history if you didn't know it, wasn't always true. Sometimes the only way to not repeat history was to have no idea it had ever existed.

The second floor of the museum was laid out in a sideways H-shape. The gallery where Pierce now found himself formed one side of the H, with stairs at either end. Two parallel rooms bisected the exhibit hall and provided access to the rooms that comprised the other side of the H. There was an emergency door in the far corner of one of those rooms. The only problem was the door alarm. He could use the induction field generator—his black box—to fool it, but that would take time.

The alarm!

Pierce's guts twisted into a knot of dread as he realized that Fiona would be facing a similar problem, and without the black box to help her. He imagined her standing in front of the door through which they had entered, wondering what to do. This was something that had not come up during their rehearsal.

Damn it. I screwed up.

He briefly considered trying to send Fiona a text message, acknowledging the problem, but it occurred to him that there was a more direct way of communicating with her. He just hoped she would be able to interpret the message.

He ran headlong through the galleries, following the illuminated signs to the emergency door, but he did not take out the black box. Nor did he slow down. Instead, he hit the door at a full run.

A piercing siren shattered the deceptive stillness. A moment later, a second alarm joined the shrieking symphony.

Fiona had received the message: *Screw the alarm. Just go for it.*

Now it was time for him to do the same.

Ignoring the commotion, Pierce flipped on his flashlight and scanned the corridor in which he now found himself. An illuminated arrow on an overhead 'Exit' sign pointed the way to a door marked in both Greek and English with the words: Fire Stairs.

He weighed his options. The fire stairs would be the most direct path to freedom, but that also made it a dangerous choice. Would the guard be waiting for him to emerge? Were the police already on their way?

Too risky, he decided. But maybe there was another way out of the building. He dashed down the corridor, checking each door until he found one marked with the word:

οροφή

Roof.

Perfect.

He twisted the doorknob but it refused to turn. Locked.

Damn. Not perfect.

Fiona still had his pick set, though even if he'd brought a spare, there probably would not have been time for him to mess around with the lock. There was a reason he had allowed her to use the picks earlier, and it wasn't to give her more experience. She was a natural with locks, faster and smoother than he would ever be.

Fine, he thought. There were other ways to deal with locked doors.

He drew back a step, lowered his shoulder and started to charge...but then stopped short. Bashing down doors always looked easy in movies, but something told him that real life might not be so accommodating. A second look at the door revealed three sets of hinges; the door opened toward him. He could have thrown himself against it all night long and the only thing he would have to show for it would be a bruised shoulder.

He glanced back down the corridor. The stairs were starting to seem like a much better idea.

Okay, if I can't pick the lock and I can't break it down...what can I do?

There was a sliver-thin gap between the door and its frame. With a blade, or even a credit card, it might be possible to jimmy the lock open, but he had neither.

Note to self: In the future, always carry a knife.

What he did have was the black box device, and that was almost as good as a blade. He took it out and placed it against the door, between the knob and the strike plate, and then hit the button to activate the induction field. There was a click as the electromagnet engaged and pulled the device tight against the metal. Something moved against his shoulder, and before he could even think to be surprised, he felt something strike the back of his hand.

His satchel, or more precisely, its contents—the Phaistos Disc—had been drawn into the powerful magnetic field.

That's interesting.

But there was no time to explore the mystery. Ignoring the satchel, he gripped the black box in both hands and slid the device toward the door knob. As the electromagnet moved, it pulled the metal latch bolt clear of the strike plate, and the door popped open.

"Top that, Dr. Jones," he said.

As soon as he switched off the device, the satchel fell away, but Pierce barely noticed. He stuffed the device back into his pocket and ventured through the door onto the rooftop, above the museum's first floor. The low wail of police sirens greeted him. Close but not yet too close.

Pierce ran to the edge of the rooftop, trying to get oriented. He could just make out the harbor off to his left, a couple of miles distant, at the base of the slope upon which the city of Heraklion had been founded. That meant he was on the east side of the museum complex. If she stuck to the plan, Fiona would be leaving from the south, only a few hundred yards away. Pierce would have preferred a route that led him further away from her, but there was nothing to be done about it now. He looked down, focusing his attention on the more immediate problem of his own escape.

Because the museum was built on a hillside, the ground was a lot further away than he had anticipated—at least a forty foot drop. The wall below was smooth concrete, with no windows or ledges.

Note to self, addendum: Also bring rope. He growled in frustration. Forget Indiana Jones. He was going to have to start wearing a utility belt like Batman...if he actually made it out of this without getting killed or arrested.

He switched on his MagTac and shone the beam along the low parapet at the edge of the rooftop. A square shadow caught his eye and revealed a small opening that fed into a metal downspout that ran down the exterior wall.

Pierce stared at it for a few seconds. He could think of at least a dozen reasons why trying to shinny down that pipe was a foolish idea, but the one argument in favor of it was even more compelling: he had no other choice.

The sirens were getting louder.

Biting his lip, he hoisted himself onto the parapet and swung his legs out into space.

Oh, crap. Nope. Can't do this.

But there was no turning back now. Although he was still gripping the edge of the roof, too much of his body weight was already hanging out over the side. Climbing back up would be harder than sliding down the spout.

He stretched his feet out, probing the wall until he felt the pipe. He tried to grip the slick surface with the soles of his boots, but struggled to find purchase. Despite his lifelong action-hero fantasies, he had always been the kid in gym class who couldn't climb the rope to save his life.

You don't have to climb, he reminded himself. *Just go down.*

Going down was inevitable now. It was just a question of whether he slid or plummeted.

He unclenched his left hand from the parapet and reached down for the pipe. It was secured tightly against the wall, with no room for him to wrap his hand around it, but he got his best grip on it and squeezed with all his strength.

Now the other one.

His right hand seemed to have developed its own opinion on the subject of letting go. Pierce squeezed the spout even harder with his left, trying to work up the courage to...

"Just. Let. Go."

He let go.

Gravity seized control of the situation. There was a shrieking noise, like air escaping from a balloon, as the soles of his boots rasped against the pipe. Pierce felt a bloom of heat against his palm, friction caused by sliding down the spout much faster than he had intended. Frantic, he groped for the pipe with his right hand. He felt more friction heat as his fingertips grazed the wall, but somehow he managed to grab hold and squeeze—

He hit the ground like a pile driver. White hot skewers of pain stabbed up through the soles of his feet, all the way to his knees. Yet, even as he pitched backward, staggering like a drunken sailor and finally landing hard on his ass, he knew that his efforts to slow the crazy descent had not been futile. He was still alive.

Ignoring the pain, he got to his feet and shuffled across an open space that appeared to be a cross between an active archaeological dig and a picnic area. A wrought-iron fence guarded this section of the museum perimeter. The street beyond was quiet, but Pierce moved along the fence until he was in the shadow of a large rhododendron bush. Then he attempted to scale the barrier. The climb out required more effort than the climb in, and was less graceful, but he was in the homestretch now.

He dropped to the base of the fence and slid down a sloped retaining wall to the sidewalk. The street before him was one of the main boulevards running down the hill toward the harbor. There was a good chance at least some of the police units responding to the alarm would be coming up it. He stripped off his ski-mask and gloves and shrugged out of his black turtle-neck to reveal a garish tropical print shirt—just the sort of thing a tourist might wear. Then he started down the sidewalk, moving as nonchalantly as his aching legs would allow. He took the next left, heading west down the narrow urban canyon between the museum and a neighboring office building.

The siren noise abruptly peaked as a police car, with emergency lights flashing, rounded a corner and raced toward the museum entrance. Pierce decided it was better to look directly at it, like a curious passerby, rather than turning away and arousing suspicion. The vehicle did not slow, but continued past, the noise of its siren building to a high-frequency shriek before Dopplering away to nothing.

Pierce did not allow himself a relieved sigh. Fiona was still back there somewhere, her fate uncertain. He quickened his step, wincing as each footfall stressed the minor injuries sustained in his fall, and continued on toward the designated rendezvous point.

"Please let her be safe," he whispered, a prayer to any actual God who might still be paying attention.

FOUR

Fiona had only just arrived at the exit, when an alarm sounded from somewhere in the building behind her.

Well that takes care of that, she thought, twisting the knob and easing the door open. After a quick check to confirm that the courtyard beyond was still deserted, she stole forward, keeping to the shadows, and scaled the fence in the same spot she and Pierce had used to enter. As she waited for a car to clear the nearby traffic circle, she stripped off her black over-garments and stuffed them into a nearby storm drain. Clad in denim shorts and a T-shirt emblazoned with a silk-screened likeness of the Acropolis, she looked like a young tourist out for a late-night stroll. She hoped Pierce was having as easy a time sticking to the plan.

She crossed the street and skirted along the edge of a city park, heading west, not moving toward a specific destination but putting as much distance between herself and the museum as possible. The noise of the alarm had already diminished, but she could hear police sirens in the distance.

"Need a lift?"

The voice startled her. She had been so focused on getting away that she had failed to notice the car pacing her. A quick glance showed a man with wavy blond hair leaning out the side window of a blue sedan. He looked old—probably as old as Pierce, who had to be at least forty. The man immediately raised her hackles. The last thing she needed right now was some perv hitting on her. She looked away, trying to send a clear 'buzz off' message with her body language, realizing only then that the man had spoken in English.

British, judging by the accent.

The man called out again. "You're here with George Pierce, aren't you?"

The question startled her, and she came to an abrupt and unintentional halt. She forced herself to resume walking, refusing to give any further acknowledgement, but her mind was racing to make sense of the situation.

"I saw you come out of the museum just now." His tone was offhand, casual.

Fiona stopped again. This time, she gave him more than a cursory look. Aside from the fact that he had approached her out of the blue, after evidently stalking her and Pierce, there was nothing particularly scary about him. Somehow that only made the situation worse.

"The police are going to be here soon," he continued in the same unruffled manner. "I'm sure they're bound to notice me following you, and since I have no intention of just driving away, you should probably ask yourself whether you want to attract their attention."

Fiona muttered a curse under her breath. Under any other circumstances, she would have welcomed the arrival of the police. "Who the hell are you?"

"My name is Liam Kenner. Dr. Pierce and I are colleagues."

"Never heard of you." It was true. Fiona had been attending classes at the University where Pierce taught. She knew everyone in the department, and most of the other archaeologists who came and went on a regular basis. The name Kenner did not ring any bells.

"We were acquainted several years ago." Kenner paused a beat, then set the hook. "When he first began his search for Hercules."

If she had not already been standing still, Fiona would have tripped over this revelation.

"I'll tell you all about it," Kenner went on, "but I really think we'd both be more comfortable if you joined me. I don't bite."

Fiona desperately wanted to beg off, citing the old wisdom about not taking rides from strangers. Something told her that Kenner might be more dangerous than a random sexual predator, but the mere fact that he knew about Pierce's connection to Hercules convinced her that not knowing was even more of a risk.

"Well, I do," she said, trying to keep the fear out of her voice. "If you try anything..." She let the threat hang. Kenner merely smiled.

As she circled around to the passenger side, Fiona stuffed her hands in her pockets, trying to make the gesture seem as casual as possible. The fingers of her right hand closed around the wallet containing the lock picks. They would be very effective stabbing weapons, if the need arose. She noted a rental sticker in the corner of the windshield. That was a good sign. It meant Kenner probably wouldn't have been able to rig the electronic locks to hold her prisoner. At the first hint of trouble, she could stab him with a pick and then jump out.

She slid into the passenger seat but didn't buckle the seat belt. "Okay. Talk."

Kenner smiled again, then turned his eyes forward. He started to pull away from the curb, but at that moment, a pair of police cars screamed past, going the wrong way on the one-way street, heading for the museum. Fiona tried to hide her concern for Pierce behind a mask of indifference, but Kenner was not going to let her off that easy.

As he started forward again, he glanced in the rearview mirror at the receding lights. "You and Dr. Pierce separated. Why?"

"Long story." She stared straight ahead. "What do you want?"

"Actually, I want the same thing George does. The truth." He paused, perhaps hoping that she would voluntarily fill the silence. When she did not, he went on. "Has he told you the story? Seven years ago, he discovered proof that Hercules was a real, historic person, named on the manifest of a ship from the fifth century BC. The ship was the *Argo*." When she did not respond to this, he glanced at her. "Does your American education include the classics? *Argo*? Jason and the quest for the Golden Fleece?"

Without meeting his gaze, Fiona replied, "Although the most complete account of Jason's voyage, the *Argonautica*, was written by Apollonius of Rhodes in the third century BC, the works of Homer make reference to both the *Argo* and Jason, not to mention *Herakles*—" She broke from an otherwise flat monotone to emphasize the correct Greek pronunciation—"which date to at least the year 850 BC and may be as much as two centuries older than that. So, while my uncle might have discovered *a* ship named *Argo*, with a crew member named for the mythological hero, I doubt very much he would have made the mistake of believing that it was the inspiration for a legend that was at least five hundred years old when that ship was built. That's what I learned in my American education."

Kenner burst out laughing. "Touché, my dear. As a matter of fact, I think I made a similar observation at the time. I don't recall what George's reaction was. Regardless, shortly thereafter, the document was stolen. George believed the theft was the work of a secret society dedicated to preserving the legacy of Hercules."

Fiona felt a chill of apprehension and dug her hand deeper into her pocket. Had Kenner spotted the tattoo on the back of her right hand?

The symbol, a circle crossed by two parallel lines, was the mark of the Herculean Society, a souvenir of her first encounter with Alexander Diotrephes. It had always reminded her of a livestock brand, not so much a declaration of ownership as a sign of protection. Despite all the grief accompanying his interference in her life, Fiona had for a time secretly liked the idea of having the legendary Hercules as her guardian. Throughout her high school years, she had done her best to keep the tattoo hidden from her classmates at Brewster Academy. With her olive-complexion, raven-black hair and distinctly Native-American features, not to mention the fact that she was a Type 1 insulin-dependent diabetic, she was already different enough.

The symbol of Hercules was not widely known outside the Society, though it had been adopted as a Druid sigil in the 1960s. But if Kenner had done his homework, he would probably have come across it.

"Secret society?" Fiona rolled her eyes and tried for her best dismissive teenager voice. "Cool story. Is that why you were following Uncle George and me? Are you in this Hercules Club?"

"I'll tell you, if you tell me why you and Dr. Pierce broke into the museum tonight."

Fiona weighed her options. She was not about to share the truth about the Society with this man, no matter who he claimed to be or how much he claimed to know. But what tack should she take? What lie should she tell?

Before she could make up her mind, Kenner chortled again and clapped her shoulder. Fiona jerked away as if his touch had been red hot, but he continued laughing, oblivious to her reaction. "Just having a spot of fun with you," he said, though his humor sounded forced. "Of course I'm not part of that group, if it even exists at all. And your business at the museum is none of mine. Where can I drop you?"

The abrupt reversal stunned Fiona almost as much as the uninvited familiarity, and it took her a moment to gather her wits. Did he want her to take him to Pierce? Was that his game? If so, she wasn't going to play.

"That old fort," she said, choosing one of Heraklion's most notable landmarks.

"The Koules fortress?" There was a hint of amusement in his voice, as if he sensed what she was trying to do.

"That's the one."

Kenner said nothing more, but at the next intersection he made a right turn, heading in the direction of the old harbor. They made the short journey in almost complete silence. Kenner merely looked ahead, focused on the road. A few minutes later, the marina appeared.

Fiona could just make out the squat silhouette of the old Venetian fortress that had once guarded the port. It was situated on a causeway that was part of the long breakwater, which still sheltered the marina.

Kenner stopped the car near the entrance to the breakwater, which was barricaded to prevent vehicle traffic. He looked out at the fort. "Rather isolated here."

"I'll be fine." Without another word, Fiona opened the door and got out.

"If you should see your uncle," Kenner called out, "Ask him to contact me. I have some information that may be of interest to him. Provided he's still looking for Hercules, of course."

Fiona kept walking toward the old monument. The faint noise of an engine revving and tires crunching on pavement prompted her to glance over her shoulder. The car was moving away.

Kenner had not been wrong about how isolated the place was, but Fiona was a lot more worried about him coming back than running into some lurking stranger. She calculated the distance to the edge of the causeway. If Kenner came after her, she would leap into the harbor and swim for it.

She kept walking, but when the receding taillights disappeared, she ducked behind a barrier and waited. A minute. Five minutes. There was no sign of Kenner.

She dug her phone from a pocket, checking for messages from Pierce. Nothing. She started to tap out a text message to him, but stopped short of sending it. If he had been caught or arrested, then the police would be monitoring his phone. They might be able to use it to track her down.

Even if he had not been captured, he would be observing the 'no contact' rule that had been part of the plan.

She left the message unsent.

The designated rendezvous was about two miles away, at the Heraklion Airport. Her arrival at such a late hour would be less likely to attract unwanted attention than anywhere else, even at a hotel, but she knew the real reason he had chosen the airport for a fallback position. If he was not there waiting, she would board a waiting jet, which would take her to a destination known only to the pilots. The Gulfstream G550 was owned and operated by one of the Herculean Society's many shadow enterprises—legitimate corporations that facilitated operations in every part of the globe, not to mention providing a steady source of revenue. The flight crew, like most of the people employed by the Society's subsidiary ventures, were unaware of the role they played in protecting the world from history, and history from the world. They did not even know the Herculean Society existed, much less that they were a part of it. But they would follow Pierce's instructions to the letter.

That might have been Pierce's plan, but there was no way she was going to leave him behind. Still, maybe there was another way she could make use of the Society's resources.

She opened the Internet browser on her phone and found the contact information for the company that managed logistics for the Herculean Society. She called the international number, and then identified herself as a passenger on the Gulfstream. She hoped that would accord her VIP status, but the operator promptly put her on hold.

A moment later, the canned music was silenced as someone picked up the line. "Fiona? Are you safe?" It was Pierce.

She heaved a sigh of relief. "I'm safe, Uncle George."

"Where are you?"

"I'm at the old fort."

"What are you doing there?"

"After I left the museum, an old friend of yours offered me a ride. I think the actual word he used was 'colleague.' Liam Kenner."

There was a long silence over the line.

"Uncle George?"

"Kenner," Pierce said in a low, almost menacing voice. "Son of a bitch."

FIVE

"**Colleague? That's what** he said?"

Fiona sank into the passenger seat of the rental car and gazed over at Pierce. "Happy to see you, too," she remarked, more amused than sarcastic. She had not been waiting long, less than ten minutes, though it had seemed a lot longer.

Pierce looked mildly embarrassed. "Sorry. I'm still trying to process this." He took a breath. "It was clever of you to draw him off like that."

"Thanks. So what's the story with you and Kenner? He seemed to know an awful lot about your search for Hercules."

Pierce stared straight ahead, as if driving the deserted streets required his full attention. "Several years ago, when I first came across some documents that mentioned Hercules in a historic context, I made the mistake of sharing that information with some other members of the archaeological community. At the time, I was merely looking for more of the same, inquiring to see if anyone else had found similar evidence."

"Then Kenner *is* a colleague? An archaeologist?"

"His specialty is paleopharmacology, a multi-disciplinary field that focuses on the medical treatments used by ancient cultures. When I originally proposed the idea that Hercules might have been an ancient scientist, Kenner was intrigued by the possibility of an elixir to explain Hercules's strength and invincibility. Evidently, he was more interested than I realized at the time."

"Interested enough to stalk you for the last seven years?"

Pierce shook his head. "It's possible that he was here conducting research of his own, and noticed us touring the museum earlier."

Fiona raised a skeptical eyebrow. "You don't actually believe that, do you?"

Pierce checked the rearview, prompting Fiona to look over her shoulder, but there was no one following them. "I wish I did," Pierce replied. "But no. It's probably not a coincidence."

"So what do we do about it? About him?"

Pierce sighed. "He's just fishing."

"He knew that we broke into the museum. What if he goes to the police?"

"He won't. Not right away. He'll want to talk to me first. Maybe try to blackmail me, but it won't do him any good. He can't prove anything." Pierce drove in silence for a few minutes. "This isn't the first time someone has gotten close, you know. There are protocols for dealing with situations like this."

"Protocols?" Fiona did not like the sound of that. "Like making him disappear?"

"Nothing so dramatic. At the very worst, we might have to destroy him professionally. Discredit him, so that no one takes him seriously ever again. But I doubt it will come to that. He has other...pressure points."

Fiona sensed that Pierce did not want to elaborate further, so she changed the subject. "So we're still going to do this?"

"I don't think we have a choice. Especially not now, with Kenner sniffing around. He probably heard about the discovery at Ideon Andron. That would explain why he's here in Heraklion. We need to move now, before anyone else figures this out."

Fiona nodded in acceptance. Pierce was right, of course. This, too, was all part of the plan.

SIX

Central Crete

According to Greek mythology, Zeus, the ruler of the gods of Olympus and father to numerous divine and semi-divine offspring, including the legendary Herakles, was born on the island of Crete. He was the child of the Titans Cronus and Rhea. Cronus, fearing a prophecy that his own offspring would destroy him, had already devoured Zeus's elder siblings. Zeus would have suffered the same fate if his mother had not hidden him away in a cave beneath Mount Psiloritis.

Like all such myths, a thread of truth ran through the tale. There was indeed a cave. Ideon Andros, the Cave of Zeus. It had been revered by the ancient Mycenaeans—the civilization that had arisen on Crete after the fall of the Minoans, and which ultimately became the Greek civilization. For centuries, long after the center of the world shifted to Athens, Ideon Andros was believed to be the actual birthplace of the king of the Olympian gods. Archaeological excavations had revealed a long tradition of votive offerings at the cave, but Pierce knew that such evidence confused cause and effect. There were many caves all across the island, but the ancients had chosen to venerate this particular cave as the birthplace of their faith. There had to be a very good reason for that.

Although just twenty linear miles from Heraklion, it took Pierce nearly two hours to make the drive, the last five miles of the trip on a dusty road that wound up the mountainside. Ideon Andros was yet one more tourist destination on an island that was renowned for places of historic interest, but what Pierce and Fiona sought was not in any of the guidebooks.

They left the car near the small museum and gift shop that serviced visitors. Then they hiked in the darkness to the mouth of the cave, checking frequently to ensure that they had not been followed. The mountain air was chilly, and Fiona hugged her arms close, but did not complain as they slipped through a small fence that kept local goats out of the cave. Pierce kept the red filter on his MagTac until they finished descending the stairs that led down into the enormous opening beneath the mountain. Once they reached the main gallery, Pierce removed the cover and played his light on the high walls, which were rippling with stalactite growth. He quickly located a shadowy recess at the rear of the cavern. The surrounding area was cordoned off with wooden barricades and caution tape, indicating that an excavation was currently in progress, but Pierce had learned through the grapevine of the archaeological community that the dig had hit a wall. Literally.

"There it is," Pierce said, motioning with the light. He moved to the narrow fissure and lowered himself into it, shining the beam into its depths. The bright flashlight illuminated a flat stone wall, clearly worked by a human craftsman and adorned with a strange symbol.

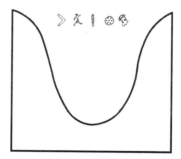

"The Horns of Consecration," Fiona said. "The symbol of the Sacred Minoan Bull. Just like the monuments in the palace at Knossos."

Pierce nodded.

They had seen several examples of bull iconography at the museum, ranging from the simple motif like that carved into the cave wall—dubbed 'The Horns of Consecration' by Sir Arthur Evans, the archaeologist whose work in Knossos had laid the foundation for the modern concept of the Minoan civilization—to much more realistic paintings and sculptures. Despite being lost to history for three millennia, the significance of the bull to the Minoan civilization had been immortalized in Greek mythology, particularly in the legend of the Minotaur, the half-man, half-bull chimera that roamed the subterranean Labyrinth, devouring human sacrifices.

There was even a connection to the story of Hercules. One of the legendary Labors imposed upon Hercules by King Eurystheus, as penance for killing his family in a fit of madness, had been the capture of the monstrous Cretan Bull. Pierce knew that much of that story was a fabrication—there had been no mental lapse, no family tragedy—but the stories hid an account of actual deeds. He had seen ample evidence that some of the Labors were based on real events, and of them all, the tale of the capture of the Cretan Bull seemed the least fantastic. It might simply have been a metaphor for a victory against the bull-worshipping Minoans, but Pierce suspected that there was probably a real bull in the story somewhere.

However, it was not the petroglyph of the horns on the wall that had drawn him to Ideon Andros, but rather a set of smaller images carved into the rock between the bull's horns.

Pierce took the Phaistos Disc from his satchel and held it at arm's length. He oriented it so that the outermost totem in the spiral—the beginning or the end, depending on whose interpretation was to be trusted—was in the six o'clock position.

Fiona looked over his shoulder. "It's a match. You were right."

"Of course I was right," Pierce answered with a grin. "You didn't think I'd come all this way on a hunch."

Fiona's shrug suggested that she thought him capable of doing exactly that.

"Alexander wrote that the Phaistos Disc was a key," Pierce went on. "He established a protocol in the event that a discovery like this was made."

"Right. More protocols. In this case, steal the Disc. Only we replaced it with an exact replica. I'm not sure how that changes anything."

Pierce held up the Disc. "I was a little worried about that, too. But the likeness of the Disc is everywhere, especially here on Crete, so if it was just a matter of hiding the message...well, that ship sailed a long time ago. I thought there might be something important about the physical disc itself, though. And guess what? I was right again. The Disc reacts to magnetic fields."

"No one ever noticed that?"

"I don't think it occurred to anyone to check. It's just a clay tablet after all. My guess is that there are flakes of magnetized iron embedded in the clay."

Fiona narrowed her eyes. "We didn't come all the way out here in the middle of the night just to compare the script, did we?"

Pierce grinned again. "Smart girl. Alexander said it was a key. I don't believe he was speaking figuratively."

He stepped closer to the wall and held the Disc up so that it was situated in the valley between the horns. The artifact was abruptly yanked out of his grasp, hitting the wall with a hollow clank, like a terra cotta bell. It did not slide to the ground but remained fixed in place between the horns. An instant later, there was a grinding sound from beyond the wall, and then a crunch, as some unseen force battled thousands of years of inertia and calcification. The wall began to move, rolling away into a hidden recess. Not a wall after all, but a circular door, with the Disc still affixed to its center. It rotated only half a turn before stopping, revealing a crescent-shaped opening.

"Open Sesame," Pierce said. "It would appear that the Phaistos Disc is actually an ancient Minoan key card."

He shone the light into the opening. The shape of the passage was too straight and uniform to be the work of nature. There was just enough space to accommodate a single person. It continued for at least fifty feet, at which point the black walls devoured his light. What lay beyond remained shrouded in darkness. "Shall we?"

"I thought we were just supposed to make sure no one gets the key," Fiona said. "Wasn't that what the protocol said to do?"

"Sometimes you have to go outside the letter of the law to keep the spirit of the law. Even without the Disc, someone might be able to get through that door. We need to know what Alexander wanted kept secret. If it's something we can remove or..." he frowned, "...destroy...then this is our chance. Besides, I'm curious. Aren't you?"

"I should call you Curious George," Fiona replied before following and sticking close behind him. As Pierce advanced into the passage, his own eagerness diminished a little. The tunnel was more confining than he had imagined. The weight of the earth above seemed to press down on him, making it difficult to breathe. The air felt warmer, and there was something else about it that seemed...off.

"What's that smell?" Fiona asked. "It's like...blood."

Pierce played the light against the walls of the passage. The black surface was mottled with what looked like a dull orange fungus. "Rust. These walls are sheeted with iron plates."

"Iron? I thought the Minoan civilization pre-dated the Iron Age."

Pierce gave an approving nod. Fiona had been paying attention to her studies. "They did. This is...interesting...to say the least. Some of the legends about this cave mention a race of spirit beings called Dactyls."

"As in 'fingers?'"

"When Rhea gave birth to Zeus, she dug her fingers into the earth, and the Dactyls were created. They were expert metalworkers, and they gave the secret of forging iron to mankind." He shrugged. "That's the myth, anyway." He stopped as the light revealed a T-junction at the end of the passage. The passages leading off in either direction were, like the first, finished with walls of featureless iron, vanishing into darkness beyond the reach of the flashlight.

Fiona peered over his shoulder. "Which way?"

"Good question. In many ancient belief systems, the choice of right or left had great symbolic significance, but in this instance, we may just have to flip a coin."

"What's that?" Fiona pushed past him and moved closer to the facing wall a few steps down the right hand passage. She pointed to a large patch of rust which, after a closer look, revealed lines and curves that were too precise to be random.

"The Horns again," Pierce said. "It's the same as the glyph on the door. But it's different. The Phaistos symbols aren't the same." He approached and brushed away some of the rust to get a better look.

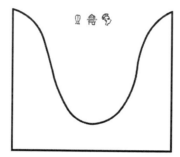

"There are only three symbols here. This is probably some kind of identifier. The name or number of this tunnel." He moved a few steps down the left hand passage, searching the wall until he found another symbol.

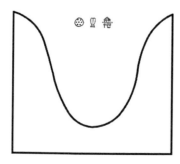

"Feel up for a linguistic puzzle?" he asked, grinning, as he took out his cell phone and handed it to Fiona. "Owens published his decipherment key online. It should give us a rough idea of what these signs are trying to tell us. See if you can find it."

Fiona stared at the screen. "No reception down here."

Pierce barely heard her as he studied the symbols, darting back and forth between the two glyphs. "We don't need it."

"You know what it says?"

He shook his head. "No, but I know what it means." He pointed at the symbol in the left hand passage. "This is on the Phaistos Disc. It's the second word in the spiral. That other one is nonsense. The Disc isn't just a key card. It's a route map. If we go down this tunnel..." He turned and headed down the left tunnel.

Fiona followed quickly and caught up to him a few steps from another junction, this time with a passage intersecting from the right. He was scanning the wall, looking for another symbol. He aimed his flashlight at the wall, revealing another glyph, identical to the one at the other end of the passage. "Here."

A quick check revealed a symbol with a different set of Phaistos characters at the beginning of the adjoining passage, and yet another on the wall that continued straight.

"One of these is the third word on the Disc," Pierce said. "If we keep going in that direction, we'll find more symbols in the same order as the Disc."

"A map," Fiona said, eyes widening. "I should have seen it."

Fiona had a gift for languages, modern and ancient, spoken and nearly forgotten, but spotting patterns was a skill that took practice. And her self-deprecation was preventing her from realizing the true scope of what they had found.

Pierce smiled wide. "Fi, do you know what this place is? This is *the* Labyrinth."

Her eyes widened in time with a broad smile. "Holy sh— Think there's a Minotaur down here?"

Pierce thought she meant it as a joke, but he gave the question serious consideration. He doubted that a literal bull-man creature had been wandering the iron corridors for over three thousand years, but the mere fact that the tunnels existed, to say nothing of the magnetic lock on the front door, strongly suggested that at least some parts of the legend were true.

"According to the myth," Pierce said, "the Labyrinth on the island of Crete was designed by the master architect, Daedalus. Ovid wrote that it was so elaborate that even Daedalus himself almost got lost in it."

"Daedalus. The guy who made the wings."

Pierce nodded. "After designing the Labyrinth, King Minos imprisoned Daedalus and his son, Icarus, so they would not be able to share its secrets. Daedalus collected feathers and stuck them together with wax to make a pair of wings so they could escape, but Icarus flew too close to the sun. The wax melted, his wings fell apart, and he crashed and burned.

"That story is also from Ovid's *Metamorphoses*, and it came much later. First century BC. But the stories of Daedalus's inventions go back much further. He was a mechanical genius. I've often thought he might be one of Alexander's alter-egos."

He knew it was a bit of a stretch, but by no means impossible. Alexander Diotrephes was a complicated man with an even more complicated story, and he'd gone by many other names in addition to Hercules and Alexander. Pierce was not sure how much Fiona knew about Alexander, and this was not the time or place for that discussion.

The short version was that Alexander had achieved a sort of immortality, by virtue of a unique physiology combined with a comprehensive knowledge of chemistry and biology, which was advanced even by modern standards. George wasn't positive, but he thought the man had been alive since before the ninth century BC. Immortality was a trait most often applied to supernatural beings or fictitious gods, but it was also the pursuit of learned men throughout all of history, ancient and recent. Alexander was one of the few who had achieved it.

"It would explain why he established the protocol," Pierce said. "He knew that if this place was ever discovered, there would be a lot of impossible questions."

"But why build it in the first place?"

"To imprison the Minotaur?"

"There are over thirty word combinations on each side of the Disc. If we take that to mean two safe paths through the maze, and we double that number for false trails, that makes at least a hundred and twenty different passages down here. Seems like a lot of work just to cage one magical beastie."

Pierce shrugged. "If the Disc is a map, then the answer to your question is probably waiting at the center."

"We'll need the Disc," Fiona said, and she headed back up the passage to the entrance, evidently having overcome her reluctance to explore the subterranean tunnels.

Pierce followed and they slipped through the opening. He reached out to pry the Disc free of the magnetic grip. It took some effort, but he managed to wedge his fingertips beneath it, and peel it away. As soon as he did, the door rolled back into place, sealing the tunnel again.

"I guess we're supposed to leave the key in the door," Fiona said.

Pierce stared at the Disc. "If I had some paper, we could do a rubbing. That way we'd have our map."

Fiona grinned and held up her phone. "Or we could do something a little more twenty-first century, and take a picture of it."

Pierce made a face. "You know what the problem with twenty-first century solutions is? Batteries die."

"I'm at ninety percent." She waggled the phone at him, then clicked a picture of the front side of the Disc. "That should give us plenty of time to get in and get back out again. Turn it over so I can get the other side."

When she was finished, Pierce used the Disc to open the door again. They retraced their steps to the second intersection, where their hypothesis was proven correct. The symbols on the wall indicated that they should continue straight. Soon thereafter, they reached yet another junction, this time with three possible choices, all marked with Phaistos script, but only one corresponded to the expected sequence found on the Disc.

"If the Phaistos symbols do represent actual letters or phonemes, could it be possible that the Labyrinth could have been a sort of literacy test?" Fiona asked. "Someone who knows how to read them would see the difference between real words and gobbledygook."

"Makes sense," Pierce said.

"What do you suppose happens if we make a wrong turn?" Fiona asked.

Pierce flashed his light down one of the alternate tunnels. "Best case, we get lost and follow the maze while keeping a hand on the wall, eventually making our way back here...which could be miles of walking."

"And worst case?"

"I suppose the very worst case would be something like the Minotaur, but my guess is that there are probably some booby traps."

"Nice." Fiona held up her phone, zooming in on the next set of symbols they were seeking.

The passages were not uniformly straight or flat. Some meandered back and forth, up long inclines and down spiral staircases. Only the reliability of the Phaistos symbols, marking the way every hundred yards or so, kept Pierce's anxiety in check. As they neared the end of the spiral, apprehension gave way to anticipation.

The final intersection presented them with a choice. Up or down. They emerged from a passage onto a broad landing, which appeared to be in the middle of a spiral staircase.

"Down," Fiona announced, checking the symbols against the picture of the Phaistos Disc. "This is it."

She started down the descending staircase.

And vanished.

SEVEN

As darkness engulfed her, Fiona felt her stomach rise into her throat. Her first thought was that she was falling, but this was more like being in a fast elevator. Her feet were still on solid ground, but she was definitely descending. A sudden heaviness signaled the end of her downward journey, and then all was still.

"Fiona!"

Pierce's frantic shout echoed in the air overhead. She looked up, searching for the source. She saw the faint glow of his flashlight, at least fifty feet above her. The light was not nearly bright enough to illuminate her surroundings, but just being able to see it filled her with hope.

"I'm down here!" she called. The iron walls created a weird reverberation effect, like shouting down a metal pipe. "I'm okay."

"What happened?" The glow intensified into a bright star, shining down into her upraised eyes. "The stairs disappeared."

"Did they? I can't see anything."

She blinked, forcing herself to look away from the pinpoint of light. "Was this a trap?"

"I don't know." Pierce's voice sounded fainter, as if the distance separating them was increasing. She knew it was not; the light above remained unchanged. "Don't move. I'll figure something out."

"I know I picked the right symbol," she insisted, more for her own sake than for Pierce's. To reassure herself, she raised her phone again, intending to double-check the symbols. "Oh, duh!"

She thumbed on the phone's built-in flashlight, and the darkness retreated.

She was standing in a small square room with walls that rose up into the black void overhead. There was no sign of the steps, but the floor beneath her feet was lined with evenly spaced grooves, each as wide as the treads of a stairway.

The stairs had been rigged to collapse downward as soon as anyone stepped onto them. A trap, but not a lethal one. At least, not right away. She and Pierce were separated. He could still get out, maybe bring back some rope...

He'll have to backtrack through the maze, but I've got the pictures of the Disc. Wonderful.

An arched doorway was the only way out of the room. Fiona flashed her light into the opening, but was unable to see much of what lay beyond. There were no Phaistos symbols on the black iron walls to indicate whether going through the door was the right course of action.

"Like I've got a choice," she muttered. Raising her head, she shouted up at Pierce. "There's a door here. I'm going to go through it."

"No! Stay right there!"

She ignored his warning and stepped closer to the door, checking the floor for pressure plates and trip wires. There was a wooden table at the edge of her light, holding something on its center. She couldn't quite make out what the object was, but the overall presentation reminded her of the display cases at the Heraklion Museum.

"I don't think this is a trap," she called. She stepped through the arch.

There was a rasping sound behind her. She whirled around and saw that another opening had appeared on the opposite side of the small room. On the wall, just to the right of the new passage, there was another glyph with Phaistos symbols.

"Freaky," she said. She stuck her head back into the room and looked up. "Uncle George?"

There was no sign of Pierce's light. Instead, there was now a ceiling, just a few feet above head level, consisting of metal panels each about the same width as the segments on the floor.

"What the hell?"

The hissing noise came again, startling her back a step. The reflex saved her life. A wall of metal descended through the air just beyond the arch, and would have sliced her in half if she had not moved.

Before she could recover her wits, an opening appeared at the top of the arch, growing larger as the wall descended into the floor. When it stopped, the second opening had vanished into the floor, and the room was configured again as it had been at first. There was just one major difference. Standing in the middle of the room was the somewhat bewildered form of Pierce.

"Uncle George!"

He raised a hand. "Don't move."

She nodded, signaling that this time, she would do as instructed.

Pierce's eyes darted around, taking in the changes. He shone the light up, revealing smooth walls with no visible ceiling. "The steps were camouflage. This is some kind of weight-sensitive elevator. Step on it, and it goes down. Step off, and it rises back up. Probably works on magnetic repulsion. It's a one-way trip though."

"I think this is where we're supposed to be." Fiona turned around and shone her phone's light at the table. There were several more like it, dotting the floor and lining the walls of a circular chamber, which was at least fifty feet in diameter. Interspersed with the displays were several more arched openings, which presumably led back into the Labyrinth, but Fiona gave these only a cursory glance. Her attention was held by the contents of the room. "Uncle George, you've got to see this...but if you step off, we won't be able to get back."

Pierce scratched his head, furrowed his brow, pursed his lips and then said, "We're not supposed to leave the same way we came in. There are two sides to the Disc. Two routes through the maze. One way in, one way out, but it leads here first."

Pierce stepped through the opening and turned to watch the segmented floor rise, propelled by invisible lines of magnetic force. The passage was momentarily blocked, then opened up to reveal the second configuration.

He joined Fiona at the central table. Resting upon it, spread out to show its extraordinary size, was what appeared at first glance to be a bearskin rug—perhaps from a Kodiak grizzly—head and all. On closer inspection, the tawny gold fur, along with the shaggy mane surrounding the fiercely snarling head, showed it to actually be the pelt of an enormous lion.

Pierce gasp in astonishment. "The Nemean Lion."

Fiona grinned as Pierce began to recount how Hercules, after strangling the Lion, had used its own claws, which were sharper than any sword, to cut through its skin, since no blade could penetrate it.

She drifted away and began looking at the other display tables. Some contained what might have been trophies from other Herculean conquests—swords, armor, teeth and claws from enormous beasts—while others contained items that were more utilitarian, with no explicit link to the myth. Fiona was drawn to one of the latter: a small chest, about one foot square and six-inches deep. It was covered in a reflective substance that showed no sign of corrosion or oxidation. Although she was no expert, Fiona thought it must be gold. Yet that was not what had drawn her eye. Something had been stamped into the soft metal, creating a raised relief. Fiona reached out a cautious finger and traced the shape.

Letters.

Greek letters.

ΘΡΑΚΓΕΙΑ

"Uncle George, this isn't right."

Pierce moved to join her, shining his light directly on the small chest. "Heracleia," he said, translating the ancient Greek script. "It's in Greek," he said, proud that she had noticed the aberration. "The Greeks didn't develop their alphabet until the eighth century BC. The Phaistos

Disc was uncovered in the ruins of a palace that was destroyed centuries before the Greeks started using this alphabet."

He tested the lid, which refused to open, then tilted the chest up to reveal a thin line of some opaque material holding the cover in place. "Beeswax. Whatever's in here has probably been perfectly preserved for thousands of years."

She watched as he exerted a little more pressure, breaking the wax seal. The lid popped open with a faint sucking noise, revealing what looked like a stack of dingy old papers covered with Greek script.

"Papyrus leaves," Pierce said, shaking his head as the mystery grew.

"You seem frustrated, Doctor Pierce. Perhaps you don't know Hercules as well as you think you do."

Fiona whirled in the direction of the familiar but unexpected voice, and found Liam Kenner standing just inside the entrance to the room. He wore the same smug smile that Fiona remembered from their earlier encounter.

Before she or Pierce could say a word to challenge him, a faint rasping noise signaled the arrival of yet another unexpected guest on the magnetic elevator.

Fiona did not recognize the man that stepped out of the small room. He was tall, broadly built and so ugly that for a moment, she wondered if he was some humanoid monster out of mythology. But this wasn't a bull-man standing before them. It was just a man. She could tell because he was pointing a gun at them.

EIGHT

Note to self, Pierce thought. *Next time, bring a gun.*

But a gun was only as good as the person holding it. His experience with firearms was mostly limited to plinking beer cans off a fence post with about fifty percent accuracy. The guy standing next to Kenner looked like someone who not only knew how to use his gun, but had every intention of doing so.

Pierce's gaze flickered around the room, looking for something he might be able to use as a weapon, calculating the distance to the nearest exit passage. He and Fiona might be able to make a mad dash out of the room, but escaping into the uncharted Labyrinth created its own set of problems. He brought his stare back to Kenner.

"What are you doing here, Liam?" Pierce tried to inject a note of righteous indignation into his voice. It was not difficult. He was angry, though mostly it was self-directed. He had badly underestimated Kenner and allowed himself to be caught flat-footed.

"Why, the same thing as you, old chap. I'm looking for Hercules. I seem to recall a time when that's what you wanted." Kenner's lips curled into a wry smile. "Not any more, though, right? Now you're the inside man."

Pierce answered him with silence. He was not about to confirm the man's suspicions by volunteering information.

"How did you find us?" Fiona demanded. "You didn't follow us. I made sure of that."

Kenner regarded her with a mixture of curiosity and disdain. "I didn't really need to, did I? It was obvious from the start why you had come to Crete. I knew you'd end up here, especially after that little caper at the museum." He advanced until he was standing right in from of her. "But I had to be sure."

He reached out a hand toward her, brushing lightly against her shoulder. She flinched a little, but her face remained defiant. Kenner drew back his hand with a flourish, like someone using sleight-of-hand to produce a coin from a child's ear. However, what he held between his fingers was not a coin, but a tiny cylinder of plastic trailing a short length of wire.

"You bugged me?" Fiona was livid. "You son of a—"

"Enough," the man with the gun growled. "You're wasting time. Get what we came for."

Kenner looked over his shoulder to his accomplice. "Tsk, Vigor. There's no need to be rude. We can behave civilly." He turned his gaze to Pierce. "I trust we can?"

"Putting that gun away would be a good start."

Kenner ignored the comment. "The transmitter wasn't much use once you went underground, but I took the open door as an invitation. After that, it was a simple matter of following the Phaistos symbols and trying not to give ourselves away too soon." He looked around the room, as if noticing its contents for the first time. "I must say, this exceeds my expectations."

He reached out for the chest containing the papyrus leaves. "The *Heracleia*." His tone was reverent. "This is the book that guided Euripides and Apollodorus. The definitive source of information about Hercules in the ancient world. There are no known copies of it still in existence, aside from this one, of course. We only know of it from references in other historical sources.

"I've always thought it strange that such an important and well-regarded work should vanish so thoroughly from the Earth. It's almost as if someone set out to erase it from existence." He cast a knowing wink in Pierce's direction, then grunted as he hefted the gold-plated chest into his arms. "Not exactly light reading, but it should prove very illuminating."

"You're not interested in the myth of Hercules, Liam." Pierce crossed his arms. "What are you really after?"

"*Myth?* It's the reality that fascinates me, just as it once did you." As he spoke, Kenner commenced a circuit of the room. He produced a small penlight and shone it on the contents of each display table in turn. "I'm not blind, George. I've seen what's been happening in the world these last few years. I've heard the whispers, the rumors. I've paid attention, and I'm not the only one who can see the pattern."

The man with the gun let out a low, threatening growl, perhaps signaling his displeasure at Kenner for volunteering too much information, or simply as a way of expressing impatience.

Pierce nodded at the gunman. "You mean him?"

"Mr. Rohn? No, he's just...what's the term they use in the movies? The muscle? The man he works for, however, is very interested in the truth about Hercules. A truth that you have conspired to keep hidden."

"Why on Earth would I want to do that?"

"Must we play this tiresome game? You have seen the monsters with your own eyes; I know this to be true. Real monsters." Kenner turned and pointed to the lion skin. "There's the proof. The Nemean Lion. The creatures that inhabited ancient stories weren't fanciful daydreams. Some of them perhaps, but not all. Many were real, flesh and blood creatures. Impossible creatures. The product of recombinant DNA engineering produced thousands of years before the discovery of the DNA molecule. If we can unlock the secrets of their genetic code, figure out how to combine diverse genetic material with viable results, there's nothing we won't be able to accomplish."

"It's been tried," Pierce said, unable to hide his disgust. "It never ends well."

"The key to finding the source of those mutations is in this room." Kenner picked up another item. He regarded it for a few moments before holding it up for inspection. "Do you know what this is?"

Pierce bit back an angry retort. The artifact was a wide band of what looked like leather, dyed black, at least eight inches wide and about two feet long. Kenner's light revealed an intricate pattern of decorative tool work. Pierce couldn't make out all the details, but he had quickly identified the object. His real effort was put into keeping that fact hidden from Kenner.

"Come, George, you're the expert on Hercules. This is the girdle of Hippolyte, the Amazon Queen. Capturing it was his Ninth Labor."

Pierce gave a noncommittal shrug.

After a few moments of studying the artifact, Kenner raised his eyes to Rohn. "This is it. This is what we came for."

"Good," Rohn declared. Then, without any hesitation, he aimed his pistol and fired.

NINE

Kenner jumped at the noise of the pistol discharging in the enclosed space. He had known it was coming, but the noise was much louder than he had expected.

At almost the same instant as the shot, the room went dark. Pierce's light had gone out. Kenner dropped to the ground and caught a glimpse of movement in the paltry beam of his own light.

The gun thundered again, and again, as Rohn pumped shot after shot into the darkness, where Pierce had stood. Kenner waited until the noise stopped, and then a few seconds more before raising his head and playing his light around the room. The air was filled with smoke and the stink of sulfur, but through the haze, he saw the big man heading for one of the exit openings.

"Stop!"

Rohn turned, his already unbearable visage twisted with disgust. "They're getting away."

"You missed?"

"No." The reply was immediate, defensive. "I don't think so. But a wounded animal can run for many miles before dying."

Kenner felt an unexpected surge of emotion. He had known all along that Rohn intended to kill Pierce and the girl, and while he found the prospect distasteful, he had come to terms with it. Sacrifices had to be made sometimes. Now, he felt a measure of relief. This was a better outcome. Not as cold-blooded. "Let them go. They'll never make it out of here."

"How do you know that? They know how to read the signs."

Kenner frowned. Rohn was right. The connection between the Disc and the correct path through the Labyrinth had been easy enough to figure out, and he had pictures of the Disc to help him navigate. "Which way?"

Rohn pointed to one of the exits. Kenner swept the floor with his light, hoping to see tell-tale drops of blood—there were none. Then he moved the beam up to shine on the walls beside the passage. As expected, there was a Phaistos glyph, but it did not match any of the combinations on the Disc. "This is not the right way," he said, then he moved quickly around the perimeter, checking the other exits until he found one that matched the character stamped in the center of the reverse-side of the artifact.

"Here. This way will take us out."

Rohn jabbed his gun into the passage Pierce and Fiona had used. "What about them?"

"Forget them. The Labyrinth will take care of them. And we'll close the door on the way out. Even if they find their way back here, they'll never be able to leave."

The big man growled his displeasure but complied. Kenner suspected his reluctance had less to do with uncertainty about Pierce's fate and more to do with Rohn's belief that he had failed. Missing his targets at such close range must have been a bitter pill. Kenner wanted only to be done with it all: out of the bizarre iron maze and back to civilization, where he could exploit what he had just discovered.

He allowed himself a satisfied grin as he trekked down the passage to the next junction. Pierce had no idea how significant the Labyrinth's treasures were. He had not even recognized Queen Hippolyte's belt, much less studied the image engraved upon it.

Pierce had always been a dreamer, an idealist. For him, archaeology was some kind of game, an intellectual puzzle. The man had no sense of how to leverage his discoveries into something more meaningful—wealth, influence, power. Pierce could have written his ticket seven years earlier when he had found the *Argo* manifest, but he had chosen to share it with only a few colleagues, instead of telling the world and launching his career as a celebrity archaeologist and TV star. And that was only the tip of an iceberg of opportunities that he could have seized.

Kenner had parlayed the mere knowledge of the document's existence into a more discreet kind of success. He had been paid a hefty finder's fee and a lucrative annual retainer simply to keep an eye on Pierce, in hopes that the archaeologist might stumble upon something even more impressive. For six years, Kenner had done just that, watching Pierce from a distance, following his movements, reporting everything back to his benefactor, the same man who had sent Rohn to join him on Crete.

From the outset, it had been clear that Pierce was continuing his search for the historic Hercules. Equally obvious, the investigation was connected to a series of global upheavals and natural disasters, though Kenner could not tell to what extent Pierce had been involved in some of those situations.

One clear picture that had emerged was that the Herculean Society, the faceless conspiracy about which Pierce had once speculated, was very real. Moreover, Kenner was now certain that Pierce was working for them. Pierce's decision to visit Crete after the strange discovery in the Cave of Zeus was the opportunity Kenner had been waiting for. He could expose both Pierce and the Society, and cash in on the subsequent revelations.

What he had found in the Labyrinth had surpassed his wildest expectations. Rohn's employer would be very pleased, and the man's gratitude was not something Kenner regarded lightly.

He was barely conscious of the journey out of the maze. The only time he paid any attention to their route was at the various crossroads, where he had to select the correct passage onward. It was only near the end that anxiety crept in to darken his mood. In his eagerness to follow Pierce, it had not occurred to him to think about the possibility that the exit from the Labyrinth might be buried, just as the entrance had been until recently. He did not share this thought with Rohn, who trudged along behind him, watching to see if Pierce was following them.

Ultimately, neither man had cause to worry. The sequence of turns indicated by the Disc brought them to another stairwell like the one that had brought them to the trophy room. As before, a magnetically regulated descent delivered them into a new chamber facing the maze entrance. They had come full circle.

After they emerged into the cave, Kenner reached for the Phaistos Disc, intending to seal the passage, but Rohn stopped him.

"Not yet," the big man said. He pressed his pistol into Kenner's hands. "Wait here. If they come out, shoot them."

Kenner blanched. "Where are you going?"

Rohn did not answer. Instead, he jogged away, leaving the uncomprehending Kenner to stand vigil at the open door. A few minutes later, Rohn returned bearing a canvas satchel. He went directly to the opening and re-entered the maze, but quickly came back out without the bag.

"Now we go," he told Kenner, extending an open hand to reclaim his sidearm.

Kenner parted with it happily. "What did you leave in there?" he asked, as he pried the Phaistos Disc loose from the rolling door.

"Semtex. We have ten minutes."

Kenner did not need to ask for an explanation. The Phaistos Disc was the only key to the Labyrinth, but there were other ways to get through locked doors, and Pierce was certainly resourceful enough to figure something out. At the very least, Rohn's bomb would cave in the entrance, blocking the way to the door, but there was a very good chance that the entire maze of passages worming back and forth under the mountain would be collapsed by the blast, pulverizing anyone still inside.

"Tough break," Kenner muttered with a shrug, and then he followed Rohn out of the cave.

TEN

Fiona lay in the darkness, half-crushed beneath Pierce's weight, holding her breath. Pierce did not seem to be breathing either, and as much as she wanted to believe that he was just trying to remain quiet, she knew better.

How many shots had there been? Four? Five? More? It seemed impossible that the ugly gunman, Rohn, had missed that many times.

She struggled to recall exactly what had happened. The room had plunged into darkness, and she had felt someone—it could only have been Pierce—grab hold of her, almost lifting her off her feet. That was when the shooting had started.

All was quiet now. She lay motionless, pinned down and immobilized by Pierce's—*don't say it, don't even think it*—dead weight.

Voices drifted toward her, Kenner and Rohn discussing what to do next, then silence again.

"Uncle George?" The question was barely a whisper. Despair had stolen her voice.

A low hissing sound issued from the darkness. "Shhh."

Fiona's heart leapt, but she stifled a squeal of joy. Pierce was still alive. Just as quickly her relief was dampened by other possibilities. What if Pierce was injured? What if the killer came after them? There was nothing she could do but hope and wait.

Finally, Pierce stirred and rolled off her. She took that as a cue to break the silence. "Are you okay?"

"I'm not hurt, if that's what you mean," he replied, with palpable anger. "But I'm not okay. Not by a long shot."

A light flashed on, blindingly bright after such a long time in the dark. Fiona raised a hand to provide some shade and braved the stinging brilliance to get a look at him. For a moment, she thought her eyes were playing tricks on her. Then, despite everything they had just gone through and the crisis they were still facing, she burst out laughing.

Pierce glowered at her from beneath the regal mane of the Nemean Lion, which he wore as Hercules once had, if the legends were to be believed. After a few seconds, his expression softened. He turned, playfully showing off the long cloak of lion skin like a runway model, and he joined her in laughter.

Fiona understood now how they had survived the barrage of gunfire at almost point blank range. In the instant before Rohn had pulled the trigger, Pierce had flicked off his light and pulled the lion skin over him like a blanket. The legendary creature's skin was evidently as impervious to bullets as it had been to swords and arrows in Hercules's time. Pierce had then scooped Fiona up and headed into the nearest passage.

That, Fiona realized, had probably been the most dangerous part of his desperate plan. The odds were against it being the correct route out of the Herculean trophy room, which meant that they were no longer in the 'safe' part of the Labyrinth. Though they had gone less than a hundred yards, Fiona was not sure which direction to go now. And even if they managed that, she doubted that Kenner and Rohn would leave the door open.

But they were still alive, and that was better than nothing.

"A dead lion," she murmured.

"What's that?"

"Something I heard once. 'Better to be a live dog, than a dead lion.' It seemed appropriate given the circumstances."

He nodded, approving. "It's from the Bible. Ecclesiastes, chapter nine. 'To him that is joined to all the living there is hope: for a living dog is better than a dead lion.' Loosely paraphrased: Where there's life, there's hope. We're a couple of lucky dogs who are still alive because of a dead lion." He turned around and pointed down a passageway. "I'm pretty certain that's the way back to the center. From there, we can follow the Phaistos markings to the exit. If Kenner and his ugly friend are waiting for us... Well, we'll figure something— Wait. The papyrus in the chest. The *Heracleia*. The Greeks didn't develop their alphabet until the eighth century BC. So that document couldn't have been written until about six hundred years after the Disc was buried in the ruins of Phaistos palace." Pierce considered this for a moment. "Alexander might have had another way to open the door. A duplicate key."

Fiona shook her head. "But no one knew about the door. It was covered up long before the Greeks started coming here. Alexander came here later, maybe hundreds of years later."

Pierce rubbed his jaw thoughtfully. "A back door, then. The Labyrinth wasn't originally built to hide these treasures. That came later, after the main entrance was covered up."

"If you're right, we still have to *find* it."

"Let's get back to the trophy room," Pierce said. "Maybe there's a clue."

Pierce, still wearing the Nemean Lion's skin, led the way back to the central chamber. As expected, Kenner and Rohn were long gone. Pierce made a cursory check of the other display tables, identifying several of the relics, many of which were clearly from later periods in history, but there was nothing that indicated which path led to the hypothetical back door.

He turned his attention to the symbols that marked each passage, hoping to find a similarly anachronistic marker. "These appear on the Disc, but they're not in the right place."

"Right," she said.

"Focus," he said. "Forget about everything else. Tell me what you see."

She furrowed her brow in thought. "If this really is some kind of literacy test, then the glyphs that lead out should form words. Even though we don't speak the language, there's going to be a logic to the way the symbols are used. In English, certain letters are frequently used together, while others almost never are."

"Go on," he said, smiling. She was on the right track.

"Some of the symbols appear with a lot more frequency. Like Wheel of Fortune. People always start with the high frequency letters? R, N, S, T, L, and E. Even though we can't read this language, we should be able to see the difference between real words and nonsense combinations."

Pierce grinned. "Well done. I knew there was a reason I brought you along." He handed her the flashlight. "Now, keep your eyes peeled for traps."

Fiona stared at the glyph, feeling the weight of responsibility. Their survival depended on her. If she was wrong, they would wander the maze until they dropped from exhaustion, or worse, got killed by some ancient booby trap.

"We should mark our trail," Pierce said. "In case we have to backtrack. Like Theseus, trailing Ariadne's thread." He held up a massive lion forepaw and squeezed it, extending the razor sharp black claws. He scratched a single vertical line on the iron wall beneath the glyph. "That should do the trick."

Grateful for the safety net, Fiona ventured into the passage.

When they arrived at each junction, she studied the choices, looking for the one that matched a word on the Disc or was consistent with the internal logic of the ancient Minoan language. They didn't encounter any traps or dead ends, but it was impossible to know if they were on the right track. Navigating the passages was like being in an 'old school' arcade game, where winning a level simply took you to the next battleground, identical in every respect, except harder. Each decision was a gut check, and as they pushed deeper into the unknown, she felt the cumulative weight of all those choices. Either she was leading them to safety, or they were already hopelessly lost. Yet, with each hard decision, she felt her confidence growing. She *was* getting it. She was going to beat this game.

Then the uniformly cramped iron walls gave way to native rock. A few steps further, the winding tunnel led out onto a rusty iron bridge spanning an open fissure with nearly vertical walls.

Fiona shone her light across the gap, which she judged to be about thirty feet wide. She saw a ledge on the far side, wide enough to walk on, stretching in either direction beyond the reach of the light. But there did not appear to be any openings in the far cave wall. She glanced back at Pierce. "Did we make a wrong turn?"

He shook his head. "I don't think so. It wouldn't make any sense to build a bridge that goes nowhere."

"Maybe the bridge is a trap. Get halfway across and then—*click!* Going down in a hurry."

Pierce studied the metal span for a moment. "I don't think it's rigged to fail. Now, whether it will hold up after all this time..." He gave a helpless shrug. "Stay here."

"What? I don't think—"

Pierce was already in motion, walking cautiously out onto the bridge. Each step generated an ominous creak, but the bridge held. Fiona held her breath, willing the metal to remain intact just a few minutes longer. Pierce stepped onto the ledge at the other side and then waved her on.

"Take it slow," he warned. "But if you think it's starting to go, run like hell."

Fighting the urge to simply run across, Fiona took a step onto the bridge, then another. She could feel it vibrating beneath her, could almost see flakes of oxidized metal crumbling away with each footfall.

Halfway.

The bridge groaned and started swaying... *Just my imagination*, she told herself.

The ledge was just ten feet away now.

Close enough.

She launched herself forward, but the extra force generated by the attempt punched a hole clean through the walkway. Her toe caught on the edge, and she pitched forward. Her knee struck the deck, the impact crumbling the metal like a stale potato chip. In her mind's eye, she saw the entire bridge disintegrating under her as she struggled to get back to her feet—

Pierce caught one of her outstretched arms and yanked her the rest of the way off the bridge. He held her upright, which was good, because her legs felt like overcooked spaghetti noodles. "I said, take it slow," he chided. "You all right?"

She glanced back at the bridge, which to her complete astonishment, looked pretty much unchanged. "Uh, huh."

He waited until she had both feet firmly planted, then let go and directed her attention to the wall. "Take a look at this."

She took a deep breath, her heart still pounding like a jackrabbit's, and shone the flashlight where Pierce indicated. There was something carved into the wall, but it was not Phaistos script.

"You know what that is, don't you?" Pierce said.

She nodded slowly, still not quite able to believe what she was seeing. "It's the Mother Tongue."

The reason for Fiona's initial encounter with the Herculean Society and the man who called himself Alexander Diotrephes, was her knowledge of the old and almost completely forgotten language of the American Indian Siletz tribe. It was a Salish dialect with several unique components that, if Diotrephes was to be believed, could be traced back to the original human language, what he called 'the Mother Tongue.' It was a manner of speech that transcended mere words, and could affect matter in seemingly magical ways. Diotrephes had also called it 'the Language of God.'

With it, Moses had commanded the elements, unleashing deadly plagues against Egypt, and parting the waters of the Red Sea. Many centuries later, Rabbi Judah Loew ben Bezalel had used his knowledge of the Mother Tongue to animate a clay effigy of a man—a *golem*—to protect Jews living in the ghettos of Prague. Such incidents were exceptional. Very few people living even knew there was one original language. Although all languages could be traced back to it, the oldest tongues that were the closest descendants of the Mother Tongue—like the language of the Siletz—were nearly extinct.

Fiona's grasp of the Siletz tribal language had led, not only to her acquaintance with Diotrephes, but also to the upheavals that had destroyed her former life, and inadvertently given her a new one as Jack Sigler's adopted daughter. She was now the only person alive who spoke the Siletz language, and according to Diotrephes, she was the perfect candidate for mastering the Mother Tongue.

Unfortunately, there was no Rosetta Stone for that ancient language. Fiona's interest in linguistic studies was a direct result of Diotrephes's desire to unravel the mystery of the Mother Tongue. It was no exaggeration to say that she had a gift for learning languages, but she was no closer to understanding it now than she had been at the start. She could see fragments of that original tongue sprinkled throughout modern languages in the same way that certain words in English could be traced to Latin roots, but trying to rebuild a language that had not been spoken for thousands of years was like trying to guess what a completed jigsaw puzzle might look like after finding a few random pieces underneath the couch.

She stared at the letters but their meaning was lost on her. "This doesn't make any sense. Alexander didn't know how to speak the Mother Tongue. So why would he put this here?"

"Maybe he knew more than he let on. Or maybe he was able to figure out some of it, the way you figured out how to read the Phaistos script." With his knowledge of the Herculean Society's inner workings, Pierce knew as much about the Mother Tongue from an academic perspective as Fiona did, even if he couldn't speak any of it. "Ten bucks says that speaking these words will unlock our back door."

"I have no idea what it says."

When it came to ancient languages, Pierce was fluent in Greek and Latin, but those were languages that could be taught. While there were traces of Mother Tongue in many modern languages, teasing them out was less about knowledge and more about intuition. It was a gift. And not his. But Fiona...she might be the only person alive who had actually spoken—and forgotten—a few phrases. But that was four years ago. "If anyone can figure it out, it's you."

"I appreciate the pep talk, but the Mother Tongue isn't just about knowing what the words sound like or even what they mean. It's deeper than that."

Fiona struggled to think of a way to explain the mechanics of the mysterious language, a combination of vibrational frequencies and focused intention that could affect matter at the subatomic level. She had no doubt that if she was able to master the words and frame the appropriate mental image, the stone wall would become as insubstantial as mist, but doing that was like trying to move a muscle by telling it to move. Mastery of the Mother Tongue was more a subconscious process than a conscious one.

But there was no other choice.

She took a deep breath, closed her eyes, and envisioned a tunnel through the rock wall that led out of the cavern. As she did that, she began to clap her hands against her thighs, pounding out a slow but regular rhythm. Then she began to sing.

Her grandmother had taught her the chant, the first words of the Siletz language that she had ever learned. It was a song to the spirits of the sea, praising the power and beauty of the waves, thanking the spirits for the bountiful gift of fish and oysters that sustained her people from one turning of the seasons to the next.

The thought of her people, the Siletz Nation, all but extinct now, nearly broke her out of the rhythm, but she focused on the words and let herself be carried along, like a leaf on the wind.

The chant was repetitive, but she gradually changed the words of the song, asking the spirits to open the door to the world beneath the sun. It was not meant as a literal prayer. She was, more than anything, hoping to get lucky and find the right words.

Hopefully, the words for 'open the magic door' were the same in both the Mother Tongue and the language Fiona's grandmother had taught her, but either her mental discipline was insufficient, or the words just weren't right.

Nothing was happening.

She tried harder to visualize the rock opening up, and chanted the words again.

Without warning, something like a gust of wind pushed her forward, slamming her against the stone wall and silencing both the chant and the persistent beat she had been clapping. She felt a tightness in her inner ear, the result of a sudden change in air pressure that went from uncomfortable to agonizing in the space of a heartbeat. Before she could start to make sense of it, she was assaulted again, this time by an ear-splitting sound, like a jet engine tearing itself apart.

Is this something I did?

She turned to Pierce, who seemed equally bewildered by what was happening. The noise was coming from behind them, from out of the depths of the Labyrinth. In the dark mouth of the passage back across the bridge, she glimpsed a dull red glow, growing brighter. The maze had been transformed into a passage to Hell itself.

Then the ground heaved beneath her as the world came apart at the seams.

ELEVEN

Pierce leapt forward and threw the Lion skin over Fiona as a shower of loose earth and rocks rained down. He could feel the impact of larger stones striking the thick pelt. It had weathered a storm of bullets, dissipating their ballistic velocity so effectively that he had barely noticed, but he doubted even the legendary lion hide could protect them against a Volkswagen-sized boulder. He looked out from beneath the skin's protective shadow, searching for some refuge from the cave in. What he saw was not encouraging.

Fissures appeared in the ledge, zigzagging like lightning bolts, transforming the solid ground underfoot into a fractured and fragile web. The low persistent rumble of the collapse was briefly punctuated by a shriek of twisting metal. The bridge tore loose, along with a generous portion of the ledge, disappearing into the chasm below. Pierce barely had time to press himself and Fiona flat against the wall before the floor crumbled as well. That was when he saw an opening in the wall.

It had not been there a moment before. Either the tremor had broken through, or Fiona's chant had worked. Regardless of the explanation, there was now a hole where there had been none. Maybe it led to salvation, maybe it led nowhere, but either option was preferable to staying put and waiting to die. He bundled Fiona into his arms and leapt into the gap.

There was no floor beneath them now, just a V-shaped crevice, widening with every passing second. Pierce felt his feet sink deeper like a wedge driven into a log. Each step was a struggle. His left foot caught and he pitched forward, Fiona's weight pulling him off balance. She seemed to sense that he was falling and slipped free of his grasp, catching herself and steadying him. The shift was just enough to free his foot. He managed to stumble forward out of the spill, realizing only after a few steps that he was on flat ground.

"We made it!" Fiona said.

Pierce took a few more steps before Fiona's words registered. His mouth and nose were full of grit, but the air was clearer, cooler. He staggered to a halt and lifted the Lion skin away from his eyes. Patches of scruffy grass grew across rocky terrain. He looked up, and saw stars in the black expanse overhead.

Behind them, the summit of Mount Psiloritis was outlined against the night sky, and much closer, there was a cliff face rent by a jagged crack. A plume of dust rose from the gap like a smoke signal. He wasn't sure where they were, but given the serpentine nature of the Labyrinth, they were probably less than a mile from the entrance to the cave.

Fiona bent over beside him, hands on her knees as if on the verge of exhaustion, but laughing. While he shared her sense of relief at their escape, another emotion burned hotter.

Rage.

Kenner had blown up the Labyrinth, probably expecting to seal them in, to die a slow death of starvation, rather than killing them outright. But the intent was the same. He had tried to kill them. Both of them. And Pierce couldn't let that go unanswered.

Yet, revenge alone was not Pierce's sole motivation. There was more to this than Kenner's ambition. The man was working with someone else, someone with a lot of resources and few scruples. Kenner was also now in possession of at least two items that Alexander Diotrephes had seen fit to hide away in the Labyrinth's forgotten depths. There was no telling where those artifacts would lead him. The *Heracleia* alone might contain enough information to help Kenner unlock the genetic treasure he sought—the secret of how to make viable chimeras—not to mention other revelations that might overturn everything the Herculean Society had accomplished over the millennia.

To say that the situation was dire seemed like an understatement. But like Fiona said, they were alive. Where there was life, there was hope. He allowed her a few more seconds to catch her breath then clapped her on the back. "Come on. We've got work to do."

LABORS

TWELVE

Gibraltar

The skipper of the flat-bottomed launch drove the bow end of his craft up onto the sloping rocky beach and shouted for his lone passenger to jump ashore. Before the words finished leaving his lips, Augustina Gallo had already hopped out. She knew the drill. This was not her first visit to Gorham's Cave.

She landed lightly on the wet rocks and scrambled up ahead of an incoming breaker. Above the tide line, she turned and threw a wave to her ferryman. Then she picked her way through the shifting mass of driftwood and rocks to the opening in the sheer cliff.

The cave was dark, lit only by ambient daylight, very little of which found its way in. It was still early, but once the sun passed its midday zenith, the east-facing cliff would fall under the shadow of the legendary Rock of Gibraltar, and even this vestige of illumination would be gone. Gallo removed her sunglasses, which helped a little, but she had to wait a few minutes for her eyes to adjust, before continuing inside.

A wooden boardwalk had been constructed through the middle of the vast hollow, branching out to areas where archaeologists had discovered artifacts and other signs of ancient habitation. Once,

Gorham's Cave had been high and dry, three miles from the shore of the Alboran Sea, where it had provided a refuge for a sizable population of Neanderthals for more than a hundred thousand years. Changing climates had spelled doom for the cave's occupants, and then the sea level raised to the point where the waves were now practically lapping at the door. The inaccessibility of the entrance meant that the archaeological record from that period was virtually pristine. The cave complex, which was awaiting designation as a UNESCO World Heritage Site, was off limits to the public. It was available only to authorized researchers, though at present, no one was working the site. Gallo had the place to herself.

She moved to the rear of the cave, where she left the marked path and climbed up to a concealed niche. Even from just a few feet away, the opening was impossible to see. Gallo paused to turn on her phone's flashlight, then moved into the recess.

The light revealed a shape carved into the wall, not Neanderthal art, though it might easily have been mistaken for that, but rather a simple circle, crossed by parallel vertical lines. Just past it, a rickety-looking staircase led up to a closed wooden door, secured with a badly rusted padlock.

She reached out to what looked like a nub of rock on the adjacent wall and gave it a twist, revealing a modern handprint scanner. She placed her right palm flat against the glass plate. There was a faint flash of light as the scanner verified her identity, and then the entire door—padlock, frame and all—swung away to reveal another, almost completely unknown, section of the cave.

Gallo entered, careful to keep her right wrist turned up at all times, exposing the mark tattooed there. It was the same mark carved on the nearby wall, the distinctive sigil of the secret society into which she had been initiated, and which her boyfriend, George Pierce, was now the director: the Herculean Society.

The handprint reader was the last of a series of measures designed to protect this secret part of the cave from unwanted visitors. The tattoo on her hand was a different sort of defensive mechanism, designed to protect *her* from what lived inside.

Long before being 'discovered' by its namesake, a British infantry captain in 1907, Gorham's Cave had been one of more than a score of citadels established by the Society and its enigmatic founder, Alexander Diotrephes. The citadels had served an important role in an era when weeks or even months of travel was required to reach far-flung destinations. In modern military terms, the citadels served as both forward operating bases and supply depots for Society agents carrying out important missions around the globe. But for a brief period starting in 2009, when it had been temporarily abandoned, this cave, the original citadel, had served as the headquarters for all Herculean Society operations. It was not a coincidence that, from ancient times, the strait that separated the Mediterranean Sea from the Atlantic Ocean had been called the Pillars of Hercules.

Now that high speed air travel had shrunk the world, the citadels served more as repositories for the secrets the Society was obliged to safeguard. It was one such secret that prompted Gallo to pause a few steps beyond the doorway and lift her gaze to the ceiling. The upper reaches of this cavern were cloaked in shadow, but she could hear them, creeping stealthily amidst the hanging stalactites.

They were called the Forgotten, and once, long ago, they had been human. Now they were...something else.

In ancient times, Alexander Diotrephes, the man who would someday be remembered as the legendary Hercules, had waged a long war against mankind's greatest enemy: Death. In the early days of that struggle, he had conducted radical scientific experiments with human tissue, and inadvertently unleashed a plague that had transformed an entire city—men, women and children—into terrifying monstrosities. Imbued with the very immortality he sought, but cursed with a primal thirst for human blood, the wraith-like creatures were the inspiration for nearly every legend of ghouls and vampires.

The Forgotten were Alexander's greatest regret, the offspring of his hubris. He labored for centuries, looking for a cure, and in return, the Forgotten served as guardians for the Herculean Society citadels. It was a dangerous alliance. Although Alexander had eventually synthesized a compound to satiate their macabre hunger, the instinct to hunt and consume living victims remained strong. Finding some kind of permanent cure for the Forgotten remained one of the Herculean Society's secondary missions, but the prospects for a workable solution were not good. The problem had confounded Alexander for more than three thousand years.

The tattoo on Gallo's wrist had no special intrinsic power to repel the creatures. But it was the symbol of an ancient agreement, made with a man who no longer inhabited the world of humankind. The Forgotten were on the honor system.

"I really do despise this place."

Her voice was soft, with a flowing drawl that was in stark contrast to most people's first impression of her. Despite her surname, to say nothing of her appearance—long black hair, olive complexion, and both the face and physique of an Italian swimsuit model—Augustina Gallo was about as Roman as a Georgia peach. A decade living abroad, teaching classical studies and mythology at the University of Athens, had reduced none of her genteel Southern charm.

Pierce, seated at a table in the center of the room, nodded but did not look up from his computer screen. The citadels were short on creature comforts, but one thing they did have was an electronic lifeline to the outside world, courtesy of concealed fiber optic lines that provided high speed Internet access for both computers and phones.

Behind Pierce, Fiona lay stretched out on a cot. She rolled over and propped herself up on her elbows. "Hey, Aunt Gus."

Gallo returned a patient smile. "Darlin', just because we happen to be in the same after-school club, don't think for a second that you are entitled to eschew proper decorum."

Fiona rolled her eyes, and then in an exaggerated approximation of Gallo's style of speech, said, "Professor Gallo, I humbly beg your pardon for my overly familiar manner of address."

"Better."

Ordinarily, Gallo would have quietly tolerated Fiona's youthful banter, but Pierce's demand that she drop everything and fly to Gibraltar to join him in the citadel, surrounded by an army of creepy vampires, had trimmed her fuse down to a nub. She stopped by Pierce, who was too preoccupied by his work to even notice the exchange between his adopted 'niece' and his long-time girlfriend and confidant. She cleared her throat. "Ahem."

Pierce looked up, but his expression was not the least bit apologetic. "Grab a chair. There's a lot to go over."

His uncharacteristically intense demeanor stopped her in her tracks. Whatever the crisis he was dealing with, it had robbed him of his customary easy-going nature. She decided to dial back her own irritation in favor of a more supportive role, and settled in beside him. "What can I do?"

Pierce, who was in the midst of sending a live-chat message, did not immediately answer. Gallo recognized the user name of the person on the receiving end. It belonged to Cintia Dourado, the Herculean Society's senior logistician.

Dourado's affiliation with the Society went back even further than Pierce's. As a teenaged prodigy living in the slums of her native Belem, Brazil, the self-styled 'black hat' had, on a whim, followed a trail of whispered rumors to their source. She hacked the Herculean Society's computer network. Alexander, impressed by her innate talent, and perhaps more importantly, recognizing that the best defense against a hacker of Dourado's skill was Dourado herself, had personally recruited her into the fold. He had used her to organize operations around the globe and to search out and erase rumors of the sort that had led her to the Society in the first place. Gallo had never met Dourado in person—the young woman was the quintessential telecommuter, now operating from a slightly more upscale residence in Belem—but they had communicated often by e-mail and teleconference.

Pierce sent his message, and then he turned to face Gallo. His expression remained grim, which prompted Gallo to lean forward and give him a light kiss on the lips. When she drew back, she saw little change. "What's wrong?"

"Fiona and I had a little run-in with your old boyfriend."

The acid in his tone felt like a physical assault. "My old...?"

"Liam Kenner. He tried to kill us."

"Kenner and I were never... Wait. Tried to *kill* you? How? Why?"

"That's what I'd like to know. He knew we'd go to Heraklion. He knew that we would be going after the Phaistos Disc."

It took a moment for the significance of this to sink in. Gallo felt her pulse quicken as her body went into full defensive mode. "You don't actually think that I had anything to do with that? I haven't spoken to Kenner in years. I haven't even thought about him. And not that it's any of your business, but we were never together. He asked me out. I refused. End of story."

Pierce closed his eyes and took a deep breath. "I'm sorry," he said, eyes still closed. "I guess almost getting buried under Mount Psiloritis has me a little on edge."

Gallo glanced over at Fiona, who was watching the exchange wide-eyed. The mere fact of the girl's presence was enough for her to bring her ire under control—she was averse to causing a scene. Though the matter was far from resolved. "Why don't you start at the beginning?"

Pierce nodded and related the events of the previous evening, beginning with the immediate aftermath of their escape from the museum, when Kenner first accosted Fiona, and ending with the early morning flight to the citadel.

"He's been tracking us," Pierce concluded. "Stalking me, all these years. Piecing it all together."

Gallo resisted the urge to emphasize that it was Pierce, and not she, that had been Kenner's target. After listening to Pierce relive the ordeal he and Fiona had narrowly survived, she felt a little more inclined to excuse his brusque manner. "You weren't exactly the soul of discretion back then."

"Yeah, but I didn't think anyone took me seriously."

"I did. And evidently, so did Kenner."

Pierce mumbled his agreement, and then added, "But he's not working alone. Someone is bankrolling him. I've got Cintia working that angle. We have to find out who, and then shut them down."

Gallo looked around. "Why did you come here? Athens would have been a lot closer."

"If he's figured out that Fi and I made it out, then he might come after us again."

"Him, or that ogre he was with," Fiona added.

"And you think he might come after me, as well," Gallo said. She did not elaborate on what Kenner's intent might be in such a scenario.

Eight years ago, when she had arrived in Athens as a freshly minted post-doc, eager to carve out a niche for herself in the academic world, she had fended off the relentless advances of more than a few of her colleagues. Liam Kenner, who was not quite as dashing and sophisticated as he imagined himself, had been just another strutting peacock trying to catch her eye.

Pierce alone had treated her as an equal, not a prize to be won. They had become friends first, and only later had their relationship deepened. When Fiona's adopted father had asked Pierce to take over the Herculean Society, as he had from Alexander, Pierce had not hesitated to include Gallo. They were more than just 'in a relationship.' They were a team.

"Or he might try to use you to get to me," Pierce replied. "It's safer here, at least until I can figure out what to do next."

Gallo did not fail to notice the exclusivity of his language, but decided to let it slide. Pierce was clearly still rattled from the attempt on his life. Rather than comment, she rose from her chair and went over to inspect the one item that Pierce had brought back from Crete. "This is really the skin of the Nemean Lion?"

"And it lives up to the hype," Fiona said, before Pierce could answer. "Bullet-proof, explosion-proof, cave-in-proof...you name it, the Lion skin stops it."

Gallo turned back to Pierce. "You said he took Queen Hippolyte's girdle and a book?"

"A copy of the *Heracleia*. Probably one of the first ever written down and the only one still in existence today."

"Why?"

Pierce blinked at her. "What do you mean?"

"Kenner's specialty is paleopharmacology. You said he as much as told you that he was looking for the secret to creating monsters like the chimeras of mythology. Yet, of all the things that you found hidden in the Labyrinth, he took a book and a belt. Does that make sense to you?"

Pierce's forehead creased in a frown. "When he found the belt, Kenner told his partner that they had what they came for." He raised his eyes to meet Gallo's stare. "Hippolyte was the daughter of Ares, the god of war. The belt was a gift from him, a symbol of his favor and her right to rule over the Amazons. In most versions of the story, the belt is said to possess magical properties, but there's no clear explanation of what that means. Probably enhanced prowess in battle or invincibility."

She nodded toward the Lion skin. "Kind of like that. Maybe the belt was from some exotic animal? That might explain Kenner's interest."

"In some versions, it's made of leather. In others, gold. Not much help there." Pierce searched his memory for other trivia relating to the war girdle, but it was Gallo who spoke next, reminding him why they made such a good team.

"Herakles was sent to retrieve the belt as a gift to King Eurystheus's daughter," Gallo said. "When he arrived at the Amazon city, Hippolyte went to meet him. She was about to give him the belt without a fight when the goddess Hera intervened and turned the Amazons against him. He ended up killing Hippolyte. In some of the more obscure interpretations, the belt is thought to be a symbol of Hippolyte's virginity, but I would tend to doubt that given the fact that Herakles takes the belt *after* killing her."

"Assuming that Kenner knew what he was talking about, the belt is the real thing." Pierce sighed. "Which means we're back to square one."

"There was something on the belt," Fiona supplied. "A picture, I think."

If Pierce heard her, he gave no indication. "Kenner was very specific about his intentions. He wants to make chimeras. We need to stop him. And we need to get back what he took. Those are our primary objectives now."

"Why would he require something from the ancient world? From what I've been reading, genetic engineers are already making chimeras."

"He seemed to think there was something unique about the creatures of Greek mythology. A shortcut that increased the chances of success. The worst thing is, he's probably right. We know that at least some of those creatures were real."

An electronic chime spared Pierce from recalling his past encounters with strange creatures believed to be myth, but which were very real. He turned to the computer screen where the message 'Incoming call from Cintia' flashed. He clicked on 'Accept,' and a few seconds later, Dourado's likeness appeared on the screen.

To say that Dourado favored an eclectic style was a profound understatement. Today, she sported purple hair—the color was as changeable as the phases of the moon—which spilled out above a lime green bandana tied around her head like a sweatband. She had too many piercings to count. Hoops and barbells seemed to sprout from every available fold of flesh: eyebrows, ears—lobes and cartilage, a tiny rhinestone decorated the side of one nostril and a pair of rings adorned her lower lip in what Gallo had been informed was called a 'snakebite.'

Gallo, who preferred a more traditional concept of beauty, was always amazed at the effort Dourado put into camouflaging her natural good looks, the product of a thoroughly mixed bloodline that gave her flawless honey-colored skin, brilliant almond-shaped green eyes and envy-inspiring cheekbones.

"Sorry to interrupt," Dourado said. "I didn't think this could wait."

She spoke in a very precise manner, enunciating every word, as if trying to avoid letting her accent slip through, not realizing that the effort had the opposite effect.

"What have you got?" Pierce replied.

"This man Kenner has some very unusual friends. I traced his financials through a series of non-profits, all of them shells, eventually circling back on itself."

"You didn't call to tell me 'dead-end.'"

"No," Dourado admitted. "But the money trail doesn't lead any-where. I haven't seen such a complicated branch network since I hacked the Society."

"That's why you're the perfect person for this job," Pierce said. "If anyone can crack this nut, it's you."

Gallo thought his tone, while encouraging, sounded dangerously close to patronization.

Dourado didn't seem to take it that way. "I decided to ignore the money and look at the shell organizations. Each of these organizations has a website, and on each website, there is a cleverly concealed application that redirects to this."

Dourado's violet-haired visage vanished, replaced by a live feed of a computer screen displaying a black logo—a stylized image of what appeared to be three dog heads, joined together and staring watchfully in all directions—on a blank white background.

Fiona, who had roused herself and was now staring over Pierce's shoulder, was the first to identify the image. "Cerberus. The three-headed dog that guards the gates of the Underworld. Capturing Cerberus was Hercules's final Labor."

Underneath the logo was a line of text and a Java script box. The prompt read simply: 'What do you want?'

Pierce and Gallo exchanged a glance, but before either of them could speak, letters began to appear in the box.

WORLD PEACE.

Pierce opened his mouth to say something, probably to advise caution, but the message was sent before he could utter a word. The screen abruptly changed to display a generic 404-error. Dourado clicked on the 'Back' button, but the 'page not found' message remained.

"That is what happens every time, no matter what I put in," Dourado explained. "You get just one try, and then you are shut out permanently. Don't worry. I am using randomly generated IP addresses. They won't be able to trace this activity to me."

"Is it asking for a password?" Pierce inquired.

"I believe the question is literal," Dourado said. "What matters is *who* asks it. This may be a blind contact page for a *concierge* service." She emphasized the word so that the listeners would understand that irony was intended. "Ask for whatever you want, and if you can afford the price tag, the doggie will go fetch it for you."

"And if you can't," Gallo murmured, "the doggie will chase you away."

"Exactly," Dourado said.

"So how does Kenner connect to this?" Pierce asked. "Is he working for...Cerberus, whatever it is? Did they hire him to find the secret of how to make chimeras?"

When no one answered, he shook his head. "Good work, Cintia. Keep digging into Cerberus. Try to figure out what their agenda is." He paused, the set of his jaw showing that he had just had a very unpleasant thought. "If Kenner is looking to exploit the DNA of ancient creatures, we might need some technical advice. We're out of our depth here. Get me a list of candidates with a background in biology and genetics."

Gallo raised an eyebrow. She knew that the Society's charter allowed for the recruitment of new members from time to time, but it was rare to draft someone out of the blue. Most new members were brought aboard only after discovering the truth about the Society for themselves. Tapping someone from out of the blue could have unpredictable results.

"Done," Dourado replied, almost before Pierce finished speaking. The screen refreshed to show a list of names along with a condensed *curriculum vitae* for each. Gallo didn't recognize any of the names, but Pierce did.

"Number three," he said. "Dr. Carter."

"It may be difficult to reach her," Dourado said. "She's in Liberia, working with the World Health Organization to develop an Ebola vaccine."

"Make the travel arrangements," Pierce said. "I'll extend the invitation personally. We have a mutual friend."

Gallo noted a change in his demeanor, as if the prospect of being on the move again had energized him. She could sympathize. Nothing sapped one's *joie de vivre* quite as fast as being stuck in a lightless hole in the ground. Something told her that was exactly what Pierce had in mind for her. "Am I to assume that you expect Fiona and me to remain here?"

Pierce blinked at her, as if sensing but not comprehending her irritation. "It's the safest place."

"Safe from what?"

"Kenner might..." He trailed off, unwilling to put whatever he was thinking into words.

"George, you can't be serious. I've got to be the last thing on his mind right now."

Pierce sagged. "Fine. But if you insist on leaving, be careful."

"Physician, heal thyself," Gallo replied. "You're the one who's going off to the hot zones of Western Africa."

THIRTEEN

Cerberus Headquarters, Location Unknown

The sudden rush of light when the blindfold was removed felt like a hot knife stabbing through Liam Kenner's skull. He winced, covering his eyes and blinking rapidly until the discomfort was manageable. He had the good sense not to complain, though.

The blindfold was a minor inconvenience compared to the sedative he had been required to take after boarding the Cerberus executive jet. Between the drug and the blindfold, he had absolutely no idea where on Earth he was.

Such ignorance was the price of admission into the Cerberus inner sanctum. Kenner considered it an investment in his future, and a bargain considering what he had been promised in exchange for the knowledge recovered from the Labyrinth.

The world came into focus around him. A laboratory. He did a slow turn, taking inventory of the varied apparatus arrayed on the tables. There were racks of glassware, microscopes and autoclaves, along with several computer workstations and a white board along one wall. His impression of the room was that it had been put together by someone whose idea of what a laboratory should look like came from watching too many movies. More a cliché than a work environment.

I hope they don't actually expect me to accomplish anything here, he thought.

As if reading his thoughts, Rohn tapped him on the shoulder and pointed to a flat-screen television monitor mounted on the wall. It displayed the image of a wizened old man with wispy white hair clinging to a mostly bald and liver-spotted head.

"Mr. Tyndareus, I presume," Kenner said.

A wheezy voice issued from the built-in speaker. "Dr. Kenner. Welcome. I realize that the facilities here may not be up to your standards. If you will provide Mr. Rohn with a list of the equipment you require, we will accommodate you." There was the faintest hint of an accent. German, or perhaps Slavic. Definitely from Eastern Europe.

Kenner shook his head impatiently. "I tried to explain this to your man. It's much too soon to be moving into the lab."

Beneath his heavy brow, the old man's gaze grew sharp. There was something disconcerting about those blue eyes. They did not quite match. The effect reminded Kenner of an old story he had once read long ago. Poe was it? He couldn't recall. He had no patience for American Romanticists, and he couldn't bear to meet Tyndareus's stare long enough to figure out what it was about the man's eyes that was so disturbing.

"Mr. Rohn led me to believe that you found what you were looking for in Crete."

"Yes, I did. But what I was looking for was *information* about where to find the source. The original mutagen responsible for recombining animal DNA to create mythological creatures. Now that I have that information, the next step is to locate the source. What the ancients called the Well of Monsters."

Tyndareus regarded him for several long seconds. He raised a gnarled hand and waggled a finger. "My time and patience are not infinite, Dr. Kenner. I trust you are not wasting either."

"I've not yet had the opportunity to examine the information we recovered," Kenner lied, careful not to sound defensive. "But the Well exists. Those creatures were real. We need only follow in the footsteps of Hercules, and we will find the mutagen. Once we accomplish that, the laboratory work should be simple and straightforward."

Tyndareus did not appear completely satisfied with the promise, but he did not press the issue. "There's something else you should know. My agents have reported that Pierce and his companion boarded their jet in Heraklion, shortly after your departure."

The news surprised Kenner, though perhaps not in the way the old man expected. Pierce's survival lifted an enormous burden of guilt from Kenner's shoulders.

Rohn's reaction, however, was sharp and immediate. There was a trace of fear in his tone. "I wanted to finish them," he blurted. "This one told me they would not be able to escape."

"Take responsibility for your own failures, Vigor." Despite its wheezy high-pitched timbre, there was something dangerous in the old man's voice. Kenner realized that Tyndareus was holding Rohn accountable for Pierce's escape, not him.

"Does it matter?" Kenner asked. "Pierce can't touch us now."

"I dislike loose ends, Dr. Kenner. They have a way of unraveling the best laid plans. I cannot allow this particular enterprise to be jeopardized. Not with the goal in sight."

"I will take care of Pierce," Rohn promised.

The old man considered the statement for a moment. "We will monitor Pierce's activities, but our first priority must be finding the source of the mutagen. Dr. Kenner...I expect results." The screen went dark.

Rohn glowered but said nothing.

As pleased as he was that Rohn was now feeling some of the heat, Kenner knew that the pressure on him would only increase with time. Tyndareus was not a patient man. At his age—the man had to be at least a hundred years old—he could not afford to be.

Kenner thought about the symbols etched into the belt of the Amazon queen. He would not find the Well of Monsters without first deciphering that strange text, but ancient languages were not his area of expertise.

He did not dare reveal to Tyndareus that the search had already hit a roadblock. With luck, the solution to the mystery would be found in the pages of the *Heracleia*. If not, Tyndareus, despite having one foot already in the grave, would definitely outlive him.

He needed help, but he didn't dare ask for it.

Then the answer occurred to him. "Mr. Rohn, I think I may know a way for us to kill two birds with one stone."

FOURTEEN

Gibraltar

It did not take long for cabin fever to set in. Only an hour after Pierce's departure, Fiona felt like climbing the walls and hanging out with the Forgotten up on the ceiling. She had to do something, anything, to alleviate the tedium of being stuck in the cave.

She had been eager to join in the hunt for Cerberus. She imagined it was a secret fraternity—a sort of anti-Herculean Society—or a vast global criminal enterprise, like something from a James Bond movie. But despite Pierce's directive, Dourado had warned her and Gallo off.

"This is a job for a hacker, not a historian," the Brazilian woman had told Gallo. "I know what to look for and what to avoid. If you go poking around on the web, you will only draw attention to yourself."

With that potential diversion removed, there was little else for Fiona to do but get caught up on her schoolwork and visit with Gallo, something that never rated high on her list of preferred activities. It wasn't that she disliked Pierce's girlfriend, but extended conversation with the woman only accentuated the stark differences between them. Fiona was a tomboy, raised by soldiers—mostly men—and still a teenager. Gallo was beautiful, sophisticated and refined...boring.

A real stick in the mud, Fiona thought.

They got along best when they didn't try to get along.

Still, since they were stuck with each other, maybe this was a chance to break down some barriers. "Are you hungry?" Fiona asked, rising from the table.

Gallo glanced at her wristwatch. "What's on the menu?"

"Uncle George brought some MREs from the plane." She went over to a stack of boxes near the entrance—cases of military-style rations and flats of bottled water.

Gallo raised a disdainful eyebrow. "As appealing as that sounds..."

"I know what you mean. I used to think they were really cool, but after a while, I realized they're actually pretty gross." She started rooting through an open box, checking the variety of choices available. "Now, I eat them only because I have to. If I don't, my blood sugar goes all wonky."

"Well, wonky blood sugar won't do." Gallo tilted her head sideways. "But don't you want something more...appetizing?"

Fiona shrugged and gestured to the MREs. "I can deal. It's not like we've got much of a choice."

"There's always a choice, my dear." Gallo took out her phone and began scrolling through the contact list. "If you can hold out a bit longer, I'll see if we can't arrange for something with a little more flavor."

"I think we may be outside the delivery area."

"Who said anything about delivery?" Gallo's tone was almost playful, but there was a hard edge to her smile. Refined and proper maybe, but Augustina Gallo was very much her own woman.

An hour later, as they dined on Indian cuisine at a little hole-in-the-wall overlooking a marina on the west side of the Rock, Fiona decided that maybe Aunt Gus wasn't so boring after all.

Gallo swirled the contents of her wine glass. "So, what's next on our agenda?"

"Back to the citadel?"

"Well, that sounds dreadful."

Fiona didn't know what to say. She knew what Pierce would want. And while she didn't relish the idea of returning to the cave, she hadn't forgotten the narrow escape from the Labyrinth. Kenner and Rohn were dangerous and meant business.

All the more reason to stop them, she thought. "Uncle George did tell us to learn all we could about Cerberus," she said, choosing her words carefully. "That would include figuring out what they want."

"My thoughts exactly. We may not have Cintia's prowess on the digital battlefield, but we are not without skills of our own." She took a sip of her wine. "Walk me through it again. Everything Kenner said and did. Let's see if we can figure out what he'll do next."

Fiona searched the corners of her memory, trying to recall her encounters with Kenner, first after escaping the museum and then later in the Labyrinth. Gallo interrupted only a few times to ask specific questions.

"You mentioned that there was something on Queen Hippolyte's belt earlier. Did you see what it was?"

Fiona shook her head. "A picture, but it was too dark. And as soon as Kenner saw it, that was it. He was out of there."

Gallo pondered this. "So Kenner now has the most complete ancient record of Herakles's deeds, and an object from his Ninth Labor."

"He kept talking about finding the mutations that caused the monsters. Maybe he's looking for the actual monsters themselves. Their remains, I mean."

"That might explain why he took the *Heracleia*. Perhaps he thinks he can follow in the footsteps of Herakles." She shook her head. "But the Lion skin was right there in front of him. I think we're missing something. Something about that belt."

Fiona squeezed her eyes shut and replayed the scene in her head once again. "He mentioned a 'source.' Is there something like that in the legend?"

Gallo thought for a moment before nodding. "There is. The monsters of Greek mythology are, almost without exception, described as 'chthonic.'"

Fiona knew the word. "Subterranean. From the Underworld."

"Yes, but in this instance, the term is not limited to their place of origin. The chthonic monsters were the literal offspring of Earth spirits. Nearly all of them, including all the monsters Herakles fought, were the children of Typhon and Echidna. They were themselves the children of Tartarus—the embodiment of the deepest parts of the

Underworld—and the Earth goddess, Gaia. In mythology, Echidna is often called 'the mother' of *all* monsters."

"That could be what Kenner is looking for. The original monster mom."

"Possibly," Gallo replied, chuckling at the nickname. "Echidna was said to live in a place called Arima, the Couch of Typhoeus, located somewhere in the Underworld. The ancients believed there was a literal entrance to the Underworld, but disagreed about where it actually is. Herakles's final Labor was to capture Cerberus, the guardian of the Underworld, which would suggest that he found the entrance, if the story is to be taken at face value."

"Did Herakles ever fight Echidna?"

A wry smile touched Gallo's lips. "Not exactly. In some of the stories, Echidna and Herakles have children of their own, Scythes, Agathyrsus and Gelonus, the progenitors of the Scythian people."

"Alexander and the monster mom got it on?" Fiona shuddered. "Eeew."

"We have to be careful not to interpret the mythology too literally," Gallo said. "These stories grew with the telling over a period of several hundred years, and often contradict each other. And don't forget that Alexander was busy altering the historical record."

"Yeah, I'll bet that was one part of the story he definitely wanted to keep out of the papers. Do you think the *Heracleia* tells where to find an entrance to the Underworld?"

"It may. Unfortunately, Kenner has it, and we don't."

Fiona pondered that for a moment. "We could still look for it," she said in a low, conspiratorial voice.

Gallo gazed at her across the top of her glass. "And how would we go about doing that?"

As Fiona explained what she had in mind, Gallo's dark brown eyes began to gleam with anticipation. "Why, Fiona, darling, I do believe that's the best idea you've had all day. Excepting dinner, of course."

Twenty minutes later, after polishing off the last few bites of Tandoori chicken, Fiona and Gallo left their table and headed for the exit. Neither of them gave more than a cursory glance to the other patrons, all of whom appeared to be thoroughly immersed in their meals.

But their departure did not go unnoticed.

As the door swung shut behind them, one of the diners—a tall man whose dark complexion bespoke Moorish ancestry, a common trait among residents of 'the Rock'—hastily rose from his table, dropped a 20 Gibraltar pound note next to his uneaten meal and headed for the door. He reached the street just as the pair climbed into a taxi.

Undaunted, the man hurried down the sidewalk to a parked sedan, got in and took off in pursuit. He wasn't worried about losing sight of his quarry. He knew exactly where they were going.

FIFTEEN

Monrovia, Liberia

Pierce spent the flight making all the necessary arrangements so that his sojourn to West Africa would be brief and goal-focused. A veteran world traveler, he knew what kind of things could go wrong, and took the appropriate proactive countermeasures. He had kept his UN passport and credentials current—many years ago, he had done a stint at the UNESCO World Heritage Commission, and was still on the rolls as a consultant—which streamlined the otherwise ponderous process of getting a visa. He made sure he was current on all his shots and even took a dose of malaria prophylaxis. He had arranged for a local expediter, a man with the unlikely name of

Daniel Cooper, who came highly recommended by the UN personnel on the ground in Monrovia. Pierce had even taken the added step of GPS-plotting the route from the airport to the World Health Organization office located on Avenue Mamba, in the capital city. His ducks were all in a row. He was ready.

The only thing he had forgotten was best summed up by the old military adage: The first casualty of war is always the battle plan.

He stepped down onto the tarmac at Spriggs Payne Airport expecting to be greeted by Cooper, but there was no sign of anyone waiting to meet him. He called the phone number—the same number he had used to contact the man just four hours earlier—but the call would not go through. He waited a half hour, repeatedly trying the number. He then called the WHO office and discovered that the problem was with the local phone service. He finally abandoned the effort and hired a taxi to drive him into the city.

Instead of the stereotypical brash and aggressive cabbie, Pierce's driver was oddly quiet. When Pierce told the young man where he wanted to go, the only response was an ambiguous nod. When the man did speak, his soft tone and odd dialect was almost incomprehensible. The nation of Liberia had gotten its start in 1820 as an American colony, intended as a home for freed slaves. Even though English remained the primary language, the passage of time had evolved Liberian English into a distinct species that, while recognizable on its face, was peppered with unique phrases, many borrowed from native languages in the region. Pierce assumed the driver understood him, but given the man's unassuming personality, it was difficult to say.

The drive, only a few miles according to the GPS, took more than half an hour, bogged down by both vehicle and foot traffic. The glacial pace ensured full exposure to the sights and smells of the trash-strewn, underdeveloped Monrovian hinterland—sheet metal shacks and cinder block homes with no doors or windows, the smell of cooking oil and wood fires, automobile exhaust and raw sewage. Pierce had seen worse in his travels, and he felt nothing but sympathy toward the locals, for whom such crushing poverty was a daily fact of life. Nevertheless, the grim crawl along the choked streets left his already damp spirits thoroughly soaked. The tropical humidity did the same for his clothes.

He thought the situation would improve once he reached his destination, but it was not to be. The WHO offices were shuttered. To add insult to injury, as he was futilely banging on the door, a man got out from behind the wheel of a beat up old Ford Ranger pick-up parked in front of the building, and came over.

"They all gone, bossman."

"I can see that," Pierce growled. "Do you know when they'll be back?"

The man shrugged. "Sometime. They gone into the bush. Left a couple hours ago. You Pierce?"

It took a moment for the question to sink in. He rounded on the man. "Who are you?"

The man flashed a broad grin. "Your good friend, Mister Daniel Cooper. I come to see you."

"Of course you are," Pierce said. He rubbed the bridge of his nose trying to banish an emerging headache. "You were supposed to meet me at the airport."

"You took a taxi," Cooper pointed out.

"Why on Earth would I want to meet you here if..." Pierce cut himself off. There was nothing to be gained by demanding that Cooper recognize his mistake, so he turned his attention to the more immediate problem. "Do you know where the doctors went?"

"They gone into the bush," Cooper repeated. "Bad news. Maybe typhoid. Maybe something worse."

Pierce knew what 'something worse' meant.

Liberia had been hit hard by the Ebola outbreak of 2014. More than nine thousand had been infected with the hemorrhagic fever virus, many of them health care workers who had been ill-equipped to deal with such a deadly disease. Almost half of the cases proved fatal—a staggering death rate—but the loss of life told only part of the story. The already beleaguered nation had been virtually paralyzed by fear. People in villages hid the infected rather than helping them seek treatment. Doctors and nurses were blamed for spreading the disease. Mobs had attacked and looted clinics. Superstition and conspiracy theories had spread like wildfire. It was considered bad luck to even utter the name of the disease. Ultimately, the outbreak had been brought under control, with no new cases reported in months, but the Monrovians could be forgiven for being a little on edge.

"Do you know where they went?"

A slight shrug.

"Can you take me there?"

He nodded to indicate the general direction of Pierce's destination. "Twenty mile. Maybe thirty. I can show you where they go."

Pierce weighed his options. The smart thing to do was to simply wait for the WHO personnel to return, but how long that might be was anyone's guess. Cooper certainly didn't know. "Fine. Let's go."

Cooper motioned to his truck. "We go quick-quick. Don't want to stop after dark."

"No, we don't want that," Pierce said to himself. He checked his watch. Just after three-thirty local time. At this latitude, sunset was almost always at the same time every day, about six p.m. But thirty miles didn't sound too far. They ought to be able to make it there, recruit Felice Carter into the Herculean Society and be on the plane before nightfall.

Cooper's truck was about what Pierce expected—battered but functional—and the Liberian was considerably more assertive behind the wheel than Pierce's taxi driver. In no time at all, they were racing north along a paved highway through endless miles of ramshackle shantytowns—the West African equivalent of urban sprawl. The pavement soon gave way to a dirt road, which did not slow Cooper down in any appreciable way. As they veered northeast into the interior, the neighborhoods became less dense and gave way to sparsely populated woodland.

Pierce turned his thoughts to the reason for his hasty trip: Dr. Felice Carter. While he had never met her personally, he already knew a great deal about her. Carter, a native of Washington State, with degrees in microbiology and genetic engineering, had twice crossed paths with Pierce's good friend and Fiona's father, Jack Sigler, and while she bore no responsibility for the crises that had unfolded from those encounters, she would carry the scars for the rest of her life.

As Sigler had explained it, during the excavation of a primitive Paleolithic archaeological site in Ethiopia's Great Rift Valley, Carter had been exposed to a bizarre retrovirus that had rewired her DNA at the subatomic level and turned her into a living 'kill switch' for humanity. In certain extreme situations, such as when facing a life-or-death threat, Felice Carter had a...the only words to describe it was 'psychic ability' to shut off the part of another person's brain that governed sentient thought. Anyone nearby, whether the source of the threat or simply an innocent bystander, would become a mindless drone with no desire other than to protect her. The effect was permanent, and there was a very real possibility that, under truly dire circumstances—such as Carter's own death—the range of influence might encompass the entire human race.

The explanation for this phenomenon required an understanding of quantum physics that Pierce didn't have, but the upshot was that Felice Carter had become one of the most dangerous people on the planet. And yet, despite being a living doomsday weapon, she had chosen to spend her life in places where she would be at the greatest risk.

Whether it was because of her African-American heritage, or some deeper connection imbued by the Ethiopian retro-virus,

Carter had made it her life's work to improve conditions for the people of Africa. Given the sheer size of the continent and the scope of the problems facing its inhabitants, it seemed a fool's errand, but she had put her scientific knowledge to good use. She had worked to stop the spread of AIDS in Central Africa, conducted ground-breaking research into the field of microbe-produced biofuels in the Democratic Republic of the Congo and most recently, she had responded to the Ebola outbreak in Liberia.

While there was no arguing that she had done important work and had made a meaningful contribution to human society, Pierce was troubled by the scientist's seemingly irresponsible attitude toward the threat *she* posed. In her place, Pierce would have chosen to hide out in a cabin in the wilderness or exile himself to a monastery—anything to stay away from potentially threatening situations. Then again, maybe Carter's altruism was a way of preserving her link to humanity.

Probably best to avoid that topic altogether, he thought.

After about forty minutes of driving, they came upon a pair of old Land Rovers parked along the roadside. Beneath a layer of mud splatter, Pierce could make out the blue United Nations logo on the doors, but there was no sign of the occupants. Cooper pulled his pick-up off to the side of the road, just ahead of the other vehicles.

"Where are they?" Pierce asked.

"In the bush, bossman," Cooper said, as if that explained everything.

As they got out of the truck, Cooper reached behind the seat and took out a rust-spotted machete, which he handed to Pierce.

Pierce hefted the blade, recalling his promise of the night before to start carrying a knife. *Not exactly what I had in mind.* He took an experimental swing at the tall grass on the roadside. "Are we going to have to do a little trail-blazing?"

"Maybe so," Cooper said, still rooting behind the seat. Pierce expected him to produce a second long knife, but instead Cooper took out a pump-action shotgun. "Maybe other things."

Without further explanation, Cooper headed out across the grass and soon located a well-traveled path that headed south into the forest. The temperature in the interior was hotter, and the air was more humid than in Monrovia. Cooper handed Pierce a one-liter bottle that looked as if it had been used in a soccer game—as the ball—but the seal on the lid appeared to be intact.

How do I want to die, Pierce thought, *from dehydration or dysentery?*

He thanked Cooper and jammed the bottle into his pocket. He knew he would eventually be desperate enough to take a chance, but he wasn't quite there yet.

The trail took them through dense woods, where the shade offered no relief from the heat. The pace was urgent but the path was well-trodden. Pierce didn't have to swing his machete even once.

After an hour of relentless trekking, Cooper signaled him to stop with a raised hand. Pierce raised his blade, ready to swing it at whatever had aroused his guide's concern, but the forest was quiet.

Unnaturally quiet.

No birds chirping, no insects buzzing.

They waited there for several minutes, but the pervasive silence did not lift. Finally, Cooper indicated they should resume, but when he started walking again, his steps were softer and more deliberate. He offered no explanation for the eerie phenomenon, but his anxiety was palpable. And contagious.

Ten minutes later he stopped again.

"What is it?" Pierce asked, unable to suppress his curiosity any longer.

Cooper turned a slow circle, then pointed at the ground. "This plant. I do not know what it is."

Because he was not familiar with the native flora, it had not occurred to Pierce that anything was out of the ordinary, but it was easy to see why the plant in question had caught Cooper's attention. It was everywhere, blanketing the ground and partially obscuring the trail, climbing up tree trunks and smothering all other plant life. The dark green three-lobed leaves and coiling vines reminded Pierce of creeping kudzu, which had infested parts of the American South.

"I have never seen this before," Cooper reiterated. "It should not be here."

Pierce was not sure how to react. Of all the potential hazards he had been worrying about—cutthroat bandits and revolutionaries, predatory wildlife, infectious disease—the one thing that had not even appeared on his radar was an infestation by an invasive plant species. In hindsight, he should have added dangerous plants to the list, but risk of getting skewered by a thorn or developing a nasty rash did not quite rank alongside getting mauled by a lion or contracting hemorrhagic fever. But Cooper seemed genuinely alarmed by the situation.

"We should keep going," Pierce said. "Find the WHO scientists. They might know what this is."

The last statement snapped the guide out of his paralysis, and he started forward again with more urgency. As Pierce moved after Cooper, he felt something tugging at his feet. He looked down and discovered that his boot had become entangled in thread-like tendrils that sprouted from the stems of the strange plant. The vines broke apart when he lifted his foot, releasing a faint noxious odor that made Pierce's eyes water.

He hastened after his guide, doing his best to avoid contact with the plant, but as they went along, the encroachment became more pronounced, with vines scaling every tree and covering every inch of open ground. The trail was completely overgrown, and the only hint of its existence was a faint depression where someone—presumably the WHO team—had crushed the plant down during their earlier passage. But even that was vanishing as the stems rebounded from being trampled. The acidic smell in the air grew stronger, and every glancing contact with the leaves released more of the stinging vapor. It was not quite strong enough to be painful; it was more like the effect of cutting onions, but each step forward took them further from fresh air. Pierce was about to admit defeat and suggest they turn back when Cooper gave a cry of triumph.

"This the place, bossman!"

For a moment, Pierce thought his guide might be hallucinating. There was no sign of a village, no buildings, not even a clearing. Just an endless tangle of the weird vines, covering everything. Then something moved in the corner of his eye. Through a blur of tears, he saw an astronaut emerging from behind a tree.

"You shouldn't be here." The astronaut's sharp tone was audible despite being muffled by the suit.

Pierce blinked, trying to bring the approaching figure into focus. Not an astronaut after all, he realized, but someone wearing a bio-safety suit.

A cursory glance showed that the over-garment was in bad shape, patched together with silver duct tape. Although designed for Bio-Safety Level Four conditions, this suit offered about as much protection as a raincoat. Instead of an internal air supply, the suit's wearer was breathing through a HEPA filter that had been taped in place alongside the plastic face shield. Pierce knew that such suits were meant to be used once and then destroyed, but he also knew that the efforts to combat disease in West Africa were woefully underfunded. Personnel on the ground had to make do with whatever they had, which evidently included the reuse of disposable environment suits.

"Sorry," he croaked. "I'm looking for Dr. Carter."

The suited figure drew closer. Through the fog of breath vapor on the transparent faceplate, Pierce could see that the person within was dark-skinned and female. "I'm Dr. Carter," she replied. "Who are you? What are you doing out here?"

"Looking for you. I need your help."

He meant to say more, but the pervasive fumes were making it tough to speak.

"You shouldn't be here," Carter repeated. "It's dangerous."

Pierce managed to shake his head, but before he could plead his case, he heard Cooper ask, "Dangerous? Is this why you are out here? This strange plant?"

The woman frowned, but her gaze came back to Pierce. "Who are you? Why are you here?"

"My name is George Pierce, and I'm here to...well, to offer you a job."

"I have a job. You should leave."

She began to turn away, so Pierce blurted, "I'm friends with Jack Sigler."

That stopped Carter in her tracks. She faced him and replied in a low, almost threatening voice. "I don't want anything to do with Jack Sigler or any of his friends. Leave. Now."

SIXTEEN

Archaia Nemea, Greece

"Is it just me?" Fiona said, staring through the windshield of Gallo's aging but reliable Volkswagen Fox. She was looking at the free-standing Doric columns illuminated in the headlights. "Or do all these ruins look alike?"

Gallo glanced over at her. "Bite your tongue, girl."

Fiona yawned. "Maybe it's different in daylight."

"This was your idea," Gallo pointed out. "Perhaps a little enthusiasm is in order?"

"Yeah, but I didn't know it would take so long to get here."

There were no direct flights between Gibraltar and Athens. The closest thing to a direct route took them first north to London Heathrow, where they caught the connecting flight headed south again to Greece. Gibraltar remained a remote destination in spite of modern conveniences. It was already dark when she and Fiona disembarked at Athens International Airport, but after retrieving her car from the long term parking lot, they set out for their next destination.

Fiona's plan, in a nutshell, was to retrace the journeys of Herakles, connecting the dots, so to speak. Many of the legendary Labors were associated with real locations. From ancient times, geographers had used the legend to inform their map of the world, and vice-versa, but since the stories could not always be taken literally, the accuracy of those known locations was also suspect. They knew, for example, that there had been a ferocious feline beast whose skin was impervious to all known weapons, but whether the events described in the story actually took place in the Peloponnesian village of Nemea was not something that had been definitively proven.

If they could find evidence that Alexander Diotrephes—the real Hercules—had been in those places, it would help narrow down the list of possibilities for places that were harder to pin down, such as the entrance to the Amazon city's Underworld. It promised to be a long, tedious search, but it was definitely better than staying cooped up in the citadel, waiting for Pierce to return.

Finding proof was only part of Fiona's plan. She was also looking for graffiti, specifically, examples of the Mother Tongue that might have been overlooked or dismissed by modern archaeologists. If they could find even one inscription, like the one carved on the wall of the Labyrinth, it would help prove that Alexander had indeed been in some of those places. Additionally, such a discovery would advance Fiona's ongoing quest to decipher that ancient and powerful language.

Although Gibraltar was associated with Hercules's Tenth Labor—retrieving a herd of cattle from the three-bodied giant, Geryon—it seemed prudent to begin at the beginning, in Greece, where the first six Labors had allegedly been undertaken.

The town of Archaia Nemea looked about as deserted as the ruins of the Temple of Zeus that were its main attraction. The local archaeological museum that housed artifacts recovered from the ongoing excavation was closed for the night, as was every other establishment in the tiny village.

"Dead after dark," Fiona observed. "Reminds me of the town where I grew up. Except for the ruins, of course. Should we come back in the morning?"

"Probably," Gallo admitted. "But we're here, so we might as well have a look."

Armed with only a pair of flashlights retrieved from the trunk of Gallo's car, the two headed into the site, where by day, archaeologists were excavating the temple and re-erecting the limestone columns, restoring a small portion of the sanctuary's former glory.

As she swept the columns with her light, Gallo explained the site's history. "This temple was built in the fourth century BC, but it was built over an earlier shrine that dates back at least to the sixth century BC. After he killed the Lion, Herakles came here and offered a sacrifice to Zeus before returning to King Eurystheus with proof of his victory."

"That's the legend," Fiona replied. "What do you suppose he was really doing?"

Gallo had no answer to that, nor was there anything noteworthy in the excavation. After twenty minutes of looking around, inspecting the columns for inscriptions and finding none, Gallo was ready to call it a night. "We'll come back tomorrow and visit the museum. If we don't find anything, we'll head to Myloi and start looking into the Hydra legend."

"Sounds good to me." Fiona tried, unsuccessfully, to stifle another yawn. "I feel like I've been up forever. Oh, wait. I have."

Gallo checked the GPS map on her phone, plotting the most direct route to the nearby city of Argos, where she had made hotel reservations earlier in the day. Although it was only a few miles away, in typical Greek fashion, getting there would require them to follow a circuitous route through the Peloponnesian hills, in this case, backtracking almost halfway to Corinth before turning southwest toward their destination, but navigating to the highway would be the trickiest part. She drove with one eye on the phone and one on the road.

Beside her, Fiona made a humming noise. Gallo glanced over and saw that she was looking back through the rear window. "What?"

"That car. It wasn't there a second ago."

Gallo felt a twinge of worry, but shouted it down. Fiona was just being paranoid. "I'm sure it's nothing."

Nevertheless, she pressed down on the accelerator a little harder. A moment later, she reached the intersection with the highway, but on a whim she decided to ignore the guidance from her phone and turned in the opposite direction.

A few seconds later, a pair of headlights appeared in the rearview mirror. "Is that the same car?"

"Yep." Fiona's voice grew more anxious.

Gallo took the next right turn, dipping back into the maze of old Nemea, trusting her GPS to lead her back to the highway again. If the trailing car stayed behind them, there would be no doubt.

"He's following us," Fiona confirmed.

A cold numbness flooded into Gallo's extremities, fear and adrenaline, but there was another emotion in the mix. Guilt.

Pierce had warned her, made provisions for her safety and Fiona's, but she had ignored him. She had chalked his caution up to jealousy and over-protectiveness. And now both of them were in danger.

She made another turn without slowing. The Fox's tires squealed. Gallo fought the steering wheel to maintain control.

She could just make out the silhouette of Doric columns against the moonlit sky. The Temple of Zeus. They had come full circle. At least now she knew where to go without consulting the GPS.

Their pursuer made the turn a moment later, his headlight beams filling her mirrors.

"Okay," she said, trying to put forth a tone of calm determination. "They're just tailing us. Maybe they're hoping we'll lead them to something."

"Except now they know we know," Fiona said.

"Damn." *I've made a mess of things,* Gallo thought. *One bad decision after another. So how do I keep from making this worse?*

The answer was practically staring her in the face. Her phone.

She handed the device to Fiona. "Call the police."

The European emergency services number was 1-1-2. Did Fiona know that?

"Uh, you're getting a call."

Wonderful. What else could go wrong? "From whom?"

"Unknown number. Should I answer it?"

Gallo felt the chill return. *Kenner. Who else could it be?*

She steered onto the highway, left this time, but suddenly she had no idea where to go. Part of her wanted to take her chances on the road, drive like hell and try to elude the pursuer. If she had been alone, she might have tried it, but she was not alone. She had to think of Fiona's safety. She had to come up with a better solution.

Without letting off the gas pedal, she nodded. "Answer it."

SEVENTEEN

Liberia

Cooper regarded Pierce with a grave expression. "We ought to go, bossman. Dark soon."

Pierce ignored him and headed after Carter, who was already striding away. "Five minutes, Dr. Carter."

"I can't guarantee your safety out here for five minutes, Mr. Pierce."

"It's Dr. Pierce, actually."

That stopped her. "You're a doctor?"

"Archaeologist. Not an MD," he added. "But if you'll give me five minutes, I'll explain."

He could see that she was intrigued but not enough to get her to lower her defenses. "Well, Dr. Pierce, I've no idea what the consequences of long term exposure to this plant might be, so I strongly suggest that you head back now, take a long shower... with some bicarbonate of soda if you can find it. I'll be back in the office later this week. You can call for an appointment."

Pierce was sorely tempted to follow that advice, but he had come too far to turn back. He decided to try a different tack. "Are you staying here tonight? Do you have a camp?"

"There's no room at the inn, if that's what you're asking. Your man is right. It will be dark soon. If you hurry, you might be able to make it back to the road."

"But you are staying here? In the middle of all this..." He waved a hand around. "Whatever this is."

Carter stared back, hands on hips. "Let me show you something that might help you understand the urgency of this situation." She gestured for him to follow, but went only about twenty yards before stopping at a veritable wall of the greenery. She carefully pulled some of the vines aside to reveal a dark opening, like a cave entrance. Pierce balked until she unclipped a flashlight from her belt and shone it inside. That was when he realized that it was not a cave, but a house.

The structure was just a one-room, cinder block shack, but the plants had intruded here as well, with vines snaking through the doorway and window openings, and even through cracks in the mortar. The ceiling was crowned with an eruption of green where the vines had crawled through the gap between the wall and the corrugated sheet-metal roof. For the most part, the floor was clear of growth, but there were a few clusters where the plants had grown like crazy. Carter directed her light to the nearest of these and Pierce could see bits of color—synthetic fabrics, something that might have been the sole of a shoe.

A shoe?

"Was that...a person?"

"The entire village was consumed by this plant," Carter said.

"That's..." He was going to say impossible, but he knew better.

Carter took something from a belt pouch and passed it over to him. It was a slim booklet bound in red leatherette, which Pierce recognized as a European Union passport. Many of the pages within had partially dissolved, but the laminated photograph of the document's owner was still intact, along with a name.

"Nils Van Der Hausen."

"There was a health worker with that name here during the worst part of the outbreak, but as far as I know, he returned home. It's not unusual for foreigners to visit these isolated areas. Missionaries and relief workers." She paused a beat. "We found that on the trail coming in, along with some other items. Synthetic materials only. Just like this. The plant consumes anything organic. But what we can't figure out is why the victims just let it happen. My hypothesis is that the plant releases a narcotic or some toxic substance that subdues or kills its victims. Then it converts their remains into organic nutrients."

"A carnivorous plant," Pierce said. "Like the Venus Flytrap."

"That's right. Only instead of catching flies in its leaves, this plant wraps its prey in vines and secretes a digestive enzyme." She sighed. "It's not native. No one here has seen anything like it before."

"How large is the affected area?"

Carter shook her head. "We're still mapping it, but the epicenter appears to be here, in this village. It wasn't here a week ago. Whatever it is, it happened fast."

Something clicked. "This is why you're out here. The plant. It's not an Ebola outbreak at all."

Carter frowned. Evidently Pierce had missed the point of the demonstration. "We were expecting a new outbreak. This is what we found. It's dangerous. Now, do you really want to stay for another five minutes?"

No, Pierce thought. But he wasn't ready to give up. "I can help you figure this out. I have resources. Money. I can get you anything you need to fight this."

Carter sighed. "Dr. Pierce, I don't know why you think you need my help so badly, but your offer of assistance would have been a lot more meaningful a year ago."

Cooper tugged at Pierce's elbow. "We should go."

"I know about what happened in Ethiopia," Pierce blurted. "That's why I want your help. And I might be able to help you with...your problem."

Even as he said it, Pierce felt a flush of shame. Not only was it a low blow, but he had no way to keep that promise.

Carter regarded him coldly for a moment, anger, curiosity and a strange sort of hope fighting for primacy behind her eyes. "I'll walk you to the edge of the infestation," she said in a taut voice. "That's how long you have to convince me."

Pierce breathed a sigh of relief and stepped away from the overgrown shack. As before, the vines tried to hold him fast, clinging to his shoes like Velcro. Carter took the lead, setting a quick pace, which Pierce was eager to match. Now that he had her attention, Pierce was faced with the question of how to win her over. He decided to lead with the truth.

As they trekked along the now almost indistinguishable path, Pierce laid it all out. The history of the Herculean Society and its mission, the role of Alexander Diotrephes, the connection to Jack Sigler and his team. He spoke in a low voice, trying to exclude Cooper from the discussion. When his narrative broached the subject of a mad geneticist who had experimented on both Pierce and one of Sigler's teammates, Carter cut him off.

"I know about that maniac. Get to the point."

Pierce was grateful to be spared the trip down that particular detour on Memory Lane, though he was a bit surprised by her statement. He vaguely recalled that Carter had once been employed by a subsidiary of Richard Ridley's Manifold Genetics, but the venom in her statement hinted at a much more personal connection, of which Pierce was unaware.

"Ridley is gone, but there are other people who want the same thing he wanted. To exploit the unique genetic properties of ancient chimera species for selfish and potentially dangerous ends. The short version is that I need someone who can make sense of the science on this. I need a consultant, and you are uniquely qualified. You've already got a background in..." He gave a helpless shrug. "Weird science.

"I'm not asking you to give up your work here," he added. "In fact, the Society can supplement you. Funding. Equipment. Personnel. You name it."

"In return for what?"

"You come with me. Help me figure out exactly what it is that I'm dealing with."

Carter stopped and looked back at the dark vine-shrouded forest behind them. "I've got a crisis of my own here, Dr. Pierce."

"Surely your team can spare you for a few days. I can have reinforcements here by tomorrow."

Pierce thought he had finally worn down her defenses, but after a few seconds she shook her head. "It's not that simple," she said, regret audible in her voice. "I need to get back to camp before dark."

Pierce made no further arguments. She was right, for practical reasons, if no other. Although there was still a hint of daylight in the sky, the air was cooling with the onset of evening, and Pierce knew that he and Cooper would be hard-pressed to get out of the infested zone before dusk. His GPS would show the way, but it wouldn't protect them against nocturnal predators. But he felt compelled to end the meeting on a positive note.

"I'll make sure that you get some help out here," he said. "No strings. And I'll find out what I can about this Van Der Hausen. Maybe he's involved in this somehow."

"Thank you," Carter said. "Good luck, Dr. Pierce." She started to turn away, but then abruptly pitched over sideways, sprawling on the ground.

Pierce reached out to help, but discovered that he was rooted in place. Literally. A fresh growth of vine shoots had lashed around his feet, wrapping several inches up his ankles. Though none of the shoots were thicker than a thread, they combined to form a fibrous net that was too strong to rip through. Pierce stared in disbelief as more tendrils uncoiled from the ground cover, shooting out like Silly String. As if guided by some intelligence, the vines sought living flesh.

His living flesh.

He could feel the tickle of leaves and stems under his pants leg, entwining with the weave of his socks.

What the—?

Cooper called out, held fast by the sudden explosion of growth. In a matter of seconds, the vines had crawled up to the man's knees. He started tearing at the tendrils, and succeeded in ripping up handfuls of vegetation, but a moment later, his cries of alarm became an unrestrained howl of agony. Pierce felt a fresh sting in his eyes and nostrils as more fumes were released into the air, but that was nothing compared to what was happening to Cooper. Despite the darkness, Pierce could see smoke rising from the other man's fingers, as the acid in the vines began to burn through his flesh.

Reacting more from instinct than rationale, Pierce hacked at the ground around his feet. The machete easily sliced through the stems, sinking into the damp loamy soil underneath, but every chop threw out droplets of acid, and a moment later, Pierce was engulfed in a choking miasma. He felt warm spots blooming on the exposed skin of his hands, arms and face, and even on areas that were covered by his clothes.

But his attack was not in vain. He broke free of the vines and charged over to where Carter was struggling to rise from beneath what looked like a blanket of vine tendrils. Careful to avoid striking her, he stabbed the machete into the ground and began sawing through the stems, cutting an outline around her.

The prickling on his skin grew quickly from a warm glow to an uncomfortable heat, and then to an intensity that made him want to drop the machete and tear his skin off with his bare hands. He gritted his teeth against the pain and kept cutting. With a heave, Carter got her feet under her and pulled free of the vines. Screaming, she fell into his arms. In the dim light, he could see something moving beneath the fabric of her bio-safety suit; the vines had found a way inside.

He tried to reach Cooper, but a new wave of shoots erupted from the ground, snagging his feet. He sliced at the vines but when he tried to draw back for another blow, he discovered that his arm had also been caught, and where the vines touched him, his skin felt like it was on fire. He tried to pull free, but more tendrils snaked out, enveloping him and Carter. The pain soared to a climax, and then Pierce's overloaded nervous system simply shut down, and he felt only numbness.

In some distant corner of his mind, Pierce wondered how much agony and fear it would take to trigger Carter's kill-switch response, and if he would still be alive when that threshold was finally crossed.

EIGHTEEN

Greece

Fiona tapped the phone's screen to accept the incoming call and thumbed another button to put it in speaker mode. "Hello?"

"Hello? Dr. Gallo, is it you?" came the reply, an unfamiliar voice. English but the accent was strange. Definitely not Kenner.

"Speaking," Gallo said in a tight, cautious tone.

"Thank heavens. Dr. Gallo, I am in the car behind you. Please don't be alarmed. I mean you no harm."

"Who are you?"

"My name is Matthew James. I work for Aegis International Services. Dr. Pierce hired me in Gibraltar to look after you."

Fiona gaped at Gallo, wide-eyed. She was familiar with Aegis, a security consulting firm that provided protection and logistical support for international businessmen and even a few small governments. It was one of the many subsidiary agencies discreetly owned by the Herculean Society, and like the rest, it was an asset that could be readily employed in the pursuit of the Society's agenda, if the need arose.

The man chasing after them was not an enemy, but a bodyguard.

Gallo's face transformed in an instant. "Son of a bitch," she said in a low but angry tone.

"It was not my intention to frighten you," James went on. "I was only supposed to watch from a distance, but... Please, slow down."

Gallo looked over at Fiona. "He knew. He knew we wouldn't stay in the cave, so he hired a babysitter."

Fiona shrugged, and then nodded to the highway ahead. "Could be worse, right?"

Gallo raised her voice. "How do I know you are who you say you are?"

"Dr. Pierce gave me your number. You can call him and verify, if you like."

Fiona thought that sounded like a good idea. "Should I?"

Gallo gave a nod.

Fiona ended the call without comment and scrolled through Gallo's contacts to find the number for Pierce's satellite phone. As the call went out, she noted that Gallo had slowed the Fox to a reasonably safe highway speed, and the trailing vehicle had backed off. Both were encouraging developments.

The call went to voicemail.

Fiona looked at Gallo again. "Now what?"

Gallo nodded her head toward their bodyguard. "Call him back."

James picked up on the first ring. "Do you believe me now?"

Gallo ignored the question. "If you're going to tag along, we're going to have to set some ground rules."

"Certainly," James replied. "Keeping you safe is my first priority, but your—"

James's voice went to static as an artificial sun rose behind them. *What?*

Fiona whipped her head around and caught a glimpse of the expanding ball of flame in the middle of the highway. She could feel heat radiating through the windows. Then the sound of the explosion reverberated through the car, simultaneous with a shock wave that swatted the Fox like an invisible hand, sending it into a spin.

Gallo swore as she fought to regain control. Beside her, Fiona could do nothing more than hang on.

An explosion. James's car just blew up. James is dead.

Just as Gallo got the Fox back under control, there was another bloom of fire, this one directly in their path and much closer.

The blast tore into the little Volkswagen. The windshield didn't shatter, but the hood peeled up, momentarily eclipsing Fiona's view of this new explosion. Then, the bottom dropped out of the world as the explosion lifted the Fox off the road like a balsa wood glider, flipping it end over end. It landed upside down, with a crunch that crumpled the roof and blew out all the windows.

Hanging upside down, Fiona was in full panic mode, desperate to grab onto anything that could restore order to the world. The interior of the car had gone dark. The air was thick with the smell of scorched metal and plastic, gasoline fumes and something else...a strange ammonia smell.

There was a crunching sound—glass being pulverized, metal and fiberglass crushed like an old soda can—as the overturned vehicle tilted forward, borne down by the weight of the engine. Fiona's center of gravity shifted again.

She heard a low moan from out of the darkness.

"Aunt Gus?" Her own voice was barely audible. She couldn't seem to draw a breath. The seat belt, which had saved her life, now felt like a saw blade, cutting across her torso. She groped blindly, trying to find the buckle.

A different noise filled her ears now, the loud scream of an engine, with an underlying rhythm, a deep, resonant thumping.

Helicopter.

In a matter of seconds, the noise reached a feverish crescendo. A tempest swirled through the crushed vehicle, blasting Fiona with debris particles. The storm's intensity abated after a moment, but the helicopter's noise had grown to deafening proportions. It had landed, somewhere close by.

A light filled the misshapen space where the window had once been, growing brighter as its source moved closer. The silhouette of a hand appeared in front of her face, fingers curling around the door frame. Then with another squeal of tortured metal, the entire door was ripped off its hinges. The whole car shuddered, and Fiona felt a fresh wave of pain as the seatbelt dug into her body.

A face materialized before her. Shrouded in the shadows cast by the flashlight, she could not make out any details, but she immediately recognized the hulking outline.

Vigor Rohn.

"No!" She scrabbled for the seatbelt release again, desperate to get free, knowing that even if she did, there was nowhere to go.

Hard, strong hands closed around her shoulders, immobilizing her. She felt a sharp twinge of pain at the base of her neck, followed by a cold sensation that spread quickly to her extremities. As she descended into a narcotic fog, Rohn laughed.

NINETEEN

Liberia

Pierce snapped back to consciousness with painful abruptness. Something hard was grinding into his abdomen, pounding his guts like repeated punches, while the rest of his body seemed to be floating in mid-air. He threw out his hands, trying to grab onto something, and in that moment, the acid bath's all-consuming pain returned with a vengeance and threatened to drag him down again. He clenched his teeth and fought to make sense of what was happening.

In the dim light, he could see the outline of trees moving past, seeming to jump up and down in time with the rhythmic pummeling.

I'm moving. Someone is carrying me.

He turned his head and tried to locate his rescuer, but all he could see was a broad back, clad in a tattered Tyvek bio-safety suit. The sharp object pressing into his innards was the shoulder of his savior. He had been scooped up like a sack of potatoes. He glimpsed something moving at the same level as his head. Another figure, wrapped in an environment suit, was slung over the opposite shoulder.

It was Carter. Which meant that the person carrying them had to be one of the WHO aid workers that had come with her.

A glimmer of hope shone through the pain-induced fog, but it was just as quickly replaced by despair. Cooper was still back there, still caught in the green trap. He wanted to tell his rescuer to stop, to put him down and let him go back, but he knew how futile the gesture would be. His own survival was still at risk.

And yet, the person carrying both him and Carter seemed impervious to the carnivorous plants. Pierce could see the man's feet moving in and out of view with each step. The vines snaked around his ankles, trying to ensnare him and drag him down, but the man tore through the green tendrils like they were party streamers. Perhaps the suit protected him from the assault, but Pierce recalled how those tiny fibrous threads had so quickly overwhelmed him and Carter. Their rescuer was as strong and relentless as a bull.

The faintest hint of a breeze brought momentary relief from the stinging miasma. Fresh air. He blinked away the tears blurring his vision. He saw trees and dark earth, untouched by the vines.

They were clear of the infested zone.

The man ran on another fifty feet before stopping and easing his burdens to the ground. Pierce rolled away, and began tearing at his clothes. He could still feel the vines on him, clinging to his skin, burning him with acidic secretions, still very much alive and intent on consuming him.

A few feet away, his rescuer was bent over Carter's unmoving form, similarly stripping off the suit that had failed to protect her. In the dim twilight, Pierce could see long green tentacles moving on the man's legs, throwing off still more tendrils in a search for nutrient-rich flesh, but the man's attention was completely focused on helping Carter. He ripped through the suit like wet tissue paper, and then tore the vines away from her face.

Carter's eyes opened. Though her face was twisted in a mask of agony, she managed a grateful smile. "The others. Help the others."

Pierce could sense hesitancy in the man's bunched shoulders, but after a few silent seconds, he got to his feet and turned back toward the vine-shrouded forest. The man was tall, easily six-four, and built like a living colossus. Then Pierce caught a glimpse of the hard visage behind the plastic face-shield, and his heart skipped a beat.

Not possible.

He was looking at a dead man.

The giant met his gaze for an instant, just long enough to register both recognition and surprise, then the man was running again, vanishing into the green hell.

Pierce tried to shake off his paralysis and call out to the man, but he was a fraction of a second too slow, and his cry simply echoed away into oblivion.

"Bishop!"

TWENTY

Bishop.

He fought back the rush of memories triggered by hearing his old name, with the same ferocity that drove him through the clinging vines. The fiery chemical burn spreading across his skin helped him sharpen his focus. Pain had a way of doing that for him, and he had not felt such clarity in a very long time.

But the memories...

I used to be Bishop, the giant thought as he ran. *But not anymore.* The memories were a burden.

What is Pierce doing here? Looking for me?

That didn't seem possible. Not a day went by where he did not half-expect to see one of his former teammates come strolling through the door, demanding to know why he had gone AWOL, but Pierce?

He clenched his jaw, as if trying to bite through the umbilical cord that still connected him to the man he had been, and he kept running.

The vines were like the tentacles of a kraken, writhing around him, latching on at the slightest contact, slithering through the tiniest holes in the fabric of his suit. The acid stung his skin, burned in his eyes like a blast of pepper-spray. He thought about tearing off the suit, but without its slight protection, even *he* might not be able to survive.

Probably best not test those limits right now.

There had not been time to process what was now happening with the plants. Earlier in the day, when the team had discovered the infestation, the risk had seemed manageable, and in a way, preferable to what they had been expecting. Their suits had provided sufficient protection from the mild stinging vapor that was released when the plants were cut or crushed, and as long as they kept moving, the vine shoots were merely a nuisance. It had only been when they reached the village that the full scope of the threat had become apparent.

The vines had killed every living thing in the village.

The scientists, including Carter, had been at a loss to explain how this had happened. While it was evident that the plants secreted an enzyme that could digest flesh and bone, it was impossible to imagine the people in the village simply rolling over and letting the vines devour them.

But now he understood how it had happened, what had changed.

It had gotten dark.

He didn't completely understand the mechanism at work. He had acquired a diverse body of knowledge over the course of his life, but he was not a botanist any more than he was an infectious disease expert. Yet, he did know that plants behaved differently when the sun went down and photosynthesis stopped. Maybe darkness or cooling temperatures acted as a signal for the plant to seek out a new source of energy or nutrients. Perhaps they were drawn to the heat of bodies or some specific chemical marker. Figuring out exactly what was happening, and for that matter, determining where the plant had come from in the first place, would be a job for the survivors. And there would be at least one. He had made sure of that.

When the vines had gone on the attack, he had acted without hesitation, almost without conscious thought, tearing through the web of growth, ignoring the tendrils that wormed through the taped seams of his suit, ignoring the cries of the other aid workers. He had immediately recognized the danger, not just to himself but to Felice, and by extension, to the rest of the world.

Only Felice mattered.

If she died, the world would die.

Or maybe not. It was impossible to say, just as it was impossible for him to separate that overarching motivation from his feelings for her.

But now that she was safe, he could not simply abandon the others.

He quickly found the place where he had rescued Felice and Pierce. A vine-covered lump lay across the trail, the shape unmistakably that of a body. There had been someone else there, someone he had missed.

He bent down and tore at the blanket of vines, exposing a body. He couldn't distinguish the man's face, but he wore ordinary street clothes instead of a bio-safety suit. A villager, or someone traveling with Pierce. It didn't matter. Alive or dead?

That didn't matter either.

He bent over and scooped the man up into his arms. He threw him over one shoulder, just as he had done with the others, and started forward again.

Or tried to.

The vines had curled around his feet, holding him fast. He kicked against them, but this time there were too many of the fibrous strands to be so easily overcome. Unbalanced, he toppled forward, his human burden slipping to the ground. More tendrils shot out, curling up his arms, clinging to the faceplate of his suit, worming into the folds of his mask's filter.

To remain still, even for a moment, was certain death. He arched his back, attempting to wrench his hands free, but to no avail. He was caught. A fly in a spider's web.

But then his fingers brushed against something hard. *A rock?* No, it was metal. The blade of a long bush knife. He curled his fist around the machete, and then using his other hand for additional leverage, he wrenched both his hand and the blade free.

He hacked at the ground with furious abandon, throwing up shreds of plants and huge clots of soil. In a few moments, he had cleared a rough circle of ground. He got back to his feet and hoisted the unconscious man onto his shoulder again, but new shoots sprang up from the fresh mulch.

Time to get moving again.

He hit the surrounding web of vines at a full sprint, his momentum allowing him to tear through them. The blocky shapes of houses appeared before him, but he did not slow.

His goal lay two hundred yards beyond the village, where the aid team had cleared an area and established a camp site. Although surrounded by the infestation, they had deemed the environment safe, even with the sorry state of their protective equipment. But that had been before nightfall.

Before the change.

He spotted a glow directly ahead, artificial light coming from the camp, and allowed himself a small measure of hope. As the tents came into view, he could see suited figures moving about, but any sense of relief was tempered by the fact that several of the tents were already partially covered in foliage. The camp wouldn't last long.

As he skidded into the ever-tightening circle of cleared ground, one of the suited figures called out. "Lazarus! Thank God!"

Lazarus was the name he had taken for himself, the name of the man who had come back from the dead, but that wasn't what had happened to him.

Erik Somers—'Bishop'—had died. The man who had come back, Erik Lazarus, was someone else.

"Where's Felice?" asked another of the suited figures.

"Safe," was all Lazarus said. He did a quick head count. They were all there. All had made it to the relative safety of the camp. It would not be safe much longer. The vines were advancing, growing toward the besieged doctors and scientists, an inch or two with every passing second.

"We have to go," he announced. He regarded the machete in his hand for a moment then passed it to the nearest man. It would not do for what he had in mind. Instead, he turned toward the stack of gear they had packed in—medical equipment and camping supplies. He selected a short-handled shovel with an eight-inch-wide blade. It was hardly ideal, but given what he had to work with, it would have to do. "I'll try to clear a trail," he told the others. "Stay on it. Stay close to me. If I go down, run as fast as you can and don't stop until you are clear. Got it?"

He got wide-eyed looks and tentative nods as an answer. That would have to suffice.

He lowered the shovel, the back of the blade flat against the ground, and then launched into motion, plowing a narrow strip through the sea of green. The vines peeled off in great clumps, rolling to the side or, more often than not, dropping back into his footpath, but he simply kicked these out of the way as he ran.

He did not stop. He did not look back.

There was nothing more he could do to save the others. Whether or not they survived was up to them now.

TWENTY-ONE

The pain gradually receded, fading to a dull glow and a persistent itch that was, in its own way, almost worse than the chemical burn. But while the physical effects seemed to steadily abate, Pierce's shock at seeing Erik Somers, alive and evidently well, only compounded with the passage of time.

Somers—whom Pierce thought of primarily by his military callsign: Bishop—had been a member of Jack Sigler's team. They had worked together closely during the years when Pierce had served as an instructor for the team. They had not been what Pierce would call 'friends.' The Iranian-born, American-raised giant had not allowed many people to get close to him. But the man was as unshakably trustworthy as he was physically unstoppable. Pierce had been stunned to learn of his death, eighteen months earlier, during a mission in the Congo region of Africa.

A mission where Sigler's team had crossed paths with Felice Carter.

Evidently someone had finally gotten close to Bishop after all.

Pierce rolled over on his side and regarded Carter, who was suffering through her recovery. Now that she was no longer encumbered by the environment suit, he was able to really see her. Carter was tall and lean, with the physique of a distance runner. He did not doubt that she was attractive, though in her present state it was hard to say. Her straight black hair was pulled back in a utilitarian pony-tail, though several strands had escaped the elastic band and were now plastered to her angular face.

"I guess now I know why he didn't come back," Pierce murmured.

He hadn't intended to say it aloud, but the effect on Carter was immediate. She flashed him an angry look that hit him like a physical blow. "You don't know anything."

"I know that there are people who love him, and are still in a lot pain because they think he died."

"He *did* die," she replied.

"Is he regenning again?" The question caught her by surprise and left her momentarily at loss for words. Pierce decided to fill the silence. "Yeah, I know all about it."

Pierce thought about saying more, thought about telling her that he and Bishop had shared the strangest of bonds—they had both been used as lab rats by Richard Ridley. The mad geneticist had, at least in that phase of his life, been obsessed with giving humans the ability to regrow lost limbs or recover almost instantaneously from even the most grievous wounds. His early attempts had yielded the desired results, but the healing process was so agonizing that it transformed the recipient into a ravening, mindless—and virtually invincible—animal. Bishop had received a dose of that serum, but had, through nothing more than the strength of his will alone, resisted the effects long enough to find a way to keep the bestial rage in check. Pierce had received a slightly different version of the serum, one derived from the DNA of the mythological Hydra, which had come with its own set of side effects and, unfortunately for Bishop, a different antidote.

Alexander Diotrephes and the Herculean Society, had supplied a drug to completely restore Pierce, but the compound had had no effect on Bishop. For several years thereafter, Somers had lived with the knowledge that a serious injury might turn him into an unstoppable rage beast, and given his position as the member of an elite special ops team, the likelihood of that happening was extremely high.

Much later, Ridley had utilized his knowledge of the Mother Tongue to 'heal' Bishop of the affliction, permanently stripping away his regenerative ability, or so everyone had believed.

Carter's reaction was not quite what Pierce expected. Her initial ire seemed to melt away, replaced by something more like sadness. "I honestly don't know. Something terrible happened to him. When he found me, later, he was...different."

She took a breath, got to her feet, and then to Pierce's utter surprise, offered a hand to help him up. "Maybe seeing you will be good for him. He might open up to you. Despite what you must think, I'm not keeping him here."

Pierce accepted her hand. "I'm sorry. I jumped to a conclusion. It's just..." He gave a helpless shrug. "We all thought..." He let the sentiment hang. There was too much happening, too many lives lost or in immediate danger. He turned his gaze to the woods. In the growing darkness, it was difficult to distinguish where the vine infestation began. "Is there something we can do to help him?"

"I don't know," she admitted. "We barely had time to make sense of what happened here. But if anyone can survive this, it's him."

"So what *did* happen? Where did this come from?"

"I'm not an expert in plant biology, but I do know that this growth is unlike anything seen before. That tells me it's not naturally occurring. Someone *created* this and set it loose here."

"A GMO," Pierce said. A genetically modified organism. It was a catchall term that could be applied to any artificially created species, whether the process involved hybrid breeding or the direct manipulation of genetic material in the laboratory—gene splicing. The subject was the focus of intense controversy, with some people imagining a doomsday scenario with created 'Frankenfood' crops destroying or outcompeting naturally occurring species, though the vine infestation certainly seemed like that particular nightmare come true.

"I'll have to analyze it, of course," Carter went on. "But this didn't just happen out of the blue. Someone is responsible for this."

Pierce nodded slowly. "I'll help in any way I can."

When she did not answer, he decided to take a concrete step forward. He took out the damaged passport and his phone. Dourado might be able to backtrack the document's owner and figure out if Van Der Hausen was involved, and who, if anyone, he was working with.

Before he could snap a photo of the passport page however, he saw that he had missed a call from Gallo. He debated calling her back but decided it could probably wait. Only one call and no voicemail message. How serious could it be?

He took the photo. The built-in flash briefly illuminated the woods, showing the creeping advance of the vines only twenty yards away. Instead of radiating outward uniformly in all directions, there was a pronounced bulge directly in front of Pierce, as if the plants were intentionally trying to reach him and Carter.

A moment later, he had Dourado on the line. After briefly explaining the situation, he sent her the picture of Van Der Hausen and instructed her to make it a top priority.

"Already on it," she told him. He could hear her tapping on her keyboard in the background. "Is there anything else I can do? Should I alert the Liberian authorities?"

Pierce relayed the question to Carter, who shook her head. "Let me analyze it first. Figure out how best to kill it. The last thing we need is the army descending on this place with flamethrowers, burning the whole jungle down and inadvertently spreading it further."

"Cintia, I'm going to put Dr. Carter on the line. Get whatever equipment she needs and have it overnighted to Monrovia." He held out the phone to Carter. "Whatever you need," he told her. "Sky's the limit. You can even get an espresso machine, if you want."

"This doesn't mean I'm going to come work for you."

"No strings attached. Except, of course, that I do expect you to save the world from that." He pointed to the infested zone.

Carter regarded him with a mixture of admiration and wariness, but she took the phone and rattled off the names of a few pieces of equipment. Pierce got the impression that she was holding back, asking only for a bare minimum, perhaps still harboring some distrust about the gift. When she was done, she handed the phone back to him. "Thank you."

He nodded and spoke to Dourado again. "I'll be wrapping things up here as soon as I can. Do me a favor and let Augustina know. Tell her I'll call as soon as I can."

"Will do. And I will call back as soon as I have more information about Van Der Hausen."

He hung up and activated the phone's built-in flashlight. He aimed the light at the forest, a beacon to guide Bishop and any other survivors to safety. In the ambient glow, he could see red splotches on his hands. Chemical burns, though nowhere near as bad as the level of pain led him to expect. The enzyme was a slow-acting acid. The vines were the real threat, since they immobilized victims, allowing the plants to digest them over the course of hours, perhaps days.

A few minutes later, he heard shouts from the forest and saw a group of people running toward them, with the gigantic form of Bishop in the lead, literally plowing a path to safety with the blade of a shovel. A partially vine-wrapped figure was slung over one shoulder. Cooper.

Pierce allowed himself a relieved sigh. He didn't know if his guide was still alive, but he was glad that the man had not been left behind to be devoured by the jungle.

"They all made it," Carter whispered. "Thank God."

"Thank Bishop," Pierce murmured.

"Don't call him that," she warned. "He goes by Lazarus now. Or just Erik."

"Lazarus." Pierce nodded. *The resurrected man. Of course.* As if to keep him from commenting on this, Dourado chose that moment to keep her promise.

"Prompt as always," he said into the phone. "What have you learned?"

"I have some information about Van Der Hausen." Dourado's tone was unusually subdued. "And there's something else."

"Van Der Hausen, first."

Dourado related the salient facts about the passport and the man, a genetic engineer who had volunteered to work in Liberia during the early days of the Ebola outbreak. He had returned to Europe and started his own boutique gene-splicing company. "Some of his working capital came from Cerberus shell companies."

"Cerberus is behind this?" Pierce said it more loudly than he had intended. His outburst did not go unnoticed by Carter. Pierce covered the phone's mouthpiece. "I think we found our culprit. And you were right. It's an engineered species."

Dourado spoke again. "Until we know more about Cerberus, it's impossible to say exactly what role they played, but yes, there does seem to be a connection."

"Keep digging. Whether or not this has anything to do with Kenner, we need to stop Cerberus."

"Dr. Gallo is not responding." Dourado said. "Not by computer or telephone. They are not in the citadel. The door was last accessed more than eight hours ago."

Pierce frowned. "I thought she might try something like that. I arranged for Aegis to keep an eye on them. If nothing else works, try to reach them through the Gibraltar office. I know she has her phone. She just tried to call me."

"Dr. Pierce, listen to me. I checked with the airlines. Dr. Gallo and Fiona went to Greece—"

"Damn it," Pierce muttered.

Dourado was not finished. "And Dr. Gallo's vehicle was involved in an accident near the city of Argos."

Now at last, Dourado's apprehension made sense. A chill went through Pierce. "What do you mean, involved?"

"The police are investigating, but I can find no indication that she was at the crash site or taken to a hospital."

Pierce heard himself speaking, asking nonsensical questions, parsing Dourado's words in a futile attempt to ignore the painfully obvious fact that Gallo and Fiona had been taken.

Cerberus had them.

TWENTY-TWO

Unknown Location

Gallo awoke in a groggy panic. Even before the world came into focus, she knew that something was amiss. The feel of a firm mattress beneath her, blurred outlines dimly illuminated, the faint odor of a citrus cleaning solution, the complete absence of any sound but her own breathing. It was all...wrong.

I was driving.

There was a...crash...explosion?

She could not grasp hold of the last bit, but she knew something bad had happened. The fact that she was in a strange place, a hospital room perhaps, indicated that she was far from where she had been.

She sat up, an action she immediately regretted as a wave of pain shot through her entire body. Her gut clenched, and she heaved so violently that she rolled off the bed and crashed onto the floor, the impact triggering a second round of full-bodied agony. Bitter bile stung her mouth and nostrils. She retched again, but there was nothing for her stomach to expel. It was not the pain her body was rebelling against, but something else.

God, I'm hungover.

Except she knew that was not quite right. This was not the result of alcohol. It was more like the nausea that sometimes followed anesthesia.

Someone drugged me. After the crash.

That made a strange sort of sense. If she had sustained serious injuries, perhaps the medical responders had given her a sedative or a strong painkiller. Yet something about that explanation did not quite ring true.

As the initial surge of pain receded into a dull ache, she took stock of her condition. The discomfort was mostly felt in her extremities and in the muscles of her back. She had taken a beating, but she felt certain her body was intact. No broken bones. No internal injuries.

She managed to draw a few quick breaths, fought through the urge to vomit again and blinked until her eyes were clear enough to see that she was not in a hospital room.

The bed she had fallen out of was a simple single mattress without headboard or footboard. The walls were a butterscotch yellow, with no pictures or other decorations—and no windows. There was a single door with no knob and a plain wooden chair beside the bed. She had probably come within an inch of cracking her head on it. Aside from that, the only other thing in the room was a large flat-screen television mounted high on the wall, opposite the bed.

"Hello?" Her voice was a hoarse croak. "Anybody here?"

For several seconds, the silence persisted. Then, a faint whine drew her attention to the television screen, which was now displaying the image of a room very much like the one she was in, with one notable difference. Stretched out on the bed was the motionless form of Fiona.

"Fi!" Gallo managed to shout this time, and strangely, the sleeping figure began to stir.

"Aunt Gus?"

Gallo heard the mumbled words as clearly as if Fiona were in the bed next to her, and although she loathed Fiona's pet name for her, she promised never to disparage it again. "Easy darlin'," she warned. "Waking up from this is like getting kicked by a mule."

Despite the warning, Fiona sat up and then swung her legs around to meet the floor. She was visibly woozy but not to the same extent Gallo had been. "Where are we?"

"I don't know yet." She was tempted to say more, but as the pieces came together in her head, she recognized what this place truly was: a prison. "Just hush now. Take your time waking up."

"Your apprehension is unnecessary," came a voice, high-pitched and asthmatic, much louder than Fiona's soft murmurings, but it was almost certainly due to electronic amplification. "Let us speak plainly. You are my hostages."

The fact that their captor made no attempt to soften the blow did not bode well. In response, Fiona unleashed an almost incoherent torrent of accusations, demands and colorful insults. She abruptly went silent a few seconds later, but Gallo could still see the girl raging at the screen in her own room. The feed had been muted.

The elderly man spoke again. "Dr. Gallo, I have brought you both here for one reason. I want you to translate a historical document."

"Can't Liam Kenner do that for you?" It was a guess, but Gallo felt certain that the man now addressing her was part of the mysterious Cerberus organization, with which Kenner was aligned.

"Dr. Kenner is not up to the task. Understand that the terms of his employment are very similar to the terms I am offering you. If you cooperate, you buy freedom and safety for yourself and the girl."

The man's enunciation was clipped, his accent almost certainly Germanic, which made him seem all the more like a cliché villain from a bad spy movie. But there was nothing amusing about the consequences of refusal.

Gallo took a deep breath and considered her options. It was a very short list.

I have to protect Fiona.

"I'll do it," she said, making no effort to hide just how pathetic she felt about the surrender. Perhaps if her captor thought she was truly broken, his vigilance would lapse and an opportunity for escape would present itself.

The disembodied voice did not acknowledge her statement, but a moment later the door swung open. A hulking figure strode into the room. Gallo immediately pegged him as Rohn, the brute who had accompanied Kenner to terrorize Fiona and Pierce in the Labyrinth. He said nothing, merely seized hold of her right biceps, and hauled her to her feet.

Gallo gasped as pain wracked her body once more. She fought through it and stood on her own. "Let go of me," she said, defiant. "I said I'd help. You don't need to manhandle me."

Rohn grunted, his grip tightening even more as he dragged her toward the door. Gallo had to struggle to keep up, as they moved down a nondescript hallway. There were several doors on either side, all plain wood and unmarked. Gallo guessed that Fiona was behind one of them, and she wondered if the rest were occupied with other people being held against their will.

What is this place?

A blank metal door at the end of the corridor slid back as they approached, revealing a waiting elevator car. Rohn ushered Gallo inside, but took no other action. There were no control buttons to push and nothing to indicate which floor they were on or what direction they would be traveling. The interior door closed, and the car ascended so slowly and smoothly that Gallo had difficulty detecting any motion. The brief ride ended at a hallway indistinguishable from the one they had left. Rohn guided her out. His manner was less brusque, indifferent. Gallo kept pace with him lest he remember his role as her tormentor.

He delivered her to a windowless room, far larger than her prison cell, though no less spartan in décor. With row after row of lab tables sporting some microscopes, racks of test tubes and other apparatus, it reminded her of a high school science classroom *sans* students. But the room was not empty. As they entered, a seated figure hunched over a computer monitor turned to greet them. Although she had not seen him in several years, Gallo recognized him immediately.

"Augustina." Kenner managed a wan smile and a half-hearted nod, as if embarrassed by the circumstances of the reunion. "They got you, too. I'm so very sorry."

The lie caught Gallo off guard, and a flicker of disgust crossed her face before she could rein in her emotions. "Spare me the act, Liam. You don't have the talent for it. Why am I here?"

Kenner seemed faintly disappointed by her refusal to embrace his pretense. She imagined he had constructed an elaborate ruse to win her over in spite of what he must have known Pierce had told her. After an awkward pause, he gestured to his computer screen. "I'm attempting to translate this document, but it's slow-going."

Gallo looked past him to study the displayed image, a page of text written in the archaic style of Ancient Greek. She spotted familiar words and names, most notably the subject of the text, the hero Herakles. The dialect was a bit challenging, but the differences from Ancient Greek were comparable to the difference between modern English and the language used by Shakespeare, with a few antiquated words and expressions easily understood in context. She was fairly certain that this was not the *Heracleia* of Peisander of Rhodes, the seventh century BC poet most often associated with the work, but rather an older version of the tale, one that had perhaps informed Peisander. There was, in fact, something very familiar about the style. If it was not the work of Homer, then it was a near perfect imitation.

With his Classical background, Kenner ought to have been able to read the document as easily as a Sunday newspaper.

Another lie? She wondered whether to challenge him openly, but decided against it. Rohn lurked in a corner of the room, and there were probably other eyes watching as well.

"Mr. Tyndareus is not a patient man," Kenner continued. "I imagine that's why he decided to bring you in."

"Tyndareus?"

Kenner made a sweeping gesture. "Our host."

Gallo thought about the wheezy, disembodied voice that had greeted her. In Greek mythology, Tyndareus was a king of the Spartans. He was also the stepfather to Helen of Troy, as well as to the demigod Pollux. The name was too distinct to be a coincidence.

"And what exactly is it that Mr. Tyndareus wants? I mean aside from the translation of a three thousand year old poem."

Kenner frowned. "I suppose there's no point in being coy about it." He crossed his arms as if preparing to give a lecture. "Mr. Tyndareus is a believer, and what he believes is that there is more than a shred of truth in the myths and legends of the ancient world. He approached me several years ago, not long after George discovered the *Argo* manifest, and he commissioned me to find the underlying truth about those myths. Specifically, the stories about Herakles."

"That hardly constitutes a rationale for kidnapping," Gallo retorted.

"If his motives were academic, that would be true. However, his reasons for wanting to know are purely self-serving. He is quite advanced in years. He wishes to find the means to delay or perhaps even avert his own death."

"Well, who wouldn't want that?" Gallo tried to fill her voice with disdain.

Kenner's eyes narrowed. "We both know that's not as preposterous as it sounds, Augustina. I've seen the proof with my own eyes. I know that you and George have as well."

There was no point in challenging the assertion. "There's one thing that I still don't understand. Why did you take Queen Hipployte's girdle?"

Kenner's smile was all the proof she needed that his claim of being an unwilling conscript in Tyndareus's plan was pure fiction. "Let me show you."

He clicked the computer mouse to minimize the window with the page from the *Heracleia*, and brought up a photo of the belt. Gallo immediately saw that Fiona's description had been spot on. The black leather had been elaborately tooled, with a rectangular border adorned with strange figures and a large central illustration that looked familiar. "Is it a map?"

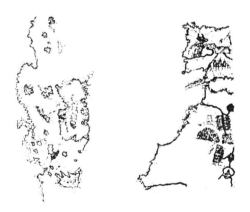

"Not just any map." Kenner traced his finger along the squiggly line at the right of the image, which bowed outward in the middle before looping back and angling away in a south-easterly direction. "Don't you recognize that?"

Gallo consulted her mental map of the Mediterranean region. The bulge might have been intended as a primitive rendering of the Turkish peninsula, but the continuous landform depicted on the other half of the map looked nothing at all like the Greek Isles. She shrugged.

Kenner's finger moved up and tapped what looked like the narrow mouth of a large fjord. "This is the Strait of Gibraltar, if that helps."

The hint opened Gallo's eyes. What she had taken to be a small inlet was actually the entire Mediterranean Sea. The bulge below was the northern half of Africa and the opposing landform was the coast of the Americas.

It was a map of the Atlantic rim, made almost 2,500 years before Columbus.

"Are you familiar with the Piri Reis map?" Kenner asked.

The name rang a bell, but Gallo shook her head.

"In 1513, a Turkish admiral named Piri Reis drew a map of the world, which included an astonishingly accurate depiction of an ice-free Antarctica—three hundred years before the continent was even discovered and long before satellites gave us a look beneath the ice—along with a detailed map of the entire coastline of the Americas. He claimed to have been informed by ancient charts dating back to at least 400 BC, which had survived the destruction of the Library at Alexandria and had been handed down through various institutions of the Muslim world." He tapped the screen again. "This is a nearly perfect match to the Piri Reis map."

The longer Gallo looked at it, the more obvious it became. She could distinguish the triangular protrusion that was the coast of Brazil, the recessed outline of the Caribbean Sea, even the dangling phallic shape of Florida, reaching out toward but not quite touching the Yucatan peninsula. The map also showed mountain ranges and inland basins in relief, but aside from a few cryptic lines occupying the open ocean between the continents—it might have been letters in some unknown language, or something else entirely—there were no labels on the map itself.

She glanced at the outer edges again and realized that the figures shown there were a stylized version of Minoan Linear A, almost identical to the figures carved on the Phaistos Disc.

Fiona would know how to read that, she thought, and then she almost started visibly as she realized what the other inscription was.

The Mother Tongue.

She doubted Kenner had any idea what those mysterious lines signified. She suspected that without a working knowledge of that all-but-extinct language, the map and all its revelations were essentially worthless. The Mother Tongue would keep the secrets of the map far more effectively than the Herculean Society ever could.

Suddenly, she didn't feel quite as bad about bargaining her assistance for Fiona's safety. The important thing now was to keep Kenner and Tyndareus from realizing that the young woman might be the only person alive who could understand what the map said.

The Minoan writing on the border would be a bit of a challenge for Gallo, since her specialty was the Classical Greek period. It was also something of an anachronism. She knew enough about the proto-history of the Greeks to know that the Minoans, despite being a sea-faring people, had never ventured beyond the Pillars of Hercules.

But Alexander did, she thought.

She turned back to Kenner. "That's all very interesting, but it doesn't answer my question."

"Come now, Augustina. Surely you see the significance of this. Herakles's quest to retrieve Queen Hippolyte's belt was really about obtaining this map. A map of the entire globe. This opens up a world of new possibilities. Herakles's journeys could have taken him anywhere. With this map and the complete account of his Labors, we will be able to pinpoint the exact locations of the places he visited."

Gallo thought about what she and Fiona had been attempting in Greece. They had been acting on the same assumptions as ancient historians who used their incomplete knowledge of the world to identify the places where the ancient hero had performed his deeds. As much as she hated to admit it, Kenner was on the right track.

"I take it you are interested in finding a specific destination?"

The direct question took some of the wind out of Kenner's sails. He pursed his lips as if trying to formulate an answer that would dovetail with his pretense of being a fellow hostage.

Gallo pressed her advantage. "You told George that you were looking for a way to make your own chimeras. That's what you're after, right?"

Kenner let out his breath in a sigh. "Those myths are evidence that the ancients knew how to recombine and engineer the DNA of living creatures, something that we are only just beginning to understand now. Herakles found a source, a mutagen that could make differentiated cells behave like stem cells. A genetic blank slate just waiting to be filled in. I intend to find it as well."

"Why? So that you can make monsters, too?" She could tell by his wounded expression that she had gotten the last part wrong. "No, that's not it. You think you can find the secret of immortality. A fountain of youth for your creaky old taskmaster."

Behind her, Rohn cleared his throat, a none-too-subtle warning that she was being too defiant.

"Would that be such a terrible thing?" Kenner replied. "I'm going to find it, with or without your help. I would prefer the former."

Gallo nodded slowly. Kenner had at last revealed the truth. He did not need her to help translate the *Heracleia* after all. This was personal. He was trying to use the situation to win her over. In his own twisted way, he still harbored the love he had once professed all those years ago.

She wondered what the mysterious Mr. Tyndareus would do when he figured out that he had been duped into playing cupid.

Whatever the outcome for Kenner, it would certainly not be as bad as the fate that awaited her and Fiona.

"As would I," she said. "Let's get to it then."

TWENTY-THREE

Monrovia, Liberia

Uncertainty about the fate of Gallo and Fiona robbed Pierce of any sense of triumph at surviving the carnivorous vines.

But survive they had. Even Cooper, who had experienced prolonged exposure to the acidic secretions, and who spent most of the trek back to the road unconscious on the shoulder of the man who now went by the name Erik Lazarus, would make a full recovery without even a scar to remember the ordeal.

Before leaving the jungle, they had taken care not to accidentally transmit even a shred of plant fiber away from the infested zone, which meant stripping nearly naked and leaving everything behind. It was a small price to pay to ensure that the species would not gain a foothold somewhere else. Once back in the WHO facility in Monrovia, scrubbed clean and salved with a topical ointment, the scientists under Carter's leadership had wasted no time analyzing the plant. They researched the possibility that it might be some naturally occurring mutation, while they waited for the arrival of the high-tech equipment Carter had requested. Pierce had little to do but sit and worry, while he waited for Dourado to run down the Cerberus group.

He had contemplated returning to the citadel, but he rejected that course of action. There was nothing he could do there, not without Carter's help at least, and he had not entirely given up hope of recruiting her into the Herculean fold.

There was also the problem of what to do about Lazarus. The man whom he had once known as Bishop clearly wanted the rest of the world to believe that he was deceased, but Pierce could not imagine keeping such knowledge a secret from Jack Sigler, his best friend and Fiona's father. But Lazarus had saved him from certain death. Pierce owed him a chance to explain, at the very least.

He found Lazarus on the roof, alone, stripped bare to the waist and seated in a lotus position, eyes closed and deep in meditation. The tableau was so surreal, so incongruous, that Pierce almost forgot why he had sought the other man out. Feeling like an intruder, he was about to turn away when something caught his eye, prompting him to take a second look.

Lazarus's arms and bare chest were splotched with patches of stark white, much like Pierce's own. The big man had applied the same healing ointment as the other survivors from the jungle nightmare.

Why?

Bishop...Lazarus...whatever he wanted to call himself...had gone missing at the bottom of Lake Kivu, at a crushing depth of more than 1,200 feet. The only possible explanation for his survival was that his body still retained the effects of Ridley's regenerative serum. But if that was true, why had he treated the chemical burns on his skin?

He should have healed within seconds.

"Do you know why I chose the name Lazarus?"

The low voice startled Pierce. The sound was like a rumble of distant thunder, yet the big man had spoken almost without moving a muscle. Pierce looked up and saw that the man's eyes were still closed.

"I...ah, assumed it was a Biblical reference. Lazarus died, but Jesus brought him back to life. Just like you. Back from the dead."

Lazarus's dark eyes opened slowly to meet Pierce's gaze. "Four days."

Pierce thought he understood the reference. In the Bible story, Lazarus had been dead and buried for four days before being raised.

"He didn't take it away," the big man went on, in the same dispassionate but haunting tone. "We all thought he did, but it's a part of me, and it always will be. All he did...was slow it down."

'He' could only mean Richard Ridley. In the early days of his insane experiments, the scientist had sought to isolate the DNA sequences that gave certain creatures like sea stars and salamanders the ability to fully reconstitute damaged tissue, even regrowing lost limbs. In nature, that process took time and a great deal of energy, no different than the recovery period for any injury. Ridley had found a way to ramp up the effect until it was almost instantaneous, but the pain, physical and mental, of both the injury and the accelerated healing, was magnified to a point beyond the capacity of an ordinary human's tolerance. The man who now called himself Erik Lazarus had not exactly been ordinary, though. His capacity for dealing with pain had been nothing short of astonishing, but even he had a breaking point.

If what Lazarus was saying was true, then Ridley—using the Mother Tongue—had not stripped away the regenerative ability, but merely dialed it back to something more like the natural rate of healing. Which meant that if Lazarus sustained a serious injury or maiming, he would still recover, but it might take days or even weeks.

Pierce struggled to wrap his brain around the revelation. He could only imagine what it would feel like to drown, and then a few minutes or perhaps hours later, have the spark of life return for a frantic moment, only to be doused again.

"Four days," Lazarus repeated. "That's probably how long it took for me to reach the surface."

Four days at the bottom of a lake, drowning, dying and then waking up to do it all over again...and again.

"Felice believes that decomposition must have started. It happens that way sometimes. The cells break down and release gases that make a drowned body buoyant enough to float to the surface."

Pierce shuddered involuntarily. "That's..." He could not find the words.

Lazarus shrugged. "One of the good things about being dead is that it switches off the black box. I have no memories of what happened. I woke up in a marsh on the edge of the lake. Probably got dragged there by a scavenger. After that, I remember everything."

He fell silent, as if daring Pierce to ask for more. Pierce did not. He had an idea now of why the man had not returned to his old life. Part of him, the part that was Erik Somers, was still dead, left behind at the bottom of Lake Kivu.

"I won't..." Pierce faltered, sucked in a breath and tried again. "I won't tell Jack, if that's what you want."

Lazarus stared back for several seconds, and then unfolded himself and rose to his feet. "You said Fiona is missing. Is there any news?"

Pierce would not have thought the conversation could become any more awkward, but the change in subject snapped him back to the helplessness he had felt since Dourado's call. "Nothing."

"Fiona is family to me. I'll do whatever I can to get her back."

TWENTY-FOUR

Cerberus Headquarters

The translation went quickly, so quickly that Gallo was at a loss to determine how Kenner had convinced Tyndareus that he needed her to do it. A first year student could have done the work in a few days with nothing more than a dictionary and a copy of the *Iliad* for reference. Like the works officially attributed to Homer, the *Heracleia* was a non-linear narrative in dactylic hexameter, a classical poetry scheme that measured out the syllables of each line. The method served not only an aesthetic purpose but also a practical one, facilitating the memorization of long epic poems that were primarily handed down orally. Gallo did most of the work in her head, consulting external translation resources only to verify her interpretation of a few tricky passages.

Kenner sat beside her the whole time. Rohn kept his vigil from a distance, but neither man interrupted her. She was provided with a light meal and as much coffee as she could drink, and she was assured that Fiona would be taken care of, as well. After three hours of perusing scans of the old papyrus pages, she completed her first pass.

"This is more or less what you thought it was," she told Kenner. "The life story of Herakles." *Part of it anyway,* she thought, but did not say aloud. "There's no mention of 'Labors'—that was probably something added later. But it does recount his battles against the children of Typhon—the chthonic monsters. After killing several of them, he embarked on a ten-year-long voyage to find Echidna, the mother of the monsters, in Erebus. *The darkness,* which was another name for the Underworld. I suspect that very round figure might be a slight exaggeration. Poetic license. But it certainly took a very long time for him to reach his destination. The gates of the Underworld, where he captured the three-headed hellhound." She paused a beat and then added, "Cerberus."

Kenner did not react to the name, but his curiosity was piqued. "Does it say where the entrance to the Underworld is?"

"Not precisely. 'In a burning land, with poisonous air, at the center of a lake of fire.'" That was a rough but mostly literal translation. "He learned the location from the Amazons and then he continued on from there."

"That's our starting point."

"We are confronted with the same problem," Gallo said. "To reach the land of the Amazons, he had to 'brave Poseidon's wrath' and 'endure a month while Eurus slept'—presumably those are references to a long sea voyage—before arriving at 'the land where Tethys resides,' and where the Amazons made their home.

"The mention of Poseidon's wrath could indicate a long sea voyage lasting at least a month. Tethys was an aquatic goddess, the wife of Oceanus and the mother of several river deities. We can assume that means the Amazons lived on a river. Knowing what we now do about the possible range of his travels, that could be anywhere."

"Not anywhere," Kenner countered. "I believe we can rule out a few of the traditionally accepted locations. Libya, for example. An ancient trireme could easily cover fifty miles a day, under oar power alone. At a bare minimum, we're looking at a distance of no less than 1,500 miles, and probably much further than that. It would not have taken Herakles months to reach a destination on the other side of the Mediterranean."

"You're assuming a direct line of travel," Gallo said. "Ancient sailors never ventured far from a visible shoreline."

"To make that map, the Amazons clearly overcame that limitation."

Gallo had no rebuttal for that, but the comment made her reconsider her own biases. She'd made the same mistake as the ancient historians who had tried to shoehorn the epic voyages of Odysseus, Jason and Herakles into their map of the known world and the limitations of their belief system. As Kenner had pointed out, the map on Queen Hippolyte's girdle suggested the Amazons, in addition to being unbeatable on the battlefield, were exceptional mariners.

The realization nagged at Gallo. What else had she glossed over because of her prejudices? She patiently scrolled through the pages. The scattershot narrative was structured like the memories of an old war veteran, but she soon located the section describing Herakles's arrival at the Amazon city. As she read the passage with fresh eyes, she became aware of a serious omission. "They weren't all women."

"What's that?"

"This account describes a fortress city ruled by the Amazon Hippolyte, but it doesn't say that everyone who lived there was an Amazon.

In fact, it explicitly describes the city's inhabitants as both Amazon women and 'men who fought as fiercely as Spartans.'"

Kenner frowned. "I'm not sure how that matters."

"In almost every version of the legend, the Amazons are exclusively female. Women without husbands, sustaining their population by mating with captured males who were either enslaved or slaughtered afterward. They killed all their male offspring."

"But that's not the case?"

"It's another example of how taking the legends at face value can get you into trouble. The word 'Amazon' definitely applies to the female warriors who ruled the city, but it would be more correct to say that they were a female-dominated society, or perhaps that they were considered the equal of men. Given the attitude of the ancient Greeks toward women, it's not surprising that the poets of the time would have exaggerated equality into a sort of pervasive hatred of men." She didn't add that the confusion may also have been an intentional deception perpetrated by Diotrephes.

"How does that help us?"

"It means that in addition to throwing out our preconceived notions about the limitations of ancient travel, we also need to stop looking for some mythical kingdom without men. The city of the Amazons probably wasn't much different from any other city of the day. Except, of course, for..." She trailed off as she considered the implications of the unspoken thought.

"Except for what?" Kenner prompted.

"Warriors and mariners," Gallo murmured. "I think the Amazons might have been the Sea Peoples."

Between the initial emergence of the Bronze era Mycenaean culture and the rise of Classical Greek civilization, was a period of time known as the Greek Dark Ages, a span of nearly three hundred years in which not only Greece but every civilization on the Mediterranean rim was terrorized by a marauding force, known to modern scholars as the Sea Peoples. The exact origin and identity of the Sea Peoples remained a controversial topic. Because of their apparent nomadic nature and lack of any permaculture, not to mention the wholesale destruction left in their wake, there was little hard evidence in the historical record to prove they existed at all.

"That's why Queen Hippolyte's belt was the symbol of her power," Gallo went on. "The Amazons were able to dominate the world of their time because they possessed a map of the world."

She scrolled to another page. "Hippolyte was prepared to give the belt to Herakles, to share that knowledge, but the rest of her people did not want to share. They turned against her and tried to kill him. Herakles defeated them and took the belt. He may have taken their other maps as well, or perhaps killed anyone with the ability to make new ones, effectively breaking the power of the Amazons. That's got to be the truth behind the legend."

Kenner nodded slowly, but then he shook his head as if trying to wake himself up. "But where is the Amazon city?"

"We're looking for a city along a major river, at least 1,500 miles journey from Greece." Gallo brought up the image of the belt again, studying the shorelines. "'Endure a month while Eurus slept,'" she murmured. "Eurus was the god of the East wind. A month without any wind."

"Is that unusual?"

"That depends on where you are in the world. Along the equator, there's a band of low pressure where the wind hardly ever blows. Ancient mariners called it the 'doldrums.'" Gallo felt like she was missing something.

Something important. Something obvious.

She laid her finger on the center of the map, approximating the location of the equator. To the right—east—lay the Congo River basin. To the left—west, across the Atlantic Ocean—was the...

"Oh, my God."

"What?" Kenner asked, urgently. "What is it?"

Gallo took a deep breath. "In June of 1542, while exploring an uncharted river, a Spaniard named Francisco de Orellana, encountered a hostile force. Friar Gaspar de Carvajal, accompanying Orellana, wrote that the attackers shot so many arrows into the Spanish boats that they resembled porcupines. He lost his eye in the attack. Carvajal also reported that the attacking force was led by a group of about a dozen female warriors who fought as fiercely as the men, and it was only when most of the women were killed that the attack ended. The encounter made such an impression on the Spaniards that they named the river for the legendary warrior women of Greek mythology."

Kenner's eyes went wide with disbelief. "You're not saying..."

"The land where Tethys, the mother of all rivers lives, where Herakles found the city of the Amazons," She gave a helpless shrug. "It's the Amazon."

Kenner stared at her for almost a full minute before slowly letting his breath out in a sigh. "Amazons in the Amazon. I seem to recall reading a rather indecent paperback novel on the subject when I was young."

"It fits," Gallo insisted. "The story, the map. Everything."

"I believe you. But it's not enough. The Amazon Basin is almost three million square miles."

Gallo rolled her eyes. "You *asked* me to translate it for you." She added emphasis to the word so there would be no mistaking the sarcasm. "To identify the location of the Amazon city, so that you would have a starting point. I've done that. You don't need to know exactly where it is to figure out where he went next."

Kenner glanced at the large television screen on the wall. Gallo wasn't sure if he was looking to see if Tyndareus had further instructions, or if the look was meant to remind her that Kenner was not the final arbiter of her fate. "Without certain proof, we would be shooting in the dark."

Gallo frowned and searched her memory for something that would convince him. "Carvajal described finding carvings of an elaborate walled city in several villages along the river, prior to that battle. The natives told him that the carvings were a symbol of their ruler, like a sort of national flag, and identified that ruler as 'the mistress of the Amazons.' The city was real."

"If there is an Amazon city in the jungles of Brazil, why has no one ever found it?"

"It's the jungle. You could walk within ten feet of a ruin and not see it. In the century following contact with the Spaniards, ninety percent of Brazil's native population was dead from small pox and other diseases. The Amazons might have suffered the same fate. In fact, if they were concentrated in an urban center, they would have been even more vulnerable than smaller tribes in isolated villages."

Kenner looked as if he wanted to believe, but he could not overcome his skepticism. "It's not enough. We have to find that city. *You* have to find it." He stood up. "We're going to Brazil. I hope you can narrow it down a little before we head upriver."

Gallo didn't know where to begin. There was nothing in the *Horacleia* that even remotely approached the level of detail necessary for her to deduce an exact location for the ancient city, and she couldn't even read the...

She turned back to the displayed image of the Amazon Queen's belt, weighing the possible consequences of the choice before her. If she did this, she would be complicit in helping Kenner and Cerberus find a secret that Diotrephes had kept hidden for more than three millennia. But if she didn't, both she and Fiona would suffer. She had no illusions about Tyndareus letting them go, but while they were alive, there was always a chance that they might be able to turn the tables on Cerberus. And she knew Pierce would never stop looking for them.

    • *I have to buy more time*, she decided.

"I have an idea," she said finally. "But I'm going to need some help from Fiona."

TWENTY-FIVE

Monrovia, Liberia

The blue alcohol flame looked deceptively cool as Carter carefully set the old-fashioned Bunsen burner under the vent hood. A six-inch long sample of the vine, which had wiped out the forest village and nearly killed her and everyone else in her team, sat beside it.

She had gathered the specimen before leaving the forest, sealing it in a plastic bio-hazard bag. Even though she had taken great pains to ensure that there was no risk from the plant, she was not about to take any chances. Using two sets of forceps, she peeled back the plastic, exposing the vine to open air.

Instantly, three white tendrils, which had been coiled up beneath the slightly-wilted leaves, shot out like party streamers, all reaching for the burner. One of the shoots got close enough to touch the fuel reservoir under the burning wick. It stuck there, as if coated with an adhesive, the tip curling upward, reaching for the flame.

Then, something very strange happened. Without releasing its hold, the tendril began to recoil, pulling the plant closer to the burner.

Thermotaxis. Movement toward heat. That explained why the plant had seemed almost dormant during the hot day. After nightfall, it aggressively sought out new heat sources, including body heat.

Over the course of the next few minutes, the other tendrils latched on to the Bunsen burner, pulling the main stem closer still, until it was in contact with the glass fuel bottle. Meanwhile, the tips of the shoots reached so close to the flame that they were starting to blacken.

"So, you like the heat," she muttered. "Even if it kills you."

"Is that a good thing?" Pierce asked from the doorway.

Carter nodded as he stepped into the lab, and then she smiled to Lazarus, who filed in behind Pierce.

The big man returned the smile. Carter felt a lightness in her heart whenever she saw him smile. It didn't happen often.

"It is," she told Pierce. "It means we'll be able to eradicate the infestation with fire. No risk of spreading the vines any further. In fact, the vines will be drawn to the heat, hastening the process. I'll still need to do some more research, once that equipment you're sending gets here. I'd like to unpack the plant's DNA, maybe figure out what the parent organisms were."

"That may not be necessary," Pierce replied holding up his phone. "I thought you might want to hear this." He placed the phone on the table. "Go ahead, Cintia."

"Yes. As I was saying, I located Nils Van Der Hausen's lab in Stockholm. The police are raiding it as we speak."

"What about Van Der Hausen himself?" Carter asked.

"He flew to Monrovia last week. There's no record of his return."

"I think that passport you found may be all that's left of him," Pierce added. "It looks like he got a taste of his own medicine."

"Good," Carter said. "Though it's too bad that we'll never know why he did it."

"Well..." Dourado said. "Van Der Hausen was definitely being bankrolled by Cerberus, and they left a trail."

Carter threw a questioning glance at Pierce. "You mentioned Cerberus earlier. I take it they're some kind of criminal organization?"

Dourado answered first. "More like semi-criminal. A lot of the stuff they're involved in isn't illegal, but it would be if anyone knew they were doing it. They're extremely secretive. The first rule of the Cerberus Group is: You do not talk about Cerberus Group. The second rule—"

"We get it Cintia," Pierce said.

There was a faint grumble from the phone, then Dourado resumed speaking. "It was a tough nut to crack. Took almost two hours."

Carter wondered if that was Dourado's idea of a joke, but the woman sounded serious. "So the same people you're after are responsible for the plant infestation. That's convenient."

"Cerberus may have been the watchdog of the Underworld in Greek mythology," Dourado said. "But the Cerberus Group is more like the bird dog of the criminal underworld. They're everywhere, and whatever you want or need, they can get it for you. I am not talking about lightweight stuff—guns, drugs and so forth. Cerberus specializes in getting things that no one else can, like rare biological samples and priceless art treasures."

"We were already investigating Cerberus," Pierce explained. "We know they're moving into research and development, specifically genetic engineering. Van Der Hausen was on their payroll, though from the looks of it, his research didn't pan out."

Carter was not entirely sure she agreed with that assessment. The plant infestation had wiped out an entire village, which made it a useful, if somewhat unconventional, biological weapon. It could be used against targets in undeveloped nations and would be much easier to control than microbial bio-weapons.

"We know they're working to procure a substance that can facilitate the creation of genetic chimeras," Pierce continued. "That's actually why I came to find you. I was hoping to bring you on as a consultant."

Carter shook her head. "I already told you—"

"I'm going with them," Lazarus said in his customary low rumble.

She gaped at him. The uncharacteristic interruption was almost as astonishing as the declaration itself. "You...ah..." She blinked, surprised to find moisture beading along the edges of her eyelids. "Are you sure that's what you want?"

"They have Fiona," he said. His tone was quiet, as it always was, and yet she could hear a hint of the old anger bubbling up. "She's just a kid."

In all their months together, he had never once expressed even a hint of a desire to leave her side. She had always known that he might someday feel the urge to return to his former life, and on an intellectual level she had thought she had come to terms with that, but now that she was actually confronted with it, she felt blindsided.

He's choosing them over me.

As the thought screamed through her head, it left a trail of guilt.

In all their months together, he had never once thought of anything but her happiness. He had stayed with her, supported her, traveled from one end of the continent to the other because it was what she wanted, and he never once complained. Never once had he demanded anything for himself.

Until now.

Yet, even that wasn't quite the truth. He was not abandoning her to pursue some personal desire. Someone needed his help.

His motives were no more selfish than her own.

There was a faint hiss from the vent hood as the blackened tips of the vine shoots, dried out after several minutes of close proximity to the burner's flame, finally ignited. She watched them burn for a moment before turning back to Pierce. "Why did Van Der Hausen turn this thing loose here? Was that Cerberus's idea?"

"This is just a guess, but I'd say it was meant as a test. Proof of concept."

"And if a few villagers die in the bush? It's Africa. Who cares?" She took a breath, trying to forge her anger into something useful. "Somebody needs to answer for this." She turned to Lazarus. "All right. Count me in."

TWENTY-SIX

Cerberus Headquarters

Fiona sat on the bed, hugging her knees to her chest. It was the only thing she could do to keep herself from pacing like a caged animal.

That was exactly what she felt like.

She knew pacing was a bad idea. She hadn't eaten anything in at least twelve hours, and her blood sugar was dangerously low. Any physical activity at this point would only make things worse. She wished there was a way to shut her brain off as well, and not just because being trapped in the little room was driving her crazy. The human central nervous system used twice as much glucose as the rest of the body. She was already running on fumes, and there was nothing she could do about it.

"Fiona? Are you there?"

She looked up to find Gallo looking down at her from the television screen. "Aunt Gus! Are you okay?"

"For now. How are you doing?"

"Not so good."

Gallo stared at her for a moment then turned to someone standing out of view. "Has she had anything to eat? You can't starve her. She's a diabetic."

"I'll make sure she gets some food straightaway," came the answer.

Fiona instantly recognized the voice: Kenner. "Aunt Gus, don't tell me you're helping that piece of—"

Gallo cut her off. "I'll do whatever I have to do, to keep you safe. That's what your uncle would want."

Fiona knew she was right. In fact, given the way she felt right now, she was not inclined to put up much of a fight. She hugged her knees tighter. Before either she or Gallo could say anything more, the door to her room swung open and an unseen hand slid a tray inside. She jumped off the bed and made a dash for the door, but it closed before she could reach it. Her failure was mitigated somewhat by the delivery she had just received. The tray contained a plastic cup of orange juice, along with a bowl of breakfast cereal and a glass of milk.

Better than nothing, she thought, snatching up the orange juice and downing it in a single gulp. It occurred to her, too late to do anything about it, that the drink might be drugged or poisoned, but then if her captors had wanted to hurt her, there would be no need for trickery.

"Fiona, I need your help with a translation," Gallo said. "You were right about Queen Hippolyte's belt. There was something on it. A map. And something that looks to me like Phaistos glyphs. Do you think you could translate them for me?"

She shook her head. "I don't know how to read Phaistos script. But even if I could read it, I wouldn't. Not for *him.*"

"Fiona!" Gallo's voice was so sharp, the speaker on the television monitor crackled for a second. "Your uncle put you in my care, and you need to *trust me.* You *will* do what I tell you. Do you understand?"

Fiona glowered at the screen. Yet, there was something very odd about Gallo's behavior. She was not the type to simply roll over and surrender at the first sign of trouble.

"Show her the belt," Gallo told Kenner.

The image on the screen changed to show the object she had only glimpsed in the Labyrinth: Queen Hippolyte's battle girdle. Despite herself, she found her gaze drawn to the intricately tooled leather. Her eyes went wide when she realized what she was seeing. "The Amazons knew about the Americas? That's amazing."

She studied it, trying to find some flaw, but the map was astonishingly accurate. Finally, she turned her attention to the Phaistos characters that bordered the image. That was when she saw the familiar but equally incomprehensible script of the Mother Tongue.

"I *just* need you to help with the *Phaistos script*," Gallo was saying. "That's all. You have to trust me, Fiona."

Fiona now understood what the woman was trying to tell her. *Just the Phaistos script. Don't let them know about the Mother Tongue.* She could do that.

Still, if she capitulated too quickly, Kenner might suspect that they were not being truthful. She squared her shoulders. "Will you let us go if we help you?"

The image shifted again, this time revealing Kenner's earnest face. "My dear, if it was up to me, I'd let you walk out the door now. But I can promise you that your cooperation will be rewarded."

"You tried to kill us in Crete," Fiona said, holding back none of the anger that memory evoked. "Why should I believe anything you say?"

Kenner ducked his head guiltily. "I didn't want that to happen. I'm so sorry. And I'm very pleased that you made it out of there."

Fiona considered a very un-ladylike reply, but decided she had already pushed back hard enough.

"I have convinced Mr. Tyndareus that you are much more useful as an ally than as an enemy," Kenner finished.

Fiona did not miss the implicit threat. "Fine. Show it to me again."

The picture of the belt returned to the screen, and this time Fiona stared at it more closely, memorizing every detail. She was feeling better now, thinking more clearly, and not just because the juice had given her a dose of fructose. She was doing something now, and even though she was a long way from any kind of escape plan, it was a step in the right direction. She recalled what Pierce had told her in the Labyrinth. *Where there's life, there's hope.*

"Okay, what is it you want to know?"

Gallo's voice came over the speaker. "We are trying to determine where Queen Hippolyte's city was. We have a rough idea, but we need to narrow down the search area. We're hoping there's a clue in the Phaistos writing on the border."

Fiona nodded to herself. She had figured out the significance of the characters almost right away. "It's a grid system."

"Grid system?" Kenner asked.

"The Phaistos letters give you coordinates on the X and Y axes. Any location on the map can be expressed with a unique address. You know, like 'B-6...Hit! You sank my battleship!'"

"Of course," Gallo murmured. "But why put reference characters on all four sides?"

"Dunno. Maybe that allows you to draw intercept points that aren't at perpendicular angles. Let's say you gave someone the address A-M-1-9. You would draw a line between A and M, and then another line between one and nine, and where those two lines cross, you have your waypoint."

"That's all very interesting," Kenner said. "But it doesn't tell us where to look for the Amazon city."

Fiona shrugged. "Without a set of coordinates, there's not much I can do."

"Could there be a clue in the Phaistos symbols?" Gallo asked. "Perhaps the coordinate address also forms a word or a name?"

"Another literacy test? Like in the Labyrinth." Fiona considered this for a moment. There was an undeniable logic to that idea. "You said that you have an idea of where the Amazon city is?"

"South America," Gallo said. "Somewhere in the Amazon Basin... Don't say it. I know how crazy it sounds."

Fiona tried unsuccessfully to stifle a grin.

She stepped closer to the screen, paying careful attention to the Phaistos characters on the left-hand vertical edge, closest to the part of the map that corresponded to equatorial South America. From there, she drew random mental lines across the map to the opposite side, looking for pairings like those she had found in the Labyrinth. She saw three possible combinations. She repeated the process top-to-bottom, coming up with two more likely pairs. One of those couplets combined perfectly with one of the three possibilities, forming a sequence that she recognized from the Phaistos disc. The lines resulting from that unique 'address' fell at a point north of a spot where the Amazon met with one of its many tributaries.

"Okay, I think I know where it is."

"Tell me," urged Kenner's disembodied voice.

She did her best to explain her conclusions and how she had reached them.

"Mount Roraima in Brazil," Gallo said, when Fiona was finished. "Well that explains a lot."

"I can show it to you on a map," Fiona said, hoping to find a way out of the room.

"I'm afraid that won't be possible," Kenner said, and then as if in an aside, he added, "I wish you would have let me bring her. It would have made this much easier."

"No way was I going to let you drag her along into the jungle," Gallo replied.

"Bring me along?" Fiona said. "Aunt Gus, where are you?"

"Honestly, darling, I haven't the foggiest. But now I know where I'm going."

TWENTY-SEVEN

Gibraltar

Lazarus jumped out of the launch and started dragging the bow of the craft up onto the rocky beach, until there was no risk of it being washed back out to sea. At the stern of the rigid-hulled inflatable boat, Pierce tilted the outboard up out of the water, and then jumped out to help. When the boat was high and dry, both men helped Carter offload several water-tight containers, which held everything she needed to set up a small-scale gene sequencing operation.

With the threat from the vines more or less under control, there was no immediate need for further genetic testing in Liberia, so Pierce had brought the equipment with them. To reduce the possibility of Cerberus tracking another chartered boat ride to the cave entrance, he had procured the Zodiac semi-rigid inflatable boat—a craft Lazarus had used extensively in his prior life—but he worried that this precaution had come too late. Cerberus might already know about the citadel. While he was confident that the Forgotten were more than a match for any incursion in the near term, the Gorham's Cave refuge would have to be abandoned. For the present however, it would continue to serve as Herculean HQ.

Carter appraised the opening in the cliff face. She shook her head and muttered, "Caves. I can't seem to get away from them."

"I know what you mean," Pierce said. "For what it's worth, this one is nicer than most. Although..." He dipped a hand into his pocket and took out a pair of bronze medallions adorned with the emblem of the Herculean Society. He passed one each to Carter and Lazarus. "You'll need to wear these. Keep them visible at all times."

Lazarus stared at his medallion for several seconds. Pierce braced himself for a deluge of questions, but if the big man had any, he did not voice them. Instead, he looped the pendant chain around his neck, and then lifted the heaviest of the cargo boxes into his arms.

Pierce led the way into the ancient Neanderthal dwelling and up to the concealed entrance to the citadel. While Lazarus shuttled containers into the hidden cavern, Carter began inspecting the Nemean Lion's impervious skin. Pierce checked in with Dourado, as he had done every half-hour since learning about Fiona's and Gallo's disappearances more than twelve hours earlier.

The answer was the same this time as it was in each of the previous instances. "Nothing yet. I'll call as soon as I know something."

Pierce sagged back in his chair, frustrated. While he had been on the move, traveling back from Liberia, he had at least been able to console himself with the illusion of progress. Now that he had reached his destination, he was confronted with the realization that there was nowhere to go next. Worse, the citadel was a reminder of his own failure to protect the people he loved. If he had taken Gallo and Fiona with him to Liberia, or insisted they remain in the cave...

If, if, if.

Carter's voice pulled him out of his self-pitying reflection. "You weren't kidding about how tough this thing is."

He glanced over and saw her struggling with the Lion skin. "The Lion's own claws were the only thing Hercules found that could cut through it."

"Hercules didn't have a diamond-tipped scalpel," she replied, holding up the tool she had used to remove a tiny slice of the preserved hide. "There's no magic at work here, Dr. Pierce. Just things that we don't understand yet."

"Will you be able to extract any viable DNA from it?"

"I think so. I'm curious about one thing, though. How exactly will this help you find your friends?"

The question stung. "Honestly, I don't know if it will. Kenner believes these chimeras originate from a specific source. I was hoping that you might be able to isolate whatever factor is responsible. A genetic footprint, if you will. A chemical agent or something like that. But that was before. Now...?" He shrugged.

"Well, you might be on to something. I don't know about chemical agents, but identifying the genetic contributors may give us a geographical ballpark."

"How so?"

She gestured to the skin. "For starters, this isn't a lion."

"I know. It's a chimera. A lion and something else."

She shook her head. "Actually, I don't think it's a chimera either. Not in the genetic sense at least. I think it's actually a transgenic hybrid."

"What's the difference?"

"In biology, a chimera is an organism that has two or more distinctive cellular populations. A bone marrow transplant or tree grafting creates a chimera because the recipient now has two distinctive cell populations. Two different sets of DNA, coexisting in the same body. If you graft a lemon branch onto a lime tree, it doesn't become a new organism. Just a lime tree that also gives you lemons. A hybrid is a combination of genetic material from two different sources, but it has only one cellular population—one set of DNA."

"Like a mule."

"Right. A mule doesn't have horse DNA in some of its cells and donkey DNA in others. It only has mule DNA. With gene splicing, we can combine nucleotides from vastly different species to create transgenic hybrids. And I think that's what this is."

Pierce was not sure the semantic distinction mattered, but Carter's expertise *was* the reason he had recruited her. "Okay. So it's a hybrid of a lion and something else. Something that gives it nearly indestructible skin and fur. Is there anything like that in the natural world?"

She shrugged. "You've probably heard about how spider silk is stronger than steel wire, ounce for ounce. Nature has produced a lot of amazing things."

"Why did you say it's not a lion?"

"I've seen a lot of lions over the past couple of years, and this isn't one. Not an African lion, at least."

"There's another kind?" Pierce examined the animal skin more closely. He knew that some large cats were mistakenly identified as 'lions'—cougars, for example were often called 'mountain lions'—but there were visible differences between the two species. The Nemean Lion, at least to Pierce's untrained eye, appeared to be a member of the true lion family, albeit a monstrously large example of it.

"There are actually several different lion species that all fall under the umbrella term African lion," Carter explained. "Some, like the Barbary lion, were only recently hunted to extinction—in the last two hundred years or so. But in ancient times, lion species could be found all over the world—the Middle East, Europe. I suspect this specimen may belong to one of those species."

"Europe? Well, I guess that would explain the presence of a lion in Greece."

She placed the tissue sample into a test-tube and carefully measured out drops of a reagent solution. "Lions were once fairly common all over Asia. I think they even show up in a couple Bible stories."

"Right. David killed a lion with his sling, and Samson killed one with his bare hands." The recollection triggered a painful memory of Fiona paraphrasing Ecclesiastes in the Labyrinth. *Live dogs and dead lions.* He grimaced.

"Those were probably *Panthera leo persica*, the Asiatic lion. The only place you'll find them in the wild today is India. They once ranged as far west as Turkey. But I don't think that's what we've got here either. The Asiatic lion is even smaller than the African species, with a less developed mane. This specimen is considerably larger than an African lion. That could be the result of the contribution from the other species, but I don't think so. Also, the fur is thicker, suggesting that this animal was adapted to colder climates. It might be a late extant European cave lion. *Panthera leo spelaea.*"

"One that survived to the first millennium BC?"

"Possibly. There are still a few pristine ecosystems where species long believed extinct are still alive and well." She cast a knowing nod in Lazarus's direction. "Or if your hypothesis about some kind of chemical agent is correct, it might have been a primitive cloning experiment involving DNA recovered from a fossilized specimen.

"The question of how may not be as important as where. If it is a *P. spelaea*, then there's a good chance your source is somewhere in Europe. Hopefully, there's still enough of the lion left in this hybrid for a match in the ADW genetic database." She placed the test tube into one of the devices Pierce had provided for her in Liberia—a Pacific BioSciences SMRT—single molecule real-time—sequencer. As the machine hummed to life, Carter crossed her arms. "You know, if I'm going to work for you, I'm going to need better facilities. Preferably, somewhere not in a cave."

"*Are* you going to work for me?"

"We'll see." Carter looked away from him, meeting Lazarus's patient gaze. The big man gave her a reassuring nod.

Before Pierce could express his gratitude, a trilling sound from his computer signaled an incoming teleconference request from Dourado. Bracing himself against the possibility of yet another disappointment, he tapped the button to receive the call. "Please have good news, Cintia."

Beneath a mane of cobalt blue curls, Dourado was grinning. "I *do* have good news, Dr. Pierce." Excitement caused her words to blur together, exaggerating her distinctive Brazilian accent. "Cerberus has a jet. I compared airport data from the week of Van Der Hausen's arrival in Monrovia against all the data from the last three days in Crete and Athens."

"What data?"

"Everything. Customs. Passport control. Car rental agencies. Flight plans. There were no names in common, but that is not surprising. They must be using aliases. But I did discover a private aircraft—a Learjet 60—that arrived in Monrovia the day before Van Der Hausen flew in from Stockholm. It left three days later. That same plane was in Heraklion when you were there, and it was in Athens late last night. It arrived shortly before...ah...Dr. Gallo's disappearance."

Pierce was suddenly giddy with the possibility of tracking Cerberus to its lair, finding Gallo and Fiona. "Who owns it?"

"It belongs to one of the Cerberus shell companies, based in Grand Cayman Island."

"Where's the plane now? Is it still in Greece?"

"No. It took off again early this morning. It flew to Barcelona, then Rome. It was there for a few hours but it left again. They refueled in the Azores, but then took off again. It is in the air as we speak."

"They have to file flight plans, right? Do you know where it's headed now?"

Dourado's excitement nearly matched Pierce's for feverish intensity. "Yes. It is coming here."

"To Brazil?"

"To Belem! They'll be arriving in less than three hours."

"Is that a stopover or a final destination?"

"No additional flight plans have been filed."

Pierce processed the information for a moment. Belem, situated at the mouth of the Amazon, seemed an unlikely destination. Given Cerberus's far-flung operations, there was no guarantee that the jet's current destination had anything to do with what Kenner was after. If the incident in Liberia had indeed been a weapons test, then maybe the Amazon rainforest was intended to be the next phase of a different plan, unrelated to what Kenner was looking for. Perhaps Cerberus intended to employ the carnivorous vine against some of the native tribes who opposed development of their ancestral home-land. Or it might be something else entirely. His gut told him that where the plane had been was probably more important than where it was going.

But what if I'm wrong? What if Augustina and Fiona are aboard that plane?

"Cintia, we need to get eyes on that plane. Contact Aegis. See if they have any operatives in the region."

"The nearest Aegis office is in Rio," Dourado replied. "They will not be able to get someone here in time."

Pierce frowned, wracking his brain to come up with an alternative. "Give them a call anyway. Maybe they can recommend someone local. A private eye or—"

"*I* will do it," Dourado said. All of her earlier enthusiasm was gone. Her voice was now so small it was barely audible.

"Cintia—"

"There is no one else. Not that can be here in time."

Pierce felt a pang of guilt for even considering the suggestion. Dourado was a computer jockey, not a field operative. Given the circumstances, the narrow window of opportunity and the lack of alternatives, he could not argue with her. But the idea of putting her in danger, even if the actual risk was minimal, made him sick to his stomach.

Being in charge really sucks.

"Just get eyes on. Don't approach them. In fact, if Augustina and Fiona are there, don't let them see you. Wear a..." He was about to say 'hat' then thought better of it. "A disguise of some kind. I don't want you to put yourself in any danger."

"I'm on it," she said.

"Thank you, Cintia. We'll be there as soon as we can." He looked over at Carter. "How much longer?"

"Anywhere from twenty minutes to four hours."

Four hours. Kenner might be on the ground in Belem before they could even leave Gorham's Cave. Leaving Lazarus and Carter behind was not an option. He would need the big man's help to rescue Gallo and Fiona, and he was not about to ask Carter to stay by herself.

"However," Carter continued, as if sensing his inner turmoil. "I can access the results remotely. We could leave right now if you want."

Perfect. "Cintia, be careful. Don't do anything dangerous. We're on our way."

TWENTY-EIGHT

Cerberus Headquarters

The door opened and another tray slid across the threshold. It was the third such delivery and Fiona's only contact with the world beyond the walls of her prison. She guessed the interval between meals to be about three hours—there was no way to tell for sure—which meant that about six hours had passed since her conversation with Gallo. In all that time, the television screen had remained dark. She assumed that she was being monitored by her unseen captors, which meant that what she was about to do now might be very dangerous, but still preferable to doing nothing at all.

As soon as the tray cleared the sweep of the door, she bolted into motion, crossing the room in three long strides, armed with a plastic fork. She slide the utensil between the door and its frame just before it could close. There was a faint tremor as the latch bolt struck the prongs of the fork. She held her breath, praying that her jailor wouldn't test to make sure the bolt had seated properly.

A moment passed. Five seconds. Ten.

Nothing happened.

She let her breath out slowly. With painstaking caution, she relaxed her hold on the stem of the fork. The pressure of the spring-loaded latch bolt held it in place. Her plan, this much of it at least, was working.

She took a step back, dropping her hands to her hips in what she hoped would look like a display of frustration, and then picked up the tray and carried it back to the bed. If someone was watching, they would think that her escape attempt had been unsuccessful. That was what she hoped, anyway.

The meal was unremarkable—a bowl of unidentifiable instant noodles, still steaming hot. There were also some peanut butter-smeared crackers and a glass of milk. She took the convenience-store style meals as a sign that the Cerberus headquarters was not a large-scale operation. A fully-prepared meal would have indicated an onsite kitchen, maybe a cafeteria for guards and other personnel. Of course, it was also possible that her captors had merely elected not to waste good food on a doomed prisoner, but she tried not to think about that.

She ate methodically, staring at the walls and biding her time. The food was not the worst thing she'd ever eaten, and it would provide metabolic fuel for what she was about to do. The supply of insulin in her pump would not last forever—another twelve hours if she was lucky. And she wasn't about to beg her captors for more, which meant that she had to succeed. If things went badly, it would probably be her last meal.

When she had siphoned the last drops of milk from the glass, she rose and carried the tray back to the door, kneeling to set it down with as much nonchalance as she could manage. Then, as she stood, she took hold of the plastic fork and gave the door a gentle tug.

As it swung open she braced herself for an alarm, expecting to be met by an armed guard, maybe even the big ugly giant, Rohn. Nothing happened. The door opened without any resistance, granting her a view of the hallway beyond. She took a cautious step forward, peering around the doorjamb, looking both ways.

No one there.

The hallway looked like something from a budget motel, except the doors on either side were unmarked and there were no signs to guide her toward an exit. There was what appeared to be an elevator door to her right, and further away to the left, a dead-end, or possibly a T-intersection; she couldn't be sure which.

Elevator, she decided, though she was by no means confident in the choice.

The quiet was unnerving. No noise of outside traffic, televisions or vacuum cleaners. Either the walls were heavily insulated or she was alone on the floor. If not for her earlier meal delivery, she would have believed that the building had been abandoned.

Her curiosity got the better of her, and she tried the doorknob of the first room she came to. Locked. She pressed her ear to the door and listened, but the room was as quiet as a tomb. She kept moving.

When she reached the elevator door, she was confronted with a new problem. There was no call button. No way to summon the car or open the doors.

The predicament reminded her of being stuck in the Labyrinth, and that made her think about the inscription on Queen Hippolyte's map-belt. She might not be able to decipher the Mother Tongue, but she recognized the words. They were the same words she had seen at the dead end in the Labyrinth, just before Kenner's bomb had blown the whole place to Hell. If they meant what she thought they did, saying them correctly would have let her and Pierce walk right through that wall. There had actually been a few seconds where she thought she had gotten the words right, but it could have been her imagination.

Could she do the same thing now?

She tried to visualize the words, picturing them engraved on the blank metal door. The letters were no longer just unfamiliar squiggles to her, but comprehension remained just beyond her grasp.

Suddenly, the door slid open.

She jumped back, startled. Her heart pounded in her chest, each beat sending a tremor through her entire body. She was about to turn and flee, even though there was nowhere to go, but before she could make another move, she realized that the car was empty. A moment later, the door closed.

"Okay, what just happened?" she muttered.

For a fleeting instant, she wondered if she had caused the door to open, perhaps merely by focusing on the Mother Tongue, but then a different thought occurred to her. She took a step toward the elevator, and it opened again.

A proximity sensor, just like a supermarket door.

She stuck her head into the car and looked around. There was no control panel, no way to select a destination.

If the doors were programmed to respond to someone getting close, maybe the elevator would automatically take her somewhere else. But where?

Only one way to find out. It was not like she had a wide range of choices.

She stepped in. The doors closed, and there was a vibration as the car began to move. She couldn't tell if it was moving up or down, but thirty seconds later, the sensation stopped. The elevator opened again.

She peeked around the door frame, but there was no one lurking in the hall beyond. She stepped out.

The corridor was so like the one she had just left that Fiona wondered if the elevator had actually moved at all—blank walls, blank doors, no signs. As she moved down the hallway, she tested doors at random. None opened, but she did see one distinctive difference between this floor of the building and the one where her prison cell had been located. There was a door at the far end, wooden and stained a dark walnut. There was no doorknob, but as she got close, the door swung inward.

Another motion sensor.

She felt a surge of hope as she stepped into the room beyond. She was in a museum, or possibly an art gallery. The room was arrayed with pedestals and display cases, exhibiting artifacts ranging from the Paleolithic era to the Renaissance. The pieces were beautiful, as if chosen specifically for their aesthetic value. Many appeared to have religious significance. Yet, as she progressed through the room, her initial optimism waned. This was not a public exhibition but rather a private collection kept solely for the enjoyment of her captor.

Still, there had to be a way out.

An arched passageway took her to another gallery, but unlike the first, this room contained memorabilia from a more recent era in history. At first, she thought the room was devoted to medical history. The walls were lined with shelves displaying skulls and skeletal fragments, jars containing organs preserved in a liquid solution. Some were marked with a numerical code, handwritten on yellowed placards and adhesive labels. The room also contained pictures, dozens—perhaps hundreds—of black and white photographs.

Fiona now regretted having eaten before making her bid for freedom. The pictures were the stuff of nightmares. There were photographs of men and women of all ages. Children, too. In fact, a disproportionate number of the photographs were of children. They were all naked and helpless, staring bleakly at the camera. Many were emaciated; all looked defeated. Those were the easiest to look at. There were pictures of corpses, amputated limbs and bodies opened up for post-mortem examinations, but those were not the worst. The worst were the photos that showed what happened in-between.

Fiona quickly recognized the pictures for what they were, a record of ghastly medical experiments, carried out on living human victims. That was when she saw a large, freestanding trophy case at the far end of the room. In it, before a background of framed diplomas, awards and portraits of a dark-haired man with a gap-toothed smile, stood a mannequin dressed in an immaculate gray-green military uniform, replete with a peaked cap and something that looked like lightning bolts on the collar.

A Nazi uniform.

She gave the exhibit only a cursory inspection. The contents confirmed what she had already guessed. This was a very different kind of Holocaust memorial, one that celebrated the torture and murder of millions and honored those who had perpetrated such unimaginable cruelty.

There was a door just behind the display, a regular door with a handle that turned when she tested it. To her dismay, it opened into yet another large room. With stark white walls, overhead fluorescent lighting and a dull gray industrial epoxy floor, the space looked like a factory warehouse. Despite the fact that the room was far more utilitarian than the preceding galleries after the horrors she had just witnessed, it was a welcome change.

She hurried past row after row of work tables, trying to ignore the contents, lest she discover new horrors. One item, however, caught her eye.

It stood in the center of the room like a suit of medieval armor decorating the entrance to a castle keep. It *was* armor, in fact, but there was nothing antiquated about it. It looked more like something from a super-hero movie.

The suit was a full-body armored exoskeleton. Fiona had heard about the military's intention to develop Iron Man-style battle suits for soldiers, though in her opinion, it looked more like the armor worn by Master Chief in the Halo games, right down to the bubble-shaped reflective visor in the helmet. As far as she knew, the project was still in the early design phase.

So how had Cerberus gotten their hands on it?

She recalled what Dourado had said about Cerberus providing anything for the right price. Had they stolen a prototype of the military exosuit? Or perhaps built this from leaked, classified plans?

The suit, which appeared to have been posed like the mannequin of the SS officer in the display case, offered no clues. She couldn't tell if it was even functional.

But if it is...

Inspiration hit her like a lightning bolt. If the suit was operational, maybe she could use it to escape this nightmare. She took a step closer, searching for some way of opening the armored carapace.

There was a flash of movement, and something struck her in the side, knocking her backward. The blow stunned her, and the next thing she knew, she was lying in a heap on the floor, twenty feet from the exosuit. The pain arrived before she could even think about trying to rise, but in the corner of her eye, she saw the dull gray suit moving, advancing toward her.

She struggled to recover, attempted to roll over and push herself up, but her left arm refused to work, and she collapsed face down on the floor. As she lay there, trying to will herself into motion, she could feel the vibration of each mechanical footfall as the exosuit stalked relentlessly toward her.

Thump. Thump.

Move it!

She tried again, bracing her right arm in front of her. The adrenaline of pure panic flooded through her body, numbing her against the throb of pain and supplying almost superhuman strength.

But she wasn't fast enough.

The exosuit loomed over her, and even as she tried to roll out of the way, an armored fist descended.

Then, she saw nothing at all.

TWENTY-NINE

Belem, Brazil

Getting past her own front door had been hell for Cintia Dourado. Each step after that got progressively harder.

"I can do this," she told herself, repeating the words like a mantra. The affirmation had gotten her across the city, all the way to the airport, but she remained unconvinced.

She had survived the taxi ride by keeping her head down, staring at the floor. But now, out here on the edge of the runway at the Val de Cans International Airport, with nothing but wide open sky above, the simple act of standing seemed as daunting as escaping the event horizon of a black hole.

Though she had never consulted a mental health practitioner or received a professional diagnosis, Dourado was well aware of her condition. Agoraphobia. An irrational anxiety associated with public places and wide open spaces. Her paranoia was almost certainly the result of psychological trauma sustained in early childhood. She had no memories of life before the debilitating panic disorder had clamped down on her like steel manacles, and in truth, she did not want to know. She had escaped the slums, and had no inclination to revisit them, even in her mind's eye.

She had discovered computers at age twelve and quickly master-ed cyberspace, roaming its vastness like a buccaneer, plying the deep web, trading in secrets and taking whatever she needed. Strangely, the possibility of being caught had not frightened her at all. Even though she had known that being arrested for her computerized transgress-ions would shatter her world, the risk did not trigger her agoraphobia. Rather, it had become her own version of an extreme sport, supplying an addictive endorphin rush that not only caused her to feel alive, but pushed her to new heights. Made her better. Smarter.

Smart enough to crack the Herculean Society.

That had been a transformational moment for her, making it possible for her to trade the squalor of her single room apartment in Tenoné for a luxury condominium in the upscale Nazareth neighbor-hood. Not that the surroundings mattered much. The digital landscape was her true home now, the only place where she felt safe and in control. She could go anywhere, know anything she wanted to know, without ever stepping outside. Everything she needed for physical survival could be ordered online and delivered to her doorstep, with a bare minimum of human interaction.

So why had she volunteered to do this?

On an intellectual level, she knew the answer. The Herculean Society had given her the one thing she had not even realized was missing from her life. A purpose. She was a part of something import-ant, no longer living just for herself. And now the Society needed something from her. People that she cared about, even though she had never met them, were in danger, and she was in the best position to help them. The calculation had been simple enough. A very real, life-and-death situation outweighed irrational panic every time.

That much was enough to get her through the front door. She had hoped it would get easier after that.

It hadn't.

She could feel the contemptuous stares of strangers. Dozens of them. Hundreds. She knew there were actually only a handful of people coming and going from the private charter aircraft hangar situated north of the runway, and that none had given her more than a passing glance, but it did not ease her anxiety.

She took out her smartphone and opened her air traffic control app. The act of checking the handheld computing device and connecting with the digital universe helped steady her nerves a little. The app confirmed that the Cerberus plane was still running on time and it would arrive in less than thirty minutes.

Thirty minutes. Could she survive that long?

She felt the void of the sky overhead, overwhelming in its immensity.

Inside. I need to get inside.

That was a bad idea though. She could not enter the secure area of the hangar, where the plane would eventually be parked, and even if she could, that was not her intent. Pierce had been very clear about not getting close to the jet or its occupants. She was to observe from a safe distance. Nothing more.

What exactly constituted a safe distance, she had no idea.

She spent the next few minutes searching for a sheltered place with a direct line of sight to the hangar, and found it in a wooded area more than two hundred yards away. The distance would be a problem, but she was able to overcome that limitation by using her phone's camera at maximum zoom. The dense trees made her feel a little less exposed, and for the first time since leaving her residence, she caught her breath.

Several planes came and went, mostly larger commercial birds from international carriers, but one aircraft caught her attention, not because it was a helicopter—another handy app revealed it to be a Sikorsky S-61L—but because the large rotor-wing passenger aircraft settled down right next to the hangar she was keeping an eye on. The whirling blades gradually wound down to a stop, but no one emerged from the aircraft.

Curious, Dourado checked the registration numbers painted on the helicopter's tail. She traced its ownership to a company that provided logistical support to remote logging and mining operations throughout the Amazon Basin.

She knew that was no coincidence. They were waiting for the passengers aboard the incoming Learjet. The Cerberus people were going to transfer to the helicopter, and then head to some unknown destination. Because helicopters were not required to file flight plans, there would be no way to track them once they left, short of accessing a Brazilian military radar tracking station.

She stared at her phone in impotent frustration, until it occurred to her that there *was* a way to track them. The realization of what that would involve brought on another wave of panic.

One simple hack, she told herself. *If I can do that, the rest will be easy.*

The hack *was* simple. She breezed through firewalls and tore through the encryption like it was digital tissue paper. After that, it was just a matter of data entry. It took all of two minutes.

She checked the air traffic control app again. The Cerberus jet was on final approach. It would be on the ground in a matter of minutes.

"I can do this."

She broke from cover and walked briskly toward the hangar, staring at the ground so she would not have to look at the sky. It didn't help. She could feel it, the open emptiness like a yawning abyss trying to devour her.

She reached the door, entered the security code she had illicitly obtained and moved inside.

Being indoors again, even in this unfamiliar environment, eased the agoraphobic panic somewhat, but it did not alleviate the anxiety she felt about the risk she was now taking. Pierce's words burned in her ears. *Don't approach. Don't do anything dangerous.*

This isn't dangerous, she told herself. *No one knows who I am.*

Dourado had covered her bases. If someone stopped her, questioned her, she had a solid cover story. She was a flight safety inspector, doing a random spot check to ensure that the helicopter was in compliance with regulations. Since she had the door access code, anyone inside would reason that she must be who she said she was, but in the unlikely event that someone decided to challenge the ruse, a call to the National Civil Aviation Agency would confirm her story.

As she moved through the reception area, she avoided making eye contact with the room's only occupant, a woman who was in the middle of a telephone conversation. Dourado glanced down, nervously checking to make sure that her bright blue hair was tucked up under her cap. She had donned the hat and removed most of her facial piercings before leaving her residence. It was not much of a disguise, but subterfuge had never been her original intention. Hopefully, the helicopter's crew would be in such a hurry to get rid of her that they would not look too closely.

After the relative security of the hangar building, the rear door that let out onto the tarmac almost stopped her cold. "I can do this."

Her heart pounded against her chest. She fixed her gaze on the helicopter, and willed her feet to start moving. As she headed toward the helicopter, she checked the flight status of the Cerberus jet. The information had not been updated, but if the clock was to be trusted, the plane should already have landed. She glanced over at the runway just in time to see an aging A320 with TAM Airlines markings touch down.

She looked back to the helicopter and realized someone was looking down from the elevated cockpit bubble. The scrutiny felt like a physical attack. She forced herself to look away, but the damage was already done. Her pulse was racing, her breathing so rapid that she was on the verge of hyperventilating.

"Can I help you?"

The voice startled her. She looked up saw another man standing near the nose of the aircraft. He wore olive drab flight coveralls, the kind that could be purchased from almost any military surplus retailer.

She worked her mouth, trying to form the short sentence she had rehearsed, but all that came out was a feeble stutter. "Safe... safe...safety inspect...in...spec..."

The man stared back patiently, and then nodded in understanding. He reached into a pocket and drew out a folded piece of paper which he extended to her. "Everything is in order."

Not paper, she now realized. *Money.*

A hundred-real banknote. The man was offering her a bribe.

This was something she had not anticipated. Strangely, this unexpected development had the equally unexpected side effect of shocking her out of her panic. Her heart grew calm, her breathing returned to normal and perhaps most importantly, her ability to think rationally switched back on.

She shook her head, and in a calm clear voice, she said, "I need to get a serial number from your fire extinguisher. It will only take a minute."

The man frowned, as if trying to decide whether to offer a larger bribe or simply comply with her request. After a moment, he turned and slid back the side hatch. "Be my guest."

Dourado climbed inside the Sikorsky and looked around. The rear of the cabin behind the passenger seating area was filled with cargo containers and cardboard boxes. The containers had been stacked up to within eight-inches of the ceiling, and they were secured in place by a cargo net that stretched between grommets in the floor and walls. Supplies. For an expedition, perhaps?

She stifled her curiosity and focused on accomplishing the task she had set for herself. "Where are the fire extinguishers?" she asked, only to discover that the crewman was no longer there. She turned to find him walking across the tarmac in the direction of a small jet aircraft that was taxiing toward the hangar. The Cerberus plane had arrived.

Dourado looked away quickly. She was nearly out of time, and yet instead of triggering a panic attack, the ticking clock only served to further sharpen her focus.

"I can do this," she told herself again, and this time, she actually believed it. What she was attempting was not much different than hacking a secure server. The only difference was that she was doing it in the real world.

It took just a few seconds for her to compose a brief e-mail with a link to a phone-finder app and instructions on how to use it. She hit send, and after a surreptitious look around to make sure that she was still unobserved, she slipped the phone into one of the boxes. It would be found eventually, but not until the helicopter reached its final destination.

She returned to the open hatch and peered out. The Learjet had pulled into the empty hangar, and its side hatch was deployed. The crewman stood at the base of the fold-down steps, waiting to greet disembarking passengers.

Dourado held her breath, but in anticipation rather than anxiety. Strangely, she was not the least bit fearful now.

She easily recognized the first man off the plane. He looked a little older than the most recent photographs she had found, but it was unmistakably Liam Kenner. That single revelation made everything she had risked and endured worthwhile. If Kenner was here, then whatever he was looking for was also here, somewhere nearby, or at least somewhere that could be reached only by helicopter from Belem. The link she had sent to Pierce would allow them to pinpoint that final destination, and finally give them an advantage in the battle with Cerberus.

The next passenger off the plane was likewise unmistakable. Though she had never seen him before, the big brutish looking man matched Fiona's description of Kenner's hired muscle, Vigor Rohn. Kenner and Rohn began conversing with the crewman from the helicopter, gesturing excitedly toward the aircraft, no doubt discussing the particulars of the impending next leg of their travels.

Time to go, Dourado thought.

It was a basic rule of hacking. Always be long gone before anyone realized something had happened. She could walk right by Kenner and Rohn without fear of being recognized. If they inquired about her, the crewman would be able to vouch for her, but the longer she waited, the more suspicious her presence would become to them.

I need to go.

Yet, she did not move. Her eyes remained fixed on the open hatch in the side of the Learjet. Someone else was coming out, three people— two large men, both cut from the same cloth as Rohn. Bracketed between them was a woman with long black hair.

Augustina Gallo.

That was what she had been waiting for, hoping for. *And now I really, really have to go.*

Still, she did not move.

She had visual confirmation that Gallo was alive and a hostage. She had established that Kenner and Rohn were bound for some destination in the Amazon. She had even managed to find a way to track the helicopter so Pierce would be able to follow when he arrived in Brazil. Realistically, there was nothing more she could do.

I'm on my own here, Dourado thought. *It's not like I can rescue her all by myself.*

Or can I?

She glanced back at the box where she had hidden her phone, and all the other cargo stacked up behind it, and she made her decision.

THIRTY

Over the Atlantic Ocean

Pierce rubbed the sleep from his eyes and looked around the dimly lit cabin of the Herculean Society's Gulfstream 550. He had not expected to sleep, but according to his watch, they had been in the air for over five hours. He had slept for most of the flight.

Lazarus was seated on the floor in the center of the cabin, between the inward facing passenger couches. The big man's eyes were closed, and his legs were folded up in the lotus position. Pierce assumed he was meditating, but he might have been asleep. Further back, Carter sat in front of an open laptop, studying the results of the SMRT sequence of the DNA taken from the Nemean Lion.

Pierce rose and stretched, then skirted around Lazarus to join her. He jerked a thumb in the big man's direction. "Does he do that a lot?"

"We both do," Carter replied, without looking away from the screen.

Pierce took a seat next to her and watched. Every few minutes, she would click the touch pad and the display would change, though Pierce would have been hard-pressed to explain exactly what was different. It was like looking at a Magic-Eye puzzle made up entirely of the letters A, G, C and T, each a different color. But one thing was obvious: she hadn't found any answers yet.

So much for 'twenty minutes to four hours,' he thought. He fought down the urge to ask Carter why it was taking so long. Pestering her would not produce results any faster.

As if sensing his growing frustration, she said, "In case you're wondering, the read is finished. I'm comparing the sequence to samples in the database."

"That must be a tedious process," he said, phrasing it almost like a question.

"That's only part of the problem. We're dealing with hybrid DNA, so there isn't going to be an exact match."

"There can't be that many species of lion to compare it against."

"The lion part was easy. Your Nemean Lion is actually *Panthera leo atrox*, better known as the American lion. They've been extinct for eleven thousand years, but were once a top-tier predator in the Americas."

"American?" Pierce asked, incredulous. "Not European?"

"The European lion was the next closest candidate, probability-wise, but I'd say *atrox* is the likeliest match."

"How did an American lion wind up in the Greek isles?"

"An extinct American lion," Carter emphasized. "*How* is a question that DNA sequencing can't answer. With today's technology, it's conceivable that someone could extract genetic material from preserved remains—maybe a tooth. Several *atrox* skeletons have been found in the La Brea Tar Pits in California. They would wander into the tar and get trapped there. Not exactly flies in amber, but pretty close. The Koreans are working on cloning woolly mammoths. The major obstacle now is ethical, not technological. But three thousand years ago..." She shrugged, helplessly.

"I suppose we've both seen stranger things."

"That we have." She stared at the endless rows of letters for a few seconds. "One way to create a transgenic hybrid is to introduce genetic material into an embryonic stem cell. We can do that using a retrovirus, but I suppose it could happen in nature. That could be what Cerberus is after. The retrovirus that made your Lion and all those other mythological monsters possible in the first place."

"An American lion. And Cerberus is on its way to Brazil. I doubt that's a coincidence." He checked his watch. Unless something had changed, the Cerberus jet was already on the ground in Belem, and had been for nearly two hours. "Cintia should have called by now."

"The sample is a ninety-eight percent match for the *atrox*," Carter said. "It's going to be a lot harder to isolate the other contributing organism, but if we come up with another match from the Western Hemisphere, then I'd say it's a slam-dunk."

Pierce nodded, but his focus had already shifted. He checked his phone for missed calls or messages. Nothing, but there was a notification for new e-mails. He opened it and discovered two messages from Dourado.

He read the first and nearly exploded. "Damn it!"

Lazarus's eyes fluttered open. "What's wrong?"

"Cintia. I told her to keep a safe distance."

Lazarus rose to his feet and moved to join Pierce and Carter. "Details. What's happened?"

Pierce read the e-mail again, gripping the phone so tightly that the edges of the LCD screen began to darken from the pressure. "Cerberus had a helicopter waiting in Belem. Cintia decided to sneak aboard and stash her phone so that we could track the helicopter."

"That's good," Lazarus pointed out.

"It's not. Cintia's a computer geek, not a spy. She's going to get herself..." He trailed off. The message was almost two hours old. Cintia might already have been captured. He opened the second message.

"'Only Gallo here,'" he read aloud, each word deepening his despair. "'Hiding on helicopter. Will try to help her escape. Come find us.' Damn her." He hit the reply button.

"Stop." Lazarus's voice was barely louder than a whisper, but the command was as forceful as a punch to the gut.

"She's going to get herself killed."

"If she hasn't been discovered yet, any attempt to contact her might put her in danger."

"Well, what am I supposed to do? Cintia's practically a shut in. She's not up for this."

"Is the tracker working?" Lazarus asked.

Pierce went back to the first e-mail and clicked on the hyperlink. After a few seconds, a map opened up and showed the location of Dourado's satellite phone. He had to zoom out to establish the exact location, a spot near the Brazilian border with Venezuela and Guyana.

"It's still transmitting," Lazarus said, "so she probably hasn't been discovered yet."

Pierce felt a glimmer of hope, but it faded almost as quickly. "This is the middle of nowhere. It will take hours for us to get there. Days."

Lazarus studied the tiny screen on the phone for a moment then shook his head. "Open that link on the computer. Let's see what we're dealing with."

Carter made room at the table and a few minutes later, they were looking at a larger satellite photo of the same region. A yellow dot marked Dourado's phone amid a background of green and brown. "It's not moving," Pierce said. "They must have reached wherever it is they were going."

"Mount Roraima." Carter tapped a nearby spot on the screen. "These plateaus—they're called *tepui*—are some of the most isolated and pristine ecosystems in the world. They're so remote that they may still support primeval life forms. Maybe that's what Cerberus is after. Some unique organism that doesn't exist anywhere else in the world."

"There have been rumors of dinosaurs and other prehistoric creatures living there for more than a century," Pierce added. "Mount Roraima was the inspiration for *The Lost World* by Edgar Rice Burroughs."

"Conan Doyle wrote *The Lost World*," Carter said, offhandedly. "You're probably thinking of *The Land That Time Forgot*."

He blinked at her. Ordinarily he would have let it slide, but he was tired and cranky. People that he loved were in danger, and his nerves were raw. "Burroughs," he insisted. "It was my favorite book growing up."

"If it was your favorite, I'm surprised you don't know who wrote it."

Lazarus cleared his throat, quashing the pointless debate before it could escalate into something uglier. "Gallo is an expert on Greek mythology, right? Why would Cerberus need to take her along to Roraima?"

"I don't know." Pierce closed his eyes, searching his memory. "Kenner is on the trail of our old friend Hercules. And we know Alexander traveled around much of the ancient world. It's possible he came here, too."

Thanks to his prior association with Jack Sigler, Lazarus knew all about Alexander, and he didn't need Pierce to elaborate. "So it's not just about rescuing your people. We also have to stop Kenner and Cerberus from getting their hands on whatever it is they're after?"

"Pretty much."

"What about Fiona?"

Pierce shook his head. "Cintia said they only had Gallo."

"So we also need to find out where they're keeping Fiona," Lazarus said. "Now we just need a plan." He studied the satellite imagery for several seconds. "No roads. The nearest airport is hundreds of miles away."

"If we go in by helicopter, they'll hear us coming from miles away."

Lazarus stared at him thoughtfully. "You could get us a helo?"

"Sure." Pierce recalled that Lazarus's diverse skill set included knowing how to pilot a helicopter. "If there's one available that is. Short notice might be a problem, but I can afford one if that's what you're asking."

Lazarus considered this for a moment, but then he shook his head. "You're right. A helicopter would make too much noise. There is another way for us to get there fast and undetected, but..." He cocked his jaw sideways. "I don't know if we could pull it off."

"We've got to get them back, no matter what. Tell me what you need, and I'll write the check."

Lazarus let out his breath in a sigh. "For what I've got in mind, money will be the least of our problems."

THIRTY-ONE

Cerberus Headquarters

Fiona jolted awake, and she was greeted by a spike of pain that threatened to split her skull. She reached up, probing the spot where the ache was most concentrated. There was a lump the size of a golf ball on the side of her head, and a rough crusty substance in her hair. Dried blood.

She managed to sit up, the pain nearly blinding her. Although the initial agony subsided after a moment, the assault on her vision continued without any let up. The room was nothing but white surfaces lit by intensely bright overhead lights. Across the room, she saw a pair of seated figures on what appeared to be examination tables—not like the padded and papered kind used in doctor's offices, but the hard stainless steel kind used for autopsies. She shuddered at the thought, and the two people across the room shuddered, too.

A mirror, she realized. *And I've got double-vision. Probably a concussion. Great.*

She blinked several times until her focus returned and her eyes adjusted to the harsh light. The full length wall mirror created the illusion of a larger space, but in reality, the rectangular room was barely large enough to accommodate the table on which she sat. She surveyed the room in the mirror, noting that there were no doors, then she stared at her own reflection. The mirror had to be one-way glass, an observation window, which meant someone was probably watching her from the other side. She stared hard, squinting a little, as if by doing so, she might be able to see through the reflective surface and look her tormentor in the eyes. After clearing her throat to make sure her voice wouldn't crack, she said. "Can I have my old room?" She managed her sweetest smile and added, "Please?"

The lights in the room dimmed, and the reflected Fiona vanished as the glass became transparent, revealing a room of similar dimensions on the other side. There was no examination table in the observation room, just an old man sitting in a wheelchair.

Not just old, Fiona thought. *Ancient.*

His wispy white hair could not hide a map of veins and liver spots on the papery-thin skin that clung to the skull. His eyes were sagging with age, but were still sharp enough that she could tell they were different shades of blue. One almost slate gray, the other a pale cornflower shade, like the eye described in Poe's classic *The Tell Tale Heart*—the eye that had driven the narrator to madness. Yet, despite the man's age and those weird, disconcerting eyes, Fiona saw something familiar in the face. It was the same man that had appeared in the pictures in the trophy case.

The thought sent a shiver down her spine, but as she stared back at him, she resolved that she would never beg for her life. Not from this man.

"Hey. I recognize you," she said, pointing at him like he was the one on display behind the glass and not her. "You're Mr. Burns from *The Simpsons*, right?"

The cadaverous face split in what she could only assume was meant to be a smile, and then an electronically amplified voice— the same wheezy voice that had taunted her earlier in her room— filled her little cell. "What are you, child?"

She stared at him in consternation. "What am I? What the hell kind of question is that?"

"Your appearance is somewhat mongoloid, but the facial structure is all wrong. Are you an American aboriginal? A red Indian? Yes, that must be it. But not pure-blooded. You're what my friends in Sao Paulo would call a *mestizo*."

The halting manner of his speech—he could only get a few syllables out between gasping breaths—and the almost clinical detachment in his voice did not make the obsolete terminology any less offensive. "What I am," she countered, mustering all the bravado she could, "is a human being. And an American citizen, I might add, with some very powerful and dangerous relatives. You really don't want them to show up on your doorstep, but if you don't let me go, that's what's going to happen."

The death's head grin did not slip. "Aside from your diabetes, and of course that little bump on your head, are you in good health? I understand that red Indians are often drunkards. How is your liver function?"

Fiona was tempted to make an obscene reply but restrained herself. It seemed unlikely that she would be able to talk her way out of this fix, but insults would definitely not improve her chances.

"Listen, I'm sorry about the Mr. Burns crack. Would you prefer me to call you by your real name?" She paused a beat and then added, "Dr. Mengele?"

Although her studies were focused mainly in Antiquity, Fiona was not unaware of modern history. She had studied World War II and the Holocaust; she knew who the major players were in that terrible chapter of history. And while his role in the rise of the Third Reich had been incidental, Josef Mengele had come to symbolize the worst sort of perversion of science and medicine. Viewing the Nazis' intention to exterminate the Jews, Romani and other so-called inferior races as an opportunity to conduct research on living human subjects, he had requested an assignment at the Auschwitz death camp, where he subjected thousands of people to unspeakable experiments, earning the nickname *Todesengel*—the Angel of Death.

After the war, Mengele had escaped to South America, and despite the best efforts of Nazi hunters, he had eluded capture until his death in 1979. That was the official version at least, but by all accounts, Mengele's remains had been positively identified through DNA testing.

Fiona had recognized Mengele's name on the various citations and diplomas displayed in the trophy case, but it was the lovingly preserved photographic record of atrocities in the gallery that had brought her knowledge of the man to the surface.

Although there was not a doubt in her mind that the man in the wheelchair behind the glass was the same man in the pictures, his reaction confirmed her accusation. His gap-toothed smile grew bigger. "You know of me? Why, that is outstanding. I would have thought people of your generation would have forgotten about me. Especially those of your particular...." He sniffed disdainfully. "Caste."

"What can I say? You're famous. I should say 'infamous.'" Instead of succumbing to despair, Fiona was feeling bolder with each passing second. Mengele might be able to torture and kill her, but she would not give him the satisfaction of breaking her spirit. "Can you clear something up for me? You're supposed to be dead."

The old man waved a gnarled hand. "It was not my intention to indulge you in conversation, child. I have work to do. Do you have any other medical conditions that I should know about?"

"Oh, come on. You're going to kill me anyway, right? Use me as a lab rat in some experiment? That's what you do, isn't it? The least you could do is answer a couple of questions. Besides, you're like the original mad scientist. Dr. Mengele, the Angel of Death. They made movies about you, you know. Don't you want to brag a little?"

"Mengele is dead," the man said. "I am Tyndareus now."

"Tyndareus." That name was more familiar to Fiona than even Mengele. "King of the Spartans, father of Castor and Clymenestra... Oh, of course. Twins."

The old man's smile slipped, but his strange eyes seemed to grow sharper. "You are remarkably well-informed."

"Because I know who Tyndareus was? Or because I know that you're obsessed with twins?" She was not exaggerating the latter point. During his time at Auschwitz, Mengele had fanatically tracked down twins for his experiments. Yet, something about the alias nagged at her.

In Greek mythology, Tyndareus's wife, the beautiful queen Leda, had been seduced by the god Zeus, who appeared to her in the unlikely form of a swan. The offspring of that union had been a pair of eggs, each one containing a set of twins—Castor and Pollux, the famed Gemini twins, and Helen of Troy and Clymenestra. But only one twin in each set—Pollux and Helen—were sired by Zeus. Castor and Clymenestra were the natural children of Tyndareus.

The twins angle seemed the likeliest reason for Mengele to choose his new name, but it did not explain his other connection to Greek mythology.

She peered at him through the glass. "Tyndareus. Cerberus. And you've got Kenner chasing after Hercules. That can't be a coincidence. What are you really after?"

Tyndareus brought his fingertips together in front of his face, which made him look exactly like the cartoon villain from *The Simpsons*. Fiona had to fight to stifle a laugh, but there was nothing amusing about the old man's next utterance. "As diverting as explaining this to you might be, it would be a waste of time for both of us. If you will not answer my questions, I will simply proceed with the experiment."

"Hey, wait—"

Tyndareus lowered his hands to the tablet computer resting on his lap and tapped the screen. Fiona heard the hiss of pressurized air, and glimpsed movement in the corner of her eye. She turned in the direction of the sound and saw that a section of the wall to her left had opened. It was not an exit however, only a small recess, like a cupboard at floor level.

Several small beige shapes darted out, the suddenness of their movement startling Fiona. She let out a yelp and drew her legs up onto the examination table, even as the rational part of her brain realized there was no threat, or more precisely, no obvious threat. The little shapes were mice, and not nasty mutant killer mice either. Just regular little mice, like Stuart Little. There were at least half a dozen of them still in the recess. Three or four had scurried out when the door opened, scouting the room, but showing no signs of hostility.

But she doubted Auschwitz's Angel of Death was interested in gauging her reaction to a rodent infestation. Mice were often a disease vector. Had Tyndareus infected them with plague or Hanta virus? Was he going to watch to see how long it took her to die?

Tyndareus's voice filled the room again. "An associate of mine was working to create a plant-based organic bio-weapon. The field tests were rather disappointing, but the concept is promising, and as I've already invested substantial resources, it only seems prudent to salvage what I can.

"There is an aerosol delivery system in the ceiling that will deliver the spores. You may feel free to take cover. In fact, I would prefer it if you did. It will provide me with a better understanding of how this organism spreads, if you are able to avoid initial infection."

Fiona had only just begun to digest what the old man was telling her when she saw his hand reach for the tablet again, and before she could utter a single word of protest, his finger touched the screen. A hissing sound filled the air, and Fiona felt drops of liquid, like a light mist, falling onto her exposed skin.

THIRTY-TWO

Roraima, Brazil

Gazing up at the night sky, it was easy to comprehend how the ancients had looked to the stars and seen their gods. Hundreds of miles from the nearest civilization, there was no light pollution to mute the starlight. High up on a plateau above the Amazon rain forest—the locals called it a *tepui*, the weathered remains of a sandstone table land that had once stretched across the northern reaches of the entire continent—the sky was not merely a dome but an all-encompassing sphere, with planets and stars and galaxies scattered like gold dust on black velvet.

I never knew there were so many of them, Gallo thought.

They were not the stars she knew, at least not all of them, and yet they might very well have been the stars glimpsed by the ancient Greeks. Her enjoyment of this rare sight was dampened by the circumstances that had brought her here.

She had awakened on a plane already bound for Brazil, after having been sedated and blindfolded to preserve the secret location of Cerberus's headquarters. Judging by the length of time they had spent in the air, she guessed it was somewhere in Europe, but there was no way to know for certain. Even Kenner was not privy to that information.

Now that she had given Kenner an exact destination, Gallo was uncertain about what he expected from her. She had been bundled onto the helicopter for the long flight to the tepui, but now that they were at the site, no one was paying attention to her. While the helicopter crew off-loaded supplies—food, gear, drums of fuel—Kenner, Rohn and the half-dozen Cerberus goons that were accompanying them had immediately gone to work rigging ropes for their descent into an enormous sinkhole, nearly two miles across, that corresponded with the coordinates Fiona had identified on the ancient map.

The sinkholes were a common feature of the tepuis, and some of the largest contained unique biospheres, with flora and fauna living and evolving in complete isolation for untold millennia. Because the tepuis were so remote, most of these unique biospheres remained pristine, untouched by all but a few bold explorers. There was no better place in the world to hide an Amazon city, and getting to it, or at least to the place where it had once stood, would require a rappel down several hundred feet of sheer cliff. Going in would be the easy part, since gravity would do all the work. Getting back out would require climbing those same ropes. There would be some risk involved, and while Gallo was undaunted by the physical challenge, she saw the impending descent as an opportunity to stand her ground.

She found Kenner at the edge of the sinkhole, peering down into the yawning void while the rest of the Cerberus team rigged the rappelling ropes under the glare of generator-powered work lights. His back was turned, and he was close enough to the brink that one good shove would have sent him over, but Gallo dismissed the idea as soon as it formed. It wasn't the thought of taking a life or the psychological toll that action would have exacted that stopped her though. Killing Kenner simply wouldn't help her situation one bit. Instead, it would make things worse, for her and for Fiona. But if he wanted her continued cooperation, Kenner was going to have to give her something in return.

"Wouldn't it be wiser to wait for daylight?" she called out.

Kenner, smiling broadly, turned to face her. "I'm sure it would, but as they say, every second counts. Besides, the sun only reaches the bottom of this shaft for a few hours at midday. We're going to need daylight to search for the Amazon city. That means we climb through the night."

Gallo bit her lip and took a deep breath to gather her courage. "You need to let Fiona go."

Kenner's smile fell. "Augustina..."

"I won't take another step, and I most certainly will not climb down into that hole, until I know she's safe. Now, I suppose you could tie me up and lower me kicking and screaming. That's up to you. But I will not help you unless you do this for me."

He shook his head sadly. "If it were up to me, I would have already let her go. But it's not. Mr. Tyndareus is running this show."

"Then tell him—"

Kenner raised a hand to silence her. The gesture was so abrupt, and so out of character for him, that Gallo flinched. After a moment of tense silence, he spoke again in a low voice that was not completely unsympathetic. "I'm sorry to have to tell you this, Augustina, but the girl is probably already dead."

Gallo felt the blood leave her face. A rushing sound filled her ears and she staggered back a step.

Kenner continued. "You must know that Mr. Tyndareus intended to kill you both as soon as you had told him what he needed to know. It's nothing short of miraculous that I was able to convince him to spare you."

Some primitive part of Gallo's brain took control of her body. She launched herself at Kenner, arms extended to shove him off the precipice or perhaps carry him along in a suicidal plunge. Neither actually happened. Instead, he side-stepped, as if anticipating this reaction, and he swept her into a bear hug from behind, pinning her arms to her sides and lifting her off the ground. She squirmed, trying to wrench free. She kicked back at his shins, but he did not relent.

His voice hissed in her ear. "Your mistake was thinking that you still had anything left to bargain with. I don't need your help anymore. I'm keeping you alive as a favor. Old times sake. You really ought to get down on your knees and thank me."

He took her wrist in his hand and tugged up her sleeve, revealing the Herculean tattoo. "Don't think I haven't noticed this. Your allegiance is...regrettable. I might be able to overlook it, but others might not be so willing. Now, if you want to run, be my guest." He twisted around, away from the edge, and then set her down, expelling her from his embrace with a shove that sent her lurching forward.

"I won't stop you," he continued, once more affecting a tone of commiseration. "Of course, there's really nowhere to go. And I can't promise that Vigor won't hunt you down for sport. That's rather his style, you know."

Gallo propped herself up on hands and knees. The reptile brain was still in control, weighing the primal options: fight or flight? Both were equally futile, but the third choice—surrender—never entered into the equation. If Fiona was truly dead, then no matter what Kenner promised, that would be her fate as well.

As much as she wanted to tear the bastard's face off, she did not want to meet her end on his terms.

Instead, she ran.

Kenner let out a dismayed shout, surprised that she had chosen to brave the treacherous landscape in the dark, but Gallo did not slow.

Although she had stood in the glow of the electrical lights for only a few minutes, her night vision was badly compromised. In her peripheral vision, she could see the distant horizon's faint outline silhouetted against the starry sky, but the ground right in front of her was uniformly black. Millions of years of wind and weather had sculpted the summit into a bizarre landscape, with natural pillars and arches that looked like melting wax. There were craters and pools of rainwater that were incredibly pure and deceptively deep. It was a deadly obstacle course, made all the more perilous by the scrubby vegetation that clung to every crevice. Gallo stumbled and crashed through the maze, ignoring the branches and rocky protrusions that caught and tore at both the fabric of her jeans and at her skin.

A root snagged one foot, and she went sprawling again, smashing into a tangle of thin branches that scratched her face and snagged her hair. In the stunned instant that followed, she heard more shouts and the sound of footsteps, and she realized that Kenner did not intend to let her run away after all. Despite every-thing else, she felt a rush of satisfaction at having disappointed him, spoiling his twisted fantasy of her groveling. She knew it would be a short-lived satisfaction if she did not get moving again, so she scrambled up, half-crawling for the first few steps, and then she resumed running blindly.

With the exception of the two crewmen unloading the helicopter, all of the Cerberus men were on the ropes already, too far away to help Kenner run her down. But he had been right about the lack of escape routes. The tepui rose from the surrounding landscape like a five-hundred-foot-tall pillar. A world class rock climber might have been able to scale the nearly sheer vertical cliffs, but climbing down them, in the dark, without any kind of ropes or equipment, was unthinkable, and that was if she was able to find the cliff without falling over.

If Kenner goes, too, it might be worth it.

The thought was yanked from her head when Kenner's out-stretched hand caught hold of her long black hair. Her feet flew out from under her, but this time she did not fall. Instead, she was pulled back, enfolded once more in his embrace.

"Bitch! I'm trying to—"

There was a loud thump and then another, as Gallo felt something smack the back of her head. Her vision flashed blue for a moment, but in that instant, Kenner's arms fell away, and she was free again. She stumbled forward and would have done another face-plant, but a firm grip closed on her wrist, steadying her. A familiar voice reached out from the darkness. "Come with me."

Gallo's thoughts were still fuzzy from being struck in the head, but there was no mistaking the clipped manner of speech and the distinctive Portuguese-flavored Brazilian accent. "Cintia?"

"Hurry," Dourado urged, offering no explanation, but tugging her along.

The woman's appearance, here at one of the remotest places on Earth, was about as unlikely as divine intervention, and it triggered an explosion of questions that threatened to trip Gallo up like the roots hidden in the darkness. Even with Kenner on her heels, she felt paralyzed by the impossibility of Dourado's intervention.

Only Kenner wasn't chasing her anymore. In the dim starlight, Gallo could make out the silhouette of her savior. Dourado was holding something, a club or a tree limb. That answered one question at least. She had struck Kenner from behind, and Kenner's cranium had cue-balled into hers.

The realization that Dourado had bought them a narrow window of escape helped her put aside the more difficult questions. She followed blindly, trusting that Dourado's night vision had to be better than her own. But there was one question that demanded an answer. "Where are we going?"

"We have to hide."

"Hide?" Gallo said, incredulous. "That's your plan?"

"No, I—"

Dourado's answer was cut off by the harsh report of a pistol. Gallo felt something sizzle past her head, and then the world in front of her was revealed in the harsh brilliance of a high-intensity spotlight.

"The next one will not be a warning." It was Rohn. He did not shout, but somehow his low gravelly voice seemed as loud as the gunshot.

THIRTY-THREE

A blast of frigid air swirled through the hold of the aged Lockheed L100 as the cargo ramp began lowering. Cabin pressure had already been equalized to match the conditions outside, so there was no sudden suction. Still, Pierce held on tight to a hanging cargo strap as the tail end of the aircraft opened up, revealing the black emptiness of the sky above the Amazon rain forest.

Earlier, when Lazarus had suggested the plan, Pierce had been able to depersonalize the risk, put aside his fear. Lazarus had done this dozens of times. He knew what he was doing, and Pierce knew it was the best chance they had of finding Gallo and Dourado. But now, literally standing on the brink of executing that plan, he was having second thoughts. He took several deep breaths, filling his lungs and saturating his blood with pure oxygen from the mountaineering-style respirator. *Don't think about it*, he told himself.

Lazarus lowered his ATN PVS-7 night vision goggles—'NODs,' short for 'night optical devices'—into place and tapped them with a fingertip, signaling Pierce and Carter to do the same. Pierce switched his on, and the dark interior of the plane was revealed in startling clarity, albeit bathed in a creepy green glow. With their goggles, respirators and bulky thermal suits, Carter and Lazarus looked like alien hunters from a science fiction movie. The guns and knives strapped and holstered to their bodies intensified the effect.

Lazarus had made all the arrangements while they were still over the Atlantic. His past experience as a Special Forces soldier had left him with a long list of contacts who could provide anything he needed on short notice, and a knowledge of how to procure those items without arousing the interest of the local authorities.

Pierce was astonished, and more than a little dismayed, by the realization that there were people out there, in every city he supposed, standing ready to provide specialized military hardware at a moment's notice. He was having difficulty believing that it was really possible for an ordinary person who knew the right people to simply make a phone call and outfit an army. Then Lazarus told him how much it would all cost. The final bill made the money Pierce had spent on the genetic sequencing equipment for Carter seem like a petty cash expenditure by comparison.

"When I told you money was no object," he had confessed to Lazarus, "I didn't realize how much money that would mean. I mean, I'll pay it, but...wow."

"It's only money," Lazarus said. "People are going to die tonight. With a little luck it will be them, not us. This equipment might mean the difference between life and death, but no amount of money is going to make it easier to pull the trigger when the time comes."

"Helluva pep talk," Pierce said, but he knew the big man was right. He had faced death before, but he had never been confronted with the prospect of having to take a life.

"Don't personalize the enemy," Lazarus went on. "Think of it like a game. Like one of those video games Fiona was always playing..." He trailed off, the memory evidently more painful than expected.

Pierce knew exactly what Lazarus meant. He had watched Fiona and some of Lazarus's former teammates spend endless hours fighting aliens and enemies—and sometimes each other—in Xbox games. *Treat it like a game, treat the Cerberus men like video game villains. Don't get psyched out.*

"We'll jump from twenty-thousand feet," Lazarus said. "We'll be using static-line deployed ram-air canopies. That means they'll open as soon as you jump. No free fall, no counting to fifty. The chutes will function like glider wings. The control toggles are intuitive. Pull left to go left, right to go right. Just before touchdown, pull both hard to flare...brake. I'll talk you through all that on the way down.

"Hook in," Lazarus directed. Despite the wind rushing through the cabin and the throaty roar of the engines, Pierce heard him clearly, courtesy of the earbud connected to a digitally encrypted walkie-talkie clipped to the combat vest under his coveralls.

Carter snapped a D-ring, connected to the ripcord on her parachute pack, to the cable that ran the length of their chartered plane. Lazarus checked the connection and then moved to do the same for Pierce.

Pierce hooked in, then gave the carabiner a tug. Lazarus checked the D-ring and gave Pierce a thumbs-up before hooking his own chute to the line.

The pilot's voice came over their comm system. "Forty miles out."

"Roger," Lazarus replied. He turned to Pierce and Carter. "Ready?"

Pierce nodded. Despite the fact that he was about to jump out of a plane for the first time in his life, nothing short of a missile would keep him from helping the people he loved.

They would be leaving the aircraft thirty miles out, distant enough that the Cerberus men would not hear the sound of the plane's engines, much less suspect that an incursion was underway, but close enough for them to glide to the objective. With their ram-air chutes and about four miles of air between them and the ground, there would be plenty of time to find a good landing spot.

Lazarus had acquired Landsat imagery of the target zone, a high plateau in the Roraima region, surrounding what appeared to be a deep sinkhole. The imagery revealed nothing about what lay at the bottom of that chasm, but Pierce felt certain it was Kenner's true objective, which presented yet another challenge. The Cerberus force had already been in place for several hours, which meant that they were probably already inside the sinkhole. The only way to get ahead of them was to bypass the summit and drop directly into the unknown abyss. While that course was fraught with risk, the biggest concern was getting back out again.

That, Pierce decided, was something to worry about once Gallo and Dourado were safe.

At their current speed, he guessed it would take less than three minutes to cover the ten miles to the drop zone. It turned out to be the shortest three minutes of his life. After what seemed like only a few seconds, the pilot began counting down. When he got to zero, Lazarus shouted, "Go!"

Carter immediately trundled to the edge of the cargo ramp and stepped out into the void.

Pierce felt fear tugging at him, but squelched it down and followed Carter, leaping into the abyss. He expected the fear to surge as the fall began, but instead he felt something unexpected. Exhilaration.

His parachute harness went rigid—painfully so—as the chute deployed above his head.

The initial discomfort passed after a moment, as his body began to compensate for the abrupt change in inertia. He experienced yet another wave of excitement and euphoria, as he processed the new sensation. He was still falling, but he could feel the resistance from the chute, holding him back.

He saw the control lines hanging down in front of him and took hold, one in each hand. Off to his left, he saw Carter and Lazarus, both of them angling back and forth across the sky like skiers slaloming down a black-diamond slope.

Pierce tugged the controls, getting a feel for the system. When he pulled, he could feel increased resistance on the respective sides of the chute, comparable to dragging an oar in the water while rowing a canoe. Once he figured out the right amount of pressure to exert, he lined up behind the others and let gravity and aerodynamics do most of the work.

Further out, the dark silhouette of their destination rose above the forest, and gleaming at its tip, like an enchanted emerald, was a dot of artificial light marking the presence of humans atop the remote tepui.

The light of the Cerberus camp drew them onward, like a beacon. When they got closer, Pierce could see the bulky outline of a helicopter. A few seconds later, they passed over the parked aircraft, still several hundred feet from touchdown, but there was no sign of human activity around it or anywhere else on the mountaintop.

"I see them," Lazarus said. "They're rappelling down into the sinkhole."

Pierce craned his head around and spotted the network of ropes that extended from the top of the tepui, down into the chasm where they were lost from view. Tiny shapes moved down the ropes, like spiders on a web.

"I count nine," Lazarus said. "No way to know if any of them are friendly."

Pierce strained to see if he could pick out Gallo, but they were still too far away. "Will they see us? Or hear us?"

"They're using flashlights, so they won't be able to see much of anything." Lazarus was silent for a moment, then added. "Stay ready though, just in case."

Pierce let a hand fall to the Heckler & Koch MP5K that hung from a sling across his chest. Pierce had never fired this particular weapon before, but Lazarus had assured him that it was as simple as point-and-shoot. It was even equipped with an infrared laser sight that would show him, with a fairly high degree of certainty, where the bullet would go.

Killing someone has never been so easy, he thought darkly. But the men they were going up against weren't innocents. Kenner and Rohn had already tried to kill him once, and they had kidnapped Gallo and Fiona. He intended to remember that when the time came to pull the trigger.

"Let's take it in," Lazarus said. "I'll go first. Corkscrew down and watch for a safe drop zone."

Pierce held back until both Carter and Lazarus were at least a hundred feet below him before pulling on his right-hand toggle to begin a clockwise spiraling descent into the sinkhole. When Lazarus had told him they would be parachuting into a sinkhole, Pierce had imagined something like diving into a swimming pool from four miles up. It was only now, as he turned lazy circles in the sky above the tepui, that he understood just how big the sinkhole was. It would be more like diving into the East River.

He could not distinguish the ground. Although the walls positively radiated infrared light, the bottom of the sinkhole—which was rushing up—looked like a Jackson Pollock painting in hues of green and black. There was no way to know what awaited them down there.

As the remaining distance closed to almost nothing, he was able to make out the landscape in relief. There were irregular patches that might have been vegetation or uneven terrain, perhaps even trees, and in-between them an unnaturally smooth black surface. He steered toward the latter, realizing too late that it was not flat ground at all, but water.

Almost directly below, Lazarus's chute seemed to curl in on itself as he pulled his control toggles hard. Then, the canopy settled gently into an amorphous heap, marking the spot where the big man had touched down. Carter flared her chute a moment later, and landed about thirty yards from Lazarus. Pierce guessed he had about ten seconds to do the same.

He hauled down on the toggles a couple of seconds later and his descent came to what felt like a screeching halt. Then he dropped another fifteen feet into chilly, waist-deep water. The thick muck that rose halfway to his knees absorbed most of the impact of landing, but it also wrapped around his legs. He wobbled for a moment and then heaved himself out of the mud and onto the shore. He quickly removed his respirator, unbuckled his harness, reeled in the water-logged parachute, bundled it up and shoved it beneath some tall ferns.

He crouched next to Lazarus beside a stand of trees that stood up out of the water on thick conical trunks with partially exposed roots. Pierce thought they might be cypress trees, which were found in wetlands along the Eastern seaboard of the United States.

Lazarus clapped him on the shoulder. "Not bad for an archeologist. I can see why Jack picked you."

"Maybe I missed my calling as a Special Forces operator," Pierce said, managing to get a smile out of the big man.

Carter clung to the stringy bark of one of the boughs, evidently trying to stay out of the water. Pierce wondered why for a moment, then remembered that Brazil was the land of piranhas and anacondas. He decided that maybe she had the right idea, and scrambled onto the nearest exposed root.

The trees obscured their view of the sandstone walls, but even through the forest canopy, Pierce could see the glow of the Cerberus group's flashlights, amplified by the night vision goggles, a stark contrast to the near total darkness at the bottom of the pit.

He watched the lights for a few moments then turned to Lazarus and Carter. "They'll be down soon. We need to get moving."

Then the distinctive crack of a gunshot echoed across the treetops.

THIRTY-FOUR

Cerberus Headquarters

At the first touch of the aerosol mist, Fiona leapt off the examination table and dove under it. The abruptness of her reaction sent two of the mice scurrying away, but for several seconds, that was the most dramatic thing that happened.

"Excellent," Tyndareus crooned. "Tell me, are you feeling anything yet?"

Fiona ignored the question, but the mere suggestion was enough to make her skin crawl. What was in the mist? Tyndareus had called it a plant-based organic bio-weapon, but what did that even mean? Some kind of nerve agent?

She felt a tingling sensation on the exposed skin of her face and arms.

I'm imagining it, she told herself, but if she was, then her imagination was running wild. She wiped a hand across her face, then began rubbing her arms vigorously. Her skin felt slightly wet, and after a few seconds, the tingling became a warm glow, like the heat of menthol or jalapeno peppers.

Okay, definitely not my imagination.

An urgent chirping noise distracted her. The mice, all of them, were now running back and forth across the room as if their tails were on fire.

They're dying, she thought. She felt a stinging in her eyes, and blinked away tears. *I probably am, too. Or will be soon.*

Then she noticed something else. There were faint green lines on the skin of her arms, long streaks marking the places she had rubbed. The floor was also marked with splotches of green, and as she watched, they started moving.

No. Not moving. Growing.

Tiny shoots, no thicker than single strands of hair, were rising from the green spots, both those on the floor and those on her arms. She wiped her fingers across her arms, obliterating them completely, but the tendrils on the floor grew thicker, like vines, throwing out branching extensions and vestigial leaves.

Plant-based bio weapon. That's what he meant. This isn't some kind of organic poison or nerve agent. It's a plant that...does what exactly?

The growth rate was extraordinary, and judging by the stinging sensation, the plant secreted some kind of toxic enzyme. The chirping of the mice had grown into a frantic cacophony. They had stopped running around. She found one nearby, caught in a tangle of green threads, squirming but unable to break loose.

Tyndareus's wheeze sounded again. "You see? It works well in a controlled environment. But we could not replicate these results in the field."

Fiona paid him no heed. She was aware now of green tendrils sprouting from her skin, probably her hair and clothes, too, but the threads on the floor scared her the most. While it was hard to imagine those tiny little fibers holding her down, she knew that enough of them might be able to do just that, immobilizing and enveloping her like some kind of invasive weed.

She scrambled out from under the table, intending to climb back on top, but found it already covered with fibrous green stalks. The sight stopped her cold. There was nowhere to escape to. Every corner of this room was infested with green.

She was going to die. Maybe not in the next few minutes, or even the next few hours, but eventually the plants would overwhelm her.

She whirled to face the glass, wondering how much force it would take to smash through. *Maybe if I used the table like a battering ram...*

Tyndareus's weird mismatched blue eyes continued to regard her with an eagerness that approached hunger. *He's enjoying this.*

He's getting off on watching me die, like some kind of psycho James Bond movie villain.

The thought triggered a lightning bolt of inspiration. *I just hope he doesn't watch the same movies I do.* She met his stare and shouted, "Is this supposed to scare me into helping you?"

Uncertainty flickered across his strange eyes. She could see him parsing her words, trying to discern what she meant. His mouth opened, but then closed again.

Damn it.

She started to turn back to the exam table, intending to scrape away the thin layer of green that had started sprouting there and buy herself a few more seconds, but the tendrils had already begun wrapping around her feet, digging into the fabric of her shoes.

I'm running out of time.

She tore free and hopped up onto the table. Her feet started to burn, so she pulled her shoes off, revealing inflamed skin. She looked at Tyndareus again. "South America is a dead end. Kenner isn't going to find anything there."

His gaze narrowed, but he said nothing.

"He doesn't know how to read the map, you know," she pressed. "That's why he had to ask me for help. But he still doesn't know how to translate it. I'm the only one who can do that." She was not desperate enough to tell him about the Mother Tongue, not yet at least.

The old man's silence continued.

"Don't believe me? Ask him what he's found. Go on. I'll wait. Only..." She looked from side to side. "I'm not sure exactly how long I've got."

Finally, Tyndareus stirred. He raised a bony finger and stabbed at the screen of his tablet. For a few seconds, Fiona dared to believe that her ploy had worked, and that he would activate some kind of counter-agent to neutralize the strange growth. But a full minute passed with no appreciable change in the room, save for the fact that the mice had stopped chirping and the room seemed to be getting increasingly warmer. Uncomfortably so. Fiona's skin began to burn anew as her sweat reacted with the acidic plants on her skin.

Instead of sparing her, Tyndareus had just turned up the heat, literally. The room was nearly sauna hot. The lights seemed brighter, too, so brilliant, in fact, that she had to shade her eyes and squint.

"Interesting," the old man said after a few more minutes. "When the temperature increases to above ninety-five degrees Fahrenheit, the organism stops seeking out new victims and simply begins growing like an ordinary plant. That explains the failure of the field test. Not a failure at all, really. Simply a different outcome than expected."

He tapped the screen again, and the lights dimmed perceptibly. "I would hear more about the map, child."

Despite the heat, Fiona felt a chill shoot down her back. She did not know if Tyndareus had chosen to curtail his experiment because of what she had said, or if he was merely playing some kind of sick game with her—like an evil child torturing ants with a magnifying glass. She regretted now having revealed the truth about the map, even if she had kept the part about the Mother Tongue to herself. Her death would have all but ensured that Kenner would never unlock the real secret of the map. Now, Tyndareus would not stop until she had revealed everything.

Nevertheless, she couldn't help but think about what Pierce had said in the Labyrinth.

Where there's life, there's hope.

She was still alive, and that was good, because it meant there was still hope. The funny thing was that she no longer hoped for rescue or a chance to escape.

She wanted payback.

THIRTY-FIVE

Roraima, Brazil

The noise of the shot startled Gallo, causing her hand to slip off the ropes. She clutched at them, trying to stop her downward plunge, but it was already too late. There was a flare of pain as the ropes burned through the skin of her palm, but that would be nothing compared to what would come when she reached the line's end.

Her descent stopped as abruptly as it had begun, with a hand reaching out to seize hold of her belay line, jerking her to a sudden, and thankfully premature, stop. She swung forward, colliding with the rock face. The impact stunned her but not enough to override her instinct for self-preservation. She grabbed hold of the ropes again, clinging to them for dear life.

"Remember what I showed you," rumbled a low voice from beside her. "Reach back and hold the ropes with your brake hand."

Gallo glanced toward the stern, unsympathetic visage of her savior, Vigor Rohn, and then she did as instructed. When she had the lines gripped in her right fist, locked in place against the small of her back, Rohn simply let go and resumed his own descent.

She felt no gratitude toward him, nor did she sense that he expected any. She was still a prisoner, still a hostage who, for the moment at least, was more useful alive.

After her recapture, and a brief interval to allow for Kenner's recovery, Rohn had given her and Dourado a quick course in rappelling techniques. She had no choice but to go along with them now. Dourado's noble attempt to liberate her had given Rohn and Kenner the leverage to compel her cooperation. Rohn did not even need to make the threat explicit; if she resisted, Dourado would suffer. Yet, despite the dire situation, Gallo felt a glimmer of optimism.

Although she had not been allowed to speak to Dourado, Gallo assumed that the young woman had snuck aboard the helicopter during the transfer at Belem—Dourado's hometown. Clearly, stowing away had been an impulsive decision, but the fact that Dourado had been able to track the movements of the Cerberus group to her own hometown meant that Pierce was looking for her, and might already know where she was.

It was a slim hope, but reason enough to hang on, both figuratively and literally.

Below her, Rohn had finished his descent. She could hear him growling at his men. "What were you shooting at?"

She took a breath to gather her wits. Then she relaxed her brake hand and resumed her cautious rappel down the wall. When she finally reached the bottom, she sagged against the wall in exhaustion.

The sheer cliff wall disappeared into a mound of rubble. Chunks of limestone, some larger than passenger cars, had crumbled from the top of the sinkhole and accumulated into a gentle slope, or more accurately, a beach that disappeared into a vast body of water. Gallo could see trees in the distance, suggesting a shallow wetland rather than a lake.

The Cerberus men had gathered near the water's edge, sweeping their lights through the darkness in every direction, aiming with their pistols. Rohn stood next to one of them, gazing down at a large glistening gray-green shape.

"You shot a frog?" There was a hint of disgust in Rohn's voice.

"It was attacking," the man protested. "Look at it."

"Attacking? It's a frog."

Gallo craned her head around for a better look at the fallen creature. From a distance, she could not make out any details, but even a glimpse was enough to reveal why the Cerberus goon had reacted so violently. The frog, or whatever it was, was huge. If not for the slick skin, she would have assumed that it was a small alligator.

The corpse suddenly came alive in a flurry of movement. Rohn leapt back, narrowly avoiding the swipe of a long black tentacle.

It's a tail, Gallo thought.

The other man was not quite fast enough. The creature's tail knocked his feet out from under him, and he crashed onto the shore in a heap. There was a sharp hissing noise, like a forceful exhalation, and then the beast splashed back into the water and vanished.

Rohn spat a disgusted oath at the unlucky man. "You can't even kill a frog? Let's hope we don't face anything more dangerous than that."

The fallen man raised a hand, as if reaching out for assistance, then his fingers curled into a claw. He collapsed back in the throes of a seizure. Rohn's eyes widened in alarm, and he retreated several steps.

Kenner hastened forward but stopped at Rohn's side. "Good god. What was that?"

The stricken man's back arched, his limbs going rigid, and then his struggles ceased. He let out a tortured rasping breath, but did not draw another. Gallo pressed tighter against the rock face. She looked over at Dourado, who was similarly paralyzed by the horror they had just witnessed.

"Poison," Rohn muttered, then turned away as if he had lost interest. He addressed the rest of the group. "Prepare the rafts."

Kenner continued to stare at the dead man. "Some species of toad secrete deadly neurotoxins. But that was something else. A giant salamander, perhaps."

He rounded on Gallo. "Salamanders can regrow lost limbs. An amphibious creature with extraordinary regenerative abilities and poisonous breath. Does that sound familiar to you, Augustina?"

Unfortunately, it did. Kenner had just described the Lernean Hydra. "A man just died, Liam."

"That creature tells me the source of the mutagen is here. The Amazons must have been protecting it." Kenner balled his fists. "We're close. I can feel it."

Gallo felt it, too. The Cerberus group, it seemed, was now the least of her worries.

THIRTY-SIX

Pierce stared toward the distant glow for nearly a full minute. No more shots were fired, but he was now acutely aware that the strange world at the bottom of the sinkhole was anything but silent. The air was filled with the noise of insects and a creaking sound that he hoped was just tree boughs rubbing together.

Lazarus finally broke the spell. He unzipped his thermal coveralls, revealing the tactical body-armor vest underneath, which was festooned with pouches for extra ammunition magazines, grenades and a variety of combat equipment. He discarded the jumpsuit into the water.

Carter gave Pierce what he took to be an encouraging nod. "It could mean anything," she said. "I'm sure they're fine."

Pierce was not reassured, but staying where he was would not ease his concerns—or confirm his worst fears. He peeled off his wet jumpsuit and turned to Lazarus. "Oversized ex-Special Ops first. Lead the way, big guy." Lazarus stepped into the swamp, followed by Carter and Pierce.

Pierce tried to picture the area as he had seen it during the last few seconds of the descent. He had noticed dozens of isolated stands of trees scattered across the submerged floor of the sinkhole. Getting around them would mean taking a circuitous, time consuming path, but less so than trying to blaze a trail through the densely clustered boughs. Lazarus kept close to the trees, venturing out across open water only when it was necessary to hopscotch to the next wooded patch.

As they progressed, Pierce realized that the sky was growing lighter. Dawn was approaching. Although the depths of the sinkhole would remain in shadow for most of the day, Lazarus called for a break and told them to remove their night vision goggles, not because it was bright enough to see, but because even that small amount of ambient light would overwhelm the extremely sensitive receptors in the PVS7s.

Pierce was stunned by the abrupt transition to near total darkness. "All I can see is a big red blob. Is that normal?"

"You've been staring into a green light for the last few hours," Lazarus said. "Just give it a few minutes."

Pierce stood motionless, eyes closed, trying to remember how the world had looked just before the lights went out. All he could see in his mind's eye were trees and water. As Lazarus had promised, Pierce's vision cleared by degrees, and soon he was able to make out the treetops and a few other details.

"Those trees look like bald cypress," he said. "We had them in swamps near where I grew up. I wonder how they got here."

"How does anything get anywhere," Carter answered in an even voice. "Seeds get scattered. The wind can do some pretty crazy things. Animals transport seeds over long distances. I seem to recall that cypresses are one of the oldest extant tree families, dating back to the time of the Pangaea super-continent. There could have been cypress trees on the Roraima plateau long before it collapsed into its present state. It's also possible that this ecosystem may not be as closed as we thought."

"What do you mean?" Lazarus asked.

"For these trees to grow like they have," Carter said, "the water level would have to remain fairly constant. The only way that could happen is if we're below the water table and there's a way for water to flow in and out."

"Like an underground river," Pierce said.

"Could someone have planted them?" Lazarus asked after a moment.

"I suppose it's possible," Pierce said, "though I can't imagine anyone going to the trouble to plant them here."

Lazarus made a low humming sound as if considering Pierce's answer, then said, "Maybe it was the same people who built that."

He stretched his arm out, pointing toward a dark shape that lay more or less in the same direction they were traveling. In the gloom, it looked no different than any of the other wooded clumps they had encountered, but as Pierce continued to stare at it, he realized that it was very different.

"What the..." Pierce started forward, slowly realizing that the land in front of him wasn't a stand of cypress trees sprouting from the marsh, but solid ground, rising more than six feet above the water, stretching away in either direction like a jetty. Protruding above it were large blocky shapes with vertical lines too perfect to be anything but the work of human hands.

Buildings.

Lazarus laid a restraining hand on his shoulder. "Oversized ex-Special Ops go first, remember? We don't know what we'll find in there. Or who."

"You don't actually think anyone still lives there," Carter said.

Pierce was tempted to don his night vision goggles once more. A quick glance at the city might answer a lot of questions, but he decided to hold off a little longer. He turned to Lazarus. "This is what Kenner is looking for. I'm sure of it. We need to get there first, and set a trap."

The big man nodded slowly. "Stay close." He glanced back at Carter. "You, too."

As they got closer, Pierce saw that it was not a solid land mass at all, but a jumble of irregular stones of varying sizes, heaped up to form an artificial island. "This was debris from the collapse," he whispered. "They must have piled it up to form the city's foundation."

"But who are *they*?" Carter asked.

"We'll find out when we get there," Pierce said. He had a theory about what they'd find, but he wasn't ready to share it.

When they reached the base of the elevated mound, Lazarus signaled them to halt with an upraised hand. He pulled himself up onto the rocks, staying low in a prone firing position. He surveyed the city for nearly a full minute, and then waved them ahead. Pierce scrambled up the rocks despite the cumbersome combat gear he wore. Crouching beside Lazarus, he looked out over the ruins.

That it was deserted and forgotten was obvious from the crumbling walls and the growth of vegetation. The stone surfaces were covered in moss, and trees rose up from some of the buildings. No one had lived here in a long time, and yet the architecture was too sophisticated to be the work of the hunter-gatherer cultures that had made the Amazon Basin their home. It was much more reminiscent of the structures he had seen in the excavation in Heraklion, a fact which reinforced his suspicions about the city's original builders.

"I think we beat them here," Pierce said, keeping his voice low.

"I didn't see any lights through the NODs," Lazarus said. "But it's an unsecured environment. Stay on your toes."

Pierce nodded. "Right behind you."

Lazarus rose slowly, first to his knees, then to his full height.

There was a flurry of movement from atop one of the buildings, and then something shot toward them like a guided missile. Lazarus barely had time to raise his gun toward the source of the strange projectile before it struck him squarely in the chest with a sickening crunch. The object was about the size of a football but amorphous, like a cloth sack filled with stones. It rebounded away and landed on the rocky ground with a wet splat. The force of the impact knocked Lazarus back a step, and then he toppled backward, off the island's edge.

Carter cried out, more in surprise than terror, but Pierce couldn't tell if she was reacting to the attack on Lazarus, or warning him. Two more shapes, barely visible in the twilight, rose up from the nearest rooftop, and then swooped toward Carter and Pierce.

He had been wrong about the place being uninhabited. Although it had been abandoned by its original builders long ago, something still lived in the city. Something deadly.

THIRTY-SEVEN

Cerberus Headquarters

Almost being devoured by toxic carnivorous plants was not, it turned out, the lowest point of an already very bad day. After sparing her life, Tyndareus had sent two of his goons—both wearing hazmat suits—in through a concealed door to retrieve her. Fiona wondered if one of them had been in the exosuit.

If she had known what would follow, she would have opted to stay in her cell. The men took her to a tiled room where they stripped her, sprayed her with a fire hose, and scrubbed her with stiff-bristled brushes.

Following that violation, she was allowed to dress in a pair of hospital scrubs. The two men dragged her into another examination room and strapped her to a table in five-point restraints. She was then checked over, head-to-toe, by a sneering, wretched woman. As she was poked and prodded, her blood drawn, Fiona retreated into her mind, blocking out the ongoing physical assault.

She felt Nurse Wretched fumbling with her insulin pump and tried to cover it with her hands. The leather restraints stopped her, but the reflex earned her an immediate rebuke from the nurse.

"Stop. Moving. I am refilling the reservoir. You want your insulin, don't you?" The woman had a harsh eastern European accent, similar to Rohn's.

What I want, Fiona thought, *is to smash your face with a baseball bat. It would improve your looks.* But she relented, allowing the woman to finish the procedure.

The insulin recharge was welcome, though it did little to improve her physical condition. She needed to eat—real food, not college dorm crap—and she needed sleep. Most of all, she needed to be somewhere else, any place, as long as it was far away from the Nazi mad scientist who now called himself Tyndareus.

"There you go," the nurse said, as if expecting Fiona to be grateful.

"How can you work for that monster?"

The woman harrumphed then moved away without another word. Fiona expected to be released from the restraints and ushered to yet another prison cell, but instead she found herself alone once more.

The solitude, while not entirely welcome, was all too brief. A door opened and Tyndareus rolled into the room, sitting in his motorized wheelchair. Fiona rolled her head to the side and glowered at him. "I thought you guys—Nazis, I mean—hated cripples."

Tyndareus appeared unruffled by the barb. "Tell me more about what you saw on the map, child."

Fiona let her head drop. She had bought her life—a few more minutes of it, at least—with a promise to cooperate. While she had no intention of helping her captor, she knew that she would have to give him something, or else the opportunity to turn the tables on him might never come. The biggest problem was that it was all a bluff. She did not really know that Kenner was on a wild goose chase in the Amazon, because she did not actually know for certain what he was looking for. Tyndareus was too canny not to know that she would attempt to play him, but if he suspected that she was unable to deliver, that would be the end for her.

"I need to see it again."

"Dr. Kenner has the original, but I can provide you with photographs."

"He's in South America, right? And my Aunt Gus...Dr. Gallo, is with him?"

The old man pursed his lips. "You said that he was wrong about South America. Explain."

"First, you tell me what it is you're really after."

"That is not your concern."

Fiona shrugged. "If you don't want to share, I can't help you." She rolled her head forward and closed her eyes, as if trying to grab a catnap. Her heart immediately began pounding so loud that she was sure he would be able to hear it. If she was wrong about this...

"Release her," Tyndareus said, but not to Fiona.

She had to struggle to hide her relief as the two goons came into the room and unbuckled the straps that held her down. When she was free, they stepped aside, saying nothing.

"Come with me," the old man said, fingering the joystick controls for his wheelchair.

The chair swung around and rolled from the room so fast that Fiona would have had to jog to keep up. She decided not to try, and instead adopted a leisurely pace that forced Tyndareus to wait for her. His men followed, matching her pace rather than his, ready to intervene if she attempted anything, but clearly giving their boss plenty of space in which to do his own thing.

He led her from the room and down a hallway identical to the others she had passed through. They all looked the same to her, and it was not until he ushered her into his private gallery of horrors that she knew where she was. She tried not to react to the macabre displays, and Tyndareus did not seem interested in showing any of them to her. Instead, he brought her to the trophy case.

"You are a remarkable young woman," he said. He did not turn to face her, but after a moment, she realized he was staring at her reflection in the glass. She gave an involuntary shudder when she realized he was smiling.

Great. Ten minutes ago, he was trying to kill me. Now, he's hitting on me.

"I was hasty in dismissing you because of your mixed bloodline. Old habits, you know. The Amerindians are descended from Asian stock, as were the original Aryans, so it's little wonder that you manifest such extraordinary intelligence."

He might have meant it as a compliment, but Fiona had no answer for him. After an uncomfortable moment, he extended a hand, pointing to something in the display case. Arranged on a swatch of red velvet, like precious gemstones, were several small ivory-colored objects that Fiona recognized immediately as bones. The way they were assembled left little doubt that they were a human hand and a foot.

"This is my brother," Tyndareus said. Despite his wheezing delivery, there was a note of reverence in his tone, as if he was sharing a sacred mystery with her.

Fiona did not recall if Josef Mengele had any siblings, but she sensed something more than just familial affection. The old man confirmed this with his next statement.

"My twin," he continued. "You were wondering, I'm sure, how I was able to fool the world into believing that I was dead." He gestured to the bones again. "Castor died and was buried in my place."

"You had a twin brother?" Given his infamous obsession with twins, Fiona felt certain that, if Mengele really did have a twin, she would have heard something about it. But it was the name that got her attention. She had been wrong about his motives for choosing the name Tyndareus, the father of twins. In Greek myths, Castor and Pollux were often called the Tyndariads. Tyndareus was meant as a family name. "He's Castor. I suppose that would make you Pollux. The immortal son of Zeus and Leda, who begged the gods to make his human twin brother immortal, too."

As soon as she said it aloud, more of the pieces fell into place. "You think you can bring him back. That's what you're really after."

The strange blue eyes narrowed until they looked like mismatched sapphires. "As I said, remarkable."

He drew in a raspy breath. "You will have heard stories I imagine, fanciful tales of how I planned to clone *der Fuhrer* and establish a new Reich." He snorted. "Ridiculous. Why would I want that when the post-war world had so much to offer me?

"Of course, I did continue my research, and slowly I built my fortune, but as the years passed, I focused my efforts on the one thing that I did not have in sufficient quantities. Time.

"I was not the only one doing research into artificial gestation and replication—cloning, in the common parlance—but I had the freedom to pursue the matter unfettered by tedious ethical considerations." He spat the last two words out like a curse. "The practical application for such a technique was obvious. If I could produce clones of living humans, it would solve the most troublesome side effect of tissue transplants."

"You wanted to clone yourself so you could have an endless supply of organ donors. Replacement parts to extend your life indefinitely." Fiona spoke without emotion. Given the man's past crimes, it was almost exactly what she would have expected from him. What surprised her was the fact that he was being so forthcoming. Did he actually believe that she would just forget that he had tried to kill her? Or that she would be impressed by these revelations?

Of course he does. He's a narcissist and a sociopath.

Tyndareus nodded, but his expression was subdued. He stared into the glass, looking past the reflection, gazing at the skeletal remains. "That is what I believed, when I began. The procedure was successful. The embryo was created in the laboratory and transplanted into a surrogate. After the child was born, however, I began to feel differently toward him. You see, he was not only my offspring—and a far better son than the ungrateful spawn of my own loins—but also my genetic twin.

"In my early research, I had mistakenly attributed the bond between twins to shared experiences in the womb, but as time passed and the child grew to maturity, I recognized that it is a genetic bond. A bond that I shared with Castor."

Fiona gave a nod. "Must have really sucked when you finally had to cut him up for spare parts."

"I did no such thing."

The admission surprised her, not because it seemed the likeliest explanation for Mengele's longevity—he was at least a hundred—but because it was hard for her to believe that there was a line he wouldn't cross.

"Even before he reached adulthood, it became apparent that something was wrong. Castor was aging." Tyndareus tapped the joystick, swinging the chair around to face her. "Tell me, child. Are you as well versed in the sciences as you are in other areas? Are you perhaps familiar with telomeres?"

"Telomeres. That sounds Greek. 'End parts?'"

The word felt familiar, but before she could search her memory, Tyndareus went on. "Telomeres are nucleotide sequences found on the end of chromosomes. TTAGGG, repeating thousands of times on each and every chromosome in each and every cell of the human body. They serve as buffers, protecting the genetic code of the chromosomes from damage during the process of cellular reproduction. It may help you to think of chromosomes as shoelaces, and the telomeres as the plastic wrapped around the end to keep them from fraying—"

"They're called 'aglets,'" Fiona murmured.

"In complex life forms, every time a cell divides, and the DNA code is duplicated, the telomere chain loses a link. After a lifetime of cellular reproduction, the telomeres eventually break down completely, after which genetic damage begins to occur."

"And the shoelace frays."

"That genetic damage is what we call 'aging.' The role telomeres play in the aging process was only discovered a decade ago, far too late to be of any use to me in my research."

Fiona was able to guess the rest. "When you cloned yourself, your telomeres were already getting pretty short. Castor was already an old man when he was born."

"The rapid cellular growth of early childhood and puberty intensified the process, causing him to age even faster. The decay, both physical and mental, accelerated with each passing year, until his death. He knew the fate that awaited him, and so he drew off the Jewish agents who were pursuing me, while I built..." He gestured around the room. "All of this.

"I wasn't able to save him," he continued, his voice showing more emotion than she would have believed possible. "I have labored for nearly forty years to find a way to bring him back to me."

"And that's what Kenner promised you."

"In the old days, we learned many things about the ancient world. The so-called mysteries. And we heard rumors about the man remembered in legend as Hercules. We knew that there was a group working to erase all evidence of his existence. When Dr. Kenner approached me with information about the Herculean Society and the possibility that he might be able to uncover its secrets, I wondered at his ability to deliver, but I never doubted the veracity of his claims."

Fiona could only assume that 'we' meant the Nazis. "If he told you that he can bring the dead back to life, then you should. Even Hercules was never able to do that."

"The bond I share with Castor did not end with his death." Tyndareus gave a patient smile. "Dr. Kenner believes, as do I, that the creatures Hercules fought in his so-called Labors, were the product of genetic experimentation, made possible by a source. A mutagenic agent that allows the DNA of two or more different creatures to be combined, producing something greater than the sum of their parts. The ancients knew where the source was, though they did not comprehend how to use it or control its creations. They called it Echidna."

"The Mother of All Monsters." If what Tyndareus said was true, given what she knew about the chthonic monsters, then how would that help Tyndareus bring his clone back to life? The answer came to her a moment later. "You want to combine your DNA with..." She nodded to the bones. "His."

Tyndareus's smile was answer enough. "Echidna will allow me to create a new form—Gemini—reuniting me with my twin, and modern genetic engineering techniques will allow me to overcome the problem of telomerase deficiency."

Fiona thought back to her conversation with Gallo on that particular topic. "Echidna lived in the Underworld. Kenner isn't going to find anything in South America. All that map will do is take him to the Amazon city."

"He believes that he can find information there that will lead him to Echidna." He narrowed his gaze at her. "Do you know where it is?"

Fiona felt the chill return. This was it, the moment of reckoning. If she refused him, she was dead, and despite what she had just told him, there was a very real possibility that Kenner would be able to follow the clues to find the entrance to the Underworld. But if she helped the old man...?

"I sense your hesitation," he said. "You believe I am some kind of monster."

She jerked her head over her shoulder, nodding toward his gallery of horrors. "Pretty much."

"Everything I did was for the greater good of humanity. My research opened new frontiers of understanding. Though the medical and scientific community would never admit it, my work at Birkenau made possible nearly every significant medical advance of the last century. Finding Echidna will be the key to the advances of the next."

Fiona was unmoved by the grandiose claim. Tyndareus would be able to do what he suggested, but he would use it as a weapon to enslave or destroy anyone he deemed unfit, feeding them to his carnivorous plants. But that was a long range problem. The question of what to do now remained.

Live dog or dead lion? The answer was simple enough. A live dog could still bite.

"Show me the map."

THIRTY-EIGHT

Roraima, Brazil

Pierce tackled Carter, throwing them both backward, off the artificial island and into the shallow water near where Lazarus lay. The two flying shapes swooped past them, and even in the low light, Pierce could make out the distinctive outlines of wings and tail feathers. Birds, but not like any birds he had ever seen before.

The birds wheeled around and lined up for another pass.

"Down!" Pierce shouted, and then he plunged his head under the surface.

A strange rapid-fire popping noise reverberated through the water. He felt a series of percussion claps against his back, and then a searing pain stabbed through his right butt cheek. He howled into the water and thrust his head above the surface. He reached back, groping for the site of the wound. His fingers brushed against something that sent a fresh throb of pain through his buttocks. Whatever had caused the injury was still there, sticking out of him like an arrow.

The natives of the Amazon hunted with blow darts and arrows, and often tipped their missiles with poison. But other than the pain of the puncture wound, he felt nothing. He had been attacked, but not by natives.

Something moved beside him, bringing him back to the moment. Carter had her arms around an unresponsive Lazarus, holding his head up out of the water. Pierce saw that she was uninjured, and then it occurred to him that the danger was not yet past. He glanced skyward and saw two dark shapes silhouetted against the violet sky, turning slow circles like vultures.

"Come on," he said through clenched teeth. "We need to get to the trees."

Carter seemed about ready to protest, but then nodded. "Help me with him."

Careful not to jostle the projectile lodged in the meat of his buttocks, Pierce looped one of Lazarus's massive arms around his shoulders. Carter took the other, and they headed for the nearest stand of cypress trees. It was more than two hundred yards away, and with the added burden of Lazarus's dead weight, they made slow progress. At first, Pierce thought he could feel the skewering object digging deeper with every step and the tingle of poison spreading through his veins—both sensations were probably just in his imagination—but before they had gone a quarter of the way, his foot snagged on a submerged root. He stumbled, and as he pitched forward into the water, he felt Lazarus go down, taking Carter with him.

The sudden immersion roused the big man. He jolted up out of the water, but after looking around for a moment, he pulled both Pierce and Carter to their feet and urged them at a near run, to the safety of the trees.

Pierce's backside burned with pain, but two things quickly became apparent. The birds were not going to attack again—in fact, they had disappeared from the sky—and the object lodged in his backside was not tipped with poison.

It still hurt like hell, though.

Carter's focus was on Lazarus. There was a large gash in the center of his combat vest. Whatever had struck him had torn through both the overlaying fabric and the layer of woven Kevlar underneath, laying bare the ceramic small arms protective insert—SAPI—plate. The tombstone-shaped armor plate could stop a round from an AK47, but whatever had hit it had cracked it in two. Without asking permission, Carter tore open the vest and laid bare Lazarus's broad chest.

The skin underneath was unbroken, but there was a bright red outline in the shape of the SAPI plate, and the beginning of a bruise.

"What was that thing?" Lazarus asked. His voice was tight, as if speaking or even breathing was painful. "It felt like a cannonball." He looked at Carter for a moment, scrutinizing her for any sign of injury, then at Pierce. "Are you okay?"

"Not exactly," Pierce admitted, and he turned to show them his wound. "I've got this pain in the ass."

Carter stifled a laugh, then said, "What *is* that? It looks like a porcupine quill." She bent over for a closer look.

"What?" Pierce craned his head around, but the quill was beyond the limit of his vision. "Not an arrow?"

Carter shook her head. "There's a couple more stuck in your vest." She carefully pulled one free and showed him. It was thicker than he expected, more like a hollow knitting needle than a stiff bristle, with a faintly opalescent sheen that made it look almost like metal.

Lazarus straightened up, as if his own injury was merely an inconvenience. "That has to come out," he declared, reaching for a small sheath clipped to his vest. He removed a Gerber multi-tool and slid the pliers out. "This will hurt."

Pierce opened his mouth to say that it already hurt, then there was an explosion of pain. Lazarus held up the pliers, along with the quill he had just removed. Half an inch of the tip was stained red. The relief however was instantaneous. The pain subsided to a dull ache.

"Stymphalian birds," George said. "For his sixth Labor, Hercules was sent to get rid of a flock of man-eating birds, with beaks made of bronze that could cut through armor. They could also launch feathers like darts."

He braced himself for a skeptical reaction, but Carter gave an encouraging nod. "Go on."

"The Greeks believed the birds were the pets of Ares, the war god. They had a fondness for human flesh. They were probably carrion eaters who were drawn to the bodies of the slain on the battlefield. In the story, a flock of the birds had migrated to a swamp near the village of Stymphalos. Hercules was sent to deal with the problem. He killed some of the birds, and the rest were scattered. The Argonauts encountered some of them during the quest for the Golden Fleece. I guess some of them ended up here. Pausanias, a geographer from the second century, described a species of ferocious birds that he associated with the legend. He described them as being similar to ibises, but there's no way of knowing if those were the birds from the legend, or just named that as an homage."

"Anything else?"

"Their droppings are supposed to be poisonous."

"Naturally," Carter said.

"They didn't attack until we got to the island. And they haven't come after us since. So they're fierce, but maybe not as bloodthirsty as in the legend."

"Protecting the nest?" Carter suggested.

"That's what I'm thinking," Pierce said. "But they're not afraid of us."

"How did Hercules beat them?" Lazarus asked.

"Athena, the goddess, gave him a magical *krotala*—a noisemaker, kind of like castanets—forged by the god Hephaestus. The sound frightened the birds away so they wouldn't attack, giving Hercules a chance to shoot them down using arrows tipped with Hydra venom."

Lazarus looked across the water to the island city. "Noisemakers."

"The sound of a gunshot might be enough to scare them off," Carter suggested. "That's something Hercules didn't have."

"It would also give our presence away. We'd lose the element of surprise." Lazarus ran a thumb over the torn Kevlar fibers of his vest. "We'll have to make a run for it. The body armor will give us some protection."

"I should have brought the Lion skin." Pierce said. He mulled the problem for a moment. "Pausanias suggested making armor out of cork wood. The birds' beaks would cut through, but get stuck."

"Like darts in a dartboard," said Carter.

"Exactly." He glanced past her at the cypress trunks. "We don't have cork, but maybe we could fashion something from tree bark."

Lazarus grasped the hilt of his knife and drew it. "Good idea."

He peeled off several large sheets of the stringy bark, each about three feet square. Then he layered them, alternating the directions of the fibers, and then bound them together using strips of parachute cord. In ten minutes, he had assembled shields for each of them.

"These should hold together long enough to get us to cover."

Pierce slipped his forearm through the loops Lazarus had fashioned, feeling a little like an ancient Hoplite, girding for battle. "We should stay close together," he said. "That way we can cover each other."

"I'll take point." Lazarus started out toward the island, taking measured, methodical steps to ensure that Pierce and Carter did not get left behind.

There was no sign of the Stymphalian birds in the sky above, but Pierce knew they had not seen the last of them. Sure enough, when they were within fifty yards of the island, two birds leapt from a perch atop one of the old buildings and began circling. Pierce raised his shield high, angling it so that he could keep an eye on the birds, who began to tighten their orbits, swooping lower with each pass.

The bird that had struck Lazarus floated on the surface a few yards from the edge of the island. They approached it cautiously, but it did not move.

Carter stepped out of their formation, ignoring a hissed warning from Lazarus, and bent to pick up the carcass. The two men moved in to cover her, as she examined it. "Broken neck."

"Probably happened when it hit the SAPI plate," Lazarus said. "Leave it."

Carter turned it over. Pierce saw that the creature's bill had the same iridescent hues as the quills that sprouted from its white plumage. "It's an egret," she announced. "But I think it's been hybridized, like the Lion. Probably with a porcupine. That would explain the quills. I'd like to sequence it when we get out of here."

Lazarus let out an irritated growl but she ignored him, tucking the dead bird's feet into her belt. "Ready."

Lazarus shook his head and moved closer to the rocks. He climbed to the top but stayed low, keeping his shield up. Pierce and Carter followed suit.

When they were all in place, Pierce pointed to the nearest structure, a ruin with crumbling walls and no roof. "There. The walls will make it harder for them to hit us."

Lazarus nodded. "When I say go, we range walk, and don't stop until we're inside."

"Range walk?" Pierce asked.

"Sorry. Military term. Walk fast, but don't run. Running increases the chances of tripping, and tripping increases the chances of dying."

"Range walk. Got it."

"Good." He paused a beat and then said simply, "Go."

They sprang to their feet and began striding across the open ground. The two birds overhead turned and dove toward them. Carter faltered. Lazarus shouted for her to keep moving, but there was no avoiding the birds.

George stood in front of Carter, raised the shield high and was nearly knocked off his feet as the leading bird struck it. A three-inch long metallic-looking spear tip punched through the layers of bark just above Pierce's forearm, and then the shield began to shake as if a giant was trying to rip it away from him. He stumbled forward as the bird, in a flurry of wings, tried to extract itself.

Lazarus gripped Pierce's arm, supporting his efforts. Then the second bird made its attack, diving toward Lazarus, but the big man was faster, swiping the air with his shield and batting it away.

He then reached around Pierce, knife in hand, and hacked at the bird caught in Pierce's shield. There was an agonized squawk and a simultaneous grunt from Lazarus. The thrashing on the other side of the shield ceased, but when Lazarus drew his knife hand back, it was bristling with quills.

"Keep going!" Lazarus shouted.

Despite the earlier advice, Pierce ran. Carter was close behind him, while Lazarus brought up the rear, his shield raised.

Pierce glanced back and was relieved to see that the sky was clear. The bird stuck in his shield was probably dead, and the one Lazarus had bashed was stunned or possibly also dead. Definitely out of the fight.

His relief was short-lived. When they were still ten yards from the building, he heard a low ominous rushing sound that grew to deafening intensity.

Flapping wings.

A lot of them.

He glanced up and saw the sky darken as dozens, perhaps even hundreds of winged creatures filled the air above them. As if guided by a single mind, the entire flock of Stymphalian birds shot toward them.

Lazarus threw his arms out in a sweeping gesture, propelling both Pierce and Carter toward the ruins. "Run!"

Pierce raised his shield over his head, but stayed close to Carter, keeping the edge of his shield in contact with hers, doubling the protection provided by the bark sheets. The shield blocked his view of the approaching swarm, but he didn't need to see them to know that they were in serious trouble.

Something slammed into the shield, staggering Pierce. Another long spike punctured the wood right above his forearm. Another impact followed, and then another. Too many to count. The inside of the shield was transformed into a bed of nails.

Behind him, Lazarus swung his shield back and forth, deflecting the diving birds and knocking them out of the air as they attacked. But for every bird he demolished, two more made it past the barrier, slashing at his torso with their beaks and stabbing their spiny quills into him. His combat harness hung in shreds and blood streamed from dozens of wounds, but he fought on.

They were not even halfway to the shelter of the ruins.

Carter stumbled. Pierce caught her arm and tried to keep her from falling but the relentless assault from above had him off balance. Instead of keeping her on her feet, he went down alongside her. For a moment, they were both exposed and vulnerable, but Pierce twisted around and got his shield up, covering himself and her.

The shield shuddered against him like a wild animal trying to wrestle out of his grip. Dozens of birds, their beaks caught in the bark, tried to wrestle free, even as more birds slammed into their midst. The number of holes weakened the barrier. It was only a matter of time—perhaps seconds—before it came apart.

Pierce felt something brush against his legs—not more birds but Lazarus, bloody and beaten, crawling to join them. His face was a bleeding mask of pain. "Go!"

"We'll never make it," Carter shouted back.

"I know." Lazarus heaved his half-destroyed shield over them, leaving himself completely unprotected. "But you have to try."

Pierce knew the big man was right on both counts. "Felice. Let's go."

But before either of them could move, a loud report—the sound of gunfire—cut through the thrashing of the bird attack. Pierce cursed under his breath. As impossible as it seemed, things were about to get even worse.

THIRTY-NINE

A commotion echoed across the treetops, filling the bottom of the sinkhole with the noise of flapping wings. Gallo scanned the sky, trying to locate the disturbance, but there were too many trees in the way. The sound seemed to be coming from somewhere directly ahead, near what she guessed to be the center of the abyss.

Another noise, a low murmur of wariness and discontent, rippled through the Cerberus team. Rohn silenced them all with a withering glance. "Keep rowing," he snarled.

They had been exploring the marsh for nearly an hour, using a small fleet of three-person inflatable rafts. Gallo occupied the center seat of one, bracketed by two guards. Dourado was in another, while Kenner and Rohn rode together in a third.

The boats were probably unnecessary since the water was shallow enough to walk through. But they granted some protection from possible attacks by amphibious and aquatic creatures, which might be lurking beneath the surface. That was the reasoning at least. Gallo doubted the inflatables would shield them from the poisonous breath of the salamanders, but thus far the strategy had worked. Aside from the buzzing of insects, they had seen no evidence of animal life since the attack on the shore. At least, not until the noise of not-quite-distant-enough wings was heard.

And now that's where we're headed, Gallo thought. The only upside to it all was that every deadly animal encounter brought them one step closer to the failure of Kenner's plan.

The salamander creature, which she knew must be some kind of chthonic chimera related to the Hydra, was evidence enough that Kenner was on the right track, but the outcome of that initial attack indicated how ill-prepared the Cerberus team was. Hercules had been hard-pressed to defeat such beasts, and he had been nearly invincible.

As they rounded a copse of cypress trees, Gallo glimpsed movement in the sky. A strange rippling cloud hovered above a point several hundred yards away. After a few seconds, something changed, and the cloud became almost transparent, dotted with black specks. Then it solidified again. It reminded her of a fish shoal changing direction in unison. Or a flock of birds.

Dourado gave an uneasy laugh. "Angry birds."

"No kidding," Gallo muttered.

Kenner peered through a pair of binoculars for a moment then lowered them. He flashed a grin in Gallo's direction. "Stymphalian birds, Augustina. That's what those are. Think about it. The birds origin-ally belonged to Ares. Hippolyte was the daughter of Ares."

"I think you're missing the point, Liam."

He waved a dismissive hand. "We have guns."

Gallo eyed the swirling mass in the distance. "But do you have enough bullets?"

Kenner made a hurt expression. "Give me some credit for knowing the source material. The sound of the shots will drive them off. That's how Herakles defeated them."

Gallo was not quite so optimistic about the strategy's chances of success, but offered no further comment. If the birds did attack, it might present a chance for escape.

She glanced over at Dourado and mouthed the words, 'Be ready.'

Dourado just stared back at her, looking miserable.

Oh, Cintia, I'm so sorry. I bet you're wishing you'd stayed at your computer.

"There!" Kenner's hand shot out, pointing at something on the near horizon. "The city of the Amazons!"

Despite everything else that was happening, Gallo experienced a fleeting excitement. Mutant creatures from mythology were one thing, but this...this was something else. Her entire professional career, more than half of her life, had been spent pursuing the connection between ancient myths and actual history. Here before her lay the physical evidence of that connection, and in a place the academic world least expected it. It was a singular moment in her life, an unparalleled discovery.

And I won't be able to tell a soul.

For the first time since accepting Pierce's invitation, she understood just how much she would have to sacrifice to be part of the Herculean Society.

Probably doesn't matter. I doubt any of us are getting out of here alive.

"They're coming," Rohn said, in a flat voice.

Gallo turned her gaze back to the sky and saw what looked like a dark finger reaching out from the cloud of birds, stretching toward them. In just a few seconds, the leading edge of the finger was close enough for her to see flapping wings, and then the birds themselves.

Kenner shifted in his boat, looking from the birds to Rohn and back again. "Shouldn't we...ah..."

"Shoot," Rohn said. "Now."

The Cerberus men opened fire with their pistols, shooting into the onrushing feathered mass. The first report startled Gallo, the noise deafening with its proximity. She clapped her hands over her ears, too late to silence the ringing noise.

In the sky above, the approaching swarm split apart, seeming to curl back on itself. Two of the birds simply dropped, mortally wounded by the random shots.

"It's working," Kenner shouted above the din. "Keep shooting."

As if to embarrass him, at almost that exact moment, the guns fell silent. The men had shot out the magazines in their weapons and were now reloading. The lull was only a few seconds long, but it was enough for the Stymphalian birds to renew their advance. The firing resumed and the birds scattered again, but the flaw in Kenner's plan was now obvious. Once the Cerberus men ran out of bullets, there would be no way to drive the birds off. Instead of frightening the creatures away, the shooting had merely advertised their presence.

Kenner seemed to realize this as well. He gripped Rohn's shoulder. "We need to fall back."

"It is too late for that," Rohn answered. There was no dread in his tone, only a hint of disgust at Kenner's foolishness.

Kenner flinched at the dire pronouncement. "Stagger your shots," he cried. "Make every bullet count."

The Cerberus men were already doing that, trying to work out a sequential pattern that would maintain the rate of fire and cover reloading periods, but the noise of the shots was no longer having the desired effect. More birds were being drawn off from the main cloud and despite the fact that some of the rounds were finding their marks, the swarm was closing fast.

Gallo felt like a spectator, watching a disaster unfolding, powerless to do anything to stop what had been set in motion. It took a moment for her to grasp that she was not merely an observer. When the birds finally attacked, she would be killed along with everyone else.

The realization hit like an electric shock, galvanizing her into action. She rolled over the side of the raft, not caring that doing so nearly capsized the little inflatable boat. The water was only about waist deep, shallow enough for her to walk, but she swam, striking out for Dourado's boat.

Behind her, the Cerberus men assigned to guard her shouted for her to stop, but neither they nor any of the others attempted to pursue her. Dourado, however, had understood the earlier signal, and followed Gallo's example. When Gallo saw the blue-haired woman splashing toward her, she changed course, angling in the direction of the ruins. "This way!"

Dourado stared at her in disbelief. "You want to go *toward* them?"

"Trust me!"

It was a spur of the moment judgment call, but Gallo was fairly sure that the birds would pass them by and attack the source of the noise. She was also certain that the birds and the salamanders were natural enemies, perhaps existing in a predator-prey relationship, and as long as they were in the water, she was more worried about things that swam than things that flew. They had encountered the salamander at the furthest reaches of the sinkhole, while the birds seemed to occupy the center, so it stood to reason that a denser population of birds would mean fewer salamanders. She did not have time to explain this to Dourado, and there was a very good chance that she was wrong about it, but the truth of the matter was that her decision had nothing to do with choosing the safest escape route. The only thing she really cared about was seeing the Amazon city.

The sound of flapping wings intensified as the flock's leading edge drowned out the noise of sporadic gunfire. Then a scream split the air. Gallo glanced back and saw one of the Cerberus men, or rather what was left of him, topple over the side of his boat. A red mist hung in the air above the remains. The birds that had attacked him were already thrashing toward the other men in the boat.

Gallo heard the snap of bullets creasing the air right above her, then the splash as they smacked into the water nearby. Although the men were not shooting at her, the errant shots were as dangerous as the birds. Judging by the attack's ferocity and the general pandemonium unfolding behind her, it wouldn't be a problem for much longer.

Gallo turned her gaze back to the island and kept swimming. She chose a breaststroke, keeping most of her body underwater, hoping it would be enough to hide them from the winged attackers.

It almost was.

When she was just thirty yards from the island's rocky shore, one of the birds noticed her. The flapping of wings announced the attack, giving her just enough advance notice to shout a warning to Dourado before plunging her head under the water. Then, her left leg seemed to catch on fire.

Because she had been prepared for an attack of some kind, she was able to clench her teeth and push through the pain. She kept swimming under the surface, clawing through the water with her hands, expecting more razor sharp beaks or claws to tear into her. There were no more attacks, but her leg was throbbing so badly that the mere act of trying to kick made her feel like throwing up.

Her hands scraped against something, and she looked up, cautiously raising her head. She had reached the island.

"Cintia?" she gasped, barely able to get the words out. "Still with me?"

There was a splash beside her as Dourado broke the surface. Strings of cobalt hair were plastered to her face, but she seemed none the worse for wear. "We made it," she said.

Gallo glanced up at the sky overhead. It was clear, with most of the birds fully involved in the attack on the Cerberus men, but she knew that could change at any moment. "Give me a hand, Cintia. I can't walk."

Dourado let out a low wail of dismay. "Ai! There are things stuck in your leg. Should I pull them out?"

Pull them out? Will that make me bleed to death? She couldn't think straight. "Just get me to the city."

Dourado nodded and put an arm around Gallo's waist, helping her onto the rocky slope. She glanced down at her leg, which was not as badly swollen as she would have expected given the intensity of the ache. When she craned her head around, she could just make out something protruding from the back of her thigh. It looked like a meat skewer made of translucent fiberglass.

It's a feather, she realized, or rather the shaft of a feather with the barbs removed. She tried to grasp hold, intending to pull it free, but even light pressure sent a current of pain through her leg. She cried out and would have collapsed if not for Dourado's support.

"Come on," Dourado urged. She pointed forward, and Gallo remembered what it was that had brought her here. A high-walled structure with a colonnaded porch and a doorless entryway stood directly ahead. Gallo nodded, and gritting her teeth against the pain, she hobbled toward the entrance.

The beat of wings grew louder behind them. They'd been noticed. Dourado glanced back, then quickened her step, all but dragging Gallo along. The porch and the doorway beyond could not have been more than twenty yards away, but it seemed like a mile. Gallo knew she should tell Dourado to leave her and find safety, but she didn't have the strength—physically or emotionally—to say it out loud. Dourado would probably refuse anyway. A waste of breath for both of them.

Still, if they didn't make it...if they both died, it would be her fault. The thought made her angry, and anger provided the motivation that desperation could not. She straightened her back, bit her lip until it bled and started to run.

The noise of flapping wings built to a fever pitch as Gallo and Dourado reached the porch, but as they passed through the arched opening and threw themselves sideways into the shadows beyond, it was like someone had hit the mute button on the world. Not a single bird pursued them inside.

Disbelief gave way to relief, and while neither was a particularly good painkiller, Gallo got to her feet unassisted and limped close to the doorway's edge. She peeked outside. The swarm had returned to the sky, or possibly gone back to their roosts.

The attack was over.

"Are we safe?" Dourado asked from behind her.

Gallo nodded. "For the moment. Eventually we're going to have to run the gauntlet again, but for now, I think we can breathe."

She turned back and took a look at their new surroundings. The door opened into a long hallway with several doorways leading to other parts of the building. Gallo shuffled toward the nearest opening and peered inside. The floor was covered with a thick layer of dirt, and lichen growth streaked the walls. There was no sign of a human presence aside from the structure itself. Though it was impossible to see what lay in the shadowy corners, Gallo felt certain that the room contained nothing that would shed light on the mystery of the city's builders. This might once have been the home of the Amazon warriors, or the Sea Peoples, but it had been abandoned long ago. The former occupants had taken everything of value with them.

She moved to the next door and the next, but found only more of the same. But the doorway at the end of the tunnel was different—wider, like the entrance, and covered with something that might have been an actual door, though it was hard to tell in the darkness. Gallo extended a hand to probe the dark barrier, and felt her fingers sink into something the consistency of peat moss. She yanked her hand back, but her touch was enough to collapse the rotted wood. As the damp pungent pulp fell away, dim light filled the hallway.

Gallo looked through the newly created hole and out into a vast plaza, surrounded by buildings like the one in which she now stood. In the courtyard, a series of stone terraces descended to a wide canal that surrounded an elevated mound, upon which had been built a structure that rose up higher than any of the other buildings in the city. The building was rectangular, with a gently sloping roof and decorative pediment held aloft by tall columns— the classic design of a Greek temple.

Gallo could only imagine what the courtyard and the temple might have looked like in the days of Queen Hippolyte and her Amazons. She wondered if the ancient Alexander Diotrephes, posing as Herakles, had stood where she now did. *Was he the cause of the culture's downfall? Did seizing the Queen's belt with its map of the world, the key to the Amazons' power, undo them all?*

Whether or not that part was true, their society had survived, in some form, at least long enough for Orellana and Carvajal to have their encounter with the fierce warrior women for whom the river was named. The advance of European conquerors, with their guns and germs, had dealt the final death blow. There was only a memory of the city's former glory now. Nature had reclaimed much of it. The terraces were thick with vegetation, and cypress trees had taken root in the canal.

"We need to get to that temple," Gallo said. "If we're going to find anything, it will be there."

Dourado did not question this assessment. "Can you make it?"

"I have to." She took a breath then faced the other woman. "Thanks for trying to help me. I didn't get a chance to say it before. I was really surprised to see you."

"I'm sorry. I thought I could... If I had known this would happen..."

Gallo took her hand and gave it a squeeze. "I'm glad you're here."

Dourado returned the squeeze with a wan smile. "I guess I am, too."

"Ready?"

Dourado nodded and together they began tearing away the rotted planks until the hole was big enough for both of them to walk through. Gallo leaned against Dourado every time she had to put weight on her injured leg, but the pain had finally subsided to a dull ache. She suspected that the quills had not penetrated very deeply and that the discomfort and inflammation was merely her body's way of telling her to pull them out, but that would have to wait until she was ready to deal with the wounds. Right now, the quills were acting as stoppers, minimizing the flow of blood.

As they moved out into the open, a rustling sound came from above them. Gallo looked up and saw hundreds of white bird heads looking down at them. The creatures were everywhere, perched along the edge of the rooftops that ringed the plaza. Many of them stood with their wings fully extended, plumage puffed up in a display of ferocity. Dourado started to turn back, probably intending to bolt for the refuge of the building they had just exited, but Gallo held her back.

"No," she whispered. "Don't move."

"But..."

"They haven't attacked. I don't know why. Maybe they don't like how closed in the courtyard is. Just keep moving, slowly."

She demonstrated, moving with exaggerated slowness, like a living-statue street performer. The birds continued posturing, but none of them took flight.

By the time they reached stairs descending to the next terrace, Gallo was certain that the birds were not going to attack, though she could not fathom what was keeping them at bay. She sped up to a normal walking pace—or as close to it as her wounded leg would allow—though she carefully avoided any sudden moves.

Each successive terrace took them further from the birds and closer to their destination: a bridge that spanned the canal and ended at a passage leading into the central temple mound. The canal was murky, thick with plants and trees, but not completely self-contained. A single channel led away, dividing the terraces before disappearing into the mouth of a large opening in the city's foundation, a channel connecting the canal to shallow marshlands outside the city on the opposite side of their original approach.

Now that they were in the homestretch, Gallo gave up on stealth, hobbling across the bridge as fast as she could manage. The passage beyond was dark, but she could make out the base of a staircase spiraling up a central passage, and once inside, she could see daylight filtering down from above.

"Augustina!"

The shout sent a fresh wave of panic through her, partly because it might be enough to upset the balance and bring the birds down on them, and partly because of who the voice belonged to. She glanced back and saw that there could be no retreat. Kenner was approaching the bridge, and he was not alone. Rohn was with him, along with two other Cerberus men. They had not come through the attack unscathed. All four men were bloody from head to toe, clothing sliced to unrecognizable tatters, their bodies bristling with quills. Kenner was faltering, but Rohn and the others stalked forward like relentless automatons.

Kenner stretched out a hand. "Augustina. Wait."

She turned to Dourado. "Go!"

They plunged into the dark stairwell, Dourado running and Gallo shuffling along as best she could. Behind them, Rohn charged, reaching the bridge and sprinting across it. Gallo bounded blindly up the stairs, two at a time. The light beckoned to her, but before she could reach the top, a hand clamped down on her biceps and pulled her off her feet. She didn't fall. Instead, Rohn dragged her along until, at the topmost step he caught Dourado, too.

He took a few more steps then hurled both women forward. Gallo cried out as the impact with the moss-covered stone drove some of the quills deeper into her leg, but fear of what Rohn would do next compelled her to keep moving. She stumbled and fell to her knees, but kept crawling.

As she beheld the interior of the temple, dimly illuminated by daylight seeping in from beyond the colonnade, the fight nearly went out of her. There was nothing particularly glorious about the sacred building. It was as overgrown and dilapidated as the rest of the city, but Gallo saw past the decay and neglect, imagining the place as it might have been three thousand years earlier.

Directly ahead, occupying the center of the sanctuary, stood a colossal statue of a warrior. Like everything else, the old stone was weathered and overgrown, but the image was unmistakably that of a muscular man wearing battle armor and a helmet. A round shield covered his left arm. In his right, poised for a throw, was a long spear.

It was Ares, the god of war.

A Greek temple to Ares in the Amazon. At least I lived long enough to see this, she thought.

"Stop," Kenner shouted. "Vigor, what are you doing?"

Gallo looked back and saw Rohn stalking toward her, a long double-edged knife, like a dagger, clenched in one hand.

"Leave her alone," Kenner said. He sounded weak and ineffectual, begging more than demanding. "You're not supposed to kill her."

Rohn wasn't listening. He advanced, moving faster than Gallo could crawl. There was nowhere to go. She heard his footsteps, felt his hand seize hold of her once more, saw the blade rise...

"Let her go!"

The voice was strained, but so filled with authority and passion that, even if Gallo had not recognized it, she would have known that it was not Kenner.

A lone figure stepped out from behind the statue of Ares. The man was as bloody and bedraggled as the Cerberus men, but Gallo recognized him immediately.

"You made a classic mistake," George Pierce said, aiming his machine pistol at Rohn. "You brought a knife to a gunfight."

FORTY

Rohn moved faster than Pierce would have thought possible, but he did not attack. Instead, he ran. The retreat was so unexpected that Pierce didn't have time to pull the trigger.

He had been prepared to shoot. The MP5K was equipped with an Aimpoint holographic reflex scope. Lazarus had assured him that the rounds would go right where the red dot pointed, so there was little risk of accidentally hitting Gallo or Dourado, but keeping that red dot on a fast moving target wasn't easy.

Rohn vanished, disappearing into the stairwell.

Kenner seemed as stunned by the big man's flight as Pierce was, but the other two Cerberus men made a desperate rush at Pierce.

This time, there was no hesitation. Pierce jerked the gun toward the nearest man and pulled the trigger. There was hardly any recoil, and the suppressor muffled the report so effectively that, for a fleeting instant, Pierce thought the gun had malfunctioned. It had not. The first Cerberus man went down, stumbling and skidding across the floor until both his momentum and his life ran out.

Pierce brought the gun around to the second man, who after witnessing his comrade's fate, was already trying to veer off. Pierce squeezed the trigger, but the bullets sizzled past their intended target, smashing into the stone walls of the temple. The man twisted around and dove to the ground, right behind Dourado.

Pierce yanked his finger out of the trigger guard and raised the muzzle, but he leveled it again as the Cerberus man dragged Dourado to her feet, holding her between himself and Pierce as a human shield.

"Let her go," Pierce said. He trained the red dot on the man's head, or rather the fraction of it that was not hidden behind Dourado's cobalt hair. Lazarus probably would have taken the shot, but Pierce didn't want to risk Dourado's life. The man hunched lower, removing even that slim opportunity, and he began backing toward the stairs. Pierce started forward, but the man slid an arm around her neck, none-too-subtly signaling what would happen if he came any closer. Pierce kept the red dot aimed at a spot just over Dourado's shoulder, determined to pull the trigger if the man revealed even an inch of himself. At the edge of the scope, he could see Dourado staring back at him, her eyes bulging from the pressure at her throat.

Then, all of sudden, she wasn't there anymore.

The Cerberus man, now fully exposed, gaped in disbelief as his hostage squirmed away. Pierce fired, wiping the shocked look from the man's face, along with most of his other distinguishing features. The man toppled backward, disappearing into the stairwell, but Pierce just stood where he was, the gun still pointed at the empty spot where the Cerberus man had been, the red dot aimed at nothing but the smoke drifting up from the end of the suppressor.

"George?"

He engaged the gun's safety and lowered it before turning to meet Gallo's wide gaze.

"You..." Her eyes dropped to the dead man on the floor. "You killed them?"

"Uh. Yeah."

She limped toward him and then threw both arms around him, hugging him tight. "Thank you."

Relief washed away any emotional turmoil. Gallo was safe. Dourado, too. He returned the embrace, savoring the reunion as long as he dared. "Augustina, where's Fi?"

"Fi?" Gallo drew back, her expression instantly changing to a look of horror. She pointed at Kenner, who still stood dumbfounded, just a few steps away from the stairwell. "He said they killed her."

Pierce's joy turned to sand. He rounded on Kenner, bringing his gun up, fully intending to put a bullet between the man's eyes. Kenner, sensing what was about to happen, let out a wail of protest and dropped to his knees, hands raised in a show of surrender.

"Don't kill me," he shrieked. "Please. I didn't do anything."

The pathetic display was just enough to dull the edge of Pierce's resolve, but it did not prevent him from moving closer and aiming the weapon at the back of Kenner's head. "Where is she? Where's Fiona?"

"I don't know. Tyndareus has her."

"Where?" Pierce jammed the muzzle hard against Kenner's neck. There was a hiss as the hot suppressor scorched exposed skin, leaving a ring-shaped brand, and Kenner let out a yelp.

"I don't..." He broke off, as if realizing that professing ignorance was a poor position from which to negotiate for his life. "Don't kill me. I'll help you."

"Is she still alive?"

Kenner swallowed. "Honestly, I don't know. Tyndareus is a monster, but he might have kept her alive for leverage against Augustina."

Pierce swept the muzzle of the weapon across the back of Kenner's head. Kenner pitched forward, squealing in pain. "You don't get to say her name," Pierce growled.

"No! Please. I'm sorry." Kenner was weeping now. "Don't kill me."

Pierce took a breath and counted to ten, then kept counting until the urge to pull the trigger finally abated. "Get up." He turned his head until he could see Gallo and Dourado in his peripheral vision. "We're getting out of here."

He felt Gallo's hand on his arm. "George. Do you know what this place is?"

Kenner raised his head, adding to Gallo's words with the desperation of a man trying to be useful. "Herakles was here. He took the map from Queen Hippolyte. He learned the location of the entrance to the Underworld from her."

"Map?" Pierce asked.

"George, the Amazons *were* the Sea Peoples," Gallo said. "They lived right here, in this city. And Queen Hippolyte's belt had a map of the entire world. That was the key to their power."

Pierce frowned. "Where's the map, now? Do you have it?"

Kenner hesitated a moment, but then nodded. "In my satchel."

Gallo hobbled forward and knelt beside Kenner. She rooted in his bag and then held up the object Kenner had taken from the Labyrinth. Pierce glanced at it, noting the images inscribed upon it.

"We used it to find this place," Gallo said. "Fiona figured it out."

"We?" Pierce regretted the implicit accusation as soon as he said it. "It doesn't matter. We're leaving."

"Tyndareus wants to find the source," Kenner insisted. "He's desperate to find it. If the girl is still alive, he'll trade that information for her. I know he will."

"We'll see about that." Pierce took a step away from Kenner and turned to Gallo. Only now did he see the line of quills that stitched the back of her leg. "Are you all right? Can you walk?"

"I made it this far." She managed a smile, but then her expression darkened. "What about the birds? How are we going to get past them?"

Pierce hauled Kenner to his feet and propelled him toward the stairwell. "Don't worry. I brought friends."

FORTY-ONE

Carter blinked away tears as she plucked the quills from Lazarus's body with the multi-tool. There were too many of the barbed spines to count, but while they were the least of his wounds, they were also the easiest for her to deal with.

The attack had been ruthless, razor sharp beaks lancing through what was left of his Kevlar armor and into his body, yet he had never faltered. When they had reached the relative safety of one of the ruined buildings, just before collapsing, he had whispered, "I'll be okay."

She knew he was right, but seeing him like this, flesh hanging in ragged strips from his bones, felt like a knife through her soul.

After removing the quills, she did what she could to close the larger lacerations, pressing the muscle and skin back into place. Then she used the sharp spines as impromptu sutures to hold everything together. Even with most of the wounds closed, he looked awful. A patchwork man, held together with toothpicks.

As she began snipping the ends of the shafts off with the wire-cutter built into the multi-tool, his eyes opened. He looked at her for a moment, his gaze steady, betraying none of the excruciating pain he was surely feeling. "Pierce?"

She started to reply, but she had to cough to clear away the emotion that had seized her throat. "He went ahead. There's a temple at the center of the city. He said that's where they would go."

"They?"

"Cerberus. Just after…" She faltered. "We heard shooting. The birds went after them, but a few of them made it to the island."

"He'll need my help." Lazarus attempted to rise, but before Carter could even attempt to stop him he sagged back. "Damn. That hurts."

Carter couldn't decide whether to laugh or sob. The sound that came out was something in-between. She could tell that he was already beginning to heal. The bleeding had stopped, and some of more superficial cuts had scabbed over. Hopefully, putting everything where it belonged and stitching him together would accelerate the process, but what he really needed was rest. Even a few hours might make all the difference.

Yeah, she thought. *Good luck with that.*

"Felice. I'll be okay."

"You keep saying that, but... You're not invincible, Erik."

"Yes, I am." He grimaced, and then with the determination of a glacier scraping across a continent, he sat up.

A voice came from behind them. "You should listen to your doctor."

Carter turned to see Pierce, accompanied by two women and a man—the latter clearly a prisoner—entering through the doorway at the back of the building.

Lazarus chuckled softly. "Not bad, Pierce. Jack would be proud."

"You can tell him all about it when you're ready." Pierce moved closer and knelt beside Carter. "How's he doing?"

"See for yourself."

"I'll be okay," Lazarus said. "You know how this works."

Pierce nodded. "I do." He turned to the others. "Felice and Erik, meet Augustina Gallo and Cintia Dourado." Almost as an afterthought, he pointed to the sullen man standing away from the others. "That's Kenner. He's a dick. But he's going to help us get Fiona back."

"She's not here?" Lazarus asked, his forehead creasing in concern.

Pierce shook his head. "She's at Cerberus HQ."

Carter frowned. "We barely made it this far. We'll be cut to ribbons if we try to leave."

"There's a canal that goes under the city. We can use it to get outside, and then we swim for the trees. From there, we make our way to the wall and climb out of here."

"That might work," Lazarus said, continuing his relentless struggle to get his feet back under him.

Carter hated the plan, but not as much as the idea of staying where they were. If she had learned one thing during her time with the man who now called himself Lazarus, it was to trust him, no matter how dire the situation looked. As she was about to voice her reluctant support, she heard a distant but familiar roar of an engine.

Despite his injuries, Lazarus was the first to reach the outside entrance to the building. As he stared up at the sky, the sound of rotor blades beating the air began echoing from the walls of the sinkhole. "There goes our ride."

"Rohn," Pierce said, disgusted. "I should have gone after the bastard. If we can get to the top, we should be able to get a signal out. Call for a pick up."

"You don't think he cut the ropes? Or sabotaged them?" Carter shook her head. "We're in no shape for a climb like that," she said, then added, "but there might be another way. We just need to find out where the water goes."

"She's right," Gallo said. "The Amazons sure as hell didn't climb up and down every time they went out. There has to be another way in, and I'd be willing to bet that canal goes right to it. It probably goes all the way to the river."

"So instead of a climb, we have to swim?"

"Amazons?" Carter glanced from Gallo to Pierce. "You mean...?"

"Like Xena," Dourado supplied. "Warrior Princess."

Carter laughed. "Actually, Gabrielle was the—"

Pierce looked up suddenly. "Augustina, you said the Amazons and Sea Peoples were one and the same, right? Well they would have needed something else besides the map to conquer the known world three thousand years ago." He looked around as if expecting someone to fill in the blanks.

"Boats?" Carter guessed.

"Ships, actually. We were wondering how the cypress trees got here. Now we know. The Amazons planted them. Cypress wood is extremely hydrophobic. The ancients knew that. It's long been believed that they used cypress wood for their ships. The Bible says that Noah built the ark out of cypress wood. Don't you see? This place wasn't just their city. It was where they grew the timber for their ships."

"And that helps us...how? Are you suggesting we should build an ark?"

"Of course not. That's ridiculous." Pierce grinned. "I was thinking more along the lines of a raft."

FORTY-TWO

Pierce had expected to spend hours hacking away at trees in the canal with Lazarus's Pathfinder knife. The big man was still in no shape for physical labor, and Pierce was definitely not going to put a blade in Kenner's hands. Despite the man's assurances that he would cause no trouble, Pierce had tied him up. Since he was too hardwired for chivalry to ask any of the women to take a turn, Pierce had resigned himself to the prospect of doing all the work himself.

Lazarus, however, had a better idea. He took a spool of what looked like yellow and black rope from his pack and wrapped a length of it around the base of a tree. The trunk was twelve-inches in diameter at the base and about forty-feet tall, a baby compared to those growing outside the city.

"Primacord," Lazarus explained in response to Pierce's questioning look. "Basically a rope made out of high explosives. Perfect for small breaching charges."

"You're going to blow the trees up? I've heard of fishing with dynamite, but never lumberjacking with it."

Lazarus tucked a slim silver blasting cap into the Primacord knot. "You should probably find cover."

The detonation was not as spectacular as Pierce had expected, but it was loud and released a shock wave that scattered the Stymphalian birds from their rooftop perch. The strand of explosives did not blow the cypress apart in a shower of splinters, but rather burned through it like an acetylene torch. The tree toppled over onto the terrace with a crash of branches, then slid into the canal.

Using det cord like a laser saw, it took less than an hour to produce the logs necessary to form the raft's deck, and slightly longer to drag them to the mouth of the tunnel leading out of the city where they began assembling the makeshift vessel. While Pierce and Lazarus lashed the logs together with parachute cord, Gallo, Dourado and Carter wove long strips of bark together to form a shield against another attack by the Stymphalian birds. Once these tasks were complete, they climbed aboard, and Pierce shoved off, using a pole cut from the top of one of the trees to punt the craft toward the daylight at the far end of the tunnel.

As they emerged, Lazarus scanned the sky above for any sign of another attack while the others huddled beneath the bark screen, but the birds didn't show. Evidently the repeated explosions had driven the creatures off.

Pierce kept his eyes on the water. Gallo had told him about the salamander attack. But his curiosity about the creature was short-lived. All he cared about now was getting out of the sinkhole and finding Fiona.

As Gallo had predicted, the ancient Amazons had erected stone pillars to mark a channel leading south through the swamp. Long before they reached the base of the wall, Pierce could see a gaping hole in the cliff face directly ahead.

Carter stared at it and shook her head. "Great. I hate caves."

Despite Carter's apprehension, the passage out of the sinkhole was uneventful. There were no monsters lurking in the Stygian darkness, no treacherous waterfalls or cataracts, and best of all, no Cerberus gunmen waiting to ambush them. After everything they had endured, it was almost anticlimactic, but Pierce knew their exit was just a brief respite from the ongoing struggle. Cerberus still had Fiona, and he would not rest until she was safe.

The river channel might once have connected with one of the many Amazon tributaries, but time and neglect had altered the landscape. Not long after they emerged from beneath the tepui, the stream became a shallow marsh and the raft bottomed out. They were able to acquire a signal for both GPS and the satellite phone, and made contact with the Aegis office in Rio de Janeiro. Pierce arranged for an extraction. The remoteness of their location meant a wait of nearly a full day, but that would give them time to figure out what to do with Kenner.

"Kill him," Lazarus said.

Pierce knew, or rather hoped, that Lazarus was bluffing. Shooting the Cerberus men to save Gallo had been one thing, but cold-blooded murder was another. Still, it was a tempting fantasy. "You're probably right. Leave the body out here. No one will ever find it."

"No!" Kenner protested. "I can help you. The girl—"

"The girl has a name," Lazarus said.

"You already said you don't know where she is," Pierce said. "You're of no use to us."

Kenner's eyes darted back and forth. "I can tell you what I do know. It might help you find Tyndareus."

"The plane!" Dourado exclaimed from behind them. She stepped forward and pointed a finger at Kenner. "You were on the Cerberus Learjet."

Kenner stared back uncertainly, as if trying to gauge how his reaction would be interpreted. "Yes. But I don't know where I boarded.

I was blindfolded from the time I left Tyndareus until the plane was in the air." He pointed to Gallo. "Ask her. She'll confirm what I'm saying."

"It does not matter. I have a record of the plane's flight plans for the last month. I just need you to tell me how many times you landed before you got to Belem."

Kenner blinked, but before he could answer, Gallo joined the conversation. "We stopped once. The blinds were lowered so I couldn't tell where. We were on the ground for maybe an hour."

"You were in the Azores. That means you left from Rome. Cerberus is in Rome!"

"It's a big city," Pierce said.

Dourado shook her head. "Now that I know where to look, I can follow the money moving into Rome from the Cerberus shell corporations. I'll find it. Just get me to a computer."

Lazarus stared at Kenner. "I guess we don't need you anymore."

"No, wait. I can still help. I know things."

Pierce glanced at Lazarus, but the big man's face was unreadable. If eliciting Kenner's complete cooperation, whatever that was worth, had been Lazarus's intent, then he had succeeded. That did not solve the problem of what to do with Kenner, but it was a start. "The helicopter will be here in ten hours. That's how long you've got to convince my friend that you're worth saving. Start talking."

SOURCE

FORTY-THREE

Rome, Italy

"**Are you sure** this is the place?" Pierce asked.

"Pretty sure," was the reply, Dourado's voice in his Bluetooth earpiece. She, along with Gallo, Carter and Kenner, who was zip-tied to his seat, were sitting in a rented van a block away. If Pierce and Lazarus did not make it out, they would call in the Carabinieri.

Dourado didn't elaborate on the reasons for her certainty, and she didn't have to. She'd already shown him the financial records tracing the flow of money from a number of Cerberus shell organizations to the *Fondazione Dioscuri*, a nebulous historical preservation society based in Rome. Construction records from the late 1980s confirmed major renovations to the famed Castel Sant'Angelo, underwritten by the same group. And blueprints revealed the extensive work done to parts of the building that were not on the tour route.

Even without the exhaustive compilation, Pierce would have believed her. Dioscuri was the Latin name for Castor and Pollux, the Gemini twins, also known as the Tyndarids—sons of Tyndareus. Their enemy seemed to have a fondness for that particular theme.

Pierce crossed the footbridge over the Fiume Tevere, moving against the current of visitors departing the imposing circular edifice.

The structure had served as a mausoleum to Roman emperors, a military fortress, a prison where enemies of the Vatican were held and executed and presently as a national museum. Everything felt so normal that Pierce wondered if they had gotten something wrong.

"It just seems awfully public for the headquarters of a criminal empire." It was an understatement. Situated less than a quarter of a mile from Vatican City, the *Museo Nazionale di Castel Sant'Angelo* was in all the guidebooks, and it was one of the most frequently visited landmarks west of the Tiber.

"Camouflage," Lazarus said, walking beside him. "They're hiding in plain sight."

Pierce didn't know if that was a good thing. He had expected Cerberus Headquarters to be a walled compound, ringed with razor wire, patrolled by uniformed guards with machine guns and dogs. If it had been, he would have brought a squad of Aegis operators, armed to the teeth with all the latest military specs. But for sneaking into a secret basement in a 1,900 year-old castle-turned-museum, less was better, or so Lazarus had assured him.

"Just the two of us," the big man had said. "Stealth will serve us better than overwhelming force."

If Kenner was to be believed, most of the Cerberus staff had perished in the sinkhole. Only a token force had remained behind with the head of Cerberus, a man that Kenner had identified as Pollux Tyndareus.

Kenner had not been able to tell them much about Tyndareus, aside from the fact that he was extremely old and very interested in exploiting exotic scientific discoveries for profit. The name was almost certainly an alias, but Dourado had been unable to learn anything about the man, or who he might really be.

As Pierce approached the entrance to the Castel, a museum attendant rushed to intercept him. "The museum is closing, *signore*. No more tickets today."

"I'm here to see the director," Pierce replied, his Italian perfect, his manner imperious. "I have an appointment."

The attendant stared at Lazarus with undisguised skepticism. Both he and Pierce wore loose fitting jackets, which concealed both body armor and weapons, but Lazarus had added a baseball cap, with the bill pulled down low to conceal the scars on his face. The wounds had healed with astonishing rapidity, but even with the tiger-stripe pattern of new pink skin hidden from view, his size alone made him stand out in a crowd. "Both of you?"

"Say that he's your *consigliere*," Dourado suggested in Pierce's ear. "Like Sil in *The Sopranos*."

Pierce ignored her. "Yes. Both of us."

The attendant shrugged and waved them through.

They passed through the gateway and entered the open walkway that separated the outer walls from the main fortress. Dourado had loaded the blueprints into their phones, along with turn-by-turn instructions to get them to the locked door that would access the secret basement levels under the building, but Pierce did not need to consult them. He knew the place like the back of his hand, and not just because he had studied the maps during the final leg of their flight. Pierce had been here before.

It had been years since his last visit, but one thing about a city like Rome, where you couldn't throw a Frisbee without hitting a historically significant landmark, was that nothing really ever changed. But as he was fond of telling his students, even in an old place, you can still find something new.

They passed through a long corridor with walls of travertine blocks, through the atrium, where a statue of the famed Roman emperor Hadrian had once stood, and descended the ramp that led to his tomb. Their destination lay along that route, beneath a sign that read: *ascensore*. Elevator.

The lift was a relatively new addition to the Castel. It was only three hundred years old, installed by Pope Clement XII in 1734. In addition to being the Vatican's Death Row for several centuries, Castel Sant'Angelo was also a secondary papal residence, connected to Vatican City by a half-mile long aboveground tunnel called the *Passetto di Borgo*. Clement XII, one of the oldest men ever to be elected as pontiff, had been a forward thinker with respect to accessibility.

The elevator had been upgraded since its installation. Now it looked like a relic from the early 1900s. Pierce and Lazarus waited until the corridor was empty before opening the door and moving into the waiting cage-style car. Pierce slotted a skeleton key into the control panel, and then turned the manual control wheel to the left. Beyond this point, they would have no communication with Dourado. No way to call for help.

As the car descended, Lazarus opened his jacket and readied his MP5K. "Remember why we're here," he told Pierce. "Everyone that isn't Fiona is hostile."

"Thanks for the 'stay frosty' speech, but I've done this before. With Jack." Pierce said.

Lazarus smiled. "Heard you punched a woman."

Pierce shrugged. "She had it coming."

It wasn't true. The woman had been another trespasser at the Roman Forum he had mistaken for a guard, but his nonchalance pulled a chuckle from Lazarus. He'd heard about this routine. Soldiers joking before battle. Reaffirming a bond, like friendship, but deeper. He'd experienced it with Jack, but never with the big man who so rarely said anything.

Lazarus added, "I'll take point. You watch my six."

The elevator descended through alternating layers of masonry and bedrock until arriving at the basement. Officially, the subterranean levels of the fortress remained unexcavated, but clearly that was not the whole story. A simple passage led away from the elevator. A metal door awaited them at the far end. Although newer than the elevator, it was shrouded in cobwebs and spotted with corrosion.

"Doesn't look like anyone's used this door in ages," Pierce remarked. "They must have another way in. Something that doesn't show on the blueprints."

"That may work in our favor," Lazarus said.

Pierce approached the door and swept it with his black box. The readings showed no electrical fields indicating an alarm system, so he tried the door. "Locked."

"I'll knock." Lazarus stepped forward and placed a length of what looked like foam insulation over the latch plate, fixing it in place with tape. He motioned for Pierce to back up a few steps, and then he hit the detonator switch. There was a loud bang, like a car backfiring, and the door flew open. Lazarus immediately charged through, his MP5K at the ready. Pierce moved in behind him, searching for a target in the smoky room.

Pierce recognized the corridor from both the blueprints and firsthand accounts from Gallo and Kenner. There were doors to either side, and at the far end, a modern elevator, but little else of note.

"It's clear," Lazarus said. "But stay sharp. We don't know what's behind these doors."

Pierce maintained a watch on the corridor while Lazarus methodically searched each room. They found personal quarters, classrooms and storage closets, but no Cerberus personnel and no Fiona. As they neared the end, Pierce finally voiced the thought that had been nagging at him for several minutes.

"Where is everyone?"

"We knew there would be minimal personnel," Lazarus said. From his tone, Pierce guessed that the big man was as anxious about the situation as he. He stared at the sliding metal doors to the elevator for several seconds, then walked toward it.

The doors slid open revealing an empty car. Lazarus stepped inside, but as Pierce moved to join him, he raised a hand. "Better wait here."

"If they're waiting for you," Pierce said, "you're going to need me."

"If they're waiting, they'll kill us both."

Before Pierce could protest, the doors closed and he was left alone.

FORTY-FOUR

The doors opened and Lazarus shot out of the elevator like a burst from a machine gun. If there was an ambush waiting, he would have only a millisecond to acquire a target and fire before the bullets began tearing into him. His Kevlar vest would stop some of the rounds, especially if the Cerberus men were armed with pistols and shooting nine-mil, but some of their shots would undoubtedly find unprotected areas of his body—arms, legs, head—and he would go down.

He would die, but that would only be a temporary problem. What mattered was that he would be rendered combat ineffective.

To give Pierce a fighting chance at rescuing Fiona, he had to kill as many hostiles as he could, as quickly as he could, and to do that, he would have to be more than just Lazarus, the man who came back. He would need to be the man he had left behind on the bottom of Lake Kivu. He would need the rage again.

All his life, it had been with him...*in* him. He had never understood why. The traumas of his early childhood played a role, but they did not explain the intensity of his primal anger. Being a soldier had given him a way to channel the emotional firestorm that always burned within him, but that was not a solution. Rather, it just added fuel to the fire.

The regenerative serum had changed all that, forced him to control that which had always controlled him, because if his focus slipped, he would become nothing *but* rage. Yet, control was not the same as peace. The fire never went out. Not until Felice.

She had shown him that rage was not, as he often believed, his oldest and only true friend. It was a drug, and he was an addict. She had shown him how to kick the habit.

Like any addiction, the urges never completely went away, but every day that passed, every quiet moment spent meditating, every second in Felice's arms, made it easier. Made him believe in a life without rage.

He knew how to tap into it, to make it work for him. He had done it in Liberia to survive the carnivorous plants and rescue Felice and the others. He had used it to withstand the assault of the Stymphalian birds, to help her and Pierce reach safety. Now, he needed to unleash it to save Fiona.

And to kill the bastards that took her.

It wasn't enough. Indignation wasn't enough. He couldn't just throw a switch and decide to be mad. He needed more. He needed pain.

He needed to remember what that felt like. The birds tearing into his flesh. The vines, burning his skin like acid. The lake...

The lake filling his lungs and extinguishing his life again and again and again...

A red mist filled his eyes as he surged out of the elevator car.

Kill the bastards!

Except there was nobody to kill. This hallway was as empty as the first. Without waiting for Pierce to catch up, he began clearing rooms, kicking in doors one after another, his frustration mounting with each discovery of absolutely nothing. With each empty room, the anger built within him like the pressure in a volcano, demanding release.

"Erik!"

He wheeled toward the sound of the voice, his finger finding the trigger, squeezing...

He barely managed to jerk the muzzle up before the bullets started flying. The ceiling erupted in a shower of broken plaster, which rained down on the man standing at the other end of the hallway. George Pierce stared at him in wide-eyed disbelief.

Anger continued to boil within him, but now it was self-directed. He had given in to the urge, taken the fix, convinced himself it was the only way to win, and it had almost cost Pierce his life. He closed his eyes and tried to quiet his rapid breathing.

He could almost hear Felice's voice in his head. *You are, without a doubt, the strongest, toughest, most badass person I've ever met. But there's something inside you...eating at you.*

I can help.

I want to.

He needed her now. Needed her to talk him down.

Maybe I'm not as strong as you thought, Felice.

He opened his eyes and looked at Pierce again. "No one here," he said. "The place is completely deserted. We missed them."

Pierce blinked, the shock of almost getting killed starting to fade. Then his eyes went wide and he brought his gun up. The motion was so abrupt that Lazarus did not have time to react before Pierce pulled the trigger. He saw the puffs of smoke leaving the end of the suppressor, and felt waves of pressure buffeting him as bullets creased the air to either side of him, but none of the rounds struck him.

There was a cry of pain from behind Lazarus, followed by the thump of a body hitting the ground. Then another.

Pierce lowered his gun.

Lazarus turned and was surprised to discover a pair of bodies—men, wearing charcoal gray combat fatigues—sprawled out behind him. He had no idea where the duo had been lurking. All he knew for sure was that Pierce had just saved his life.

One of the guards was definitely dead, a hole drilled neatly between his eyes. The other was still alive and reaching for the pistol that had fallen from his grasp when Pierce's bullet had punched into his chest. Lazarus strode over and kicked the gun out of the man's reach.

Pierce knelt beside the stricken man. "Where is everyone?" he demanded. "Where's Fiona?"

The man stared up at him, face twisted in pain, but eyes defiant. Lazarus doubted the man was capable of answering the question, but Pierce was not going to let him slip quietly into the hereafter. He punched the man's oozing chest wound. "Where is the girl? Is she here?"

The man shuddered and let out a gasp, and then his eyes rolled back in his head, his body deflating. Pierce, however, did not relent. He kept shouting the question until Lazarus reached out and put a hand on Pierce's shoulder. "George. He's gone."

Pierce sagged back. "Damn it."

"We'll find her."

Pierce climbed to his feet and raised his pistol to a ready firing stance. "I appreciate what you were trying to do back there, but we're supposed to be doing this together, okay? No more rogue ops."

Lazarus nodded. "Roger that." He stood up and gestured to the bodies. "Good work. I think you've officially graduated to badass."

Pierce managed a wan smile.

"Did you see where they came from?" Lazarus continued. "I thought I checked all the rooms."

Pierce pointed down the hall. "That way. Maybe there's a secret door. Something that isn't included in the blueprint."

Lazarus stared down at the dead gunmen again, this time taking note of the ID badges clipped to their belts. He plucked one up. "I think you're right. This is a proximity key card. Let's go see what it opens."

Pierce took the second key card. "Sounds like a plan."

As they approached the end of the hall, a section of wall slid aside. Lazarus and Pierce went through the opening with their guns at the ready, but there was no one to shoot at. The room beyond the secret door was as deserted as the rest of the compound.

It was not however, empty.

FORTY-FIVE

Gallo had no memory of the tunnel or the small parking garage just off the Via Cossa where it began—or ended, depending on which direction you were going—but things began looking familiar once she reached the other side.

Coming back was a bittersweet experience. She had left as Kenner's hostage, cooperating with him only to ensure Fiona's safety. Now, her former prison was under Herculean Society control and Kenner was the captive.

But Fiona was missing, and all the battles they had won meant nothing.

As Pierce walked them through the facility, Gallo realized that she had seen only a small fraction of the place. Aside from an entire floor of guest quarters, several of which were much more accommodating than the room where she had been kept, there were libraries and laboratories, conference rooms, even a movie theater.

There was an entire lab devoted to genetics research, which prompted Carter to ask Pierce if he had kept the receipt for the SMRT sequencer he'd bought for her. "Because there's no way I'm going back to that cave."

Lazarus flashed a smile at the comment, but said nothing. He was a strange man, and although she had known him for only about a day, Gallo sensed that even Pierce, whose history with the man went back several years, had barely scratched the surface.

They moved on to a computer server room with hardware that almost brought Dourado to tears. "Can you hack your way into this?" Pierce asked her. "And figure out where they went? Where Fiona is?"

"I am looking forward to trying," she replied with an eagerness bordering on hunger.

Pierce let her skip the rest of the tour.

After they passed through a gallery filled with priceless art and artifacts ranging from Neolithic to neo-classical, Pierce held them back for a moment. "The next room isn't going to be easy," he said. "But I think it will explain a lot about who we're dealing with."

With that ominous warning, he led them into a room that was filled with the stuff of nightmares. Gallo immediately realized that she was looking at images from the Holocaust, but it took a little longer to grasp the ghastly intent behind the collection. After that, she stopped looking until Pierce brought them to a trophy case filled with Nazi memorabilia.

Kenner, who had been unusually quiet up to that point, let out a gasp. He nodded at the photographs in the case. "Oh, God. It's him. That's Tyndareus."

The outburst prompted Gallo to take a closer look at the pictures and documents in the display. One name stood out. "That's not possible. He's dead."

"Are you certain?" Pierce locked eyes with Kenner, but Gallo got the sense that he was not at all surprised by the news. "Augustina's right. Josef Mengele died over thirty years ago. His remains are locked in a safe in Brazil. The DNA was checked against known relatives."

Kenner shook his head. "No. That's Tyndareus. He's older now, of course, but I'd recognize that..." He looked as if he was about to throw up. "That smile. My God. What have I done? I was helping that monster."

"So kidnapping and attempted murder were okay when you weren't working for a Nazi?" Pierce asked. Kenner feigned disgust for a moment, but Pierce cut him off with a raised hand. "Liam, I just want to know one thing. Where is he now?"

Kenner shook his head. "I promised him the source. The Well of Monsters. I thought I would find the location in the Amazon city, but there was nothing there."

"In the myths, the monsters came from the Underworld," Gallo said. "That's where their mother Echidna lived. If there is some kind of...something...that can create monsters, that's where we'll find it."

Pierce considered this, then lowered his voice as if sharing a secret. "Hercules—the real Hercules—did visit the Underworld. I don't mean Hell. A real place. We have records of a massive underground network—we're talking global in scope—that almost certainly corresponds to the Underworld of Greek mythology. There are dozens of entrances though, and probably thousands of miles of connecting passages. It would be virtually impossible to simply stumble onto a specific location."

He paused, looked at Kenner again and then at Gallo. "He learned the location of the entrance from the Amazons, right? So the answer has to be on the map."

Gallo shot an accusing glance at Kenner, but she knew she shared some of the blame. "Tyndareus must have forced Fiona to translate it for him."

"We need to figure out how to read it, too," Pierce said. "Were there any clues in the *Heracleia* that might narrow it down?"

"If it's still here, I'll go through it again."

"I might be able to help," Carter said, raising a tentative hand. "Remember how I told you that the DNA of the hybrids might help us narrow down the geographical location of the parent animals? Well, I haven't had a chance to sequence that bird I brought back yet, but I can tell you that it looks like a cross between a great egret and a porcupine. Probably a lot of other contributors as well, but those two species account for most of the dominant traits. Now, egrets don't help us since they're found on every continent, but the quills are similar to those found on the body of the North American porcupine."

"North American?" Pierce said. "Just like the Lion?

Carter nodded. "I can use the equipment here to verify it, but I'd say the odds are good that these hybrids originated in North America."

"That doesn't exactly narrow it down," Pierce said.

Gallo felt as if scales had fallen from her eyes. "I know where it is. In the *Heracleia*, it says that Herakles found the Underworld 'in a burning land, with poisonous air, at the center of a lake of fire.'"

"That's pretty typical imagery for the Land of the Dead," Pierce countered.

Gallo shook her head. "That was where he found the entrance. Before he went into the Underworld. Ancient historians tried to pinpoint its location from the stories. The Greeks believed it was in a cave at Cape Matapan, but that doesn't fit the physical description. A much better candidate is Mount Chimaera in Lycia—modern-day Turkey—because it's a very geologically active location with burning methane pockets that erupt from the ground. But those were just educated guesses based on their limited knowledge of the world. They didn't know the Americas even existed.

"There's a place in North America that matches that description. It's one of the most geologically active places in the world. The Yellowstone caldera."

"Yellowstone," Pierce echoed. His tone was more thoughtful than disbelieving.

"Of course," Kenner exclaimed. "It's a perfect fit."

Gallo shot him a withering look. "No one asked you.

Kenner ignored her. "But that's still a lot of ground to cover."

Pierce looked up. "No, it isn't." He turned to Gallo, a hungry gleam in his eyes. "We're not looking for the entrance to the Underworld. Tyndareus is, and he's the one who's got his work cut out for him. We're looking for Fiona, and now we know where she is, assuming that she reached the same conclusion you did.

"He's got her. We're going to get her back." He looked around the gathering, as if daring anyone to question his decision. No one did. His gaze settled on the SS uniform in the display. "We're done here."

FORTY-SIX

Yellowstone National Park, Wyoming, USA

For as long as she could remember, Yellowstone National Park had been one of those places that Fiona knew she would have to visit someday. If she had been a little older, she might have called it a 'bucket list' item.

Guess I'll get to cross it off before I die, she thought.

Her knowledge of the park was piecemeal. She knew about the grizzly bears that roamed the forest, and knew that you weren't supposed to feed them. She knew about the geysers, especially Old Faithful, which spewed superheated steam on a schedule you could set your watch by, though she also recalled hearing that it wasn't as 'faithful' as it once had been. She knew that scientists were worried about a super-volcano underneath the park, a gigantic underground bubble of magma, which in addition to boiling the water for the geysers, was also going to erupt any day and bury half the United States in ash—or maybe it wouldn't happen for a hundred thousand years. All of these things were interesting to her, but there were a lot of places in the world that she wanted to visit, and she knew she would get there eventually. Yellowstone was practically in her back yard, after all.

But this was *not* how she wanted to see it.

When she had identified a particular set of Phaistos symbols on the map's border, which combined to form the phrase 'the land of the god ruling the dead,' and crossed at a point near the center of the ancient depiction of North America, she did not immediately grasp that the spot fell within the boundaries of the world's first national park. Midwestern geography had never been her strong suit.

But Tyndareus had known exactly where it was without needing to consult a more current map. "Yes. That is the place. We shall leave immediately."

Within the hour, the old man, along with his entire staff, including Nurse Wretched, had loaded up and headed out. Fiona had been blindfolded for the drive, so she had no idea where they had left from. When the blindfold was removed, she found herself in the passenger cabin of a medium-sized jet. It was larger than the Herculean Society's Gulfstream, with rows of seats like a regular commercial airliner, but she and the Cerberus team were the only passengers. Tyndareus had evidently chartered a plane to take them to their destination, which explained how they had been able to avoid airport security and nagging questions about the identity of a blindfolded hostage.

The flight was long, but the food was significantly better than the fare she had been fed so far, and the regularity with which it was served helped her mark the passage of time. Shortly after the fifth meal—somewhere between ten and fifteen hours after leaving the Cerberus facility, if her estimation was correct—she was brought to Tyndareus.

"We will be landing in a few hours," he said, his manner as offhand as his age and its associated afflictions would allow. "Then we will drive to the coordinates you supplied. Unfortunately, the map is of such a scale that the target area is more than a hundred square miles. Hardly an ideal situation, wouldn't you agree?"

Fiona shrugged. "It's the best I could do with what you gave me."

"Mmmm. Yes." He tented his fingers in front of his face. "I've just heard from Mr. Rohn. As you predicted, the Amazon yielded nothing of substance, though we did find evidence to support both your interpretation of the map and Dr. Kenner's underlying premise." He paused a beat, then added, "He also reported to me that Dr. Gallo made an ill-advised attempt to escape."

The news caught Fiona off-guard. She almost said, 'Good for her,' but Tyndareus had also used the word *attempt*. "Is she okay?"

A faint smile curled the old man's lips. "She took a foolish risk with your life, child. I was quite clear about the consequences of such an action. Now, she's put me in a rather awkward position. You have become far more valuable to me as a resource than as a hostage, yet I cannot let this rebellion go unpunished. I am a man of my word."

"Bullshit!"

Tyndareus flinched under the verbal assault. Out of the corner of her eye, Fiona saw the goons moving to defend their boss, but she was done playing nice. "Aunt Gus only cooperated with you because you threatened to hurt me, and then as soon as she was gone, you used me as a lab rat. You planned to kill us both right from the start, so don't even talk to me about keeping your word."

Tyndareus's weird blue eyes flashed dangerously. "You will not pay the price for her mistakes, child, but be assured, she will most certainly pay for yours, so choose your words with greater care."

The threat stopped Fiona's rising ire cold. She bit back another retort. "Fine. I'm sorry."

"Do you need a demonstration? Shall I have Mr. Rohn bring us one of her hands? I will let you choose which. Left or right?"

"I said, I'm sorry," Fiona replied through clenched teeth. She was pretty sure that the old man was just trying to make a point, but what if he was serious? "I'll help you."

The silence that followed quickly grew uncomfortable, prompting Fiona to raise her eyes to him once more.

"I trust you understand how vital it is that you cooperate with me," he said. "For your own safety and Dr. Gallo's." He watched her for a moment, a lopsided smile making a brief appearance. "The map coordinates you gave us are not precise enough. I need to know if there is any other information on the map that can narrow our search parameters. Perhaps something that you have been intentionally withholding from me."

Fiona felt a chill shoot through her veins. *He knows about the Mother Tongue. But how? Did Aunt Gus let something slip? Did that animal Rohn torture her? Or is Tyndareus bluffing again?*

Two can play that game.

"The writing on that map is a form of Linear A, the language of the Minoan culture, which lived almost four thousand years ago." Her voice was terse, as if weary of explaining herself. "If you think I'm holding back, go hire somebody else to read it. Oh, that's right. *Nobody* knows how to read it. Half of what I did was guesswork. The other half was luck."

She took a breath, held it a moment then went on in a more conciliatory tone. "I do know this. The ancient Minoans used language as a way of protecting their secrets from the unworthy. They left signs in the Labyrinth as a test. If you could read the signs, you could find your way out. If not, you'd wander around forever. They probably left similar signs pointing the way to the Underworld."

"You think we'll find these signs once we get there?"

She nodded. "Actual, literal road markers that only someone who reads Linear A would recognize."

This seemed to satisfy Tyndareus. He made a shooing motion, signaling that the audience was at an end.

That had been eight hours ago. Their flight had arrived in Montana in the middle of the night. She identified the state by the license plates on the convoy of vehicles waiting for them on the tarmac. She was ushered into one, along with two of the Cerberus goons. She didn't recognize the driver, a big guy with a shaved head and what she assumed were prison tattoos on his neck. He looked like a biker or a recruit from the local Aryan Nations chapter. There were two vans and a larger Ryder truck, each with a pair of White Power dudes, which brought the total size of the Cerberus contingent to fourteen, not counting Tyndareus and Nurse Wretched. The latter pair rode in a different vehicle.

It was only when she saw road signs with the mileage to the park that Fiona finally realized where they were going.

The passing scenery reminded Fiona of the Mt. Hood National Forest, near where she had grown up. It was not just the natural landscape, but also the towns, which had a sort of faux rustic charm. Window dressing for the tourists.

They passed beneath the stone arch at the North Entrance as dawn was lightening the sky, and continued into the park on the Grand Loop Road. Not long thereafter, Fiona noticed a change in the scenery. She did not need a map to see that they were entering geyser country.

Vents of steam erupting from the earth. Pools of boiling acidic water. Bubbling cauldrons of mud. Exactly the sort of place to find a doorway into Hell, she thought.

About half an hour later, the convoy pulled to the side of the road. "What's going on?" Fiona asked. She did not get a direct answer. Instead, the goons got out and told her to follow.

When the door opened, she got a whiff of sulfur that made her eyes water. The next thing she noticed was the heat. The thin, high-altitude air felt cool when she breathed in, yet the pavement underfoot radiated heat like a parking lot in the dead of summer, so much so that she dared not stand still for too long.

The Cerberus men walked her to the van in the lead, where Tyndareus was riding. The front row of passenger seats had been removed to accommodate his wheelchair, which was anchored to the floor with nylon tie-downs.

"This is as close to our destination as the road will take us," he told her. "My men will move out on foot, looking for the signs that you promised we would find."

"I don't know if I would use the word *promised*."

"What should they be looking for?" Tyndareus asked, ignoring the comment.

"Phaistos symbols, like on the map."

"Where?"

She shrugged. "Carved on rocks. Like petroglyphs."

Tyndareus turned to his nearest associate. "You heard her. Begin the search. Instruct the men to send photographs of anything they discover."

"Am I going to have to go out there?" Fiona asked.

"I would prefer you remain here with me," Tyndareus replied. "That way, you can verify anything my men discover."

"Whatever." Though she was somewhat relieved by the fact that she would not have to venture out into the alien landscape, hanging out with Tyndareus was not much better. But as she watched the Cerberus men—all but the two who had been assigned to watch over her—move out across the blasted terrain, she realized that she might never get a better chance to escape. All she would have to do was ditch Nurse Wretched and the two goons, and flag down a passing car. It would be that easy.

Except she knew that it wouldn't. And there were other considerations as well. Tyndareus had made it clear that Gallo would pay dearly for any display of resistance.

He's going to kill us both, she thought. *Even if he gets what he wants.*

She knew it was true, just as she knew that Gallo would never want her to cooperate with Tyndareus just to buy her a brief reprieve. Being part of the Herculean Society meant being willing to sacrifice everything to preserve those ancient secrets, to keep them out of the wrong hands. Fiona had already given Tyndareus too much, brought him too close. She couldn't wait any longer.

One by one, the searchers disappeared into the roiling convection waves or dropped behind terrain features that eclipsed them from her view. She settled back into her chair, biding her time, counting the cars that passed by. Traffic was light, but she suspected that it would increase as the day progressed. Tyndareus might be willing to kill a lone Good Samaritan stopping to help a running girl, but she doubted he would do so in front of dozens of witnesses. He had not evaded capture for more than seventy years by being reckless.

A silver sedan passed the parked vehicles a few minutes later, slowing as if the driver was curious.

Too soon, she thought. But she could not afford to pass up an opportunity.

Without moving, she calculated the distance to the door, rehearsing the sequence of moves that would be required to unlock it, open it and hit the ground running. The guards would make a grab for her. She would have to be ready for that. Fiona shifted in her chair, stretching casually, as she readied herself.

On your mark...

The sedan stopped and pulled off the road, right in front of them.

Get set...

The door opened and the driver got out. It was Rohn.

As the big man strode along the roadside to the van, Fiona slumped back, her enthusiasm extinguished. She had come within a heartbeat of making a fatal mistake, one that would not only get her killed, but also...

She sat up again. "Where's Aunt Gus?"

"In a secure place," Tyndareus said, without looking at her. "Safe, as long as you continue to behave."

The door opened and Rohn climbed in, taking a seat alongside Fiona. She shied away, as if his mere proximity was revolting to her, but he remained indifferent to her. Tyndareus did not overtly acknowledge Rohn's presence, nor did Rohn seem to expect any greeting.

Only now did Fiona see the cuts on his face and hands, swollen flesh, exposed sutures stained with antiseptic, crusted with dried blood and oozing fluid. He looked like he'd gone toe-to-toe with a weed whacker and lost.

Did Aunt Gus do that? If so, good for her. No wonder Tyndareus is pissed.

As the initial shock of Rohn's arrival wore off, she resumed plotting her escape. It would be harder with the big man right beside her, but she would have to find a way. If she did not make her move soon...

The electronic trilling of a cell phone broke her train of thought.

"Ah, good," Tyndareus said. "We've found something."

Damn.

The old man stared at the phone for several seconds, his eyes widening with undisguised excitement as he studied the image. "It would seem that we have found one of your road signs. I don't believe it will need any translation however."

He turned the phone, showing her the displayed image, a lump of sandstone jutting above the flat brown earth with a single glyph etched into its surface. Though the passage of time and centuries of wind and rain had worn away at it, the sign remained legible.

A circle crossed by two vertical lines. The sign of the Herculean Society.

She tore her gaze away from the image. "You know what that means, don't you? The Society was already here. You won't find anything."

"Is that what it means? I think it is meant as a warning. 'Keep out. No Trespassing.'" Tyndareus chuckled. "It is a warning I have no intention of heeding. I think we should see for ourselves what the Herculean Society has been protecting. Vigor, keep an eye on the child. Do not underestimate her. She is quite remarkable."

Rohn grunted in assent, and then he took her wrist in his hand. She tried to pull free, but his grip was as unyielding as an iron manacle. He got out, dragging her with him, but was careful to keep her behind the van, shielded from the view of any passing cars. The other Cerberus men got out as well, and then proceeded to lift Tyndareus, wheelchair and all, out of the van.

"You're going, too?" she said, making no real effort to hide her contempt. "I don't think the trails around here are ADA approved. Or are you going to be carried the whole way like Yoda?"

Tyndareus returned a cryptic smile, then he tapped the joystick control and began rolling along the gravel shoulder until he reached the truck's rear end. Rohn followed, pulling Fiona along. The other men had already rushed ahead to deploy the hydraulic liftgate and open the rollup door. Fiona did a double-take when she saw what was inside.

A familiar gray figure—man-shaped, but not a man—stood in the center of the cargo bay like a guardian statue.

It was the exosuit.

Tyndareus chuckled again. "It won't be a problem."

FORTY-SEVEN

The men moved across the landscape like pawns on a chessboard, guided by an invisible hand. *That's probably exactly how Tyndareus sees them,* Pierce thought. *Disposable soldiers, sacrificed without a second thought. Why would anyone want to work for a guy like that?*

"Cintia, can you get a head count? How many are we dealing with?"

"Eighteen," Lazarus said. "One of them might be Fiona."

"Yes, eighteen," Dourado said, her tone faintly irritated. "Fortunately, I can do a lot better than just counting."

A moment later, Pierce saw what she meant. The image displayed on the LCD computer screen zoomed in on one of them, close enough for Pierce to distinguish the gun—Lazarus identified it as an AR15—slung across the man's back. A yellow rectangle appeared, superimposed on the man, and then the perspective pulled back momentarily to acquire another target in the same fashion.

"Keep going," Pierce said. "Tag them all."

He looked away from the screen and let his eyes drift across the strange landscape of the Norris Basin geothermal area of Yellowstone

National Park. The terrain was an assault on the senses. Thin, high-altitude mountain air that could make people feel giddy. The sky was wide and open, no shelter from the sun. Then there was the pervasive stench of sulfur. The worst part was the intense heat rising up from the ground, which could burn right through the shoe soles if someone stood in one place too long. Norris Basin was one of the hottest spots in the park, the temperature often high enough to liquefy the asphalt on the roads.

As disconcerting as the environment was, it was the enormity of the task set before him that was truly staggering. He wondered if Alexander had felt this way before setting out on his Labors.

Pierce, Gallo, Lazarus and Carter—Kenner, too, though as far as Pierce was concerned, he didn't count—had left Rome shortly after determining Tyndareus's likely destination. Dourado remained behind in Rome, ensconced in the computer room of the Cerberus Headquarters beneath Castel Sant'Angelo, under the protection of Aegis operatives brought in by Pierce. When Pierce had asked her if she was ready to go back into the field, the resulting look of horror had prompted him to laugh it off. "Just kidding. I'll let you get back to your new toys."

It had taken her about an hour to crack the security on the mainframe, at which point she had informed Pierce that they 'powned Cerberus.' Maybe Dourado's grasp of English was not quite as firm as she believed, but her statement was more than just trash talk. The secret base and everything in it, as well as the not inconsiderable assets stashed in tax shelters and banks around the world, were spoils of war, transferred to the Society with a keystroke. Just as ancient Herakles had subdued but not killed the three-headed hellhound guarding the gates of the Underworld, the Herculean Society had captured the modern Cerberus largely intact. The entity was theirs now, to do with as they pleased.

But it was a hollow victory. Fiona was still a captive and Tyndareus was closing in on his goal—Echinda, the Well of Monsters.

Even before she succeeded in taking over the Cerberus computer, Dourado was able to confirm their deductions about Yellowstone by tracing the movements of the Cerberus Learjet. It had departed from Belem shortly before their own rescue helicopter had arrived, presumably carrying Kohn and anyone else from his team that might have survived the expedition to the Amazon city. The jet had not returned to Rome as expected, but rather had made a short hop to São Paulo for a layover, before heading north again, hopscotching across two continents but headed for Billings, Montana, the closest major airport to Yellowstone.

Dourado then identified a chartered flight from Rome to the same airport, and several vehicle rentals, all of which traced to Cerberus fronts. All of the vehicles were equipped with GPS locators, which she promptly hacked and tracked to a spot in the park at the edge of the Norris Basin geothermal area, just a few miles north of Old Faithful, where they had been sitting idle ever since. Unfortunately, the data could not reveal anything about the passengers, particularly whether Fiona was with them.

Upon their arrival, Dourado had guided Pierce and the others right to the vehicles, but just like Cerberus Headquarters, the vans appeared to have been abandoned. Tyndareus and his men had set out on foot to explore the alien-looking landscape. But Dourado had anticipated that possibility.

There had been a package waiting for them when they arrived in Billings. In addition to the computer and Bluetooth-enabled smart-phones, all of which were networked through an accompanying high-speed satellite data modem, Dourado had supplied them with a DJI Phantom 3 quad-copter camera drone. With a line-of-sight range of just over a mile and a 1080p digital video camera, the little remote aircraft gave them a bird's eye view that extended several miles in all directions. Dourado talked Pierce through the process of slaving the drone controller to the computer, and then took over, flying the Phantom from the other side of the world. It took only a few minutes for her to spot the large group of hikers, about two miles southwest of the parked cars. They were moving slowly as they blazed a trail through a part of Yellowstone that was not only off-limits but generally hostile to living creatures.

"Stop!" Pierce said as something on the screen caught his eye. "Cintia, go back. Rewind a couple of frames, or whatever it is you do."

"What did you see?" Gallo asked, looking over his shoulder.

The perspective zoomed out to a wide-angle shot, and Pierce now saw a little yellow box displayed above each vaguely human figure. *Forget chess*, Pierce decided. *This is more like watching Monday Night Football.* "Number eleven," he said. "What is that?"

"I set this up to be completely interactive," Dourado said. "The computer has a touch screen. You can just tap on whatever—"

"Cintia, please. Just do it."

There was an irritated "humph" from the speaker, then the shot zoomed in on Pierce's selection. At a casual glance, it looked like a man, but a closer look revealed something else.

"What the hell is that?"

"It looks like RoboCop," Dourado said, with just a trace of awe.

Pierce turned to Kenner. "Liam, do you know what that is?"

Kenner shook his head, but Dourado jumped in with the answer. "It's *Talos*."

Pierce wondered if he had heard her correctly. In Greek mythology, Talos was a giant living statue, made of bronze and powered by *ichor*, the magical blood of the gods. He had seen too much to dismiss the possibility that the myth might have some foundation in reality. Had Tyndareus located an ancient automaton—perhaps one of Alexander's early experimental creations—and restored it to working order?

"The name is an acronym for Tactical Light Operator Suit," Lazarus said. "It's an armored, powered exoskeleton designed for use by the U.S. military. I thought they were still on the drawing board."

"It is like Iron Man's armor," Dourado added. "There's a whole section of the Cerberus mainframe dedicated to it. They stole the specs from Lockheed Martin. It uses a FORTIS load-bearing wearable exoskeleton, but the exterior shell is made of hollow titanium panels, filled with Kevlar fibers suspended in a non-Newtonian shearing fluid."

Pierce understood about half of what she said. "Fine. They've got a TALOS suit. Good to know. Any sign of Fiona?"

The camera view pulled back, and Dourado resumed the process of scanning and tagging each member of Tyndareus's group. The display tightened on a pair of walking figures that appeared to be holding hands, and Pierce felt his heart skip a beat as he recognized not only Fiona's dark hair and slim build, but also the man who held onto her wrist.

"Rohn." He spat the name out like a mouthful of bile.

"And the man in the suit must be Tyndareus," Kenner said in a flat voice. Pierce regarded their prisoner for a moment, then turned to Lazarus who was staring at the computer screen, which had reverted back to a wide-angle view. "Any tactical suggestions?"

There was a long delay before the answer. "We have to get her away from the main group." Another pause. "We'll need a diversion, something to divide their forces. I'll take care of that. A hit and run attack on their rear should draw some of them off. The rest of you can then move in and get Fiona out."

"We would also be dividing *our* forces," Pierce said. "You're the only one with any hostage rescue experience. I'll provide the diversion. You lead the rescue." As much as Pierce wanted to lead the charge, real leadership came from identifying your team's various skill sets and using them for the best possible outcome. Personal feelings just got in the way. He'd learned that from Fiona's father, though he doubted the man thought Pierce would ever have to put the lesson to use to save his daughter.

Before Lazarus could reply, Kenner spoke up. "There's a better way."

Pierce regarded him with open suspicion. Although the man had been nothing but cooperative since his capture, even more so since learning Tyndareus's true identity, Pierce was a long way from trusting Kenner. He had considered leaving the paleopharmacologist in Rome, but he didn't want to make him Dourado's responsibility. "Let's hear it."

Kenner looked at Gallo for a moment, as if hoping to elicit her support, then turned to Pierce. "Let me go to them. I can tell Tyndareus that I escaped from you in Brazil. Or better yet, I'll say you're dead. Then, as soon as I get the chance, I'll tell the girl..." He winced and glanced nervously at Lazarus. "Ah, Fiona. I'll tell Fiona to run."

Pierce did not know how to react. It was a good plan, maybe better than Lazarus's desperate diversion, but it would require trusting Kenner, and that was something Pierce was not ready to do. Before he could articulate a response, Gallo spoke up. "It won't work. Fiona would never trust you."

Thank you, Augustina.

Then she added. "I'll go with you."

"What?"

Gallo pushed ahead, ignoring Pierce's outburst. "We'll pretend that you captured me before escaping from the sinkhole. You can say that we figured out the Yellowstone connection together. We might even be able to convince him that you turned me."

Pierce managed a tight smile. "Augustina, may I speak with you privately?"

Gallo acceded without protest, allowing Pierce to guide her a few steps away from the others. If her determined bearing was any indication, she was not about to back down, but Pierce felt he had to try.

"This is a very bad idea."

"Actually, it's a very good idea," she countered, speaking in an urgent whisper. "You're right not to trust Liam. If we let him go alone, he'll sell us out in a heartbeat. But he won't put me at risk. He still has feelings for me, George."

The rationale surprised Pierce. "If he realizes you're playing him, he'll turn on you."

"I won't be playing him. I will simply provide an implicit reminder for him to do the right thing." She placed a hand on his forearm. "You and the others can follow at a discreet distance. Cintia can watch us from the drone. If I get in trouble, I'll give the signal, and then you can go to Plan B."

"Gus..."

"You risked your life to come get me. And I know you would do anything to get Fiona back. Let me take some of the risk for a change. I owe it to you, and I owe it to her. If I had done a better job of watching over her, none of this would have happened."

Pierce started to protest but she silenced him with a quick kiss on the lips.

"So it's settled," she said, as she pulled back. "Liam, let's get moving."

FORTY-EIGHT

In the course of her language studies, Fiona had become intimately familiar with the Land of the Dead, as imagined by countless Greek and Roman poets, and later figures such as Dante and Milton. There was a fantastical quality to each and every depiction. The poets were not trying to describe something real, but rather the stuff of nightmares. She never would have believed that a place like what was described in those works could actually exist on the surface of the Earth.

And this was only the doorstep of Hell.

Ignoring the warning signs—some of which were printed with the explicit message 'Danger. Thermal Area. Boiling Water. Unstable Ground. Do Not Enter' and others that simply depicted cartoon hikers being scalded alive in a steam eruption—Tyndareus, completely encased in his exosuit, led the small group out across the desolate hard pan. The servo motors in the exosuit made faint whirring noises as he moved, but the sound was mostly drowned out by the loud crunch of metal shod feet on the gritty earth. Each step stirred up a cloud of what looked like powdery snow but was actually sulfur dust.

After breaking through a thin crust of ground and sinking knee-deep into the boiling liquid concealed beneath, Tyndareus was a little more tentative about the path he chose, but at no time did he appear daunted by the hostile environment. Safe within the closed environment of the suit, breathing a self-contained air supply, there was not much for him to worry about. With Rohn dragging her along, Fiona had little choice about where to tread, but whenever possible, she tried to follow in Tyndareus's actual footsteps. If the ground could support the weight of the exosuit, then it could hold her up.

The danger of the ground giving way, however, was only one example of the weird unearthliness of the place. Steam rose from holes and cracks in the ground, then settled to form an eerie fog. There were small pools of water—some clear and dangerously inviting, other exhibiting jeweled hues of red, blue, green and yellow—and lakes of bubbling mud.

The foul air and pervasive heat sapped her energy. Five minutes into the trek, she was ready for a break, but the only thing worse than walking through the hellscape was standing still in it. She looked over her shoulder and located Nurse Wretched. The sneering woman looked even less happy about the situation than Fiona felt, which actually made Fiona feel a little better.

"Hey," she called out. "Got any water?"

The woman made a face that was even uglier than usual, and gestured to a nearby pool. "Drink up!"

Fiona was about to respond in kind when Rohn jerked her attention forward again. He held out a bottle of water and a Nature Valley granola bar. She muttered her thanks and stuffed the latter item into a back pocket. Then, with some difficulty, since Rohn had not released her left wrist, she got the bottle open and took a lukewarm sip.

Better, but not much.

They arrived at the rock with the Herculean symbol a few minutes later. At Tyndareus's behest, Fiona examined the inscription, but there was not much to say about it. She stared up at the reflective visor of the exosuit and shrugged. "I told you what it means," she said. "You won't find anything."

The mirrored visage stared back at her. "Your attempts to deceive me are ill-advised, child."

"I'm not trying to deceive you," she said, making no effort to hold back her growing frustration. "I just want to get out of here. I'm hot and thirsty, and I have to pee. This is a waste of time."

Tyndareus continued to regard her for a few more seconds then turned away. "Keep looking. There will be more markers like this."

He was not wrong. Two more stones with the Herculean mark were discovered, spaced out about half a mile apart in different directions. "I believe I understand the significance of the markers," Tyndareus announced after surveying the third. "We have found three, each approximately corresponding to a cardinal direction. I believe there is a fourth to be found as well, but we do not need it now. Our destination lies where the lines connecting north and south, and east and west, converge."

Fiona barely heard him. She was beyond thirst now. The constant heat was not only draining the moisture from her body but breaking down the insulin in her pump. She recognized the early symptoms of dehydration associated with diabetic ketoacidosis. The reek of sulfur had left her nose-blind, but her breath probably reeked of acetone. She needed to get somewhere cool, drink a couple of gallons of water, and change out the insulin in the reservoir, but that was not going to happen unless Tyndareus either found what he was looking for or admitted defeat, and since both seemed pretty unlikely, Fiona resigned herself to the alternative. She would eventually collapse. She might even die.

If that happened...when that happened...the secret would be safe forever. Tyndareus would never be able to open the gates of the Underworld.

The thought brought her a little comfort, until Tyndareus led them down into a dry ravine, which butted up against a rough extrusion of igneous rock. Faintly visible on its weathered surface was another Herculean sigil. Beside the symbol, a large section of the rock face was rougher in texture than the rest. It matched the color of the stone where Alexander's chisel had left its mark. As she stared at it, Fiona began to see shadowy lines in the stone, like an echo of what had once been written there.

An inscription written in the Mother Tongue.

The letters became more visible, as if her awareness of them was coaxing the ancient writing out of hiding.

"It was here," Tyndareus said, his voice a mixture of triumph and anger. He whirled around and bent toward Fiona until his visor was almost touching her face. "There was something written here. The Herculean Society removed it. What did it say?"

The letters vanished as though she had imagined them, but her memory of them was perfect. She had seen the same message before, on the walls of the Labyrinth and on the map that had belonged to Queen Hippolyte.

She felt a flicker of defiance as she stared, not at the face of the monstrous Tyndareus but at her own frail and beaten reflection. *It's almost over now.*

A line from an old Star Trek movie popped into her. The usually cool, reserved Captain Picard, in a rare display of anger, defiant in the face of a Borg invasion. It was probably a quote from Shakespeare or Moby Dick, or maybe the Bible. *Uncle George would know.*

She straightened. "You're right. It said, 'This far. No further.'"

A strange noise issued from the helmeted head, then repeated with greater frequency, until Fiona recognized it as laughter. Tyndareus pulled back, rising to his full height. He began slamming his armored fist into the Herculean symbol. The pistonlike assault pulverized the distinctive sigil, but the rock itself was unyielding.

This far. No further.

That should have been the end of it, but Tyndareus abruptly broke off his temper tantrum and whirled toward the open end of the ravine, where a group of his men were advancing, escorting someone. Two someones: Gallo and Kenner.

Fiona began crying, but whether they were tears of joy or despair, she did not know.

FORTY-NINE

Kenner was unusually quiet as they trekked across the basin. Gallo was grateful for the silence at first, but after a while it began to unnerve her. She had expected him to continue professing his sincerity, offering flimsy rationalizations for his earlier misdeeds, but he hardly spoke at all.

George was right. I shouldn't have trusted him. She glanced over her shoulder at the harsh landscape through which they had been walking. Pierce and the others were back there somewhere, following, but there was no sign of them.

I should turn back. Right now. This was a bad idea.

Perhaps sensing her anxiety, Kenner chose that moment to break his silence. "It's going to be all right, Augustina. We'll get Fiona away from him."

She scrutinized his optimistic smile. "How did you get mixed up with him in the first place, Liam?"

Kenner ducked his head in embarrassment. "What answer won't make me sound like a complete arse? I did it for the money? Fame? The chance to discover something amazing? A little bit of all of those, I suppose.

"It didn't seem like I was doing anything wrong at first. Just passing along information about new discoveries. And of course, keeping tabs on George. Mr. Tyndareus was always very interested in him and the Herculean Society. I never thought I would be asked to put other people in danger." He gave her a sidelong glance. "People I care about."

He went on before she could respond. "Now, I just want to make things right. You understand, don't you?"

"Honestly, it won't be easy. Not after everything you've done."

"I know," he said, and lapsed back into silence.

Nothing more was said between them, until a few minutes later, Gallo spotted the rear guard of Tyndareus's group, about a hundred yards away. They were stationed at the edge of a slope, which descended into a ravine. She pulled Kenner behind a clump of vegetation. "Showtime," she said. "How should we play this?"

"That depends on you, I suppose. Would you rather be my partner or my hostage?"

The question, or perhaps the way Kenner asked it, made Gallo feel uncomfortable, but it was too late to back out now.

Oblivious to her reaction, he plowed ahead. "Since your friends wouldn't let me have a gun, it might be difficult to convince Tyndareus that you are my prisoner. However, I think it might be even harder to convince him that I won you over. Shall we say that I made threats against Fiona to ensure your compliance?"

"That sounds plausible enough," Gallo said. "Remember, we just need to get close enough to tell Fiona what's going on. At the first opportunity, we make a break for it."

"Of course." He stood up, putting himself in full view of Tyndareus's men. He reached out and took hold of her upper arm, dragging her erect. She started to protest the unexpectedly rough treatment, but he cut her off. "Just act your part, Augustina. We have to be convincing, you know." He raised his free hand and began waving. "Hello! Over here!"

The men in the distance immediately took note and began advancing, their guns at the ready.

"There's something I've been wanting to ask," Kenner said, without looking at her. "Be honest. Did I ever really have a chance with you?"

Her discomfort intensified into something approaching real distress. "Liam, this is hardly the time."

He uttered a short, humorless laugh. "I suspected as much." His grip on her arm became painfully tight, and then without any warning, he started forward, almost yanking her off her feet.

"Liam!" She tried to pull free but his hold was ferocious in its strength. She had to jog just to avoid being dragged. The warning alarms were ringing loudly in her head, but the opportunity to turn and run had already slipped away.

"Stop, Liam. Think about what you're doing. He's a monster. You said so yourself."

Kenner made no reply. The two gunmen broke into a run, reaching them a few seconds later, brandishing their guns and ordering both of them to freeze and raise their hands. Kenner did so, without releasing his hold on Gallo.

"Well done, gents. Now, take me to Mr. Tyndareus. Immediately. This can't wait."

The two men regarded him with open suspicion, as did Gallo, but they quickly reached a mutual silent agreement, and circled around behind Kenner and Gallo, motioning for them to move.

Gallo at last managed to pull free of Kenner's grip. She rubbed her bruised arm, refusing to look at him, though a part of her could not help but wonder if this was all part of the act. If so, Kenner deserved an Academy Award. *And if not?*

Before leaving, she had promised to send a signal at the first sign of trouble. Dourado was still watching the feed from the drone, so all Gallo would have to do is start frantically waving her arms, and then Pierce and Lazarus would sweep in, guns blazing, to rescue her.

Kenner knew of that arrangement. If he was truly betraying her now, then he would have taken steps to prevent her from communicating with the others. Perhaps the fact that he had not done so was proof that the abrupt change in his demeanor was just a part of the act.

Even if it was not, she dared not run yet, not until she could tell Fiona what was happening.

The men ushered them down into the ravine, where the rest of the group was waiting. The video feed of the TALOS suit had not truly conveyed how imposing it was. It towered above everyone else, yet moved with a natural smoothness that belied its mechanical nature. She looked past the armored suit and spotted Fiona, leaning against a rock wall behind the group, weeping openly.

Gallo burst forward, disregarding any perceived or actual threat from her captors, and ran to Fiona. It had been days since she'd last seen the young woman. The physical ordeal of captivity had taken its toll, but she rallied and threw her arms around Gallo. "Aunt Gus. I'm so glad to see you."

Gallo returned the embrace. Her first impulse was simply to offer comfort, but empty words were the last thing Fiona needed right now. "Listen to me," she whispered. "There's no time to explain, but when I tell you run, you run. Got it?"

"I don't think I can."

At that moment, Tyndareus's amplified voice issued from speakers on the suit. The microphone also picked up the sound of his ventilator-assisted breathing, which made him sound like a geriatric Darth Vader. "Dr. Kenner. You've returned." There was a note of undisguised suspicion in the voice.

Kenner assumed a contemptuous air. "No thanks to your man there." He jerked his head in Rohn's direction and scowled. "He ran like a coward, and left me to die in the jungle."

"Yet, here you are. And with Dr. Gallo. Very resourceful of you."

"Not really. If you want the truth of it, I've spent the last few days as a guest of Dr. Pierce and the Herculean Society."

The unexpected admission stunned Gallo. If Kenner was still playing a part, he was way off script. She hugged Fiona again, but before she could repeat her warning, Kenner continued.

"They know everything. That's how I was able to find you. They're out there right now, preparing to attack."

Gallo gasped. "Liam, you son of a bitch!"

Rohn started barking orders to the other men, but Tyndareus raised one armored hand. "And I am to believe they just allowed you to wander out here, with Dr. Gallo as a hostage?"

"Of course not. I convinced them that I was on their side. Not hard to do given who you really are, *Herr Doktor Mengele*."

"You know this, and yet here you are?"

Kenner shrugged. "What you did in the past does not concern me. What you may accomplish in the future is a different matter entirely." He stabbed a finger at the rock slab behind Fiona and Gallo. "Beyond that wall lies the greatest discovery in the history of mankind. A mutagen that will allow us to take absolute control of evolution, to rewrite the source code of life. Pierce and his merry little band believe it's their mission to keep it secret. To hide it from the rest of us. That kind of paternalism disgusts me." His eyes drifted to Gallo, and he locked stares with her. "Even if I had no other reason to hate him, that would be enough."

He tore his gaze away and looked at Tyndareus again. "He'll be here any moment. You really ought to be getting ready for that."

Electronically enhanced laughter burbled from the TALOS suit. "You've made a believer out of me, Dr. Kenner. Vigor, take care of it."

As Rohn began marshalling his forces to prepare for the imminent attack, Tyndareus spoke again. "Your return is more fortuitous than you may realize, Dr. Kenner. If this is indeed the gate to the Underworld, then it is closed to us. I trust you possess the knowledge to unlock it."

Kenner stared at the wall for a moment. "No. I'm rather afraid I don't. But she does." He pointed at Fiona.

"That's absurd," Gallo said. "Leave her out of this, Liam."

"She's a genius with ancient languages," Kenner continued. "She's the one who figured out how to use the Phaistos Disc to navigate the Labyrinth in Crete. She figured out how to read Queen Hippolyte's map in less than five minutes."

He narrowed his gaze on Fiona as if peering into her soul. "There was something else on that map. An inscription in a language I've never seen before. Augustina avoided mentioning it, but I think the girl knows how to read it. And I think it contains instructions on how to find a way in."

Tyndareus turned his bulk around and marched toward Fiona.

Although she felt foolish doing so, Gallo stepped in front of the man in the mechanical suit. "Leave her alone."

"Is he correct?" The sound of Tyndareus's wheezy voice issuing from the speakers of the metallic behemoth was almost absurdly comical. "Is there an inscription on the map? Something that points to the door to the Underworld?"

"Of course not," Gallo answered, but then she heard a small voice from behind her.

"Yes."

Gallo's heart broke. "Oh, Fi...."

"Yes, there is," Fiona said, a little louder. "And I know what it says. I might be the only person alive who knows what it says."

Tyndareus leaned closer, the suit poised like a lion getting ready to pounce. "You can read it? What does it say? Is there a secret door? Can you open it?"

Gallo turned her head, lowering her voice to an urgent whisper. "Fi, don't help him."

"Is Uncle George really here?" Fiona asked.

"With friends."

"Good." As exhausted and broken as she appeared, there was something indomitable in her smile. "You need to trust me, Aunt

Gus. Everything is going to be okay." She stepped out from behind Gallo. "Yes. I can. But first, you have to let my aunt go."

Almost before she finished the sentence, one of Tyndareus's metal gauntlets shot out and wrapped around Gallo's throat. Both her hands shot up, but the mechanically assisted grip was unbreakable. She felt the pressure increase and heard her vertebrae popping as he lifted her off the ground. She managed to wrap both hands around his wrist so that her neck was not bearing the entire weight of her body, but she knew it was a losing battle. In a moment, she would pass out, and then her neck would snap.

"If you do not open it," Tyndareus countered, "she will die."

There was a rushing sound in Gallo's head, and bright spots began to swim in front of her eyes. But through the haze, she heard Fiona's response, loud and clear. "Screw you. Let her go, or you'll never get in there."

The pressure at Gallo's throat disappeared as suddenly as it had come, and she dropped like a sack of potatoes. She coughed and gasped, but any sense of relief she might have felt was dampened by the knowledge that Fiona had just made a deal with the devil to save her life.

"Open it!" Tyndareus roared.

"Don't do it, Fi," Gallo croaked.

"Get out of here, Aunt Gus. You don't want to be anywhere near here when this opens."

Still struggling to draw breath, Gallo pushed herself up on all fours. "I appreciate the offer," she coughed, "but I'm not going anywhere without you."

Fiona gave her a sad but strangely satisfied nod. Then she turned to the wall and began to speak.

FIFTY

"**Something's wrong.**"

Lazarus shot out a hand to restrain Pierce. "Wait."

On the playing-card-sized screen of Pierce's phone, which was displaying the video feed from the drone camera hovering overhead, Tyndareus, in his TALOS suit, lifted Gallo off the ground by the neck.

Pierce felt his reaction to that was appropriate. "He's killing her. We have to do something."

Lazarus just repeated the single word. "Wait."

A moment later, Tyndareus released Gallo. She was still alive and conscious, but it was impossible to tell how badly she had been injured.

"I'll kill him," Pierce growled.

"Yes. But wait."

They were less than a hundred yards from the edge of the ravine, and maybe another fifty to the far end, where the drama was unfolding. Pierce knew he could cover that distance in thirty seconds. *And then what? Kill more than a dozen armed men, including one who's a walking tank, all without hitting Gallo or Fiona?* Lazarus was right.

On the screen, Gallo sat up and began crawling closer to Fiona. "That bastard, Kenner. I knew we couldn't trust him."

"How do we know he's not just playing?" Carter asked. Her dubious tone suggested she was only bringing up the possibility just to cover their bases.

"It doesn't matter," Pierce said. "Plan B is a go." He turned to Lazarus. "Ready?"

Lazarus nodded and turned to Carter. "You?"

She nodded.

He continued to stare at her. "Felice, you know what might—"

"I know," she said. "I can handle it."

Pierce focused his attention on the video feed. Fiona had turned her back to the rest of the group and had her hands placed against the wall as if she was trying to push the slab or rock away, or perhaps...

"Shit," Pierce said. "She's trying to open it."

Lazarus and Carter looked over Pierce's shoulder at the screen.

"Open?" Carter asked. "How?"

"She's using the Mother Tongue. I thought there would be a cave entrance or something like that. This explains that inscription on the map. It's the same as the one we found in the Labyrinth." In response to Carter's blank look, he added, "It's like 'Open Sesame.' Makes it possible to walk through walls. The rest is a long story." He jerked a thumb at Lazarus. "He can tell you all about it."

"What happens when she succeeds?"

"It's a doorway to Hell. Short answer, nothing good." Pierce shoved the phone in his pocket and gripped his MP5K with both hands. "We've got to do this. Now."

"Can she do it?" Lazarus asked. "It's been years since she learned, and forgot, those few phrases of the Mother Tongue."

"She's a fast learner," Pierce said, followed by, "Cintia, start the countdown. Let's move."

Pierce heard Dourado's voice in his Bluetooth earpiece. "Countdown started. You've got thirty seconds."

Lazarus led the way, staying low but running at a near-sprint. The ravine hid them from Tyndareus's men, but if any scouts ventured out of the depression, they would be exposed and the element of surprise lost. But with the clock ticking, the most important thing was to be in position when the fireworks started. Pierce tried to count down the passing seconds, but when Dourado spoke again, informing them that they had twenty seconds, he realized he was counting too fast.

Of course, none of that would matter if Fiona succeeded in opening the door before they got there.

They ran parallel to the ravine, following a circuitous route toward Fiona and Gallo. That meant cutting across the blighted landscape and dodging fumaroles. With each step, the ground might give way beneath their feet, dropping them into hidden, superheated pools of water to be boiled like Maine lobsters. It also meant that, if they survived the approach, they would have to fight their way past all of Tyndareus's men before escaping the ravine.

One thing at a time.

"Ten seconds," Dourado said. "Hard left, now!"

Lazarus adjusted course, pouring on the speed. Their objective, the far end of the ravine, lay straight ahead, hidden by the terrain. If all went according to plan, they would arrive directly above where Fiona now stood, attempting to unlock a portal to the Underworld.

"Five...four...three...two...one..."

There was a flash on the western horizon. A pillar of dust and smoke arose to mark the spot, and an instant later, Pierce both heard and felt the shock wave of the improvised explosive device Lazarus had placed two hundred yards away from the entrance to the ravine.

"That got their attention," Dourado said.

Lazarus stopped short and motioned for Pierce and Carter to get down, then began belly-crawling across the hot ground toward the edge of the drop. Pierce hit the dirt, getting a face-full of sulfur dust in the process. Blinking the stinging substance away, he crawled alongside Lazarus and got his first look at the mayhem unfolding fifty feet below.

Some of Tyndareus's men had taken the bait, though not enough for Pierce's liking. Eight of them were moving away, toward the site of the explosion, their assault rifles shouldered. The others had pulled back to form a defensive perimeter around Tyndareus. Pierce picked out Rohn in the latter group, shouting orders and waving to his men. Tyndareus, safely inside his armored suit, paid little heed to the disturbance, keeping his attention fixed on Fiona.

"Cintia," Lazarus said, his voice taut but strangely calm given the circumstances. "Now."

"They aren't in range—"

"Do it."

There was another flash, closer this time. The noise of the explosion was incredibly loud as it was funneled down the ravine. Lazarus had placed the second IED as close to the mouth of the depression as he dared get. The advancing front of Tyndareus's men fell down like bowling pins, but none were within the explosion's kill radius.

Then something extraordinary happened. The ground all around the explosion split apart like thin ice on a lake. Jagged cracks, spewing steam, radiated out from beneath the debris cloud. Three of the stunned gunmen vanished, as the earth upon which they lay collapsed and transformed into liquid. The others scrambled to their feet, retreating from the roiling wave of steam and destruction. Not all of them made it.

Although he had been primed to charge into battle only a moment before, Pierce was frozen in place by the spectacle. "Did you know that would happen?"

"No," Lazarus admitted, sounding a little awed. "Sometimes, you just get lucky. Let's go."

The big man sprang to his feet and hurtled over the edge, bounding down the side of the ravine toward Tyndareus and the remainder of his forces. Pierce followed with Carter.

Instead of trying to run down the steep incline, he fell against the slope and slid on his backside, dragging his feet in front of him to slow his descent, even as he tried to acquire a target in the mayhem below. He managed to squeeze off a few shots, though it was impossible to tell whether he was hitting anything. He was still sliding when the earth beside him erupted from the impact of high-velocity rounds, and he heard the harsh reports from enemy rifles.

Shit!

Remembering Lazarus's common sense advice—'don't make it easy for them to shoot you'—Pierce rolled to the right, heaving himself out of the path of another fusillade, then launched himself the rest of the way down the slope.

In the instant before he landed, he saw Gallo, huddled into a protective ball less than thirty feet away. Just past her, Fiona stood, her back turned to the chaos, her hands still pressed against the wall.

"Fiona! Don't—"

She recoiled as if from an electric shock, and for a fleeting instant, Pierce dared to believe that his shout had reached her through the din. Then he saw the look of elation on her face, and he knew that his warning had come too late.

The door was already open.

Something was coming through.

FIFTY-ONE

The explosions were the signal to run. Pierce and Lazarus had told her to be ready, warned her that their diversion would be unmistakable. But when the moment came, when the first explosion drew half of Tyndareus's men away, and then a second, much closer blast, triggered a localized geothermal event, Gallo did not flee. She was not going to leave without Fiona.

Even as she heard the young woman speaking the strange words, chanting a language that sounded like it might be a Native American dialect, she knew that she should grab Fiona by the arm and drag her away, but she did not.

Part of it was curiosity. Even though she had been an unwilling participant in Kenner's quest, she had traveled so far, followed the clues, done so much... She just had to know. Even though she knew there was a very good reason for it, she hated the fact that the Herculean Society demanded such discoveries be kept secret from everyone.

But that was not why she remained where she was. She was not curious about whether Fiona could master the Mother Tongue and transform the rock slab in front of them into some kind of magical portal to the Underworld. In truth, she did not doubt it for a second.

What kept her from fleeing, from physically pulling the young woman along with her, was Fiona's confident smile.

You need to trust me, she had said. *Everything is going to be okay.*

Though she did not know why, Gallo believed her.

But the second explosion was so close that she almost panicked. The ground heaved beneath her, not just the shock wave but the beginning of an earth tremor. A blast of heat rushed down the length of the ravine, followed by a vapor cloud that smelled like rotten eggs, which stung her eyes. Then the shooting started.

She caught a glimpse of Lazarus bounding down the hill, a colossal figure, like Hercules reborn. After him came the considerably less imposing forms of Carter and Pierce, sliding down the slope, charging into the fray.

Still, she did not run.

Fiona stopped chanting and leaped back from the slab. She shouted something, a taunt probably meant for Kenner's ears, or possibly for Tyndareus, though it was unlikely that either man could have heard her amidst the unfolding fury of battle. Gallo heard the words, but did not grasp their significance until she heard another noise, a rhythmic thumping that reminded her inexplicably of hoofbeats.

Even stranger than the sound was the fact that it was emanating from *inside* the rock slab. And it was getting louder.

Something was coming through.

Now Gallo understood why Fiona was smiling and why she had shouted the words: "It says, 'Beware of dog!'"

In their eagerness to unlock the gates of the Underworld, and to find the Well of Monsters, Kenner and Tyndareus had forgotten a critical element of the myth.

Hell had a watchdog.

"Cerberus."

Gallo's mind raced. It couldn't be Cerberus. Hercules had captured the hellhound. Gallo knew this to be true. Pierce had once told her the truth behind the legend, how Alexander had jokingly referred to the beast as 'puppy,' downplaying the facts behind the legend. And that had all happened three thousand years in the past.

Three thousand years was a long time for a portal to the Underworld to go unguarded. Something had taken the hellhound's place.

What emerged from the wall, which was still visible, but somehow immaterial, was not Cerberus, not a gigantic dog with three heads, but it was no less monstrous. Gallo's first impression was of a bear, but one that was easily three times the size of the biggest Kodiak grizzly she had ever heard of. The creature's head was broad and bear-like but wrapped around it like a crown of thorns was a rack of sharp-tipped antlers, as thick as tree limbs.

The beast lumbered into view, passing through the wall as if the stone were no more substantial than mist. Gallo scrambled back, so close that she could feel the creature's hot breath on her face and see the primal fury in its dark eyes. One heavy paw, tipped with curving claws each as long as Gallo's leg, slammed down on the place where she had been standing a moment before, eclipsing her view of Fiona. The beast however, barely seemed to notice her. Its eyes were on the pandemonium unfolding further up the ravine.

With a roar that shook Gallo's bones, it reared up on its hind legs and threw its forepaws wide, as if to gather all of Tyndareus's men in a crushing embrace. The crest of its horned head rose as high as the top of the ravine, its reach almost spanning from one side to the other.

It was a bear, but like the other chthonic monsters, it had incorporated characteristics of other animals. Its limbs were longer, the musculature rippling beneath a pelt of fine reddish-brown hair that reminded Gallo of deerskin.

Despite the fact that they were still repelling Pierce's assault, Tyndareus's men seemed to grasp that this new arrival was a much greater threat. They brought their rifles around and began firing into the beast's exposed underbelly.

Fat drops of blood began raining down on Gallo as the bullets found their mark. The creature snorted and began pawing at its torso, as if trying to swat away a swarm of bees. But it appeared otherwise untroubled by the attack. The noise of the shooting seemed to irritate it even more than the sting of the bullets, and after another thunderous bellow, it dropped back onto all fours and started forward.

Gallo craned her head around to watch. Behind her and just a few feet away from a stunned Kenner, a stern-looking woman—the only female she had seen in Tyndareus's employ—drew a pistol and started firing, shouting curses in a language that Gallo did not recognize. The shooting and the swearing were silenced by the swipe of a paw. Gallo saw a puff of red, as pieces of the woman flew in different directions. Kenner dove aside at the last instant, narrowly avoiding the same fate.

As the creature thundered past, smashing gunmen aside with its paws and spearing them on its antlers, Kenner raised his head and looked back at Gallo.

No, not at me, she realized. *Behind me. What he wants is on the other side of that wall.*

He stooped, picked something from the ground—a gun?—and then he was running toward her. She started to backpedal out of his way, but then realized, almost too late, that she had misread his intention. There was something else behind her...someone else.

"Fi! Get away!" She tried to put herself between Kenner and Fiona, but he anticipated the move, stiff-arming her out of the way. She stumbled back, flailing in vain for something to arrest her fall, and she landed painfully on her backside.

Kenner seized Fiona by the wrist and dragged her toward the wall.

Into the wall.

They vanished without even a ripple.

Gallo leapt to her feet, and without a moment's hesitation, she followed.

FIFTY-TWO

As the monstrous bear-elk hybrid bulldozed a swath of devastation through the midst of Tyndareus's forces, Lazarus pulled Pierce and Carter out of the way.

At first, it appeared the creature was going to win the battle for them. Its thick hide might not have been bulletproof, but the rounds failed to penetrate deep enough to do any real damage. It was like trying to bring down an elephant with a BB gun. And while the animal might not have understood the connection between the projectiles impacting against its body and the loud flashing things in the hands of the men scattered across the ravine, the noise was driving it into a frenzy.

The battle was so one-sided that Pierce found himself hoping that one of the gunmen might get off a lucky shot and strike some vital organ or at the very least, wound a leg to slow it down. He didn't feel any sympathy for the men, but he knew that to reach Gallo and Fiona, they would have to get past the battle's victor.

Rohn was trying to organize the men, directing their fire and orchestrating their inevitable retreat, but the creature pushed them toward the bubbling cauldron that Lazarus's explosives had opened. There was no escape for the men, and no way to stand against the guardian of the Underworld's gates. One by one, the men threw down their rifles and tried to scramble up the ravine's steep sides, but the creature's rage was fixed on them now. There was no escaping it.

Then, a lone figure, taller than any of the men, but still dwarfed by the creature, advanced and took up a position directly in front of it. Tyndareus in his TALOS suit appeared to be challenging the bear-elk to one-on-one combat.

Powered armor or not, Pierce expected the outcome to be the same. The creature would swat the old man aside like the insect he was. The suit might survive, but Tyndareus would be pulverized inside it like an egg in a tumble dryer.

But Tyndareus had a trick up his sleeve, or rather, on it. The right arm of the TALOS suit came up and pointed at the beast. Pierce glimpsed something mounted to the forearm plates, like an extra piece of armor.

There was a loud, hollow sound, deeper but not quite as loud as the report of a rifle, and then Pierce was face down on the scorched ground next to Carter, with Lazarus covering both of them.

Another explosion blasted through the ravine, but the shock wave that socked Pierce in the gut felt more like the Primacord detonations that had felled the trees in the Amazon—firecrackers instead of dynamite.

Even before the last echoes of the blast died away, a new sound filled the air: a tortured, braying howl. The smell of burnt hair and cooking meat briefly overpowered the stink of sulfur. Pierce raised his head and saw the massive shape of the bear-elk writhing on the floor of the ravine. Pierce could not tell how serious the injury was. The creature might have been in its death throes, or it might merely have gotten a nasty shock.

"Forty mike-mike grenade launcher," Lazarus muttered. "HE rounds. I wonder why the old man was holding back?"

Tyndareus stood his ground, hand still extended, ready to fire again, but the creature abruptly righted itself, and with astonishing swiftness for something so enormous, it bolted for the stone wall and the safety of the Underworld. It ran at the seemingly solid obstacle, as if aware that there would be no resistance, and disappeared into the stone. If not for the carnage littering the ravine floor, the whole episode would have seemed like a bizarre night terror.

The calm following the creature's defeat did not last long. Tyndareus swung around, his arm still extended, the barrel of his grenade launcher now aimed at the three figures huddled near the ravine wall.

Although he had not seen the 40mm high-explosive round hit the bear-elk, Pierce had felt its destructive power, and he knew that there would be no surviving the explosion. There wasn't even time to flee, but that didn't stop Lazarus from springing into motion. But he wasn't running away from the impending grenade blast. Instead, he ran toward its source.

The unexpected charge surprised Tyndareus. He took a step back, recoiling in the face of aggression, despite the fact of being impervious to almost any attack that Lazarus might hope to bring against him. Lazarus surely knew it as well, but the knowledge did not slow him down.

Just as he was about to pass within Tyndareus's reach, Lazarus veered to his left and launched himself up at the outstretched arm. The TALOS suit weighed as much as a small car, but the weight was distributed very differently. When Lazarus hit Tyndareus's arm at a full charge, it was enough to spin the armored figure around. Tyndareus flailed, and in so doing, flung Lazarus twenty feet away. But he could not prevent gravity from taking him down. He crashed to the ground, releasing another grenade as he fell. The explosive round arced high and then came back down a hundred and fifty feet away, exploding with a harmless flash and bang.

Pierce saw Lazarus scrambling up and charging Tyndareus again, and then something like a wall blocked his view of the combatants.

Rohn.

Pierce was just starting to focus on the figure standing in front of him when something metallic flashed in front of him, tugging at his chest, spinning him halfway around. Starbursts bloomed in his vision as a heavy fist crashed into the back of his head and sent him stumbling away to sprawl face down on the searing hot ground.

He rolled over, not as gracefully as Lazarus, but with the same urgency, groping for his machine pistol. That was when he noticed the dark sticky substance smeared all over his hands and down the front of his combat vest.

Blood. His own blood.

Rohn had slashed him with a knife, a very sharp knife, judging by the fact that he was only now beginning to feel the faintest tingle of pain across his chest, where the blade had struck.

Screw it. I'm still alive.

He brought the gun up, but Rohn was now advancing on Carter. Pierce tried to settle the red dot sight on Rohn's moving form, but his grip was sloppy, his hands slick. In the corner of his eye, he saw three more gunmen, the last remnants of Tyndareus's small army, moving toward him.

Rohn's back erupted in a spray of blood as Carter triggered a round, point blank into his body, and then fired again and again. The big man lurched with each impact, but kept advancing. Carter stumbled back and fell, the gun slipping from her hands, a look of terror on her face. Rohn's hand came up, the blade poised to end Felice Carter's life.

FIFTY-THREE

Gallo expected some kind of sensory feedback as she passed through the rock wall. Would it feel like walking through a dust cloud? Would it be like swimming through something denser than air but not quite liquid? The only noticeable difference was the absolute darkness. She couldn't even tell if her eyes were open or shut. She held her breath, afraid to inhale the...whatever it was. That meant she had about forty seconds to cross the threshold of the Underworld, but how would she know when she reached it?

The answer to her question appeared suddenly before her, a faint glow directly ahead. It had to be Kenner, heading into the depths with Fiona. She looked back and could just make out a rough stone wall right behind her, looking as solid and impenetrable as it had on the outside. She reached out, probing it with her fingertips. There was no resistance at all. The rock might have been a hologram, a magician's projection of smoke and mirrors. It occurred to her that she should mark her path or risk spending the last hours of her life wandering around in the dark looking for the exit, but she had nothing at all with which to do so.

I should have thought this through a little first, she mused. *But how do you prepare yourself for walking through solid objects? It's not like there's a YouTube video that tells you what to expect.*

The glow was receding, growing dimmer as the source of the light moved further along the passage. Gallo put aside her hesitancy and hastened forward. The passage, formed from an old lava tube, was wide with smooth walls, sloping downward. With each step closer to the light source, her ability to see increased, allowing her to move even faster. She picked up speed, running toward the light.

The slope bottomed out and opened into a vast chamber, at least as large as Gorham's Cave. It was hard to be sure in the dim light, yet Gallo realized that there was more illumination in the cavern than could be explained by Kenner's single flashlight. The chamber walls glowed red-orange, like coals in a barbecue.

The air was blast-furnace hot, sucking both moisture and energy from her body. Gallo wondered how long she could survive here. How long before organ and brain damage occurred? Probably less than an hour. Maybe a lot less. And Fiona had already been showing signs of serious dehydration related to her diabetes.

Gallo forced herself to move even faster. She had to reach Kenner, had to get Fiona away from him before the damage was irreversible.

"Liam! Stop!" She tried to shout, but the sound that came out seemed to evaporate into nothingness along with everything else.

Kenner couldn't have heard her, yet after just a few more steps, he stopped. The beam of his light hung in the air, sweeping back and forth, but moving no further into the cavern. Gallo could just distinguish the pair—Kenner and Fiona—silhouetted against a flame-red glow. With each step forward, more detail was revealed, as was the real reason Kenner had stopped. When she was still twenty feet away from them, Gallo saw a precipice. Kenner and Fiona stood at the edge of a wide fissure that bisected the entire chamber.

"End of the road," she called out.

Kenner whirled around, surprise on his face. "Augustina?" His voice was strained with the fatigue of enduring the oppressive heat, but the conditions had done nothing to dampen his enthusiasm. "I didn't think anyone would come after us."

Beside him, Fiona barely moved at all. Gallo wasn't sure how she was still standing, but doubted that she would be able to walk out under her own power. "I'm not leaving without Fiona, Liam. If you want to stay, fine, but let her go."

"Oh, I can't very well do that. She is, quite literally, the key to getting out of here."

"She's dying. You can see that. And if she dies, then we'll be trapped in here." Gallo pressed the point home. "We can all leave together. There's nothing here."

Any progress she might have been making vanished at that moment.

"Nothing?" Kenner sounded offended. He pointed to whatever it was that lay beyond the edge of the precipice. "You call that *nothing*?"

Despite herself, Gallo took a step closer and looked for herself. What she saw defied belief, but one thing was certain.

Kenner was right.

It was far more than 'nothing.'

FIFTY-FOUR

The knife came down, but not with the expected fury of a deathblow. Instead, Rohn's entire body seemed to deflate, as if the impact of his mortal wounds had finally hit home. He did not collapse but tottered unsteadily for a moment, and then he turned slowly around.

Pierce could see that something had changed in him. Although he was still standing, still very much alive, his eyes were dead, without any trace of emotion. On the ground behind him, Carter appeared to be in the grip of a seizure. Though there was no outward sign of injury, her muscles were rigid, her body shaking violently.

The trio of gunmen fanned out, their weapons ready to finish what Rohn had started, but they were clearly confounded by the man's strange behavior.

Rohn lurched into motion, walking toward them with the shuffling steps of an unhinged derelict. The nearest man called out to him, but Rohn seemed not to hear. He just continued stalking forward on a collision course with the man who had spoken. The man stepped to the side to get out of Rohn's way, but Rohn adjusted course. Then, as soon as he was within reach, he slashed his blade across the man's throat.

The other two gaped in disbelief as the stricken man went down, blood spraying from the wound, but as Rohn turned toward them, his face ashen from blood loss yet otherwise utterly blank, they turned their guns on him.

Rohn's chest exploded as twin bursts of rifle fire ripped into him, staggering him back. But he kept coming, walking headlong into the barrage.

Pierce wrestled his own gun around and without bothering to aim, emptied the magazine into the men. Both went down.

Rohn stopped in his tracks. He stood there, an automaton waiting for a command that never came, as the last of his life leaked away. Then he simply crumpled to the ground, dead.

Fifty feet away, Lazarus and Tyndareus were locked in a struggle that was not as one-sided as it should have been, but Pierce barely took note. The mystery of what had just happened to Rohn was screaming for his attention. The change had come over the man as suddenly as if someone had thrown a switch and turned his brain off.

No, not someone. Carter had done it, or some part of her unconscious mind. The latent ability that slumbered within her, the ghost of a prehistoric human ancestor, linking her to every living human on the planet. It was a link that, if threatened, could transform a human into a mindless drone, and if severed, might do to the entire population of humanity what it had done to Rohn.

"Felice?" He let the spent machine pistol fall. Carter's convulsions had abated, and from the rise and fall of her chest, he could see that she was still very much alive. But was she still Felice Carter? And if he went to her, tried to help her, would the same thing happen to him?

He was not about to risk it. There was nothing he could do for her. If anyone could reach her...

Lazarus was still fighting, anticipating and dodging most of Tyndareus's lightning fast attacks. Most, but not all. As Pierce watched, the fist of the TALOS suit struck Lazarus in the shoulder. It was a glancing blow, but it spun him around and sent him cartwheeling away. He landed on his feet, catlike, but his right arm hung from his shoulder at an impossible angle. Lazarus gripped the injured limb with his good hand and twisted his body until the dislocated joint slid back into place. Then he dove out of the way an instant before Tyndareus slammed the same fist down on the place where he had been standing. Sulfurous vapor erupted as the ground split apart under the impact.

Lazarus hurled himself at Tyndareus, wrapping both arms around the suit's helmet. Tyndareus reached up and peeled his attacker away, as effortlessly as if brushing off an insect, and Lazarus went flying again.

Pierce felt helpless. It was nothing short of amazing that Lazarus was still in the fight, but he couldn't hope to win. Safe inside the armored TALOS suit, Tyndareus had beaten back the monstrous bear-elk. How could an ordinary human, or even an extraordinary one like Lazarus, hope to defeat technology like that?

"Talos," he muttered the name, thinking of a similarly mismatched showdown recorded in the legend of Jason and the Argonauts, and the answer came to him. He raised a bloody hand to the side of his head. His Bluetooth earpiece was still there. "Cintia? Are you still with me?"

Dourado's frantic voice sounded in his head. "Dr. Pierce! What's happening there? What happened to Dr. Carter?"

"No time to explain. I need you to do something."

"Of course."

Fifty feet away, Lazarus charged again, ducking under Tyndareus's reaching arms and throwing himself at the armored legs. He attempted to sweep the armored legs out from under Tyndareus, but he might as well have been trying to roll a locomotive onto its side. Tyndareus kicked at him, but Lazarus managed to wrap his arms around the extended leg. He planted his feet on the ground and then heaved upward with such ferocity that the ground beneath him crumbled, dropping him into a knee-deep pit of boiling acid, but his attempt to throw Tyndareus succeeded. The man in the TALOS suit landed flat on his back.

Lazarus howled in agony as he clawed his way out of the steaming hole. His legs were wreathed in smoke as his boots and trousers disintegrated, revealing skin that was bright red and beginning to blister, but as soon as his feet were on relatively solid ground he started toward his foe again. Tyndareus was already back on his feet, swinging his arms back and forth to meet the attack.

Pierce charged, too, leaping over the steaming cracks in the Earth, acutely aware of what the consequences would be if the ground beneath him gave way. Tyndareus's head swiveled in Pierce's direction, but then looked away just as quickly. Lazarus may have posed a bit of a challenge, but Pierce was hardly worth the bother.

Big mistake, Pierce thought. *Brains beat brawn.*

He circled behind Tyndareus, searching for and finding the chink in the smooth metal armor. He peeked around Tyndareus, trying to telegraph to Lazarus what he was doing.

Keep him busy, he wanted to shout. *I just need a couple seconds.*

Lazarus must have understood, because Pierce got all the time he needed. He darted in close, much too close for comfort, and fought with the clamps that held a square metal plate in place. When he failed to move the clamps with his hands, he pried at them with a knife, using leverage to move what his fingers couldn't. He put all his strength into the effort, until the tight clamps snapped free. The plate fell away to reveal a metal box from which sprouted three thick cables. Pierce plunged a hand in, gripped one of the cables, and just as Dourado had instructed him, gave it a hard twist.

The cable popped loose, and the TALOS suit froze in place.

In Greek mythology, Talos, a gigantic living bronze statue, was defeated by the guile of the sorceress Medea, who had discovered his fatal weakness. Talos's lifeblood—a molten metallic liquid called *ichor*—had been poured into his body through an opening in his ankle, the hole stoppered by a single bronze nail. The TALOS suit was powered by electricity, not *ichor*, but it had the same exploitable weakness. To shut it down, Pierce merely had to pull the plug.

Pierce backed away, half-expecting the suit to begin moving again, reactivated by an auxiliary power source or some other measure designed to prevent an enemy from doing what he had just done, but the armored figure remained statue-still, a seven-foot tall gray mannequin.

Lazarus arrived a moment later, his face contorted with pain. "Are you all right?"

"I should be asking you."

"I'll live," Lazarus said, making it sound almost like a regret. "But you're wounded."

As if in response to the question, Pierce felt an ache across his chest. He looked down and saw the damage that Rohn's blade had caused. His body armor had taken the brunt of the attack and no doubt saved his life, but the skin underneath was a bloody perforated line. It could wait.

"I'm going after Augustina and Fiona. Take care of her." He nodded his head in Carter's direction.

Lazarus stared at the woman for several seconds then he shook his head. "You need me."

"She needs you more."

A different kind of pain twisted Lazarus's features, one that had nothing to do with his injuries. "I don't know what to do for her."

Pierce extended a hand and gripped Lazarus's shoulder. He sensed that this admission of helplessness was a harder thing than any battle the man had ever fought. "You'll figure it out."

"What about you? You can't do this alone."

Pierce reached out with his other hand and patted the stationary TALOS suit. "Actually, I think I can."

FIFTY-FIVE

The worst part was the smell. After breathing sulfuric acid fumes for more than an hour, Pierce thought the suit's oxygen supply would be a welcome relief, but as soon as the seals were clamped down and the O2 began to flow, he realized that there were worse smells in the world. It was the TALOS suit itself he realized, or more likely, its former occupant. A foul odor, like antiseptic ointment and cleaning fluid mixed with the smell of illness and decay, clung to the interior surfaces like a fungus growing on the inside of the helmet.

Probably just my imagination, he told himself.

The controls were surprisingly intuitive. Once he was strapped in, he needed only to move his arms and legs as he normally would, and the suit responded. The first few steps reminded him of walking in ski boots. After that, he could almost forget that he was encased in titanium armor.

A heads-up display projected on the inside of the visor showed battery charge, oxygen pressure and a few other status indicators that were probably important to know, but there had not been time for Dourado to go over the operator's manual with him. The meters were all in the yellow. "You have half an hour of battery life remaining," Dourado told him.

"Augustina and Fiona probably don't have that long," he replied. "It's more than enough."

A fingertip sensor in the suit's gauntlets allowed him to toggle on the weapons systems. The grenade launcher on the right arm, and a plasma torch on the left. Pierce doubted he would need them. The suit itself was his best weapon.

He approached the wall cautiously, unsure what he would encounter when he touched its surface, but there was no resistance, no sense of making contact.

He turned and glanced back at Lazarus. The big man was cautiously approaching the still motionless form of Carter. Pierce regretted that there was nothing he could do to help either of them, but time was running out.

He also spotted Tyndareus. The old man hadn't gone far from the spot where Pierce had dropped him after manually disengaging the clamps that held the TALOS suit together. With his gnarled limbs and liver-spotted bald head, he looked like Gollum from *The Hobbit*. Gollum in a business suit, crawling across the scorching hot earth.

It was a better fate than Auschwitz's 'Angel of Death' deserved.

"Cintia, I'll probably lose radio contact in a second or two. If you don't hear from me in half an hour..." He realized he didn't have a contingency.

"You'll make it, Dr. Pierce."

"Thanks. And from now on, you can just call me George."

"I'll start doing that when you get back. Good luck."

He took a step forward and was plunged into darkness. The high-intensity spotlights mounted to either side of the visor might as well have been covered with mud for all the good they did. The intangible wall through which he was passing was not like fog or dust. It didn't reflect light. Instead it seemed to absorb it. He took another step and another, and then he could see again. He found himself in a wide passage, like an immense wormhole bored in the blazing hot rock, sloping away into the depths of the Earth.

The light revealed other details. A litter of what looked like bone fragments, globs of matted hair or fur and black nodules the size of softballs were scattered everywhere.

Droppings, Pierce realized. *Bear-elk scat.*

That stopped him. The creature was here, somewhere. It had retreated to its lair, maybe to lick its wounds, maybe to die in the darkness, but it was between Pierce and the people he loved. Maybe he would need the weapons after all.

He tried to creep down the passage, but stealth was not one of the suit's selling points. No matter how carefully he lowered his feet, his steps sounded like an anvil dropping on concrete.

Abandoning the sneaky approach, he set out at a jog, pounding down the passage, each footfall ringing through the suit like a pile-driver impact. He kicked through more litter, pulverizing fragments of bone and discarded antlers.

The part of him that was both a scientist and a scholar of mythology, regretted that there was not time to make a more thorough examination. Hercules had walked here once, fought another guardian of the Underworld gates. Not a mythological monster with supernatural abilities living in some kind of netherworld, where the laws of physics did not apply, but a hybrid animal living in a strange closed ecosystem. The bear-elk was evidently the latest creature to occupy that niche, but how did it survive? What did it eat? Were there others like it down here?

He would probably never get the answer to those questions. The job of the Herculean Society was to make sure that such mysteries remained unsolved. When he got Gallo and Fiona to safety, he would have to take steps to ensure that no one ever returned.

The passage opened into a vast cavern with walls that burned like magma. As Pierce swept the chamber with his headlamp, he spotted movement off to the left and froze when the reflected light showed a pair of glowing green eyes.

The bear-elk.

The creature remained perfectly still, a deer in the headlights. A deer with the temper of a territorial grizzly bear. It could, if it chose to, stomp him into oblivion...or peel open the suit like a sardine can. Yet, it did not move. Perhaps it remembered its previous encounter with TALOS. The animal was curled up, protecting its wounds. Pierce did not doubt that the grenade had done some serious damage—burns, broken bones, perhaps internal injuries as well.

"You made it."

The voice—Kenner's voice—almost made Pierce jump, which might have proved either comical or disastrous given the circumstances. Pierce turned slowly and searched for the source. He found Kenner a moment later, near the center of the cavern, with one hand holding a flashlight aimed back in Pierce's direction. The other hand was gripping Fiona's arm.

She stared dully into the darkness, conscious but limp in his grasp, her legs folded up beneath her, unable to support her own weight any longer. Pierce recognized the signs of severe dehydration and diabetic ketoacidosis, no doubt exacerbated by the extreme heat. Gallo stood nearby, looking defeated.

"As promised, *Herr Doktor,*" Kenner went on. "The Well of Monsters."

He thinks I'm Tyndareus.

Kenner's tone was triumphant but grudging. He hadn't been prepared to share his discovery, but he knew better than to challenge his benefactor. Without replying, Pierce backed away from the bear-elk before turning to join the others. He was still twenty feet away when his headlamps revealed Echidna.

In Greek mythology, Echidna was described as both a serpentine creature and a beautiful woman. From what he knew of Kenner's quest and his own experience with how the mythology of Hercules's labors had been distorted over the millennia, Pierce had assumed that Echidna would be some kind of naturally occurring phenomenon: a pool of chemicals or a bubbling pot of primordial soup.

It was none of those things, and yet in a way, it was all of them.

The cavern was split by a wide fissure—thirty or forty feet across and at least a hundred feet long—filled to the brim with what looked like molten stone. In reality, it was a transparent liquid—probably a solution of water and dissolved minerals—reflecting the glowing red of the chamber's walls. Dotting its surface but mostly concentrated at the edges, were clumps of what looked like vegetation. They resembled clusters of water lilies floating on the surface of a pond, except these were a coal black. They were plants of some kind, adapted to using thermal and chemical energy instead of sunlight. They probably formed the base of the underground food chain, but as strange as they were, the floating organisms were the least interesting thing in the pool.

Just below the surface, filling the bottom of the fissure, was Echidna.

It was alive, no question about that, but whether it was plant, animal or other, was a question that only Felice Carter might have been able to answer. It looked like an enormous flower, a many-petaled orchid, or perhaps a gigantic upside down jellyfish. Hundreds of snake-like tendrils reached up like fingers, not quite breaking the surface, while directly below, the main body was covered with oblong globules that resembled bunches of grapes. There was movement beneath the faintly translucent membranes covering the globes, the pulsing of something alive.

Eggs, Pierce thought. *Like an octopus's garden.*

Scattered around the eggs, atop the amorphous creature's body, were chunks of debris. Pierce sensed that he was close to grasping the secret of Echidna, but such knowledge would serve no purpose other than to satisfy his curiosity. He tore his gaze away from the strangely beautiful monster and returned his attention to the more immediate problem.

He considered sustaining the ruse that he was Tyndareus so he could get Kenner's cooperation, but he would be found out as soon as he spoke. *Better to stick with the truth*, he decided.

"Liam, it's me. George."

At the sound of his voice, Gallo looked up, a flicker of hope in her eyes. Fiona perked up, too, but the reaction made her dire condition all the more apparent.

Kenner was taken aback, but only for a moment. "George? Well, I'll be damned. You are a lot more resourceful than I ever gave you credit for. No wonder Augustina fancies you."

Pierce ignored the comment. "Liam, I don't have a clue where your loyalties lie, but we need to get out of here. All of us."

"Leave? George, do you *see* this?" He waved at the creature in the pool.

"We can come back," Pierce lied. "But it's not safe to stay here. The heat is going to cook you alive."

Kenner's eyes darted back and forth as he considered this. "You're right, of course." Then his gaze settled on Pierce. "But not you. That suit you're wearing. I'll wager it protects you."

"That doesn't matter. There's only one suit. And we're not alone in here."

"You mean the creature? Cerberus or whatever it is that's taken its place. I thought I heard something crawling around back there. But it's beaten. And even if it tried to attack, the suit has weapons, doesn't it?"

"Liam, this is insane."

Kenner shook his head. "I don't think so. Give me the suit, George." He jerked Fiona up and then thrust her toward the fissure.

"No!"

Pierce reacted instantly, taking a step forward, reaching out as if to snatch her back, but he wasn't close enough. Gallo let out a shriek of surprise, but she was too far away. In the pool below, Echidna's tendrils quivered, stretching upward, as if in anticipation of a meal. Kenner, however, did not let go of Fiona. He just held her there, poised above the water's surface.

"Give me the suit," he repeated. "Or she goes in."

There was a rustling sound behind Pierce as the shouts roused the bear-elk.

"Hurry, George," Kenner urged. His voice was frenetic, adrenaline superseding reason.

Pierce glanced back and saw the beast standing on all fours, blocking the passage back to the surface with its bulk. He tapped the sensor with a fingertip, and the weapons menu appeared on the HUD. "Get her away from there. I can deal with that thing, but you need to move away. Find some cover."

"That's not going to happen. Take the suit off, and I'll let the three of you go. Do it now."

The creature took a tentative step, shoulder muscles bunching, as if preparing to spring.

"Damn it, Liam. There's no time for this."

"I'll drop her! I swear to God, I'll do it."

"No! Wait." Pierce swung his attention back to Kenner. Fiona hung from his outstretched arm like the bait in a snare. She was trembling... No, she was saying something. Mumbling, too faintly for Pierce to hear. Praying? "I'm taking it off, Liam. Just pull her back."

He didn't wait for an answer, but quickly switched to the main menu and brought up the controls to disengage the seals. There was a hiss as the internal pressure equalized, then the scorching air of the cavern rushed in. The chest plate swung up and Pierce squirmed to get his head and arms out of the exoskeleton.

Fiona's eyes lit up when she saw him, but her lips kept moving.

"Pull her back," Pierce repeated. His voice, no longer amplified by the suit, sounded small in the dead air.

"Faster, George," Kenner said.

Pierce struggled out of the suit and toppled forward, landing hard on the cavern floor. The impact awakened the pain of his injuries, but he scrambled up, reaching out to Fiona.

Satisfied with this victory, Kenner pulled Fiona back and sent her stumbling toward Pierce, and in the same motion, he leaped for the TALOS suit.

The bear-elk charged.

Pierce caught Fiona, hugging her close, but it was too late to escape. He pulled her down, covering her with his body.

Gallo was there, too, huddling with them.

They would face the end together.

Kenner made it to the suit, but before he could even begin to figure out how to climb inside, a swipe of the creature's massive forepaw sent it and him flying across the cavern. Both splashed into the pool and were instantly erased from sight. The light from the suit's headlamps continued to shine, illuminating the waters from below, but the rest of the chamber was plunged into a ruddy darkness.

The cavern floor vibrated with each heavy step that brought the bear-elk closer.

Then silence.

Pierce felt the creature's hot breath against his back. It was right above them. He squeezed Fiona and Gallo tighter and waited for the end.

FIFTY-SIX

Fiona's weak voice reached through the silence. She had been speaking all along, but only now could Pierce hear what she was saying, or rather, chanting.

He did not recognize the words, but he intuitively understood that she was speaking her native language. He had wondered if she might be praying; now he was sure of it.

The sound was oddly soothing, and it was only after listening for several seconds that Pierce began to wonder why they were still alive. He could still feel the creature's breath, knew that it was very close, but it wasn't attacking. He raised his head, and in the dim light, he saw the large snout just inches away. Its nostrils flared with each breath, but there was no menace in its eyes. Instead, it seemed curious.

Still chanting, Fiona shifted under him. One of her hands wriggled free and reached up as if to stroke the snout. The bristly folds of skin covering its teeth pulled back slowly as its mouth opened.

"Careful," Pierce whispered, knowing it was already too late to make a difference. Fiona already had her hand in the creature's maw.

As she reached in, Pierce saw that she held something. It looked like a strip of wood, about six inches in length, with a rough texture. She deposited it on the animal's tongue and withdrew her hand. "It's okay," she murmured, somehow folding the words into her chant. "It's just a granola bar."

Although the morsel was the equivalent of a crumb for the enormous bear-elk, it worked its jaws several times, and then tilted its head forward, nuzzling the trio.

"Sorry, fella," Fiona said. "That's all there is."

After a few more insistent nudges, the creature seemed to lose interest. It turned away and padded back to the corner of the cavern where it had been when Pierce arrived.

"What the hell just happened?"

"She can explain later," Gallo whispered. "Let's just get out of here."

Pierce felt no inclination to argue. Moving slowly to avoid upsetting the delicate peace, he rose to his feet and then lifted Fiona in his arms and glanced into the fissure for one last look at Echidna.

A section of its tentacles had curled in, but through the snake-like tendrils, he could see Kenner's motionless form, or rather what was left of it. His clothes were dissolving, his skin starting to slough off as the hot acidic water slowly digested him. The tentacles were not just holding his dead body under though, but shifting and rippling in peristaltic waves to draw him further down.

Pierce wondered if this was the beginning of the process that created the hybrids. There was an entire ecosystem underground, with microbes, fungi and lichen, and even plants and animals adapted to life underground, all of which could have served as prey for Echidna. Perhaps she also consumed the carcasses of unlucky animals that fell through cracks in the surface and were washed into the Underworld. Echidna did not merely devour these creatures, she assimilated their genetic material into her own reproductive system, creating weird, and random, new life forms.

Maybe in a few weeks or months, a new hybrid would form—part-Kenner and part-who-knew-what.

Was it everything you hoped it would be, Liam? Pierce shook his head and turned away.

"He'll leave us alone," Fiona mumbled into his shoulder. Her voice sounded distant, as if she was drifting off to sleep. "Bears and elk are important totems for my people. I told him we were friends."

"Did you?"

"Uncle George, am I in trouble?"

"Trouble? What would make you think that?"

"We're in Yellowstone. You're not supposed to feed the bears."

Pierce laughed, a little louder than was probably wise. "Just this once, I think we can make an exception."

FIFTY-SEVEN

They stepped across the threshold a few minutes later, and Lazarus rushed to meet them. "You made it."

"Told you I would," Pierce replied.

"Anyone else in there we should be worried about? Or anything?"

Pierce shook his head. "Not today. But Fiona needs medical attention, stat."

Lazarus nodded and took her from Pierce's arms. "I'll start an IV."

Although the big man was smiling, which was unusual to say the least, there was a haggard look about him. The ordeal he'd survived, and the pain he had suffered was hard to believe. But Pierce had seen it. Had seen the man survive the impossible. In a way, they all had. Pierce noticed Carter sitting on the ground behind Lazarus, evidently awake and alert, but the faraway look in her eyes made Pierce wonder if she was really there at all. Then she blinked, and turned her head toward them, once more looking like her old self.

Lazarus carried Fiona over to where Carter sat and gently set her down. Then, with a delicate precision that seem impossible for someone so large, he inserted an intravenous catheter into Fiona's arm and started a saline drip. "This should tide her over," he said.

"Bish?" Fiona's eyes opened wide, looking up at him in awed disbelief. "Oh, God. I'm dead, aren't I?"

"No," Lazarus said with a grin. "You're alive. And so am I. I'll tell you all about it when we're somewhere that isn't here."

Pierce gripped her shoulder. "Fi, I hate to do this to you, but the gate to the Underworld is still open. Can you close it?"

Her expression twisted in consternation. "I can try, but honestly I'm not sure how I got it open in the first place."

"I can take care of that," Lazarus said. "There are other ways to shut a door. Permanently."

"Works for me," Pierce said.

"I especially like the 'permanently' part," Gallo added.

"I'll plant the charges, but we should wait until we're clear before detonating. Something tells me that one more explosion might crack open this whole valley."

Pierce looked back at the steaming ground that had consumed their enemies. "As long as you don't set off the super-volcano, it's fine with me."

As Lazarus stood to leave, a shout of protest echoed across the floor of the ravine. "No! You mustn't do that!"

Pierce craned his head around and spotted Tyndareus, crawling toward them, dragging his wasted body along with one outstretched hand. The other was clutched against his chest, as if trying to protect an injury.

"You have to let me go in there."

Pierce raised an eyebrow. "As tempting as that sounds, that would probably involve touching you again."

Tyndareus's strange blue eyes bulged, but then appeared to soften. He held out the hand he had been hugging to his chest, and Pierce saw that it contained a bunched up piece of velvet. "Please. It's not for me."

"What's that? Lucky charm?"

"My brother. Castor. I must take him to the Source, so that he can be reborn."

"Castor. So that would make you Pollux? Twins." Pierce shook his head. "One of you is too many."

Lazarus returned a moment later. "It's done. Cintia can send the detonation command as soon as we're clear."

"Good. We're out of here."

"You really mean to do this?" Tyndareus said. "To destroy it forever?"

Pierce did not correct the slight misconception. "That's what we do. Mostly so evil bastards like you won't be able to screw up the world any worse than it already is."

Lazarus lifted Fiona in his arms, while Pierce helped Gallo and Carter to their feet. As they started up the steep ravine wall, Tyndareus finally understood that they meant to leave him.

"Take me with you," he pleaded. "I can pay you. As much as you want. Just name it."

Pierce looked back. "I guess you haven't heard. We raided your headquarters and seized all your assets. Everything. Cerberus belongs to the Herculean Society now. As a friend of mine said, we completely powned you."

Fiona let out a snort. "Good one."

"Thanks. Did I say it right?" He turned back to Tyndareus. "One of the first things I'm going to do is box up everything in your little shop of horrors and donate it to the Holocaust Memorial Museum. They may be able to find some use for it, but I hope they burn it all."

Tyndareus didn't reply to that, and Pierce was too focused on negotiating the loose earth to care. By the time he reached the top he had almost completely forgotten about the old man.

"You can't just leave me here!" Tyndareus shrieked.

"Actually, I can," Pierce shouted back. He turned to the others. "Anyone have a problem with that?"

No one did.

EPILOGUE
TABULA RASA

EPILOGUE

Cerberus Headquarters, Rome, Italy

Pierce kept his final promise to Tyndareus. The contents of the gallery enshrining the worst horrors of the Holocaust were boxed up and shipped anonymously to the United States Holocaust Memorial Museum in Washington, D.C., although Pierce held back the items in Mengele's trophy case. Those, he burned.

All that remained was an empty room. A blank slate, waiting for a new story to be written upon it. Five days after returning to Rome, Pierce called the group together to discuss what shape that story would take.

They had returned to the hidden facility below Castel Sant'Angelo for a little well-earned rest and recovery, while the rest of the world briefly went crazy worrying about a possible eruption of the Yellowstone caldera.

Despite assurances from numerous geologists and volcano experts, the cable news channels stirred up a frenzy of fear and speculation about the possibility that the geothermal event being reported in the Norris Basin might be the harbinger of an even greater disaster.

By week's end, however, the furor had died down and park rangers reopened the roads to the Norris Basin area. For safety reasons, the backcountry areas remained closed to the public, just as they had before the unexpected geyser eruption, which had triggered a discharge of acidified water into a nameless minor valley a few miles from the nearest trail.

The eruption had scoured all traces of Tyndareus and his men from the ravine, and Dourado, with the powerful Cerberus computer network at her disposal, took care of the rest, arranging for the recovery of the vehicles that had borne them into the park, and obliterating any paper trail that might have prompted an investigation.

Another slate wiped clean, but then erasing history was what the Herculean Society did best. And that was something that had been nagging at Pierce since their return.

He looked at the expectant faces, trying to think of how to broach the subject. "I guess I should have had some chairs brought in," he remarked, hoping it would serve as an icebreaker. The smiles and gentle laughter told him that it had.

"Actually, furniture is one of the things I wanted to talk to you all about." That got quizzical stares, and he almost faltered. "I...ah, I'm thinking about...well, keeping this place."

"Well, duh," Fiona said. "You don't walk away from real estate like this. Not in Rome."

Pierce stared at her, wondering if she understood what he was trying to suggest. *Probably. She's a smart kid... No, make that a smart young woman.*

"You know how I feel about caves," Carter said. "But this place has more of a basement rec-room vibe. I can deal."

The comment surprised Pierce on several levels. Carter had hardly spoken to him since their return, though in truth, he was probably as much to blame for that as she. The memory of what had happened to Rohn nagged at the back of his mind. Carter had saved them both, but whether she had tapped into her ability consciously or not was something that Pierce felt he needed to know. If she couldn't control it, then the next person she turned into a mindless drone might be Lazarus. Or him. Or all of them.

It was a question he would eventually have to ask, but he did not yet know how, and he suspected that Carter probably didn't know how to answer it.

Even more surprising to him was the implicit acceptance of an offer he had not yet made.

"George, let's cut to the chase," Gallo said. "You want this to be our new headquarters. I think I speak for everyone when I say that these accommodations are far more...accommodating than the citadel in Gibraltar."

Pierce looked around to see if Gallo was in fact expressing the consensus of the group. Carter spoke up again. "I'll admit, I was a little hesitant about letting someone else call the shots for me, but where else am I going to get unlimited access to state-of-the-art equipment and unlimited funding—"

"I don't know about 'unlimited,'" Pierce cut in quickly.

"And research opportunities that are...well, unique." She glanced up at Lazarus. "But the truth is, you're doing good work. Important work. I want to be a part of that."

"You all feel that way? Cintia, would you be willing to leave Brazil and come work here?"

Dourado, her piercings all restored and sporting magenta hair with all the curl ironed out, replied without hesitation. "I can live anywhere. But with the hardware here, I can do magic."

Pierce turned to Lazarus, who merely nodded.

"Uh... well, I'm glad to hear it," Pierce said. "But actually that's only part of it. I've been thinking a lot about... I guess you could call it our 'mission statement.' The Herculean Society has a very specific agenda—to preserve and protect the legacy of Hercules. Our founder, Alexander Diotrephes, had very good reasons for wanting to do that, reasons that are still valid today. But I think he was so consumed with trying to hide the truth about who he really was, that he forgot the most important thing about the legend.

"Hercules was a hero, and heroes help people." He saw that Gallo was about to comment, and he quickly added, "I know, some of the stories don't exactly make him out to be heroic, but even today, three thousand years later, what people remember most about him is the good stuff he did. He used his power to help people."

"With great power comes great responsibility," Dourado said.

"Exactly. That's the legacy of Hercules that we're supposed to be preserving. Don't get me wrong, I'm not thinking of quitting the Herculean Society or changing what we do. But we've got the resources to do a lot more than just running around hiding the evidence. I mean, look at what we accomplished. We took down a Nazi war criminal who everyone thought was dead, and we dismantled a criminal empire. I think we're off to a pretty good start.

"But there's more to it than that. There are threats out there that no one is equipped to deal with. Things that we might know about because Alexander knew, but kept secret. We can use that knowledge to deal with those threats before they reach critical mass."

Gallo cocked her head to the side. "How exactly would that work?"

Pierce took a deep breath. This was the moment of truth. He reached into his jacket and took an envelope out of his inner pocket. "These are just mock-ups," he said as he removed the contents and began distributing them. "Subject to change. Nothing is carved in stone."

Surprisingly, Lazarus was the first to comment. "The Cerberus Group. Director of Operations, Erik Lazarus." He held up a business card which, in addition to what he had just read, featured the same image that Dourado had found on the anonymous website of Tyndareus's organization.

"I'm the Chief Scientific Advisor," Carter said, showing her card.

"Like I said, subject to change. If you don't like your title, we can come up with something better."

"Cerberus Group." Fiona wrinkled her nose. "Sounds like the name of a scary multinational corporation."

"And we'll keep all of Cerberus's current underworld connections," Pierce said. "If someone is looking for something dangerous, we'll be able to hear about it. They might even come to us to find it for them."

"I like it," Gallo said. "Cerberus was the gatekeeper of the Underworld. I think that's what George has in mind for us. We'll be the watchdogs, guarding humanity from scary things in the night."

"Something like that," Pierce said with a shrug. "You can sleep on it if you want."

"No need," Gallo said. "Count me in."

Fiona and Dourado voiced their support as well. Carter appeared enthusiastic as well, but instead of casting a vote, she nodded to Lazarus. "I'm with Erik. If he stays, I stay."

Pierce turned to the big man. "Well?"

Lazarus gazed back, the furrow of his brow the only indication that something might be amiss. He held up the card again. "It says Lazarus."

Fiona seemed to understand what he was driving at. "Erik, Uncle George explained it to me. I won't tell my dad or the others. I promise."

Lazarus frowned. "It's wrong for me to put you in that position. You shouldn't have to lie to protect me."

"Then tell them," she replied. "They aren't going to be mad at you, you know."

Pierce knew it was not quite that simple. Lazarus was caught between two worlds. He had found love and happiness with Carter, but the ties that bound him to his former life were stronger than the bonds of blood or brotherhood. If he revealed himself to Jack Sigler and the rest of his former team, the gravity of his old life would draw him back. It was probably inevitable. Yet, the fact that he was torn by the decision meant that part of him did not want to give up his new life in exchange for the old one.

"You can tell them when you're ready," Pierce said. "But you know what? Right now, I think we need to focus on new beginnings. The past isn't as important as the future. *Tabula rasa*. A clean slate and a fresh start. What do you say?"

Lazarus looked at Carter and then at Pierce, and nodded. "I'm in."

ABOUT THE AUTHORS

Jeremy Robinson is the international bestselling author of fifty novels and novellas including *MirrorWorld*, *Uprising*, *Island 731*, *SecondWorld*, the Jack Sigler thriller series, and *Project Nemesis*, the highest selling, original (non-licensed) kaiju novel of all time. He's known for mixing elements of science, history and mythology, which has earned him the #1 spot in Science Fiction and Action-Adventure, and secured him as the top creature feature author.

Robinson is also known as the bestselling horror writer, Jeremy Bishop, author of *The Sentinel* and the controversial novel, *Torment*. In 2015, he launched yet another pseudonym, Jeremiah Knight, for two post-apocalyptic Science Fiction series of novels. Robinson's works have been translated into thirteen languages.

His series of Jack Sigler / Chess Team thrillers, starting with *Pulse*, is in development as a film series, helmed by Jabbar Raisani, who earned an Emmy Award for his design work on HBO's *Game of Thrones*. Robinson's original kaiju character, Nemesis, is also being adapted into a comic book through publisher *Famous Monsters of Filmland*, with artwork and covers by renowned Godzilla artists Matt Frank and Bob Eggleton.

Born in Beverly, MA, Robinson now lives in New Hampshire with his wife and three children.

Visit Jeremy Robinson online at www.bewareofmonsters.com.

ABOUT THE AUTHORS

SEAN ELLIS is the international bestselling author *Magic Mirror* and several thriller and adventure novels. He is a veteran of Operation Enduring Freedom, and he has a Bachelor of Science degree in Natural Resources Policy from Oregon State University. Sean is also a member of the International Thriller Writers organization. He currently resides in Arizona, where he divides his time between writing, adventure sports and trying to figure out how to save the world.

Visit him on the web at: seanellisthrillers.webs.com

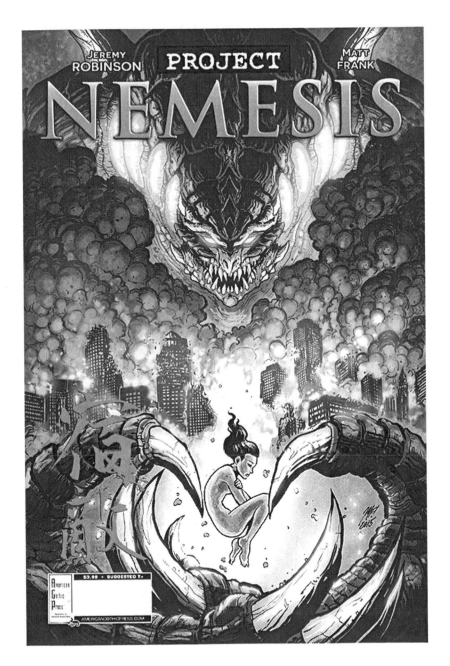

Available at Comic Book Stores, October 2015

PROJECT HYPERION

JEREMY ROBINSON

INTERNATIONAL BESTSELLING AUTHOR OF *ISLAND 731* AND *PROJECT NEMESIS*

Coming in 2015

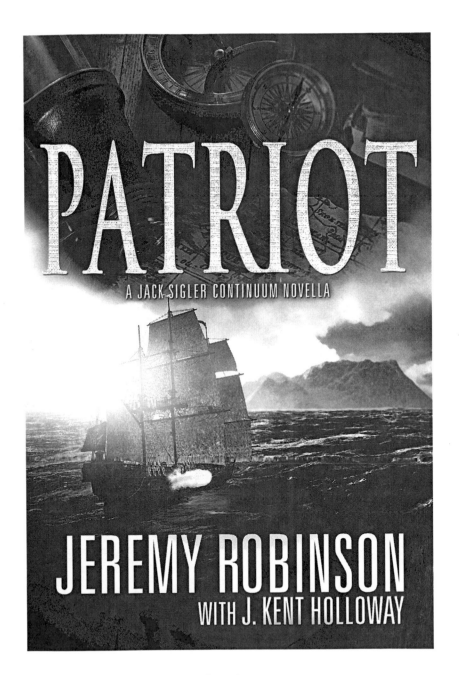

Coming in 2015

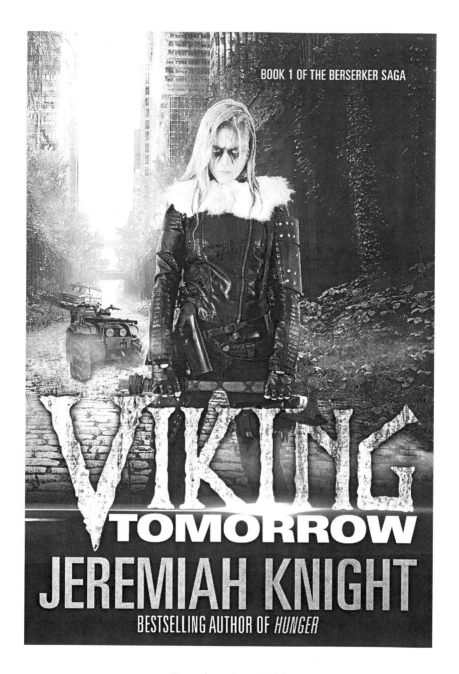

BOOK 1 OF THE BERSERKER SAGA

VIKING
TOMORROW
JEREMIAH KNIGHT
BESTSELLING AUTHOR OF *HUNGER*

Coming in 2015

CPSIA information can be obtained
at www.ICGtesting.com
Printed in the USA
FSOW01n1105280815
10487FS